THE
END
IS
NOW

Also by Rob Stennett

The Almost True Story of Ryan Fisher

THE
END
IS
NOW

a novel by

Rob Stennett

ZONDERVAN®

ZONDERVAN.com/
AUTHORTRACKER
follow your favorite authors

ZONDERVAN

The End Is Now
Copyright © 2009 by Rob Stennett

This title is also available as a Zondervan ebook.
Visit www.zondervan.com/ebooks.

This title is also available in a Zondervan audio edition.
Visit www.zondervan.fm.

Requests for information should be addressed to:

Zondervan, *Grand Rapids, Michigan 49530*

Library of Congress Cataloging-in-Publication Data

Stennett, Rob, 1977 –
     The end is now / Rob Stennett.
          p.   cm.
     ISBN 978-0-310-28679-0 (softcover)
     1. Armageddon — Fiction. 2. Goodland (Kan.) — Fiction. 3. Satire. I. Title.
PS3619.T476477E63   2009
813'.6 — dc22   2009005157

I, Rob Stennett, would like to thank the city of Goodland for being so friendly to me when I visited. If you ever get the chance, you should visit their fine town. Wonderful people. I recommend the diner at the Goodland airport. And I'd also like to remind everyone that this is a work of fiction. Any resemblance to actual people, places, rapture predictions, and/or apocalyptic events is entirely coincidental or for fictional purposes.

Interior design by Beth Shagene
Edited by Andy Meisenheimer, Becky Philpott, and Jared Winkel

Printed in the United States of America

09 10 11 12 13 14 · 23 22 21 20 19 18 17 16 15 14 13 12 11 10 9 8 7 6 5 4 3 2 1

In memory of Marjorie "Ginga" Stennett
& Grandpa John McGuire.
I'll see you on the other side.

THE **BEGINNING**

Listen, I tell you a mystery:
We will not all sleep, but we will all be changed—
in a flash, in the twinkling of an eye, at the last trumpet.
For the trumpet will sound,
the dead will be raised imperishable,
and we will be changed.

1 CORINTHIANS 15:51–52

There are certain rules to surviving a horror movie ...
Never, ever, ever under any circumstances say,
"I'll be right back." Because you won't be back.

JAMIE KENNEDY, *SCREAM*

GOODLAND, KANSAS

One week from tomorrow, at precisely 6:11 in the morning, the rapture or apocalypse or Armageddon or whatever else you'd prefer to call it, is going to occur.

But only in Goodland, Kansas.

The rapture will not take place anywhere else in the world. It will not crash the stock market, cause cars to wreck, or leave planes without their pilots. Husbands will not leave for the kitchen to grab a jar of pickles, only to come back to the living room and discover that their wives are now nothing more than piles of clothes. Power plants will not shut down, leaving televisions, light bulbs, street lamps, and hairdryers without electricity. Running water will not stop, forcing citizens to take baths in rivers and wash their clothes in lakes. Meteors will not crash into the ocean and create tidal waves. Nuclear missiles will not be launched from the USSR, North Korea, East Germany, or any of those pesky countries in the Middle East. Barcodes will not be tattooed onto wrists or foreheads. The number *666* will be nowhere in sight except for those rare instances when a customer at McDonald's buys nothing but a Filet O' Fish and a medium strawberry shake, and the total including tax comes out to be six dollars and sixty-six cents. A world government will not be formed. Computers will not melt down because they are confused about what the year 2000 actually means. Aliens will not blow up the White House.

Nothing like this will happen.

That is, nothing like this will happen anywhere but in Goodland.

This goes against conventional wisdom. Most people think that when the end comes it will be widespread: Trumpets will sound and horsemen will appear and it will be a whirlwind of all kinds of tribulation—from pre-trib, to post-trib, to middle-trib. But that doesn't make sense. It's just not how such things work. It's not true to the pattern of how other miraculous destruction has occurred in history.

There are always warning signs.

God didn't simply destroy Nineveh—Jonah was swallowed by a whale and then sent to warn Nineveh of its impending doom. Moses warned Pharaoh before the plagues hit—and even the plagues started out innocently enough, simple stuff like frogs and locusts before the heavy hitters like blood rivers and death angels. Peter warned Ananias and Sapphira, Lot warned Sodom and Gomorrah—and in the end they were all destroyed to warn others about the dangers of wickedness.

This is what will happen in Goodland. Their rapture will be a signal to the world. They are a warning. A sacrificial lamb. It makes sense. Once everyone sees how powerful the rapture is, they will be afraid, or excited; they will hit the floor and repent of their sins. Everyone, everywhere, will know the truth. Not only that, but this event will provide God a chance to see how things go. He can look at the rapture and see what worked and what didn't. He can watch the good, the bad, and the ugly of the apocalypse so He can know how to improve it when He takes it global.

Goodland is the test market for the rapture.

The ultimate warning sign for all to repent.

WILL HENDERSON

Will was running late. At this rate he'd never make it home in time for dinner. And this wasn't just dinner. This was Monday night dinner. This was the most important meal of the week for the Henderson family. The meal for which his mom spent the whole day cooking things like roast, garlic potatoes, fresh baked rolls, and pistachio fruit salad.

Will knew he should have left Nate Jackson's house sooner. But Nate had just returned from a family trip to Kansas City where he got the most impressive set of brand-new, mint-condition DC graphic novels Will had ever seen. "Look how cherry these are," Nate said as he opened the cellophane packaging and slowly took out the comics. Nate was right. These were cherry. Batman and Superman looked lifelike on these pages. No, they looked better than lifelike. Every detail on every page was breathtaking. Otherworldly. How could someone be expected to keep track of time when looking at comics like this?

"Can I read it?" Will asked.

"Yeah, just be real careful. Mom said I'm not even supposed to open these because they're so nice."

Will sat on the edge of Nate's bed and flipped the comic books open. He turned to one page after another, reading about the adventures of the superheroes. Will's mind always got lost in these stories, and at that moment he was lost in thought about Batman.

Will felt bad for Batman. The Flash could move at the speed of light, Wonder Woman had an invisible jet, and Superman had a ridiculously unfair amount of powers (flight, laser vision, X-ray vision, wind breath, super strength — and those were just his basic powers — it seemed like he could just come up with a brand-new power whenever he needed it). And then there was Batman. He had exactly zero superpowers. He was rich. He had a lot of money. His trust fund was his power. He could buy really cool cars and planes and bat gadgets that could do anything and everything. But Batman couldn't *do* anything for himself. Will thought all the other superheroes probably looked at Batman like he was a poser. Batman was the rich kid who had to buy his way into the Super Friends club. That must have made Batman really sad. Will thought Batman probably lay in bed late at night and tried not to cry at the mean things the other superheroes said. Batman probably would even look towards the heavens and pray, "Please God, give me some kind of superpower. It doesn't have to be much. Just the ability to jump over a building or become invisible or shoot beams of ice or fire out of my hands."

Will was almost in a trance flipping through the pages thinking about Batman when Nate said, "Dude, don't you have to be home? It's almost dark."

Will looked up at the clock. "Shoot. I gotta go." He jumped off Nate's bed, ran down the stairs, and opened the door to leave. "See you later Mrs. Jackson," Will said.

"If the Lord tarries," Mrs. Jackson called from the kitchen.

Once Will was out of Nate's house he started walking home down the gravel road. The road was on the outskirts of Goodland and on either side were large cornstalks as tall as NBA players. Will walked as quickly as he could. But even at his quick pace he wouldn't make it home in time. His family lived so far away from everybody.

Still, he *needed* to make it home in time. This was Monday night dinner. This was a huge deal. So, the only chance he had to make it home before he was grounded for the next month was to cut across the cornfields.

Will stepped into the fields and knew that if he walked in a straight diagonal line, he would cut at least twenty minutes off his walk home. He'd just have to keep walking quickly and he'd be there in no time. He'd be there before his mom could call Nate Jackson's mom and ask where he was. Will didn't like when his mom talked to Nate's mom. They always talked about religious things.

Of course most people talked about religious things in Goodland. Will had visited some of his cousins in Denver last summer and noticed that no one around there ever said things like, "If the Lord tarries," when they said goodbye. But in Goodland that was just how most people said goodbye. Kind of like saying "Geshundheit" after someone sneezes. But the thing is, most people say "Geshundheit" after you sneeze. It seemed to Will that no one said "If the Lord tarries" anywhere else in the world. He wanted to make sure so he tested the theory out a month ago when his family visited Worlds of Fun amusement park in St. Louis. The teenager buckling Will into the roller coaster told him, "Have a good ride." And Will answered, "If the Lord tarries."

The teenager looked at Will as if he were from Neptune.

On their road trip home from the amusement park, Will asked his mom, "How come nobody else talks like we do?"

"What do you mean?" his mother answered.

"Nobody in Denver or at Worlds of Fun says things like, 'If the Lord tarries.' Only people in Goodland say things like that."

"That's because they're not concerned with the rapture," his mother said.

"Oh."

"You know what the rapture is, don't you?"

Of course he knew what the rapture was. Everybody knew what the rapture was. He'd heard about it lots of times in Sunday school. People around town talked about it every once in a while. And from the way people talked, Will always worried that it was coming soon. That made Will scared. He didn't want to die.

Not that it was really dying. Or was it? He'd have to go away. His life on earth would be over. Isn't that essentially what dying is? Does it matter if you skip the pain? Or is the pain part of dying? Do you have to experience something bad like a bullet through your chest or a car wreck or liver cancer or AIDS or burning or drowning? Is that part of dying? Probably it was. So that was one of the things that Will *liked* about the rapture. He'd get to skip the pain part of dying. It was like God would hit fast forward or skip to the next chapter, and he'd be whisked away to some magical place with clouds and harps and singing. He'd be whisked away to heaven.

So it wasn't really heaven that bothered him—it was just that there was so much *here* that he hadn't experienced. He hadn't graduated and thrown his cap high into the air. He'd never learned to drive or been able to pick up a girl by himself on prom night. He wouldn't be able to go on a camping trip with just his friends like they'd always planned they would when they were old enough. He hadn't ever owned his own house, or had a job where he made lots of money that he could spend on video games and guitars and flat screen TVs.

Worst of all, he'd never even had a girlfriend, he'd never kissed a girl like all the other guys at school said they had. And he'd certainly never had the *S*-word with a girl. And he sort of wanted to do that too. Not until he was older. Not until his wedding night, and maybe not until a while after that. The *S*-word sounded crazy and weird and like a lot of fun, but also kind of scary and intimidating for Will right now.

But it wouldn't always be scary. Someday he would be ready.

Still, he didn't think about the *S*-word much, but he thought about his wife all the time. He wondered what she would look like. She'd probably have blonde hair and she'd like to play soccer or volleyball. Will even wondered if he knew his wife right now. Sometimes, during math when the teacher was writing long division problems on the board, he'd look around the classroom and wonder if his wife was sitting in class with him. Was she a few desks away and just as bored as he was? What if someday, once they were married, they'd talk about math class and tell each other, "That's where I first noticed you, in math, during those super boring lessons. That's when I knew we'd be married." But that day would never come. He'd never get to have that conversation with his wife. He'd never even get to know who his wife really was.

He'd probably be raptured before then.

And that wasn't fair. This was a point Will often brought up in his prayer time. "God, why can't you wait until I'm old, like twenty-five, until you bring the rapture? Let me do some of the stuff that people have gotten to do for thousands and millions of years before me. Isn't that fair?" And then Will felt like God spoke the answer to him: No, that wasn't fair. The rapture had to come someday; it couldn't wait until everyone turned twenty-five. Because then it would *never* happen. And besides, there were some people who were babies or little kids and they'd never get to experience all the good stuff Will had. They'd never get to ride a bike, or white-water raft, or go see the Kansas City Royals play live and in person. He should consider himself lucky he'd gotten to do all of that. Even more, he would be *very* lucky that the rapture was going to happen in his lifetime. He was special.

And then he stopped.

He looked around. He was so deep in thought about the rapture and Worlds of Fun and his future wife that he'd lost his place in the cornfields.

Where are you? There was barely any sunlight left. He wasn't even supposed to be in the cornfields. If his parents knew that he'd cut across the cornfields, he couldn't imagine how grounded he would be, but it would be bad. He would probably still be grounded after the rapture. The adults didn't want anyone in the Johnsons' fields because they stretched on as far as the eye could see, in every direction, rows and rows of endless cornstalks like trees in a forest. Will could navigate them; he'd done it before, but he had to pay careful attention to the subtle changes and markers along the way. And he thought he *was* paying attention. But all the thoughts of the rapture crept in and distracted him. It happened to him sometimes. Emily made fun of him because of it. His mom said it wasn't his fault. One thought could jump onto another and another. But she *also* said just because it wasn't his fault didn't mean he wouldn't have to fight against it. She said he needed to pay attention, and that wasn't easy; that's why they called it *paying*.

He was paying attention now.

He knew exactly what to do to get out of the fields; he hadn't been so lost in his thoughts that he'd completely lost his bearings. He needed to walk straight about three hundred steps, and then right five hundred steps, and then left six hundred steps. Like that, he'd be out of the cornfields. He could run home, he'd be there before dark—he'd outrace the sun if he had to. Then he could go back to normal things like worrying about the rapture.

He started counting each step. He knew right where he was the whole time, and once he got near his last few steps he could feel the outside world, taste the fresh air, and imagine what it would look like outside of the green and yellow and brown blur he'd been staring at for the last half hour. And as he walked out of the cornfields something odd happened.

There was more corn.

The six hundredth step looked just like every other step. He hadn't left the fields at all. He closed his eyes and listened. Surely he could hear people playing and talking; there would be cars driving on the road, and these sounds would guide him out of the field. He had miscalculated. But he was close. He just needed a little help to guide him the rest of the way.

He listened — and — nothing.

Now he was going to have to do something that would give him away. He'd have to yell. And then everyone for sure would know that he was in the cornfields. They would tell him, "I told you so. This is exactly why we say, 'Don't play in the cornfields.'" He would tell them he wasn't playing, he knew exactly where he was. He just got a little distracted. But those logical explanations would fall on deaf ears.

That was a price he was willing to pay. "Is anybody out there?" Will said, loudly and confidently without quite yelling it. There was still a shred of hope that someone would be nearby, someone who'd guide him out of the fields so he could avoid trouble.

"Anybody?" He half-yelled again.

No answer. He started worrying much less about being grounded and much more about dying of thirst in the cornfield. He knew that you died of thirst way before you died of hunger, which seemed weird to Will because he usually felt hungry a lot more than thirsty.

So this time he yelled, "Please, I'm lost. I need some help. PLEASE!"

Silence. Someone could hear him. They were just trying to prove a point. They were trying to teach him a lesson.

"Okay. I'm sorry! DO YOU HEAR ME? I SAID SORRY! I WILL NEVER GO IN THE CORNFIELDS AGAIN!"

Nothing.

He walked up and down the rows of corn explaining things over and over. Screaming for help. Admitting guilt. Apologizing. More screaming. And towards the end he started to cry. He didn't want to. He knew it was such a baby-kid-lame-o thing to do. But he couldn't help it. If someone could hear him, they were playing a sick-cruel-scary joke.

But what if someone *could* hear him?

He closed his eyes and listened one more time. Not for the obvious things like cars driving and honking or kids playing and laughing or parents talking. No, he listened for the quiet types of things. Like someone breathing or soft footsteps. And then he could hear it. Slow breaths, in and out, from someone else, as if they'd been there all along. He could feel someone else's eyes burrowing into the back of his neck, he could almost see whoever it was behind him, smiling.

"Hey, mister, listen, I've got a knife so you don't want to—"

And then he ran. It was a trick he'd learned from watching movies. The hero would always act like he was talking to the bad guy, and then mid-sentence, out of nowhere, the hero sprung into action. Except the hero probably wouldn't have run; he would have turned around and snapped the bad guy's neck, but Will didn't know how to break someone's neck. He couldn't even punch very hard. So he just ran. He didn't even look back to see who it was behind him. He knew if he ran in any one direction long enough and fast enough and hard enough, he'd get away from whoever was following him and out of the cornfields.

So he ran until he was out of breath, until it hurt too much to go on. And then he ran a little farther. When he finally stopped, his face was covered in tears and sweat and dust and pieces of cornhusk. He took off his shirt and wiped his face the best he could. It made his shirt filthy. Another thing to be grounded for. He didn't care now. He wanted to be grounded. He would give anything to be home, to be yelled at, to be sent to his room for a month. All of that seemed small now. Because he knew how bad the situation had become.

You could die out here.

They might not even find you until weeks from now.

This didn't even scare him. He just knew it was true. He'd watched survival videos in boy scouts where grown men had gotten lost in the wilderness. In one video a man got frostbite and his leg had to be cut off. In another video a man got lost in the desert, and his face had gotten so scorched that it looked like he had leprosy, and when they found him they tried to give him water, but even a thimble of it made him sick.

"I'm serious, God, please help me find a way out of here. I'll be good. Really good. I'll help others and feed the homeless. I shouldn't have come here. I know that now. I learned my lesson. But you have to help me. DO YOU HEAR ME? Please, if you're really out there you have to help me."

This wasn't the first time he'd prayed this kind of prayer. There were two other times (he got lost in Disneyland when he was eight, and Nate had broken his leg when they were tree climbing last summer) and both of those times God didn't say a word.

Right now Will didn't have time to wait on God. He'd have to get himself out of this mess. He needed to run more. But he was tired. His head was cloudy, and everything looked blurry. Even worse, the sun had set. The cornstalks created crisscross shadows all over the ground. The moon was starting to shine now, but just enough to make things seem eerie and alive. There was no point to running anymore. This is where he would end. This would be the final resting place of Will Henderson.

The winds picked up again, howling and making the corn-stalks dance around him. Will was paralyzed. It was like when the nightmares were so bad he couldn't even scream.

Then a face appeared in the cornstalks. It looked just like Moses did in all of the movies, only it was made out of the corn-stalks coming together: bright yellow eyes, a ripe green mouth, and a cornhusk beard. Will wondered if God was finally about to speak to him. Then again, maybe it wasn't God at all. Maybe it was an angel. Or maybe the face was Satan or a demon. Maybe it was there to trick Will.

He'd have to listen carefully to be sure.

When the face finally spoke, it told Will he had nothing to be afraid of.

Will said he was afraid of the wind. The wind stopped.

Then the face told Will about the rapture (only the face didn't call it that but Will knew what he was talking about), about what would happen in the next week. Will listened; his mind was calm and it soaked up everything.

When the face finished talking, it went back to looking like cornstalks, and Will was so calm and tired that he couldn't help but sleep.

JEFF HENDERSON

The sun set a Reese's Pieces orange as Jeff Henderson flipped down his dusty visor. He was driving home from another day of automotive sales on the access road next to I – 70. He could almost feel the cars as they whizzed by him at eighty miles per hour.

They were all on their way somewhere.

They didn't think of Goodland as a town or a city. They thought of it as more of a glorified truck stop. Most travelers know Goodland has a Holiday Inn Express or a Comfort Inn to stay at if they need a place to rest before they head 189 miles west to Denver or 394 miles east to Kansas City. They read the road signs and see that within the city limits there's a McDonald's and a Dairy Queen, or a Rusty's if they want to experience an authentic small-town diner. And observant travelers notice Goodland's slogan handpainted in white on the side of a splintered maroon barn that reads, "Goodland. Stay a night. Stay a lifetime." But that's about all those who drive past Goodland know about the town. To them it lasts for about three exits along I – 70 and then it disappears in their rearview mirror. It's quickly forgotten with the promise of a bigger, better Dairy Queen forty-five miles ahead in the next town.

What they don't know is how close-knit Goodland is. They don't know about the Goodland fair and livestock show that happens every summer, or that fall is everyone's favorite time of year because it's when the cornstalks reach up towards heaven like they are trying to touch God himself. They don't know that nobody from Goodland actually eats at Rusty's because they'd much rather go to one of the diners near downtown or the café at the airport. And most of all those tourists driving through Goodland don't know that the motto on the handpainted sign has everything to do with the belief by some (but certainly not all) that they have been chosen for the rapture. Those who think of Goodland as a truck stop have no way of knowing that to "Stay a Night" means you are a tourist passing through, but to "Stay a Lifetime" means you'll get the honor of experiencing Goodland's fate with the rest of the town.

Jeff Henderson was born in Goodland so he knew all these things. He knew exactly what the sign meant. He passed by it every day, but he never looked at it or read it because to him it was just a piece of the scenery. It was part of the background like skyscrapers are to natives of New York or mountains are to natives of Colorado. He didn't think of it as normal, nor did he think of it as eccentric. It was something he took for granted. Some small towns have legends of old haunted mansions on a hill or stories of spooky graveyards on the edge of town, and that's what the Goodland rapture talk amounted to for Jeff. It was a quaint legend which added to the charm of Goodland, but nothing more. Nothing that needed serious thought and consideration, because there were other things in life. Pressing things.

Everyday things.

And those were the things Jeff thought about as he drove home from work. At the moment he was thinking about his Ford Taurus, which was too old, clunky, and unfashionable for someone in his line of work to be driving. It was older than both his kids. If he had a promotion he could buy something much nicer and reliable and slick. But just as much, a promotion would validate everything: the hours away from his family, the stress, the phone calls, the hustling, the twisting and scheming, the smile he had to have plastered on his face forty hours every week, the nine to five, the long days without a sale. The blood, sweat, and tears would all be worth it if he could just get promoted to senior sales rep. Even better, he wouldn't have to put junior sales rep on his business card anymore. *Junior.* It was so embarrassing. He was a father of two, he was a husband, and he'd been in the business world for a little while now. And he still had a card that said *junior.*

Still, worrying about things like business cards and titles was an entirely new thing for Jeff. A couple months ago he didn't care what was on his business card. He was just happy to have a job. Well maybe not just a job. He'd had lots of those — he'd been a farmhand, he'd framed houses, and he'd been an assistant manager at Señor Clucks.

For his whole life he'd been paid by the hour. But he'd done whatever it took to survive. Jeff had been living in survival mode ever since his senior year of high school. It was second semester and he was ready to graduate. He was imagining life in college. He didn't know what he wanted to study, didn't even care, he just wanted to live the college life. He'd take all the easy classes and party for a couple of years; he'd get serious about his major and figure out life junior year. That was the plan. But then on one ordinary day, Amy came up to his locker and her face was pale. She was already pretty fair skinned, but on that day she looked almost translucent.

"What's up, babe," Jeff said. He was wearing his letter jacket and chewing gum.

"I'm late," Amy said.

"So am I," Jeff answered.

"No, I'm *really* late," Amy said.

He gently grabbed her elbow and smiled. "Don't worry, I'll go to class with you."

"Is that your way of saying you'll marry me?"

"Wow. Um, okay, I don't know if I'm ready for that kind of commitment."

"Jeff, I don't think you're following—"

"Listen, you have history, right? Mr. Smith loves me. I'll give him some excuse for why you're late—"

"No, I'm late. *Late*, you know—"

Jeff stared at his girlfriend blankly.

"—Pregnant late."

And Jeff aged ten years. He'd never had a steady girlfriend, and euphemisms like *late* just weren't in his vocabulary. But *pregnant* was.

Everything came flooding in. He could hear a crying baby, smell diapers, and he could see a tiny messy apartment overstuffed with cribs and rattles and toys that blipped, blinked, and beeped. He could also see his college life disappearing. He'd never get to drink beer while standing on his head, never get to write a paper after thirty-six hours with no sleep; he'd never get to tie sweaters around his shoulders and flirt with sorority sisters. His next eighteen years were etched in stone.

It didn't even matter that he never really saw himself as the family type. He knew what the right thing to do was. And if he had any doubt, Amy's parents knocked it away by insisting he make Amy an honorable woman. Jeff agreed that it was the reasonable thing to do. But as soon as they were married, he was just in over his head. All they could afford for a honeymoon was a weekend in Kansas City and when they got home real life began.

Jeff didn't know how to act in real life. He'd never been anything but a student. He didn't know how to support a family or be a husband. There were a whole bunch of experiences like going to college that were supposed to get him ready for all of that. But there wasn't time anymore. It was as if Rocky had to go straight to fighting Apollo Creed without the jogging in sweats.

So from the moment Emily was born, Jeff worked whatever job he could to support his family. To make sure Amy and the baby had food on the table, clothes to wear, and a warm roof to protect them at night.

At Hansley things were different. A friend had helped him get a job there about two years ago and now he finally had a career. For the first time in his life he wasn't just paid by how many hours he spent at work. Now there was incentive. Selling pre-owned cars would mean he could double and triple his salary.

The problem was every Friday, Charles Hansley Jr. (Mr. Hansley's son who'd never sold a car in his life) printed off reports of the top sales rankings of the week. The names of all the salesmen were listed, starting with the week's best salesmen at the top. Guys like Kevin Grabowski were always in the lead. He wore expensive shoes, had the million-dollar grin, and he was a natural. Sales was in his blood. He was a shark. But Jeff wasn't like Kevin and that was maybe why his name was always near the bottom. And that made him afraid. He worried that Mr. Hansley would decide Jeff didn't have what it took to be a salesman. Jeff lived in constant fear of a conversation that would start and/or end with the words, "Maybe you'd be better off in another line of work."

Lately he'd decided to change. He could do this. He could be a top salesman. He'd just have to fight a little harder. He'd have to develop a killer instinct. He decided he needed to read business books — everything from motivational books, to books on time management, to books on improving his sales techniques and approach. So, long after Emily and Will had gone to bed, Jeff would sit in the dark with Amy sound asleep next to him and a reading light clipped to his book so he could scour the pages for any insight they had to offer on increasing his sales.

And the reading helped Jeff. It reminded him that he was dedicated to his job. He was dedicated to his family. He was dedicated to providing them all the stable, normal existence they'd always wanted.

When Jeff got home he stopped at his mailbox, opened it up, threw a pile of mail into his passenger seat, and then he drove down his long concrete driveway. Coming home always made everything worthwhile. He had a great house out in the country; the nearest neighbor was five hundred yards away. He had a large windmill that faced the Johnson's cornfield. It was something he'd always wanted. The windmill didn't even do anything really, it was just there for decoration, but it was so great to own one. Sometimes he would just sit on his porch and drink lemonade and stare at it.

Jeff walked by the windmill and into his house where the smell of the roast Amy was cooking wafted towards him. It was Monday. That meant they were going to have a real meal. The type of meal that black-and-white television families had, the type where June and the Beav and Wally would laugh and share their day. The type where he could ask his kids, "How was your day at school?" Where they could share the highs and lows of life, where they could be a family.

Jeff hated that this only happened on Mondays now. He hated that they were getting too old to be a family.

Emily practically had one foot out the door. She couldn't wait to leave. Goodland was too small for her. She wanted to go to the University of Kansas, study marine biology, and who knows, maybe take over the world from there. It wasn't that she was bratty or mean—she was just disinterested. Emily saw her dad as more dorky and goofy, rather than the hero and white knight and rockstar he used to be. Still, he was proud of what she had become. Proud of her good grades, proud that she was planning to be nominated to homecoming court this fall, proud that she'd been elected student body treasurer. He just didn't want it to be over so quickly. He wanted to raise her all over again. It was so much fun the first time, but so often he was too busy to realize it. And now she would be out of the house. She would go on with her life. She would call on birthdays and visit on Christmas. There wouldn't be much left to look forward to.

Except the wedding.

If the rapture really were going to happen (and of course it wasn't), the thing he would be most upset about missing would be the wedding. He could see how beautiful and perfect and angelic Emily would look in her crystal white dress. He would be there with a handkerchief to wipe away her tears right before they walked down the aisle. He would say, "You look perfect, honey," and she would hug him tight, maybe for the last time, as she said, "I love you Daddy." The music would swell, all would stand, breathless, as they watched his little girl walk down the aisle. And he would grin from ear to ear with each step, feeling so proud, knowing that giving her away would be the bittersweet crowning achievement of being her father.

"Hey Dad," Emily said glancing toward Jeff as he walked through the door.

"I'm home," Jeff said.

"Hello honey," Amy said as she covered her hands with oven mitts and put the roast on the table. "How was your day?" she asked.

"It was all right."

"Any sales?"

"I have a couple of good leads. I'm hoping one or two of those will pan out tomorrow."

"Gotcha," Amy said. "Emily, Will, come on, it's time for dinner," Amy said.

"Roast for dinner again?" Emily asked as she took a seat.

"Yes, roast for dinner. Where's Will?"

"I don't know. I'm not his babysitter."

"What time is it?" Amy asked.

Jeff checked his watch. "7:13."

Amy walked outside. Jeff followed.

"I'd say it's dark out, wouldn't you?" Amy asked.

"Pretty close."

"Will asked if he could go to Nate's house. I told him yes but he had to be home *before* dark. He said he would. I said, 'Do you promise?' and he said, 'Mom, I *promise*.' Jeff, he's got to learn some responsibility."

"Totally agree," Jeff said.

"You don't think he's hurt? Do you?"

And then a flash came to Jeff: Will, listening to his iPod, singing along to whatever as he crossed the road at the exact wrong moment as teenagers were speeding by in a Cadillac. They'd slam on the brakes, but they'd be going too fast, and it'd be too late.

The thought made Jeff sick. He wished he wouldn't think like this. But fears often popped into Jeff's head. Probably because at such an early age he learned how fragile life was. He learned that you could just be going along and then something could happen that could change everything. For Jeff it was going from being single and carefree—and then *snap*—a wife and a baby. It made Jeff wonder what other things could suddenly change without a moment's notice. When he was driving he could picture his tire popping and the car flipping over and over. When Jeff was at work he could imagine Amy driving with Will and Emily in the car, someone drifting into their lane, and—*BAM*, the end—Jeff would be left alone to plan the funeral for his entire family.

Sometimes the fears weren't even realistic.

Sometimes Jeff could see kidnappers or thieves in his house, his family tied to wooden chairs with coarse ropes and shotguns aimed at them. Other times he could see random ways his family could be harmed—Amy taking a bath and the hairdryer drops in, Will landing on the trampoline wrong and snapping his leg, Emily parked with some drunk jock pawing at her after home-coming. It would be easy to say how morbid Jeff was for thinking about such things. And Jeff would agree, it was morbid, and he didn't want to dwell on things like this—in fact he didn't *dwell* on them at all.

They just kind of popped up. Like flashes. Quick. He'd shut his eyes and the image would be gone. The fear would still be there, for a moment, and he would tell himself there was nothing to worry about.

He told himself and his wife there was nothing to worry about at that moment when he said, "Will's fine. He got caught up play-ing at Nate's and lost track of time."

"Well he's got to learn his lesson."

Amy went back inside. Jeff walked into the kitchen to see her setting the table with the speed and determination of a pit crew.

"Mom, what are you doing?" Emily asked.

"We're going to sit here and wait for your brother. He's going to walk in and see us with the table set and the food on the table getting cold. He has to learn that there are other people in the world."

"Sure Mom," Emily said.

She was reading *Cosmo*. Seventeen's got to be too young to be reading *Cosmo*. There's some pretty grown up stuff in there, Jeff thought. In high school he used to read *Cosmo* with his friends after school. They thought it would teach them the secret to un-derstanding women. And understanding women was the key to getting women. They took the quizzes as if studying for the bar exam. And tonight Emily was reading *Cosmo*. Which meant there were boys out there, somewhere, taking *Cosmo* quizzes to get Emily.

"Put the magazine away, honey," Amy said.

Emily slid the magazine under her seat. Jeff grabbed a chair. Dinner looked great: baked potatoes in foil, green beans with bacon, sweet potatoes, fruit salad, and a roast in a Crock-Pot. Jeff hoped Will would get here soon. This was a lot of good-looking food just to waste on an object lesson.

As if reading her father's mind, Emily reached for the fruit salad.

"What are you doing?" Amy asked.

"I was going to get some fruit salad."

"Nobody eats until your brother gets here."

"But fruit salad's already cold. What does it matter if it gets *more* cold?"

"That's not the point and you know it."

"Well, what are we supposed to do until he gets here?"

"We wait," Amy said.

JEFF HENDERSON

For the first half hour they were more annoyed than worried. A meal like this was meant to be eaten piping hot — if they didn't eat it now, no microwave could ever make it taste the same. But as the steam evaporated, the concern started to rise. They didn't say anything about it; they tried to talk about other things — things they would be talking about even if Will were with them. But Will knew what a big deal Monday night was to his father, he wouldn't just ditch it; there was losing track of time, getting carried away with your friends, and then there was *this*.

Amy snatched the phone from its charger and called Nate's mother.

"Hi Cindy. It's Amy. Will's not over at your place is he?"

"No, he left at 6:15," Cindy said.

"6:15? But it's 7:45."

Oh, please no, Jeff thought. His stomach was in a free fall. Jeff could suddenly see: Will's face on milk cartons, search parties, sitting on plush chairs on a talk show and speaking about what it is like to be living with a missing son. Usually Jeff could push the fears and flashes away. But this was real. This was the type of evening that started normal and ended with a phone call from the police. Or even worse, the evening would never end, life would be split into two distinct moments: Before, when they were a normal, average, all-American family — and after, when every dinner for the rest of their lives would feel empty because Will's empty chair would be an eerie, nauseating reminder of how simple and great things once were.

"Yeah, no, I don't know where else he could have stopped. He was supposed to come straight here," Amy said and then listened. "Yeah, you betcha. I will." She hung up.

Jeff looked at his wife and said, "I'm going to find him."

"What do you want me to do?"

"Call the police," Jeff shouted as he sprinted out the front door.

Moments later Jeff was in his car with his brights flicked on, cruising the gravel road that was between his home and the Jacksons' house. This was not the ideal night for Will to disappear. Clouds covered the moon like thin black sheets. It was nearly pitch black. There were no streetlights—any light from Goodland was too dim to make a difference. As Jeff drove down the road, the headlights cut through the dark, but only for a bit, and only right in front of Jeff's car. Will could be right outside of the headlights' reach, passed out and hurt, and Jeff could drive right by. It was difficult to concentrate with so much at stake. Because something was wrong. That wasn't even the issue anymore. The only question now was, how *wrong* were things? Jeff needed to think straight, to get creative and aggressive if he was going to find his son.

The clock was ticking. But that's when Jeff was at his best.

He popped the trunk, ran to the back of the car, and took the flares and flashlights out of his emergency kit. He opened up the first-aid kit: gauze strips, Neosporin, Band-Aids. He could help a minor injury, but if it was something major—no time to think about that. He threw the kit in the backseat of the car. He flicked his headlights to bright, he rolled up the passenger window, bracing a flashlight between it and the car door, and he held a flare out the driver's side window. Probably wasn't a safe thing to do, as if that mattered right now.

He drove slowly down the road yelling Will's name over and over. For a second he wondered if he should be saying something more. Should he be asking, where are you? Or, are you okay? But that was nonsense. There was no need to be creative. It wasn't as if Will wouldn't come running to his dad because he couldn't quite understand what his father was asking. It wasn't as if Will would think, Oh, sorry Dad, I thought you meant the other Will.

Jeff scanned to the right, the left, and right again. His car was a lighthouse, shining in every direction at once, giving him the largest possible radius to find his son. Assuming he was stranded on the side of the road. And if that were the case, it was possible another car would have driven by and seen him. He would have been taken somewhere. They would have received a phone call, and he would be at the hospital with Amy at least *knowing* what happened.

No, he wasn't on the side of the road. Which left three possible things that could have happened: (1) He ran away; (2) He'd been kidnapped; or (3) He'd used the cornfields as a shortcut. Jeff knew Will had done it before. Will thought he could get away with it and no one would notice. And maybe Amy didn't notice, but Jeff could tell when Will took the shortcut. But he never said anything because boys will be boys and there's no harm in that. He'd probably cut through those fields a hundred times.

Only this time something went wrong.

Jeff supposed there was a *distant* fourth possibility, which was that many people in town, including his son, had been raptured and his family had all been left behind. The apocalypse had begun. Jeff felt embarrassed for even thinking that. The rapture wasn't going to happen. It was just some quaint old legend. He was certain. He was almost certain. But on a night like tonight, anything felt possible.

Jeff ripped the flashlight out of the car window and marched into the cornfields. There were large stalks everywhere; they'd never seemed that tall before, but tonight they were towering over him. After twenty steps his car seemed well out of reach, and he suddenly understood why Fred Johnson was so adamant that kids stayed out of his cornfields. It really would be easy for any kid to get lost in here. Heck, it'd be easy for Jeff to get lost in here. How embarrassing would—

you just turn around

—that be? Still, turning back—

is your best option; he's probably not even in here

—was out of the question. Will could be hurt, his leg could be broken, and he could be screaming for help. What was Jeff going to do, wait for sunlight? Not a chance. He would do whatever it took to find his son. But then, as if mocking his resolve, his flashlight burned out. If it was pitch black before, there was nothing to describe what it was now.

Jeff hurried back to his car, tripping over cornstalks and getting back up. He was obsessed now. One cornstalk twisted his ankle, badly, and Jeff couldn't feel the pain. He knew the pain was there, but it was more of an idea. He could feel the blood rushing to his ankle as it ballooned, but it was distant, as if it were happening to someone else. The adrenaline wouldn't let him think about anything but the search.

He rummaged through his trunk for the next three minutes: books and golf clubs and tennis rackets and sneakers and tire irons and flip-flops.

God, Jeff, why is your trunk so filthy?

He could almost hear his mother's voice saying, This is what happens when you don't stay organized. Your boy is out there dying and you can't save him because you never bothered to keep your trunk clean.

Okay, so no D batteries in the trunk. Or if they were there he didn't have time to find them. But he knew where the flares were. He was always paranoid about breaking down on the side of the road whenever they took trips to visit Amy's mother in Manhattan (Kansas) and so he always had his trunk packed with supplies to help in an emergency. He grabbed three flares, stuck them in the back pockets of his Dockers, and cracked another one open. The flare's crimson light danced all over his face as he headed back into the cornfields, and he almost made it until he heard—

"You go out there alone and we'll have two missing persons we're looking for."

Jeff turned around holding the flare. And he saw Mike. "I'm looking for Will," Jeff said. Mike was in uniform, the lights of his squad car were flashing, and Jeff hadn't even noticed. There was nothing he could think about but the fields.

"Amy called it in, said you'd be out here."

"Well, I'm going to look for him."

"With a flare?"

"It's all I got."

"I called the boys back at the station, they're getting some fellas together right now. We'll get organized and comb through this field in twenty minutes. We'll find your boy in no time."

But how could Jeff just wait when Will was out there? Was he really supposed to just sit on the side of the road while his son was hurting and lost in the cornfield? Still, he couldn't just rummage through the cornfield alone with a busted up ankle and a flare.

There was nothing to do but wait.

Jeff leaned against the squad car and tied his shoe as tight as he could so his ankle wouldn't swell anymore. Mike leaned against the squad car next to him. When Jeff finished tying his shoe the two stood there in the dead silence for a moment. What was there to say? After a minute, maybe two, Mike lit a cigarette.

"So," Mike said.

"So," Jeff answered.

"How are things at Hansley?" Mike asked.

"They're picking up. I've got a couple of good leads."

"That's good to hear."

"Yeah," Jeff said. He always felt awkward talking about work with Mike. Even when there were much bigger things to think about — like a missing and/or critically wounded family member — Jeff still felt uneasy about this subject.

He'd been best friends with Mike for twenty years. Or maybe he'd been best friends with Mike twenty years ago. They had both been on the baseball team, Jeff the lefty pitcher and Mike the catcher, and they both planned on going to college together. But when Jeff got Amy pregnant everything changed. Emily was Jeff's own mini-apocalypse. After she was born he started to drift apart from Mike and the other guys in high school. Jeff was always working on odd jobs and Mike decided to go to the police academy. Mike saw how much Jeff was struggling with work and tried to convince him to join the force. "There's a steady salary, full benefits, retirement plan, and you get to make a difference," Mike said with bright eyes and a hopeful tone in his voice. Jeff didn't know how to tell Mike he didn't want to make a difference. And if he did want to make a difference he didn't want to do it by handing out speeding tickets.

So, whenever work came up, Jeff tried to steer the conversation elsewhere. Tonight he did so by saying, "How's the remodeling of the basement going?"

"Great. We're installing a projector in the basement. It'll project in HD. We'll have you guys over once it's finished. We'll barbeque and watch a Royals game."

"For sure," Jeff said. But he wasn't thinking *for sure*. He was thinking Will loves the Royals. How could he ever watch a Royals game again if his son was dead? What else out there would be daily reminders of his little boy?

Then, thankfully, other squad cars started pulling up. He'd never been so happy to see flashing red and blue lights.

Once the search party assembled outside the cornfields, Jeff thought they had a pretty decent group. There were deputies with search dogs. There were friends, co-workers like Kevin from Hansley Auto, and Fred Johnson himself even came out. His help would be invaluable; he knew the fields backwards and forwards.

Mike, the senior officer on duty, made a plan for the search party. They would fan out in groups of two, but stay well within earshot of each other, and thoroughly comb through each section of the field. When one section of the field was complete, they would go on to the next. Mike gave each one of the teams a flare gun and instructed everyone to fire a shot in the air the second they found the boy. Finally, Mike had one of the deputies call the paramedics. They should be on standby. Just in case.

Mike's final instruction was, "Okay men, Jeff's boy is out there. He needs us. Let's not waste anymore time." At that the search party fanned out and marched into the field, focused and determined. But again, Jeff barely made it into the field when his flashlight burned out.

"You have got to be kidding me. Again?"

"Again what?" Sam the deputy asked.

"My bulb burned out."

At that, *flash*, Sam's light was out.

"What's going on, Jeff?"

Jeff didn't have time to answer. He could see the other's lights, and one at a time, like dominos falling, they burned out. A chorus of "hey," "what happened," and "my light just died" swirled around him. He grabbed a flare out of his back pocket and cracked it open. "Come on," Jeff said to Sam. They found the closest group. "Here's a flare," Jeff said. "Use this, find the other groups, and guide them out of here. It's dangerous in the dark and we don't need anyone getting hurt. I'll head east and do the same."

They went much too slowly for Jeff—they had to take their time so everyone could see using the minimal light the flares cast off—but finally all the teams were found and brought back to where the cars were parked.

"What just happened?" Mike asked.

"The flashlights burned out," Sam said.

"Thank you Sam," Mike said. "But how?"

"They ran out of batteries?" Kevin Grabowski proposed.

"All at the same time?" Mike asked.

"It's possible," Kevin said.

"It's not possible," Mike said.

"Electromagnetic storm," Sam said.

"And what is that?"

"It's a storm, something about the magnetic poles shifting and ions getting into clouds, and it does all sorts of weird stuff to machinery. Shorts it out, and you know, stuff like that," Sam said. "I saw it on the Discovery Channel."

"And we just happen to have an electromagnetic storm here?" Mike said.

"This is Kansas, man. We have the weirdest storms on the planet," Sam said.

Silence. He kind of had a point.

"Fine, we'll load up on batteries and go back out there," Mike said.

"It won't matter. I was out there before you got here. Same thing happened to me," Jeff said.

"So what do we do?" Mike asked.

"We need light the old fashioned way. Torches, flares, any kind of fire," Jeff said.

"You're not taking fire into my cornfields," Fred Johnson said.

"Are you serious? Crops? You're worried about your crops?" Jeff said.

"Since it's my livelihood, yes I am. But that's not all I'm worried about. You get one of the dry husks on fire, and you're not going to be able to contain it. If your boy's out there, he'll burn alive. And so will anyone else who's trapped in the middle of the field."

"Maybe I should have the fire department on standby as well," Sam said.

Again, silence. This was the worst search party ever assembled — a search party who couldn't search.

"Mike, you have extinguishers in your squad cars?" Jeff asked.

"Yeah, sure," Mike said.

"We split up into groups again. One man holds a flare — we won't use torches, the flames are too hard to control, but a flare should be safe. And if something does catch fire, the other man walks with an extinguisher, puts it out right away."

The party stared at Jeff. This was the most half-baked plan they'd ever heard of. They weren't convinced. Jeff knew what their stares were saying. He took a deep breath and nodded. "Or, I go by myself, which I was ready to do an hour ago anyway. My son is out there. I can't wait till morning. You guys can. So, I'll see you later. Thanks for wasting my time."

"No, Jeff, I'll help you find your boy," Mike said.

"So will I," Sam said.

"So will I," Kevin Grabowski added.

At that, there was one "So will I" after another, after another. And that's what's so great about a small town like Goodland. Everyone sticks together — they were family. If one person is hurting, everyone is hurting. This was the type of *Dead Poets So-ciety* moment that would have really touched Jeff if his son wasn't lost and he wasn't freaked out of his mind at whatever was causing the bulbs to burn out and if the flare he was holding wasn't singe-ing all the hairs on his hand.

They quickly loaded up with flares and extinguishers and headed back out to the field. Jeff held his flare low to the ground, walking at a sprinter's pace through the cornfields. He scanned the ground and looked through cornstalks. He listened for cries or screams—for breathing or whimpering. His mind was clear. He was completely focused on the task at hand. This had gone on long enough. He would not be deterred anymore. He would face whatever was in here: storms, demons, or any other unspeakable evil. They would be sorry to cross his path.

And then, *crack*. A flare soared through the night sky—it looked as if Tinkerbell was lit on fire and shot out of a cannon. They found him, Jeff thought. All the possibilities rushed through his mind: Will with leg snapped, Will shivering and crying, Will not moving at all, Will hugging an officer and telling his story.

Crack.

Another flare shot above them. Jeff ran towards it. He didn't wait to make sure Sam was following, or that his path was clear. He just ran. He pushed through stalks and anything else that was in his way. And then he burst through one final stalk and saw his son. He was standing there, without a shirt, coated in dirt and gravel, and looking a little cut up. Jeff didn't run toward him right away, because no one else had. Something didn't seem right. In-stead, the entire search party stood there, creating a circle all the way around the shirtless, cut-up boy. The entire party clutched their flares, creating a neon glow on Will, and his eyes and his teeth seemed to reflect the red light perfectly.

"Will. Are you okay?" Mike asked.

Will smiled.

Jeff went over to Will and crouched next to him. Jeff felt Will's ribs, his legs, and his face to make sure nothing was broken. And nothing was. Everything was fine. His son was fine. Jeff hugged him and through tears he said, "I was so worried about you." He let go and looked his son in the eyes. "So worried."

Will put a hand on Jeff's shoulder. It didn't feel like the hand of a boy, it was much older, firm and confident. "I have a message for you Dad." Then Will looked past his father and at the entire search party. And with the confidence of a prophet he said, "I have a message for all of you."

SERGEANT MIKE FRANK

Sergeant Mike Frank still remembers a time when students had drills for the apocalypse. However, the apocalypse the elementary students were running drills for had nothing to do with God or Jesus. Rather, the impending doom was a by-product of the United States of America's inability to coexist with Russia.

And vice versa.

Both sides had been arming themselves with nuclear warheads for years. And soon everyone had too many weapons. The governments of these powerful countries couldn't just buy all of those weapons for nothing. That would be frivolous, a waste of the taxpayers' hard-earned money. Therefore, the responsible thing to do would be to attack. It would go like this: Once one country (Mike was pretty sure Russia was going to attack first) launches their weapons high into the air, the other country would have to respond, they would have to rain down retribution, and in the end, if everything went according to plan, most of the planet would be a lifeless, smoldering, radioactive wasteland.

To protect against nuclear blasts, teachers had students hide underneath their desks. This was the great plan for safety. Even at the age of eight Mike was pretty skeptical of a small wooden desk's ability to shield him from an atomic bomb. He tried to bite his tongue. He tried to obey every other Thursday as the drill bell rang and everyone put down their classwork to crouch under their desks. But one Thursday, towards the end of the third grade, he couldn't take it anymore. He couldn't willingly just accept that this was worth anyone's time. So, while the other kids slid under their desks, Mike just sat up, proud, with his hands folded in front of him. When Mrs. Peacock looked up from underneath her own desk she was horrified.

"Michael, what are you doing?"

"I'm not going on with this charade anymore," Michael said. *Charade* was a new word that Michael had just added to his vocabulary. He learned it from playing the game Charades.

"Charade?" Mrs. Peacock squawked, wondering where he learned that word. That was a fourth grade word.

"We're going to die anyway so why does it matter if I hide under my desk," Michael said.

Mrs. Peacock walked over to Michael, seized his arm, and tugged him into the hallway. "What has gotten into you Michael Frank?" she asked.

"I just don't know why we're charading around with this desk drill," Michael answered. He still hadn't mastered his new word.

"Because if something does happen, and God forbid it does, we need the students safe. The blast probably isn't going to hit our town, which means parents will be looking for students, which means there will be lots of fear and we'll need order—"

Order.

Now, thirty years later, it made a lot of sense to Mike. The desks weren't about safety—they were about order. Keeping things under control was the highest priority. Because truthfully, when it came to the masses, people were cattle. The entire town could be easily spooked, and if that were to happen, disorder and looting and lawlessness bring just as much damage as the original disaster ever could.

And as rumors and gossip about the impeding Goodland

rapture started to spring up, Mike knew that soon his primary job would be to keep Goodland orderly.

Tonight, the battle against hysteria would start with figuring out what to do about Jeff Henderson's boy. Will said some weird things in that cornfield, and it wasn't just what he said, it was the *way* he said things that had riled everyone up. Just an hour ago Mike had seen grown men — calloused brave men — turn stark white at some of the things Will was saying. Heck, Curt Benson, a twice-decorated veteran from the Korean War, looked like he'd wet himself by the time Will finished —

(*prophesying*)

— talking.

The key to keeping things under control would be keeping their stories straight. They needed to be careful about what they said, especially to their wives. Mike had already briefed the other men in the cornfield. He told them, "Will was lost and we found him sleeping. That's all anyone else needs to know." He hadn't discussed things with Jeff yet because he was so emotional. And rightfully so. His son had been lost.

But after they found Will, Mike convinced Jeff to let him take them home. He'd have one of the other men take Mike in his car later on. And now that they were getting close to Jeff's house they needed to decide how they were going to frame the story to Amy.

"What exactly are we going to tell Amy?" asked Mike.

"What do you mean?" Jeff asked.

"Well, about what happened. What are we going to tell her?"

"We'll tell her the truth."

"The truth, sure," Mike said. "But what version of the truth?"

AMY HENDERSON

Amy clutched her lukewarm cup of coffee and stared out the window. There wasn't much to look at outside. Right in front of the house there was a large elm tree lit up from the glow of the front porch lights. The leaves had fallen off the tree so all that was left were branches twisted and stretching in every direction. A little past the tree Amy could see the silhouette of the windmill as the blades slowly spun. And beyond the windmill there was nothing but blackness. It looked like it engulfed everything. All the lights in Goodland and everywhere else on the planet seemed to have been shut off.

Her son was out there somewhere in the darkness.

She prayed that nothing had happened to him. But even as she was praying it seemed impossible. How could something have actually happened? Will was her little miracle baby. He was the special guy who'd given her life purpose. After Emily had gone to kindergarten Amy could remember how depressed she was. Emily was always so independent already, and when Amy dropped her off for her first day she thought Emily might cry. She thought Emily might clutch on to her and say, "Don't leave me Mommy!" All the other kids were doing things like that. But Emily just grabbed her Barbie lunchbox and sprinted onto the playground. She shouted "Bye, Mommy!" as she ran, but she never looked back.

Six weeks later Amy was pregnant again.

Only this time it was planned. This time she knew the hardships the upcoming months and years had in store, but she also knew how special they would be.

She just didn't expect that the hardships would start right away. Will was born six weeks early. He was in an incubator for the first month of his life. Amy stood outside the window of the nursery every single day. She spent hours looking at her son bathed in that ultraviolet light and watching those little ribs rise up and down with every breath.

But she never feared the worst. Even then she could see what a fighter he was. Because from the day he was born she could see the glint and purpose in his eyes. She knew how special he was.

When they finally took him home Amy spent the first night with him in the nursery. She rocked for hours with him cradled in her arms and she just stared at her perfect little miracle. She felt so proud. It was probably how Mary felt the first time she held baby Jesus.

There had been other scary moments. The time he'd fallen out of the tree and snapped his arm in half. The day he came home with his first black eye. The afternoon he'd wrecked his bike into a chain-link fence. Amy worried about Will, took care of him, and mothered him after every one of those incidents. But she always knew there was nothing to worry about.

There was something special about her son.

And God doesn't just let special people die somewhere out in the black darkness of a Kansas night, does he? If he was going to do that, why would he have made them special in the first place?

He wouldn't have. That's why Amy knew her son was going to be okay. That's why when other mothers would be frantic and fearing the worst, Amy just sipped on her coffee and stared out in the darkness.

And as if God himself were answering Amy's thoughts and

fears, a police car pulled up the driveway right as Amy finished her last sip of coffee. She knew who was inside the car. And she was so excited to see them that she didn't even put her empty cup of coffee down as she walked outside.

Will jumped out from the police car and ran up the driveway. For some reason he wasn't wearing a shirt. He was also nicked and cut and bruised but he didn't seem to have any serious injuries. No broken arms or legs or anything like that. He ran into Amy's arms and hugged her tightly.

It felt so good to have her son back.

Amy had already planned what she was going to say to Will when she first saw him. She was going to tell him how much she loved him. She was going to tell him how very much he meant to her. She was going to explain, probably as the tears rolled down her cheeks, how she didn't say kind, loving things often enough. But for some reason none of that came out of Amy's mouth after they hugged.

For some reason Amy firmly grabbed Will on both of his arms and asked, "Where were you? What happened? Do you have any idea how worried I was about you? You said you were going over to Nate's for just a few minutes. How did that turn into hours?"

"I got lost," Will answered.

"Lost?"

"In the cornfields."

"You cut across the cornfields?"

"Yes."

"Even though we've talked over and over again about not going in there?"

"I was running late. I knew I'd get in trouble if I was late for family dinner."

"You get in more trouble for getting lost in the cornfields."

"I didn't mean to get lost. Am I grounded?"

"You are beyond grounded," Amy said, though she didn't really know what there was beyond grounded. The electric chair? There's only so much punishment a mother can deliver before she reaches her limits. And besides, she wasn't really trying to deliver punishment, she was trying to let her son know how much she loved him. But he needed to know how dangerous things were. He needed to know there were consequences for his actions. She wasn't just making rules like don't go into the cornfields because she was the wicked witch of the west and she laughed with her flying monkeys at the thought of taking away all of his fun. She was making those rules to protect him.

Amy looked again at her son, unsure of what to say or do next. "Why aren't you wearing a shirt?"

"It got dirty from running."

"What were you running from?"

"I'm not exactly sure."

"You're not?"

"No. There were bad things in the cornfield. But there were also good things."

"Like what?"

"I'm not really supposed to tell you."

"You're not?" Amy asked.

"No. Officer Mike said he wanted to fill you in on everything that happened."

Amy suddenly felt nauseous. It was kind of like morning sickness, at night, without being pregnant. "Honey, I'm your mother. You can tell me anything."

"Officer Mike was pretty serious about me not telling *any-one anything*. I mean, I want to tell you, but I don't want to get grounded *and* arrested."

As Will finished talking, Amy realized her husband was suspiciously absent. He should have jumped out of the police car and followed right behind Will. He should have been telling her everything that had happened since they'd last seen each other. It had been a nightmare of a night; they'd faced their worst fear, and so why didn't he come inside and fill her in on everything?

Amy looked back towards the police car and she could see Jeff and Mike standing right in front of the car engaged in some sort of serious conversation. It seemed like Mike was trying to convince Jeff of something. Mike's face was stern and serious while Jeff looked tired and defeated. Even from where Amy was standing she could see the bags under Jeff's eyes. So what was Mike telling Jeff? Was he trying to keep Amy out of the loop just like Will? Why would they be doing that? What could have happened out there? What didn't they want her to know?

It didn't matter. They were kidding themselves if they thought they could hide the truth from her. "Go inside honey," Amy told Will. "Get those cuts cleaned out and get a shirt on."

"Okay," Will said and went inside.

Amy walked towards the police car and she heard the tail end of the conversation as Mike said, "—not the parents at the school. And especially not your wife."

"Especially not your wife what?" Amy asked.

Amy walked out of the kitchen holding a kettle full of blisteringly hot Earl Grey tea. She poured Mike and Jeff a cup. They would need tea. Kansas days in the early fall are still warm, but by night things begin to frost over, making summer seem like a distant memory. The tea would make them warm and rational and calm enough to tell her what had happened.

"Thank you, Mrs. Henderson," Mike said, after Amy finished filling his cup.

"You're welcome," Amy said. She sat on the couch next to her husband. The men didn't say anything. They just kept sipping their tea. Apparently, they didn't realize that this was the moment they should start filling her in on what happened. This shouldn't have been a shock to Amy. Jeff was usually horrible at reading the moment. He didn't understand the right moments of when to say "I love you," or to ask her how her day was, or when to turn off the TV so they could catch up on their lives. Whenever Amy pointed this out, Jeff gave some Neanderthal response like, "How am I supposed to read your mind?"

Amy always tried to explain that he wasn't supposed to read her mind; he was just supposed to be a little bit empathetic. If he used a hint of intuition he could tell the right moments. And when you feel the moment it's so much more rewarding. It's so much better for your husband to say things like, "Honey, I'm so lucky to have you," when it's not prompted. When it comes out of the blue. But intuition and reading the situation would have to wait for another night.

Tonight, she needed to know what was going on with her son. Even when she had tucked Will into bed, he still wouldn't tell her anything more. And if he wasn't going to tell her, they would have to. "What happened out there?" Amy asked. Then she looked at Mike and asked, "Why did you tell my son not to tell me anything? He said you were going to 'fill me in on the situation.' And so I've made your tea and now I'm waiting for you to fill me in."

"All right Mrs. Henderson. Your son was lost deep, three-quarters of a mile at least, in those cornfields," Mike said. "He was running around trying to find his way out for hours. When one of my deputies found your son he was asleep. After we found him and woke him up, he started to say some unsettling things."

"Unsettling things."

"He started talking about the rapture, Amy," Jeff said. "And I've never seen him look or sound the way he did when he was out there. I can't even really explain it. It wasn't even Will. It was like he was someone else."

"What was he saying?"

"He was making some pretty bold claims," Mike said.

"He said there were going to be three signs," Jeff added, "and once those three signs were complete the rapture would come. It was crazy. It didn't really make sense."

"How did he know there would be three signs?"

"Some face told him," Jeff said. "He saw some face made out of corn or something and it told him all of this."

"So what were the signs?"

Jeff and Mike looked at each other the way a couple who'd been married for years would. They were talking without words. The problem was, Jeff was Amy's husband. He should be exchanging secret looks with her, not Mike. They were still covering something.

"Don't look at each other, look at me," Amy said. "What were the signs?"

"He only told us one of them," Jeff said. "He told us the school would be destroyed."

"He what?"

"In three days," Jeff said. "He told us the school would be destroyed in three days and that is the first sign."

"What does that even mean?" Amy asked.

"Honestly, Mrs. Henderson, nothing," Mike said. "Your son was out there for hours. He was traumatized. He could have seen a lot of things but that doesn't mean they were real. It just means he was scared. He probably dreamed it all. And that's why I wanted to fill you in. We need to all work together to convince Will that he was dreaming. We probably need to keep him home from school tomorrow. Then this will all go away."

"What if he wasn't dreaming?"

"Honey, come on—"

"No, what if he wasn't dreaming? What if he really saw something out there?"

"And what if it was just a dream?" Mike asked. "In the age of school shootings and every other kind of fear we can't have your son running around telling everyone the school's going to be destroyed. That's going to freak this entire town out. The bottom line is your son had a traumatic night. But he's home and he's safe. We should all be thankful for that. Let's take the next day or two to help him calm down. If he's still convinced he saw something after that we'll go from there."

"It's the right thing to do honey," Jeff said. "He's still only eleven and we're his parents. It's our job to help him know what's real and what isn't."

The conversation went on in circles for a while until they finally agreed that it was in everyone's best interest to keep Will home from school tomorrow. If anything, he'd had a traumatic night and needed some rest. Once that was agreed on, Mike left the house. Amy felt like an oppressive weight left with him. Who was he to boss them around anyway? It wasn't like Jeff ever talked to him anymore. So why did he suddenly care so much, Amy thought as she brushed her teeth.

"I know this is scary," Jeff said with a toothbrush crammed in his mouth, "but it's late and things seem so much worse late at night. Let's get some sleep. By tomorrow night we'll all be laughing about this."

"Okay," Amy said as she bit down on her own toothbrush. *Laughing about this?* Was he serious? Amy rinsed out her mouth with Cool Mint Listerine, thinking she should cut Jeff a little slack. He meant well. He'd been through a tough night himself and he had to get some sleep for work tomorrow. He was just trying to be a good husband. He was trying to make her feel better.

But it wasn't working. She felt worse after everything he said, but he was trying and that was worth something.

After Jeff went to bed Amy couldn't sleep.

So she stood in Will's doorway and watched him sleep. He was just as perfect as the day he was born. She still smiled as she watched his miraculous little lungs slightly move the covers up and down. He made the cutest little snoring sound as he slept. And as Amy stood in the doorway she felt like she could finally relax. She felt maybe Jeff was right; the sun would come up tomorrow and everything would be okay.

About a half hour later she crawled into bed with Jeff. It reminded her of how she felt when she was first married. She was frightened about the concept of sharing her bed with someone. Every time she wanted to turn over or pull the sheets a little closer she was scared that she might wake Jeff up. It felt so strange then. It felt surreal that she would be sharing her bed for the rest of her life. It made her anxious as she realized this wasn't just an arrangement that would be going on for a couple of weeks, this was forever. As long as she was still on earth, every time she twisted or turned or tugged on the covers, Jeff would notice.

That feeling went away after a while though. And Amy grew to like sharing her bed. She thought it was nice to have a warm body to snuggle up with on the bitter cold nights of December. And it was nice on a night like tonight, when the world outside of her home seemed so frightening, to have Jeff there to protect her.

As Amy got into bed she curled against her husband and closed her eyes. Amy had recently been studying about lucid dreaming. She learned that she could dream about whatever she wanted and that seemed like such a wonderful thing. So she'd read up on how it worked and had tried with some success lately to control what she dreamed about. Amy lay with her eyes closed and imagined all of the things she wanted to dream about—picnics in the park, their trip to Disney World, Emily growing up and becoming famous, Will marrying some amazing Christian girl and bringing over perfect little grandbabies on Thanksgiving. Amy was sure these would be the things she would dream about.

She was wrong. Once she finally fell asleep the image that kept rolling over and over in her mind was Will stranded alone in that cornfield having visions of the future. And the question that kept popping into her dreams was—what really happened to my son out there?

WILL HENDERSON

Will skipped school the next day.

It was only the second time in Will's life that he'd been told *not* to go to school even though he was feeling perfectly fine. The first time was in the second grade. The kids at school were busy making a haunted house. Will was on the zombie team and his job was to make a dish called "brains delight," which consisted of red Jell-O and Raisinets. When his mom heard about what the class was doing she insisted Will stay home from school. At the time she was listening to Kent Howard, a nationally known, loved, and respected evangelist who was warning about the little ways evil things get into our homes. "Often, the evilest, I'm talking about the most demonic of things, can get put into our homes through our children's toys."

And when she learned about the haunted house she knew this was exactly what Kent Howard was talking about. Will thought it was sort of neat he got to stay home without being sick, but he was kind of conflicted too. He didn't want to let the other kids on the zombie team down. When he told his mother this, she said, "The kids on the zombie team *should* be let down."

Will didn't exactly know what she meant.

But then his mom asked if he wanted to go to the store and get all new toys and some new movies. Will could hardly believe it. Skip school and get new toys — it was too good to be true.

The problem was his new toys were Bible action figures like the apostle Paul and Meshack and his new movies were *McGee and Me* and *Superbook*.

When Will got home he started to watch his new movies. They were sort of okay. *Superbook* was a cartoon about a bunch of Japanese-looking children who had a robot and a time-traveling flying house. They traveled back to Jesus' time to watch him do miracles. Will tried to get into the cartoon but the whole time he kept thinking, If you had a time-traveling flying house, why would you go back to Jesus' time? Why not go see cowboys and gunfights in the wild west or to medieval days when there were knights and dragons and castles and moats? Will decided that the kids in *Superbook* were just more spiritual than he was and then he felt guilty that he was more interested in cowboys and dragons than in Jesus.

As *Superbook* came to an end Will heard a rustling sound in his room. He ran upstairs and saw his mom with a trash bag throwing away his Power Rangers, Teenage Mutant Ninja Turtles, and *Harry Potter* books. "Why are you throwing everything away?" Will asked.

"Oh, these old things? You don't need them anymore. You have new toys and books now," his mother explained.

"Oh," Will said. And then, "But I sort of like my old ones too."

"These aren't good for you. I know you don't understand this now, but someday you're going to. And you'll thank me," she said.

Will didn't get any new toys on the morning after the cornfield. But his dad did tell him that he could watch any movie he wanted. His dad said he deserved a day off after his rough night last night. He told Will that he had seen some special things but he needed to keep them a secret from *everybody* until they could talk about it more.

So Will tried to enjoy his day off. He poured himself a bowl of Lucky Charms and then spent twenty minutes picking out all of the non-charm pieces so he could enjoy a bowl of nothing but colorful marshmallows. Then he popped in *The Return of the King*, his favorite in the *Lord of the Rings* trilogy. He should have been having fun. He should have been getting lost in middle earth and not worrying about anything that was going on in Goodland. But he couldn't because there was a big problem — the face had given him a warning. And this wasn't something he was supposed to keep a secret; this wasn't something that was supposed to just be between him and the other guys in the cornfield. Everybody was supposed to know the things the face was saying. Because what good is a warning if you don't warn anyone?

Had his parents not thought about this?

Was Officer Mike saying things — saying *lies* — that were tricking his mom and dad? Suddenly, Will got a little scared. A police officer who was a bad guy, that was a lot to take in. Still, it was possible. It had to be. Will sat in the back of the police car last night and listened to Officer Mike tell his dad, "Your son shouldn't go to school for the next few days because he's going to scare people." And Officer Mike was right. Will was going to scare people.

He was *supposed* to scare people.

Sure, it was scary that the school was going to be destroyed. But wouldn't it be scarier if the other elementary kids were in the school while it was being destroyed? Of course it would. So the only explanation was that the police officer and his parents didn't believe him.

Did they think he was just making this stuff up for fun? Or did they think he was dreaming? Did they think he was having a nightmare? Maybe they thought he was having a dream or a nightmare and when he woke up he started talking about the face and reasons the rapture was going to happen. But they couldn't be more wrong. Whatever last night was, it wasn't a nightmare. Nightmares jump all around. You could be in a field, then in a house, then falling from the sky, and then in your underwear in the middle of the school bus with all the other kids laughing at you. Nightmares are jumbled with lots of scary pictures strung together.

The face wasn't like that.

It was calm, and it talked for a long time, and Will could remember everything. He could remember how the wind sounded, how cool it was, the questions he asked and the answers the face gave. Still, it was starting to make sense, his parents and the officer wanted him to believe that it was a dream. It was safer that way. After all, they hadn't seen the face themselves. And kids imagine up weird stuff like fairies and pirates and monsters in the closet all the time. Sure, Will wasn't a kid anymore, but he wasn't an adult either. So, how were they supposed to know Will had actually seen the face? They couldn't. The only way they could believe would be by the school being destroyed.

And by then it wouldn't matter anymore.

It was suddenly clear what had to be done. Will ran upstairs, put on his favorite sweatshirt, his second favorite pair of jeans, and his bright red Chuck Taylor sneakers. Then he ran back downstairs, threw a blanket over himself, and waited. He would look exactly like he did on any other sick day. He wouldn't act until the moment was right. He continued to watch *Return of the King*. Right around Will's favorite part (the moment where Sam Wise Gamgee says, "I may not be able to carry the ring Mr. Frodo, but I can carry you") his mom sauntered down the stairs.

"How are you honey?" This question felt more annoying than it should have. Lately, Will didn't want to be mothered. He loved his mom, sure, but she could also be so suffocating. It was like she was trying to hold him back. She didn't want him to grow up. She wanted him to be her "precious guy" or "little lamb" forever.

"I'm fine Mom."

"Do you want to come to the store with me?"

"I'm going to watch the rest of the movie."

"Isn't it almost over?"

"No, there's a lot left." That's what was so great about *Return of the King*. Even when it felt like it should be over there was still like an hour left.

"Okay, is there anything you want me to get at the store?"

"No, I think I'm okay."

"But you always want me to get you something."

"Right, of course," he said. She was right. He always wanted something at the store. And now suddenly he didn't. He was acting suspicious. He needed to ask for something — but what? How was he supposed to be able to think about treats when the end of the world was so near? It was tough to think about what to ask for when every friend you have is going to be killed in a few days. So he just blurted, "I'd like some ice cream."

"What flavor?"

"Vanilla."

"Vanilla? That's it?" she said.

Vanilla? What are you thinking? Why didn't you say Cookie Dough or Rocky Road or any of the special flavors of ice cream? Why did you have to pick vanilla, the most suspicious of all ice cream flavors? He needed to tell her some things he'd like with the ice cream. Because the only reason a person would ever order vanilla ice cream is so they could put all sorts of stuff on top of it. So he said, "I'd like vanilla, *and* chocolate sauce, caramel, and marshmallows for toppings."

"Isn't that a little much?"

"You asked me what I wanted."

"Okay, because you've been so brave," his mom said right before she kissed him on the forehead, grabbed her keys, and left.

She bought it, Will thought.

He sprung up from under the covers, peered through the window, and watched as the Volvo pulled out of the driveway and down the road. He darted outside. He grabbed his bike and pedaled down the road as fast as he could. It wasn't fast enough. He had to get to school and back before his mother got home. Unfortunately, his family lived out in the country. And in Goodland that's saying something. Still, he had to somehow get onto the school grounds without any of the teachers or principals seeing him and beat his mom home. If he could do that successfully, then no one could prove he was ever there. Sure, someone else would get the credit for saving the school, but he couldn't worry about being a hero at the moment.

The message was all that mattered.

The plan started off well. Will made it to school in record time. He pulled up to the school right as everyone was getting out for lunch. Luckily he wouldn't have to sneak into the school because in the fall most kids eat their lunches outside. They eat on the benches or sitting in the grass (it was more like weeds, dandelions, dirt, and grass splotches, but none of the kids paid much attention to the landscaping), and they ate quickly so they could get on to the important business of playing dodgeball and steal the bacon.

Will hid his bike in the shrubs and snuck up to the chain-link fence. He'd have to find the nearest kids and talk to them. In the corner he saw Phil, Jessica, and Veronica. It was perfect. They were in the fifth grade *and* they were popular. Everyone looked up to them. If he could just convince them, they would have the clout to spread the word.

"Jessica," Will whispered. Jessica looked towards the playground, benches, and slides, but she didn't see anyone.

"Jessica," Will whispered again. She looked a bit more, and then she saw Will, crouching and peering through the fence.

"What are you doing here?" Jessica asked.

"I have something important to tell you," Will said. By this time Phil and Veronica saw him and went over to the fence.

"Why aren't you at school today?"

"The police wouldn't let me come to school," Will said.

"The police told you to skip school? We're seriously supposed to believe that?" Veronica said.

"It's the truth."

"The police bust people for skipping school. Not the other way around," Veronica said.

Will once again realized how annoying and prissy Veronica was. His mom told him that God puts all kinds of people in our lives to teach us how to get along with everybody. But Will suddenly had a horrifying thought: What if he had to marry someone like Veronica? What if God was planning on teaching him the ultimate lesson? He could imagine coming home and having everything he ever said met with a nagging, know-it-all resistance. Suddenly he was very grateful that the rapture was going to save him from such a miserable marriage.

"Would you just listen Veronica? I don't have very long," Will said.

"Fine," she said.

"This is going to sound weird but you have to believe me. You know the rapture everyone is talking about?"

"Yeah," all his classmates said. They knew about the rapture all right.

"Well, last night someone told me that our school is going to be destroyed. It's the first sign that the rapture is coming."

"Who told you that?" Jessica asked.

"I can't say. But I can tell you that it's gonna happen in three days."

"Three days from when?" Phil asked.

Will had never really thought about this. The face said three days. It didn't say when the three days were starting. Why are all prophecies and visions so vague? What good does that do anybody? If the face had said, "Seventy-two hours from now the school will be destroyed," that would be something Will could act on. He could have set his stopwatch and told everyone the exact minute the school was going to be destroyed. But three days was all he had to go on. It was up to him to interpret what that meant.

"Three days from yesterday," Will said.

"And how is the school going to be destroyed?" Jessica asked.

"I don't know. Something big. Probably a meteor from the sky or something," Will speculated for the second time in as many statements.

Through the fence Will noticed the other kids on the playground were staring in his direction. Their lunches were finished —their Capri Suns empty and their Snack Packs scraped dry. They were bored, restless, and something interesting was happening by the fence. They could smell it; they were drawn to it like jackals to blood. Will watched as they whispered, pointed, congregated, and began to walk toward him. He should run. But no one was convinced of his message yet. Suddenly, he understood: This was his chance, his one shot to convince everyone of the catastrophe that would strike Jefferson Elementary in three days. He'd have to convince them quickly. Kids could tell first when something interesting like a fight or a kissing contest was happening, but teachers and principals would be soon to follow.

Will climbed the eight-foot chain-link fence and slid down the other side. He stood in the middle of all the students of Jefferson Elementary who had "A" lunch. The students were silent and reverent. Will could almost hear their collective silence asking, What's going on? What's he going to say?

Will broke the silence by exclaiming, "Tomorrow, or possibly the day after tomorrow, Jefferson Elementary will be destroyed. I'm not sure how. But I'm positive it's going to happen. You cannot be here. If you are, then you will be destroyed along with the school. And this is happening for one reason: It will be the first sign of the rapture. It's coming soon. Long before any of us can ever get married," Will said.

For a while, maybe as long as four seconds, no one said a word. Then the kids started to laugh. And they weren't chuckling — they were belly laughing and flinging insults between breaths. The laughter punctured Will; seconds before he was a helium balloon floating proud, but now his air had been let out and he felt flimsy and wrinkled.

"I thought you said a meteor was going to destroy the school," Phil said.

"Yeah, I think it's going to be meteor, or something scary like a laser —"

"A laser? Who has a giant laser to destroy the school?" one of the kids said. Will couldn't tell who was who anymore. They were just blurry laughing faces amidst the dirt, weeds, and monkey bars.

"I said something *like* a laser."

"Didn't you say someone told you this?" a voice asked. Maybe it was Veronica.

"Yes," Will answered.

"Who told you?"

"I can't say."

"Why not?"

Will tried to calm himself down. They wouldn't believe him if he was flustered. But he couldn't center his thoughts. He tried to continue. "I can't tell you because I think maybe I saw—" Will tried to start again, "Well last night I got lost in the cornfields for a long time. For maybe hours. And then this face came to me, it was made out of corn but it looked kind of like Moses, and it told me things—"

"So a cornface told you a laser is going to destroy the school tomorrow?" someone asked. At that the laughter really erupted. It was deafening. And Will didn't quite understand why. What was happening? It wasn't supposed to go like this. And now the teachers were noticing what was going on. They could see trouble brewing. They'd break things up in no time. Will had to explain himself quickly.

"No, not a laser exactly," Will said. "This is really important. You have to listen—"

"I think they've listened enough," Vice Principal Morris said. His hand was on Will's shoulder. "Come with me, son. Everybody else, lunch is over. Back to class."

The kids dispersed at the vice principal's command. But they were still whispering and pointing as they walked. Some kids continued to laugh right at Will. The kinder kids only looked at him like he was pathetic and strange.

"You have to listen to me," Will shouted as he was being tugged to the principal's office. "I'm not making this up! Do not come to school tomorrow or maybe the day after!"

But he was out of earshot of most kids now. And the ones who could hear him acted like he wasn't even there.

AMY HENDERSON

Once Will was watching *The Lord of the Rings* Amy knew it would be a good time to duck out of the house. That movie went on forever so she could use that time to go grocery shopping. Not that she liked grocery shopping. It was just one of her weekly chores that needed to be done. It wasn't really the shopping Amy didn't like — it was the compromise. There were aisles and aisles of delicious food that she could not get because most of that food was *name-brand* food and she was shopping on a budget. Shopping on a budget meant that things like Tide and Pepsi and Doritos were luxuries. So she'd get all the items in black and white bags that were the generic equivalents.

Sometimes she'd tell Jeff that they should upgrade and buy some name-brand groceries and household items. But Jeff would always say, "Amy, you're paying for the packaging and advertising. Do you know how much those Superbowl commercials cost? Millions, that's how much. And that's all you're getting with name brands. A fancy ad. It's not like the chips taste any different."

But that's where Jeff was wrong. Doritos did taste better than Mr. Cheesy's Chips. Tide did protect the color in their clothes much better than the generic black and white laundry detergent. They were saving a couple of pennies, and for that, the price they had to pay was high — stale tasting chips and faded, colorless clothes.

Every time Amy checked out at the register, she couldn't help but think that the groceries she was buying were simply helping her to sustain life rather than groceries that would allow them to celebrate life and enjoy their food. And that's why on that day Amy broke down and bought the name-brand ice cream. Not just any name-brand ice cream—she bought Ben and Jerry's. For the price of a tiny pint of Ben and Jerry's, Amy knew she could buy a giant gallon of the generic ice cream that comes in the big plastic tub. But she didn't care. She wanted to buy something for her son to celebrate his bravery. She wasn't willing to do that with the ice cream in the cheap plastic tub.

As Amy was standing in the checkout line with her Ben and Jerry's and the rest of her groceries, her cell phone rang.

"Excuse me," Amy told the cashier. "Hello."

"Mrs. Henderson, we need you to come to Jefferson. There's been an incident with your son."

"My son isn't at school."

"Actually he is. I'm staring at him right now. He's right outside the principal's office."

"He's what?"

"He made quite the bold statement today at school. He said it was a prophecy, but we're having to treat it like a bomb threat."

"I don't understand how prophesying and a bomb threat are even in the same category."

"They're in the same category, Mrs. Henderson, because any threat towards students, teachers, or school property must be treated with the utmost severity."

Amy didn't even think about what she was doing as she left the store with her phone pressed against her ear. But before she knew it, she was in her car driving toward Jefferson. As she drove she tried to explain, "He wasn't threatening. He was prophesying. He saw something last night in the cornfield."

"I'm sure he did," the receptionist said. "You can discuss that with the principal. And he's ready to discuss all of that whenever you get here."

"Fine. I'm ready to discuss a few things with *him* too. I'm almost there."

The first person she saw at the school was Will. Where should she start? Should she lay into him because of his irresponsibility, lying, manipulating, and recklessness? He had told her, "I'll stay right here." He said, "I promise." And she leaves the house for a few minutes to get some groceries and expensive ice cream, and he's sitting in the principal's office for making threats to the school? Amy was in shock that Will would do this. She was TNT dynamite, her fuse was lit, and right before she was about to explode—she looked closely at her son.

His face was splotchy and his eyes were puffy. Her anger evaporated. Suddenly it was clear her boy was hurt and needed his mother. She gently grabbed his face and asked, "What happened?"

"They—" Will said and then trailed off. It seemed to be all he could manage.

"They what? Interrogated you? Accused you of making a bomb threat? Said you were going to jail? What did they say honey?"

"They laughed at me. They wouldn't even listen. I was just trying to save them," Will said.

"The principals laughed at you?"

"The kids at lunch. They called him cornface and then said a bunch of stuff about me. But that's not even what bothered me. They wouldn't listen, Mom. They thought I was crazy. And so now they're still going to be here when the school gets destroyed. Everyone is going to die."

Principal Morris cracked open the door. Behind the principal was the guidance counselor Mrs. Heller, Sergeant Mike, and two other police officers. Amy suddenly wasn't sure what was going on. Things were more serious than she suspected.

"May we speak in private, Mrs. Henderson?" Principal Morris asked.

"I'll be right back, honey," Amy said, kissing him on the cheek, and walked into the office.

As Amy sat down, she felt unprepared to deal with the principal and all those people in his office. Not that this was a new feeling. For most of her parental life Amy had felt unprepared. She felt that she didn't have the right advice, she hadn't gone to college, and she couldn't afford the fancy school supplies that all the other parents seemed to buy their kids.

But when her kids came home with good grades—no, make that *great* grades—Amy smiled. She felt vindicated. She felt proud her kids had risen above adversity and bad circumstances to succeed. That is, until one day, she started realizing what sort of adversity her kids had overcome.

Will and Emily had come from a (lower) middle class home. They had young parents who'd never been to college. Parents who were just kids themselves—who weren't prepared to be parents when this whole thing started. Will and Emily were succeeding *in spite of* her and Jeff's faults. This revelation was bittersweet. Amy realized her kids were doing what she couldn't. They were walking in God's best plan for their lives. They had the perfect balance of work and play and spirituality in their lives. They were both walking towards a bright future.

Unfortunately, Amy had long ago abandoned God's best plan.

She actually didn't even know God had a best plan until she turned fourteen. Once she turned fourteen she was allowed to go to youth group. It was the most exciting thing she'd ever experienced. Youth Group was nothing like Kids Church. It was so much better. From the second she walked in she heard Christian rock music blaring on the speakers and there were cool lights and they gave her a WWJD bracelet.

Then when the service started, Pastor Colby started to speak. He was so cool. He had ripped up jeans, a flannel shirt, and a goatee. His sermon talked about "God's best plan for your life," and he used a lot of funny stories to make his points. He also talked relevant pop culture types of things like when he said, "If you take all the words to every Boyz II Men song ever written, that only begins to describe God's love for us."

That's a lot of love, Amy thought.

And then Pastor Colby talked about how God loved her so much that he had a perfect plan for her. God knew what we were supposed to do even before we were born.

And as Pastor Colby was talking, Amy realized what God wanted her to do with her life: He wanted her to be a missionary. It was the special thing God had placed in her heart so she could change the world. She would build huts and hold those crying, perfect-looking African babies. She'd dig wells and give people fresh water. She'd give shots and medicine to the sick, and at the end of the day she'd teach the Bible lessons to the villagers while the sun set. As she taught she'd look into the African people's faces and their bright eyes would be smiling and grateful to Amy for bringing the truth. And then, after Amy finished her lesson, she'd lead everyone in a final song and she'd glance just beyond the village as the zebras and elephants and lions gathered around to hear the sweet music.

For the next three years she studied all about being a missionary, she learned about various organizations she could join to do overseas work, and she went on trips to Mexico with the Youth Group every summer. Mexico missions were okay—just not as glamorous as missions to Africa—but that was fine because she was just in training anyway.

Then one night after prom, things with Jeff went *way* too far. And that was all it took for Amy to walk out of God's plan for her life. She felt guilty for how things went with Jeff, but guilt apparently wasn't enough. Amy had to pay a price, and nine months later Emily was born.

Still, it wasn't like God had shunned her or banished her for her mistake, it's just she was no longer walking in God's *best* for her. It was like God had the name-brand plan for her life and because of her sin she had picked the generic plan. Pastor Colby had explained it that night, "If you walk out of God's plan, it's okay, he'll still rescue you and love you, it's just you'll be living outside of what he wants for you."

And Pastor Colby was right.

Amy had been in God's Plan B since that night of her junior year. It wasn't that she didn't love Jeff and the kids — she adored them all very much, they were everything to her — it's just things had always been so difficult for all of them from that moment forward. And today, in the principal's office, was just another example of her trials.

"Mrs. Henderson," the principal said. "We saw that you excused your son from school today."

"That's right," Amy said.

"Well then, let me tell you how your son trespassed onto school property and caused a lot of needless fear and panic," the principal said.

"He didn't trespass," Amy said.

"Being on school grounds during an excused absence is trespassing."

"Oh. I didn't know that," she said.

Amy sat in there for what seemed like an hour, listening to the principal and the police officers go back and forth, scolding her and telling her their concerns about Will.

She tried to explain, but they wouldn't listen. They said he had to be suspended. They said they had to take dramatic measures to make sure he didn't leave the house for the next couple of days. She was trying to carefully listen to everything they were saying, but the whole time she couldn't stop wondering if she could ever get out of the path that she'd made for herself—she wondered if she could ever get back into God's Plan A for her life.

Two hours after Amy had taken Will home, the phones were still ringing. She didn't know if they'd ever stop. Cell phones, home phones, and text messages all chimed and blipped and beeped, and on the other end was some parent asking, "What is your son doing?" They wanted to know why Will had freaked out their kids. They wanted to know where he got off saying the school was going to be destroyed. They wanted to know how he knew this, or, if he was making it up, they wanted to know what his problem was. Did he think it was fun? Was it amusing to needlessly worry other children and parents?

Amy stopped answering after the fifth call.

What was there to say? Why answer when every conversation went the same? She tried to explain herself initially, she tried to let the other parents know that she was freaked out too, that she didn't understand this either, that as they were speaking, her son was being put on house arrest. She asked if they knew what it felt like to watch the police put a tracking device on your son. They said they had no idea what that was like because their children were well behaved. Their children weren't crazy prophets creating mass hysteria.

Amy didn't expect all of these phone calls by the way Will painted the events on the playground. Will said the kids just laughed at him, they all thought it was some kind of joke. But that was only the half-truth. The older kids laughed at him, but the younger ones, the first and second graders, were deeply concerned.

After all, Will was a fifth grader. Fifth graders were at the top of the totem pole at Jefferson Elementary. When they spoke, the younger kids listened. When a fifth grader said something was going to be scary, a first grader's only response was, "How scary?" By that afternoon, no one who was on the playground talked about the laughing; they only talked about how their classmate, *their friend*, was dragged off screaming, "The school is going to be destroyed!"

Some of the fifth graders actually did remember the laughing. But they were laughing when they thought this was going to be no big deal. When they realized that this whole situation was getting traction, that if they acted worried they could get a day off, they decided to play right along. They said they didn't feel comfortable going to school tomorrow because they thought Will was right. The school was going to be destroyed. He seemed so convinced — how could they not believe him?

Additionally, to make matters worse, some of the men who'd discovered Will the night before were siding with him. When they heard what went on at Jefferson Elementary, they said it made perfect sense. They expected something like this. They told their wives, kids, and neighbors about what had happened in the cornfields. Many of the men said something to the effect of, "That boy's telling the truth. I don't care what he's saying. It's true. You should have seen him when we found him. That wasn't no boy speaking. His voice, his eyes, there was something there, I'm telling you. It was like Jesus was talking. Or maybe the Antichrist."

And this endorsement from men, trusted men like Gus Wiley from city council and Curt Benson the veteran, forced everyone to reconsider. Everyone started to think there was a chance that Will was actually telling the truth. And perhaps they shouldn't be yelling at anyone in the Henderson family, but instead figuring out a way to protect the children that God had given them.

GOODLAND, KANSAS

When tourists (which Goodland has very few of—most are family members looking to kill time or travelers on I–70 who have been trapped in town because of a snow/ice storm) visit The Goodland Museum of History and Culture, the wing that always gets the most attention is the one dedicated to the rapture.

Now, Goodland doesn't have an actual museum with a curator and a budget and all of the other scientific and logistical processes that go into making exhibits. Instead, the Goodland Museum of History and Culture is just May Brown's old bed and breakfast that she turned into a museum five years ago when she realized that people weren't looking to go to Goodland for a romantic weekend getaway.

The museum mostly consists of western Kansas oddities; tourists can buy keychain-sized sunflower paintings (which are replicas of Goodland's prize largest easel painting in the world) and T-shirts that say, "Kansas, There's No Place Like Home." The tourists are mildly interested in all of these things, but what they love is walking down the hallway and into the room that's dedicated to the rapture. Because inside that room there are facts and pictures and exhibits that explain why Goodland is convinced the rapture is coming in their town before it hits the rest of the world.

A question one of the tourists always asks is, "Why is everyone in Goodland so willing to believe in the rapture in the first place?

And not only the rapture—but the rapture happening *only* here? Isn't that a little weird?"

And May Brown always uses this as an opportunity to jump into her explanation of the history of the rapture in Goodland. She tells the room full of tourists that Goodland has long been fascinated with looking for the apocalypse and the end of the world. They've been anticipating it for nearly 167 years.

Still, Goodland hasn't always been looking toward the sky. Once upon a time the town didn't even know they should be waiting for anything. Rather, the town was simply founded by traveling farmers who could see how fertile and profitable the ground was. They were people of faith so they planned on planting churches and crops out West.

The founders settled, constructed cabins, formed a city government, and tried to build a life for themselves. They needed a city name, but sadly they did not have a marketing director or PR manager that could help them be forward thinking and create a memorable brand for their town. So they called their town "Goodland" simply because the land was good to farm. The men liked the name because it was to the point; the women thought it sounded charming.

But they quickly discovered the land was anything but good.

It started with the natives. At night, when the moon was the shape of a fingernail, the settlers would huddle together, clutching their rifles and listening as the Navajos and Apaches came near their town. The settlers saw that these natives were not wearing normal things like bonnets and trousers, so they assumed that these natives weren't humans at all. Maybe they were demons or warlocks or witches. It was tough to say exactly what they were, but the people of Goodland considered the possibility that Satan had sent them to destroy their town. Some of the town's theologians thought that maybe the western plains of America were the new earth, and maybe they'd been chosen to fight some sort of supernatural epic war. Goodland was being attacked for a reason. They were being singled out.

Of course that was nonsense.

There was no reason to think Goodland was *that* special. People all around the country had been having troubles with natives/demons. But then they saw something no one could explain. It was sort of like the cloud that's described in Exodus—the one shaped like the pillar that the Israelites followed around in the desert for forty years—only this cloud looked more like an ice cream cone. Not that they had ice cream cones back then, which is really too bad because that's the perfect way to describe the shape. However, on further thought, maybe ice cream cone is a horrible word to describe this cloud. Because then you might think it was friendly.

It wasn't friendly.

It destroyed whatever it touched. It turned cabins into piles of splinter, barns into rubble, and livestock into dinner. Nothing survived the angry, twisty cloud. And no one had ever seen anything like this, let alone *heard* of anything like this. Surely, this was a miracle—this cloud was the hand of God. Perhaps God was angry. Perhaps once again he wanted the earth destroyed. The end was near and it was starting at Goodland. The beginning of the end would happen in this fair town. They were being targeted for something special. After all, when they wrote their friends and family out East about the destructive clouds, their friends had no idea what they were talking about.

It was all the talk at church services. They were a chosen people. Jesus was coming back for everybody, sure, but what if he was coming for them first? The mantra of the town became "Stay a Night, Stay a Lifetime." Posters and preachers and just about everything else repeated the mantra. Everyone knew it wasn't a sure thing, but many asked, "Isn't it possible God takes us before everybody else? God has favorites, doesn't He?" And these ideas became something grandparents told their grandchildren. "God is watching Goodland closely. He is waiting to take us home."

In the 1930s, Oscar Thomas got so inspired by these stories that he wrote a radio drama about them. The drama was presented as a newscast and it gave an account of the rapture coming instantly and leaving many in the town behind. Oscar thought the rapture drama would be a wonderful homage — a delightful, spiritual experience that would highlight all that Goodland had to look forward to. But he was wrong.

The radio dramatization had disastrous consequences. Most in the town didn't know it was a drama; they thought these events were actually happening (and who could blame them; it was being presented as a newscast). Many thought they were surefire candidates for the rapture and were horrified to discover they'd been left behind. If that wasn't frightening enough, when the newscaster started to describe the four horsemen of the apocalypse descending on Goodland, everything went crazy. Model T's wrecked, stores were looted, and violence and mayhem spread throughout the town. Many of the town's citizens made brash decisions. Couples got married because they figured they could love, honor, and respect one another until the world came to an end. Others called their bosses and told them where they could stick their jobs. Few thought to look up at the sky to see if there was any accuracy to the rapture account, and those who did would later swear they saw something.

It wasn't until the next day that the citizens discovered the whole thing was fictional. It took months for the people of Goodland to rebuild their town, get marriages annulled, and find new jobs. And during the reconstruction the cynicism started to set in. That's when some started to think that all of the apocalyptic talk was nonsense. The rapture became taboo. Talk of it dissipated, and believing in it made a person seem archaic and foolish.

And for a while Goodland forgot all about its fascination with the end of the world.

But thoughts about the rapture were ingrained too deep to simply disappear. As Goodland entered the twenty-first century, there were so many things that seemed fragile. Technology was linking everything together but that only made it easier for everything to crash. Modern conveniences like chat rooms, text messaging, and eHarmony made everyone more connected yet somehow all the more isolated. The world was getting smaller, but the threat of annihilation by weapons of mass destruction was only growing.

It just seemed like things couldn't go on forever.

It seemed like God had to come sooner or later.

When May Brown finished talking, everyone was always dead silent. They were a little frightened by how she ended her story. Then she'd smile from ear to ear as if to let everyone know, "It's okay, it was just a ghost story," and they'd politely clap for her. Some would say, "You had us there for a moment. You actually had us believing the end of the world was coming." Everyone would be so relieved the apocalypse was not coming that they would buy lots of keychains and T-shirts.

Of course May Brown didn't tell everyone what she really thought about the subject, that Goodland *would* be raptured first. They would be the warning sign God used to tell the world about the end. There were still people—a lot of people—in Goodland who believed that. And rumors of the Henderson boy seemed to make the clock tick louder than it ever had before. She wouldn't be giving these little presentations very much longer. Soon she'd be on the other side and it would be up to police and FBI agents and scientists to figure out why half of Goodland had just up and disappeared.

EMILY HENDERSON

Emily Henderson knew about the history of the rapture, but it was always in the back of her mind. Something for other people to think and worry about. Today was no different; it just hit a little closer to home.

The rapture was something for her family to freak out about. Her parents were freaked out about it because it had something to do with Will causing a big commotion at school. And that created lots of arguments and tension in the house. Her parents were arguing with each other. They were arguing with Will. They were pacing back and forth and making phone calls and squawking at whoever was on the other end of the line about what was going on.

And it drove Emily crazy.

She tried to escape from the problem by locking herself in her room, chatting on her laptop with potential homecoming dates. But they didn't want to talk about homecoming. They didn't want to talk about where they'd go to dinner and what they'd wear. They were asking her what she thought about Will being arrested.

She didn't know exactly what to say. She barely understood what happened herself. All she really knew was that last night Will saw a ghost or the devil or Jesus or something in the Johnsons' cornfield. Emily wasn't sure exactly what Will had seen because her parents were being so secretive about it. This morning when she asked, "What happened last night?" they quickly said, "Nothing." But the way they answered, they were so nervous, it was like walking up to a car and asking a get-away driver what time it was in the middle of a bank heist. Any question would make the get-away driver crack because he had so much to hide. And that morning her parents were a couple of get-away drivers. They were carrying the weight of some secret, but Emily didn't have the energy to find out what it was.

By that afternoon it seemed like the secrets had only multiplied. When Emily got home, her kitchen was packed with her mom, dad, Will, Sergeant Mike, and some other officer. They were arguing. The police were saying that for the rest of the week Will was under house arrest. He could not leave the house for any reason.

"What if it's on fire?" her mom asked.

"Okay, only if it's on fire," Officer Mike said.

"Or what if—"

"Amy, you know what we're trying to say. He needs to stay inside unless there's an emergency."

"This is so unfair," she said. "He didn't do anything wrong."

The police said maybe not, but there were a lot of people in town really upset by what happened. "There could be lawsuits," they said. At that Emily watched her dad turn a pasty white.

She didn't want to listen anymore. It was making her sick. She walked away from the kitchen and up to her room. She plopped onto her bed and stared at the ceiling wondering, if I lay here long enough, will my problems eventually melt away? Maybe if she stayed in her room and gave things enough time, she would go back downstairs and discover things had returned to normal. It would be like a sitcom. Everything would reset and the Henderson family would be ready for another adventure. Because the adventure that was important in her life right now was becoming homecoming queen. And there was no way she was going to be able to do that while her brother was screaming about the end of the world during recess.

A couple of hours later—after she was done answering for the hundredth time, "Do you think your brother can see the future? Or is he just crazy?"—Emily came back downstairs and realized her problems were still there waiting for her. At least the police were gone, but now her family was gathered around the TV.

They were all sitting on the couch and the blue glow from the television was bouncing off their faces. They were watching *Wheel of Fortune*. "Will's going to be on the news tonight," her mom said.

"He's what?" Emily asked.

"That's what I heard from Fran Morris," she said without looking up from the TV. "Fran knows Tiffany Peters. And Tiffany Peters is friends with a gal who does all the makeup for the newscasts."

"Oh." Emily said. But that's not what she wanted to say. What she wanted to say was, "On TV? Are you kidding me? Really? He's going to be on TV? That's just great. It's bad enough everyone's talking, and now you're telling me the whole town is going to be watching this. You're telling me my brother's freaky problems are going to be broadcast!"

Then no one said another word because the newscast started. Emily sat on the dark blue recliner in the corner and watched with the rest of her family, wondering what the media would say about her little baby brother.

The news kicked off that night with Sean McGuire reporting live from Jefferson Elementary. As the news anchors turned it over to Sean, he stood in the middle of the playground with the twisted silhouettes of merry-go-rounds and monkey bars serving as a somewhat ominous backdrop.

"There's a lot of panic and fear tonight over a scene that happened on Jefferson Elementary's playground today," Sean said. "The worry started when a fifth-grade boy began to tell the other students that the school was going to be destroyed. The boy didn't say he was going to destroy the school, rather, he said he'd had a vision. Administrators and the police are yet to comment if this is being treated like a threat or if this is simply a misguided student. To be honest, there seems to be a lot of confusion with this story thus far. But here's what some eyewitnesses and parents had to say about the incident."

The newscast cut to a boy in a yellow jacket. "I probably wouldn't say he was screaming. But he was yelling really loud. He was saying something bad is going to happen to Jefferson."

The newscast cut to a sour-looking mother. "I don't know if I should believe this boy or not. Who knows him? I don't know him. Do you know him? And is he going to commit some sort of violence if his 'prediction' doesn't come true?"

The newscast cut to a mom loading her kids into a minivan. "Am I going to send my kids to school tomorrow? Absolutely not! Not if people are saying it's going to be destroyed or violent or whatever. I don't care if it's true or not. If there's even a chance anything could happen I'm keeping my kids home."

The newscast cut to two girls—both in the second grade, both wearing pink, and both with pigtails. "Yeah, he said not to come to school."

"He said he knew he sounded crazy."

"Or weird."

"Or maybe weird crazy."

"But he said a meteor was going to blow things up."

"Or a laser."

"Or a meteor with a laser. And he said it's going to happen in three days."

"Which means tomorrow."

"Or the day after tomorrow."

"Yeah, the day after tomorrow."

The newscast cut back to Sean McGuire. "There is actually quite a bit of debate over when this alleged 'event' is going to happen. I would say about two-thirds of the people I've polled believe it's going to be tomorrow, everyone else thinks the day after."

The newscast cut back to the studio where Nancy Palmer was looking concerned. Emily was impressed by how Nancy always looked beautiful and confident. Emily thought, I bet she was homecoming queen once upon a time. Then Nancy interrupted Emily's thoughts by asking, "Sean, do we have any idea if the school is shutting down tomorrow?"

"The school will be open for classes," Sean answered. "Administration has guaranteed the school will be safe and assures extra police protection will be on hand. They also want parents to know that all absences must be excused like normal, should parents decide to keep their students home."

"Thank you, Sean," Nancy said.

Then Nancy looked into the camera and said, "To get a different perspective on this story we have contacted Bill Thorpe, a theologian at Goodland Community College, and Rhonda Vernon, a child psychologist at Cedar Brooks Mental Health Center."

The newscast cut to a split screen with the theologian on one side and the psychologist on the other. "Good evening," Nancy said.

"Good evening," the theologian and psychologist said.

"Let's start with the day that this incident is allegedly going to take place. The student said three days, but what does that mean exactly? A full seventy-two hours?" Nancy asked.

"I believe it means tomorrow," the theologian said. "Prophecies are not concerned about hours nearly as much as days. Take Jesus, for instance. He died Friday at three p.m. He was raised from the dead by Sunday sometime in the morning. Many scholars believe he was only dead for a total of around forty to forty-two hours, but that still counts as three days."

"So do you believe the school is going to be destroyed tomorrow?" Nancy asked.

"No. Not at all. I just think that is what the boy meant," the theologian answered.

"Okay," Nancy said. "Dr. Vernon — if the school is fully guarded for the next few days and the student who's allegedly making threats is nowhere near the school, do parents have anything to fear?"

"Actually, they could," the psychologist said. "In a school violence situation, the attacker often doesn't work alone. In many cases there are accomplices, several students that work together to form an attack."

"Who said anything about attacking? Jeff, they're putting words into his mouth!" Emily's mom shouted as she jumped up from the couch.

"I know," her dad said.

The newscast continued. It was almost as if Nancy had heard her mom's objection. "Okay, but what if this isn't an attack or a threat? There are some people who believe this prediction is religious. We talked with many in town who believe the boy's prediction has something to do with Armageddon."

"Sure, that's possible," the psychologist agreed. "With all of the religious fears that are inherent in Goodland, it's possible the boy had some form of a hallucination that made him believe the end of the world was coming. He could have even thought it was a vision. In this case the student would believe that he was helping by predicting the school's destruction."

"I think calling it 'religious fears' is a bit condescending," the theologian said.

"Then how would you say it?" the psychologist asked.

"I'd say the boy and many in this town have beliefs in a higher power."

"Semantics aside," Nancy interrupted, "is there any chance this student actually had a vision?"

"I suppose anything is possible, but I doubt it," the theologian said.

"Rhonda?" Nancy asked.

"What is this, the sixteenth century? No, there is no chance. Visions are what we called things before we could diagnose them as psychological disorders."

"Well, we'll be watching as this story develops. Thank you for joining us." Nancy quickly moved along to other news stories. Apparently there were problems with a drainage system and some of the local livestock were getting sick.

"Psychological disorders. Jeff, they're making our son look like he's a nutcase."

Emily was a little shocked that her mom would say this in front of Will. But he didn't seem to mind; he just stared at the laces on his sneakers as if they held the answers to all the problems of the universe.

"This will all go away in a couple of days," her dad answered.

"A couple of days!"

"Let's talk in the other room honey," her dad said. Emily knew what he was doing. Her dad's parents were divorced at a young age, so he never wanted to fight in front of the kids. Of course, they could always hear them when they were in another room.

But Emily knew it made her dad feel better so she never pointed that out.

He gave the remote to Will. "You can watch anything you want buddy. We're just going to talk for a few minutes." And then Emily watched her parents leave the room.

Will started clicking through the channels. Cartoons. History. Rambo. Martha Stewart. CNN. Will didn't seem to care what he was watching. Seeing the picture on the TV change every two seconds was all that mattered to him. Emily was sure he was upset by what was said about him in the news. All of his friends, teachers, and everyone else in town was thinking he was a freak with some sort of psychological disorder.

"You okay?" Emily asked.

"Yeah, I'm fine," Will said.

"Don't even worry about what they were saying," Emily said. She felt awful for her baby brother. He didn't deserve this. He was just a kid. He'd probably never had a girlfriend. He'd never had a locker, and he'd never had to keep his own schedule going from one class to the next. You don't have to do that until junior high. It's intimidating the first time you have to do that, when you're suddenly responsible for getting yourself to class on time with the right books. But it teaches you responsibility. It prepares you for the real world. Will hadn't had any of that preparation.

Yet tonight he was instantly thrust into the real world as all these newscasters and people in town were talking about him. They were making judgments about him without even having met him. Most of them weren't even there when he said those things at his school.

Will continued to stare at the TV.

"You know those people on the news just make stuff up so everyone will watch," Emily said.

"I know. For sure. I don't even care. I mean, I've just about forgotten what they said anyway," Will said. Emily was pretty sure his eyes were watering up.

Emily didn't say anything about that. And she didn't know what else she could say to make things better. So she just sat silently in the living room with her baby brother, watching him flick through the channels, searching for something amidst all the choices cable television had to offer.

EMILY HENDERSON

In one sense, Emily felt bad for her little brother. She could see the toll the rapture predictions and the town's whispers and gossiping were taking on him. She should be doing everything she could to validate him and help him get his message out there.

The problem was that in another much more urgent, real, and everyday sense, Emily understood that her brother's soothsaying was creating a serious problem in her social life. There were enough real problems out in the world already. Why did Will have to be making them up? And why did he have to be doing all of this *now*? This was the most important week of Emily's life. She planned on becoming homecoming queen. It was the highest honor that any girl could achieve in high school. It would be something she could always look back on proudly, something she could tell her grandchildren about.

Now, it's entirely possible this was a selfish goal. Perhaps Emily was shallow for thinking about how Will's meltdown was messing with her chances of getting to wear a plastic crown from the dollar store while holding a bouquet of pink roses. If that's the case, you just had to forgive Emily. She'd had this goal locked in her sights every day for the last six years. Emily decided that she was going to become homecoming queen after her first day in junior high. Actually, she made this goal exactly eight minutes into her first lunch as a junior high school student.

At Jefferson Elementary, Emily always ate lunch with Marsha, Tonya, and Becka. She didn't really even remember how they became friends. They'd always been friends. But at her first junior high lunch she realized she didn't know anyone.

Not a soul.

Well, okay, she "knew" other kids. But not enough to sit by them at lunch. You had to really know someone to do that. You had to know them well enough to share the same piece of chewed gum. It was that intimate.

So she clutched her lunch tray and walked slowly through the room. She was looking for someone— *anyone*— to sit by. Marsha's family had moved to Wichita that summer so that wasn't helping. And Tonya had "B" lunch so she was out. Emily continued to search the lunchroom for a friendly face. Only now it was getting obvious. She didn't have a friend in the room. She was looking foolish and scared standing there clutching the tray as her knuckles turned white. She had to do something.

And then she saw Becka sitting at the popular table. The table where all the kids had clothes that looked ratty and torn even though they really paid lots of money for them. These clothes were so expensive because trendy New York designers knew just how to rip jeans, tatter hats, and give a rugby shirt the exact fade it should have. The unpopular kids would try to rip their own jeans and fade their own shirts, but it was really embarrassing. The uncool kids were such posers.

Anyway, relief rushed through Emily's face as she discovered the popular table. It was all so clear now. She would sit here every day with Becka. She would become part of the "in" crowd, the upper crust of the junior high school. She would get a boyfriend named Clay or Kyle or Blake. Maybe she'd get all three to be her boyfriends.

But as she placed her tray on the table something funny happened. A guy (who was kind of hot, which made this even worse) with a brown thread beanie looked at the place where Emily placed her lunch tray. He said, "Hey, um, not to be weird or anything, but that seat is taken. I think."

This is what Emily hated about popular kids. They could never just be jerks. Probably because they had such a need to be liked. So even when they were shooting you down they still tried to be so cool about it.

"Oh, I'm sorry," Emily said.

"It's cool, but you know," he said.

No, I don't know. You couldn't make a little room for me? Do you realize you're destroying me? I have no other friends, and I try to reach out and this is what I get? Do you realize what a wreck I'm going to be because of this? And who are you to decide that I'm not cool enough? What, you really think Becka is prettier than me? Well, maybe she is, but I can get some cool clothes, I promise. Please don't reject me like this. I will do whatever it takes to fit in. Please just change your mind. P L E A S E!

"I totally understand," Emily said.

Emily looked to Becka for support. But Becka was looking down at the table. No way was she going to sacrifice her spot at the chosen-kid table for her old friend. So Emily picked up her tray and found a table in the corner. It was grimy and dark and dim. Emily sat there alone eating her lunch. She wasn't hungry at all, but she couldn't just sit there. She had to at least try to act busy. And for the whole time she was there, she didn't look up. She just stared into her cheese and cracker handi-pack and thought about her future. At that moment she decided to become popular. She would do whatever it took. And by her senior year she'd be homecoming queen. Becka and that stupid hot guy with the brown beanie would be lucky if Emily would even talk to them.

So that was the plan. That was what she was going to do. And once Emily decided to become the most popular girl in school, she threw her handi-pack away, went into the bathroom, locked herself into a stall, and spent the rest of her lunch hour crying.

Six years later, Emily had forgotten what it felt like to be unpopular. But on the day that (according to her newly crowned prophet baby brother) the school was supposed to be destroyed, it all came flooding back to her. Everyone had apparently watched the news the night before. So as Emily walked down the hall, every student in the school looked at her as if she were an alien. She was Carrie. She might as well have had yellow eyes, green skin, and the ability to lift objects with her thoughts. Emily hadn't felt this way since that first day of junior high. One outburst from Will, one silly rapture prediction, and she was in exile. How could she have fallen from the top to the bottom of the popularity ladder so quickly?

How was she supposed to act after what happened on the news last night? Was she supposed to just be walking around school like things were A-OK hunky-dory? Was she supposed to act like it was no big deal that her brother threatened (or claimed that some supernatural force had threatened) to destroy the elementary school? Why would anyone trust her after what Will had said? All the other kids in school probably thought she came from a long line of prophets/terrorists and there is no way you vote a prophet/terrorist to become the homecoming queen.

Not even the Goth kids would do that.

Emily opened her locker. Inside were pictures of fashion models and movie stars, the people she'd need to dress like, look like, and act like if she'd have any shot at becoming homecoming queen.

"Hi, Emily," Megan said, peeking into her locker.

"Hey," Emily replied. She didn't want to talk. That meant she'd have to respond to all of this Will/rapture stuff. She was running out of things to say.

"So, the news was crazy last night," Megan said.

"Yeah, hey, I'm running late to trig," Emily said as she shut her locker. She was almost home free. She'd go to trigonometry and work the whole period on some response to her baby brother's threat.

But right before Emily could get away, Megan said, "Why don't you just cut class?"

"I can't. Mr. Saunders is giving notes on what's going to be on the first chapter test. He usually gives all the answers there," Emily said.

But she was lying. Mr. Saunders didn't give any answers. Ever. Still, Emily knew this would be the type of class a homecoming queen would be interested in. She could get all of the answers, which meant good grades, which meant she could go to college and get into a great sorority. And she could do all of this without having to study hard. Even her popular friends could understand why she wouldn't want to cut that sort of class.

"No, you need to cut class. We're all going."

"Going where?"

"Jefferson Elementary."

"What?"

"Everyone wants to see if it's going to blow up like your brother said."

"Right."

"And you'd know more about all that than anyone else. So you've got to be there, everyone's going to want to hear what you've got to say about it."

And that's when Emily saw the life raft that was being thrown right at her. She was drowning in the sea of unpopularity. She could pull herself out of it, and go straight into the upper crust again.

It was all so clear. She needed to go to the elementary school to control this situation. To control how people were thinking about her brother. To show them how misguided they'd been. She couldn't do that in trig. And if she didn't go down there, she'd have no way to control what they were saying. They could gossip about her all they wanted. She'd spend the rest of her high school years as an outcast. Even worse, she'd be *remembered* as an outcast. The last six years of work would have been all for nothing.

"Why didn't you say so?" Emily asked. "Come on, let's go."

Emily arrived at Jefferson with a carload of her friends. She couldn't believe how many people were there; cars were parked for blocks in every direction. Everyone was lined up around the school watching. They were waiting to see if something was going to happen. They weren't quite sure what, but they didn't want to miss it.

How are people taking everything this seriously? Emily thought. Will's just a kid. He reads comic books and pours chocolate milk on his Cocoa Puffs. He's not a prophet. He can barely do long division, and everyone is really looking at him to predict the end of the whole world? Was the whole town actually shutting down because of what he said?

Apparently it was.

Businesses, restaurants, and government offices must have shut down because it seemed like most of Goodland was circled around the perimeter of the school. The actual school was a ghost town, as if there were only a few teachers and kids inside the school. It almost looked like the rapture had *already* happened. There wasn't much for everyone to look at. A few uniformed officers roamed around the school grounds, but other than that there was nothing but tumbleweeds.

But still everyone watched and waited.

When Emily and her friends arrived at the scene, there was almost a reverence in the air. But once carload after carload of high school students arrived the reverence was replaced by rock music, booming speakers, tickling, laughing, flirting, smoking, and everything else that ruined the atmosphere for those waiting to see a sign from on high.

Still Emily noticed that as the morning progressed, concern started to seep into many of the high school students. Their little brothers and sisters went to Jefferson. And a lot of them had grown up in Goodland and went to Jefferson at one point. They had great memories of their days as a Jefferson Mountain Lion. And now their old school was supposedly just going to be destroyed? How were they supposed to feel good about that? How could they just tailgate and flirt and giggle?

Some students began to ask Emily this. She still had enough popularity left for them to respect her opinion, and besides, who could understand this situation better than her? Her brother had caused it. So what was she feeling?

"What am I feeling?" Emily repeated to the group of students that was gathering around her.

"Yeah, do you think the school's going to be destroyed?"

"No."

"No?" The students asked.

"Not a chance," Emily said.

"Then what's going on here? Is your brother just crazy?" some guy asked.

Emily looked at him with disdain. He was probably on the chess club or a Mathlete. But she had to say something. If she ever wanted to become homecoming queen, if she ever wanted to gain back the admiration of all of her friends and everyone else at school, this was her moment. So she looked at all of the confused and accusing faces of her classmates for a moment, and then she said, "What if I told you that someone could pull a prank so big that an entire elementary school would shut down? And not only that, but then high schools, businesses, an entire town would shut down because everyone came to watch his prank.

"Look what's going on around you. My brother came to me about a week ago. He said, 'I bet I can shut down the entire city. It'll be just like a snow day. Only without the snow.' I said, 'No way.' And he said, 'Oh yeah, watch.' And now look what's happened. He did it. And he's at home and he is *so* busted. The police are pissed. He's under house arrest. I mean, he could be expelled or something."

Emily was starting to get fired up. She stood on the hood of some guy's Camaro.

"Don't you understand what's happened here? My brother has given us a gift. He has sacrificed himself so we can have a day to do whatever we want. And so if you want to waste it whining and worrying about something that's just not going to happen — fine. But as for me, I'm going to make the most of it."

Emily jumped off the hood of the Camaro and into some guy's arms.

She barely knew him. His name was Curtis, or at least something that rhymed with Curtis. And he held her for a second until she grabbed his face and kissed him. She didn't really have a reason — she did it just because it was a day off — a day to do whatever you felt like at the exact moment you felt like doing it. And everyone cheered. Emily went from freak to rockstar in minutes. It was an impressive feat. And everyone loved her that day because she made them feel okay. She gave them license to make the day something to remember. And quickly Frisbees started to fly, teenagers used the hoods of their cars for recliners, they laid blankets on the grass and had picnics. They flirted and had water fights.

They ate. They chilled. They did whatever they wanted. And the best part was the police couldn't do a thing. They had bigger problems on their hands like the rapture/bomb threat.

For a while Emily enjoyed the day off with her friends. She sat on the ratty old blankets that lined the hill overlooking Jefferson. She lounged with the popular and smoked cloves, Swisher Sweets, and anything else that wasn't an actual cigarette because only the trashy, unpopular kids smoked regular cigarettes.

Through the smoke Emily started to watch what was going on around Jefferson. It seemed the other groups were following the high schoolers' lead. Actually, some of the groups that gathered were more active than the high school students. Some groups were playing the guitar and singing with their hands stretched toward heaven. Other groups were waving posters and shouting. Then there were some who just stood silently and stared at the elementary school.

Suddenly Emily wanted to know: Who are these people? Why do they care so much about my brother's prediction? And as the day wound down and the sun was setting, the crowds kept gathering. Cars were parked on curbs, in fields, and in front of fire hydrants. The streets around the school looked like New York City during rush hour. Lights flashed and cars honked and drivers yelled at each other. Everyone was gathering at the school. Emily had never seen an event like this in Goodland. And Emily journeyed away from the teenage camp and toward the other groups so she could better understand who all was gathered out here.

The first group she ventured into were total believers. She could tell because they were wearing T-shirts and had bumper stickers on their guitars and Nalgene bottles that proclaimed them as such. Everyone had seen their most famous bumper sticker: *In case of rapture this car will be unmanned.*

Emily and most other people around Goodland had heard the

urban legend of these bumper stickers. She knew they weren't originally intended to be any sort of religious or political statement. Rather, the guy who first created it did so for completely practical reasons. He could picture the rapture coming in a flash and he saw the results being disastrous. Motorists that were left behind would be unaware that cars would be stopping suddenly or flying off the side of the road and into ditches. The guy must have thought these bumper stickers would be warning labels similar to signs that read *Falling Rocks* or *This Car Makes Sudden Stops.*

He had no idea these bumper stickers would be used as a cute way for homeschool moms to announce their faith. He would have never invented them if he knew that.

These people were rapture fanatics. They would look at anything—the Reagan presidency, the cancellation of *Star Trek*, or whatever else—and decide that it was a sign of the end times. But Emily didn't think there were that many rapture fanatics in Goodland. She thought maybe twenty or thirty, tops. But at this corner of the school there were hundreds of them. Some of them looked normal enough, businessmen and other professionals. Only now their coats were off and their sleeves were rolled up so they could do their real work. Apparently their real work was standing around a giant bonfire as it popped and crackled and singing songs like "I Wish We'd All Been Ready" and "Repent, Cleanse, Repeat." In between these songs some members of the group would debate about the miraculous sign they were waiting for. Emily walked around catching pieces of the conversation that went like this:

"I can't believe God would really destroy an elementary school."

"Why not?"

"Because, you know, it's full of children."

"No, it's not, they've all gone home for the day."

"Yeah, but you know what I'm saying."

"You're saying God wouldn't hurt children?"

"Yeah, pretty much."

"What about the death angel?"

"Death angel?"

"In Exodus. It was the final plague. God killed all of those firstborn children. And that was just to save the Israelites. Why wouldn't God destroy an empty elementary school in Kansas to save the whole world?"

"Yeah, I guess that's a good point." And then there was the sound of guitar strumming.

"Oh man, Randolph is about to play 'Turn, Turn, Turn, before You Burn, Burn, Burn.' I love that song." Then the two people stopped their conversation and ran towards the acoustic guitar.

Emily didn't quite know what to make of what she had heard. Sure, there were some messed up things about America, but blowing up an elementary school seemed sort of messed up too. And besides, didn't Jesus say that two wrongs don't make a right? She was pretty sure he did. But she wasn't positive because church was lame and she'd stopped going the moment she had a choice.

So feeling upset and uneasy, Emily walked away from the believers. She wouldn't go near them again. There was something a little bit funny going on with them. Sure, they *seemed* friendly, but that was part of their trick. It was the same trick drug dealers and vampires and Mary Kay reps had used for years.

The formula was simple: You find somebody weak, maybe even a little bit pathetic. You act all nice and warm and caring towards them. That person becomes so grateful that somebody actually cares about them that they are willing to listen to anything. And they *do* listen to anything. Then, before the person knows it, they've become a drone. Next thing you know they're looking to create drones of their own.

Emily didn't know how people didn't see when this was happening to them. Maybe that's the worst part of rejection—it makes a person so blind that they are willing to do absolutely anything to be accepted.

The next group Emily walked into was quite the opposite. They could not fathom that anyone could actually believe anything would happen. They were saying that if the earth were going to be destroyed it'd be because of global warming, greenhouse gas pollution, the rotting away of the ozone, our embarrassing dependence on fossil fuels, and the senseless destruction of rain forests.

"No wonder they want the rapture to happen," Emily overheard someone from this group say. "They've left planet Earth in such bad shape they want God to rescue them."

Emily wandered on towards other groups. She discovered one group of soccer moms debating whether or not the school was safe to send their students to tomorrow. There was another group that consisted of men in expensive suits. They seemed to be talking about the legal ramifications of this whole thing. They got quiet as she walked by.

And after that she stopped being able to tell who the other groups were, because most people were leaving. Word around the school grounds was that the destruction was going to happen at sunset, because sunrise and sunset are when God does his most dramatic work. And once sunlight was no longer anything but a memory, everyone decided the school was going to be fine. Some were disappointed they didn't see anything and others were glad the school was still in place.

But either way, most decided that they'd wasted too much time huddled around this elementary school. It was late. It was time to get dinner. It was time to get on with their lives.

Emily was ready to get on with her life just like everyone else.

When she'd made her way back to where her friends were hanging out, she couldn't find her ride. Most of the high schoolers were gone. The only proof that they were ever there were crushed up beer and soda cans, candy wrappers, and empty boxes of cigarettes and cloves littered all over the hill. Emily asked one of the unpopular girls who was still around where everyone went.

"I think most people went to the after party," the unpopular girl said.

"The after party? There's an after party?" Emily asked.

"We're in high school. There's an after party for everything."

"Right," Emily said, "but didn't my friends at least wait for me?"

"I don't know. Neil Pratchett just said 'party at my place' and everyone got in their cars and took off."

"Then what are you still doing here?"

"I'm waiting for my dad."

"Oh," Emily said.

Then an image flashed across Emily's thoughts: She was sitting on the hill in the dark with this unpopular girl waiting for her own parents to pick her up. She'd spent the whole day reconstructing her image, and in the end she'd be just like this poor unpopular girl next to her. But what was she supposed to do? It seemed like everyone with a car had left. And she had to get a ride home because it was getting dark and all of the people left around Jefferson were starting to act crazy.

The believers' bonfire was burning bright orange, the skeptics had environmentally friendly lamps around their site, and in between those two sites there were just shadowy figures walking around. Who knows what those shadowy people were planning on doing? Probably raping and pillaging and things like that.

Emily took out her phone to call her mother to come pick her up because she thought she'd rather be unpopular than be raped or pillaged. The phone started to ring.

But then Curtis walked up.

"Hey," he said.

"Hey," Emily said back to Curtis. He was the boy she kissed after the big speech and it was no accident she picked him. His eyes were ice blue, his hair was curly, and he had the most adorable dimples. Even in the twilight she could admire all of that. Plus, he was a godsend. She could get a ride home and be popular.

"Hello," Emily could hear her mother saying on the phone, but Emily hit the End Call button.

"What are you still doing here?"

"I'm kind of stuck. I was walking around."

"Walking around?"

"I wanted to hear what all of the groups were saying about my brother's prediction."

"What are they saying?"

"Freaky stuff. I didn't really understand it all."

"Is that tough for you?"

"Is what tough?"

"People saying freaky things about your brother."

"I don't think they were talking about my brother at all. They were just using his prediction to say whatever they were already thinking about."

Curtis nodded. "Yeah, you're probably right."

"Why aren't you at the after party?" Emily asked.

"After parties aren't really my thing."

"After parties are everyone's thing."

"Not mine."

"Why?"

"Everyone's always mingling around and talking about different things and I never know what to say in those kinds of conversations. I like one-on-one conversations. That's where I can be really interesting. Though I'm really waiting to say something interesting and charming in this conversation and it hasn't happened yet."

"Keep trying. You'll get there," Emily said and smiled a little.

"You need a ride home?"

"Why don't you give me a ride to the party first?"

"I just told you—"

"I know, I know, but don't worry. I know everyone and I can introduce you around."

"Maybe—"

"Come on. Just look at everyone I introduce you to as a one-on-one conversation—it will give you lots of chances to be interesting and charming."

They hopped in his car and drove away from Jefferson.

As they were leaving she saw a news truck driving up. Sean McGuire was going to give another live report from the playground. But there was nothing to worry about anymore. She'd saved her reputation, she'd find a date for homecoming, and in a few days this whole situation would blow over. Life could go on. The rapture talk would once again disappear and this would be just another chapter in the long line of Goodland's unfulfilled apocalyptic predictions.

No big deal.

THE HENDERSONS

The blue glow from the TV was making Jeff's eyes water. People weren't meant to watch TV for this long. They weren't meant to eat this many stale generic Doritos and sit on the couch for this long either. And clothes certainly weren't supposed to be this sweaty. But this is what happens when you watch the news every hour, on the hour, scared that your son's prophecy might come true. Or at least that's what he thought for the first six or so news updates. But now his body was just numb. He was tingling from head to toe so badly, he wondered if blood was still circulating through his veins.

I need to get up and walk around, he thought. But every time he tried to get up, another news update would start. At the moment he was watching what must have been his fourteenth news update of the day.

Sean McGuire was saying, "There is a group that's started a bonfire and is singing religious songs, and another group lighting lamps and shouting statistics about the melting of the polar caps. So all there is to say is there is a lot of activity going on *around* the school, but nothing has happened *at* the school as of yet. Back to you, Nancy."

Of course nothing has happened yet, Jeff thought. I knew nothing would. Not that I want anything to happen. I guess that's the whole point. I knew this would all amount to needless worry and fear. That's why I told Amy to keep Will away from the school in the first place.

"Do you want another sandwich?" Amy asked.

"No thanks." Jeff said. He'd had three of Amy's sandwiches in the last few hours. How many more sandwiches could he really eat? And how many more "updates" could he watch?

He wanted to turn it all off—the phones, the TV, and everything else connecting them to the outside world. But every time he'd mention it to his son, saying something like, "Let's go throw the baseball around," Will would always answer, "No thanks, I don't want to miss the update."

But there never was an update. Just some news anchor with too much pomade in his hair saying, "Still a lot of unrest around Jefferson but nothing has happened yet." They continued to watch the updates. They watched all the way until the last update at ten o'clock. And finally Jeff told them it was time for bed.

Once his whole family was asleep Jeff sat in bed with his tiny lamp on and tried to read another business book. But his thoughts wouldn't stay with the words on the page.

Instead his mind drifted: I did the right thing. I wish we wouldn't have spent the whole day watching that but Will needed to. He needed to know things were okay at his school. So, I was supportive. Isn't that a dad's job?

No, a man's job is to lead his family, Jeff could hear his own father saying. His father had drilled these words into his head. Growing up, that's the way his father governed their home. His word was law. His orders were not questioned.

In fact, in all of the years growing up, Jeff only questioned his father once. It was the Christmas that Uncle Dale came to visit. For Jeff, Uncle Dale was more than a family member. He was a role model. Uncle Dale had a mustache like Magnum P.I. and a Harley Davidson just like the one Lorenzo Lamas drove around on. Jeff could imagine his uncle driving his Harley around fighting crime and solving mysteries. And Uncle Dale was funny. He knew dirty knock, knock jokes (opposed to the lame clean ones about oranges and interrupting cows) and Uncle Dale taught Jeff how to play poker.

That's why Uncle Dale's first and only visit to the Henderson household for Christmas was a pretty big deal for Jeff. When his uncle walked inside the house, he was holding a bright red gift with Jeff's name on it. And all through Christmas dinner Jeff imagined all of the things that could be in the package. Maybe there was a rifle they could go hunting with or a really small dirt bike. Jeff's imagination was running so wild that he didn't even notice all of the rum that Uncle Dale was pouring into his egg nog.

And halfway through dinner Jeff noticed that Uncle Dale was starting to make some jokes about his mom. He didn't understand at the time what the joke was exactly, all he knew was Uncle Dale asked his mom if his father's Snickers satisfied her. Jeff didn't even know his dad gave candy bars to his mother on a regular basis. But apparently he did and it was serious business, because at the word *satisfied* Jeff's father slammed his fist on the table and told Uncle Dale, "You need to leave. Now."

"Come on, I was just joking around," Uncle Dale said.

"I don't care what you were doing. You can do it somewhere else."

"Where am I supposed to go? It's Christmas day."

"Don't make me ask you again."

At that, Uncle Dale got up from the table. He grabbed the big red box he'd brought for Jeff and left the house without saying another word. The house shook as Uncle Dale slammed the door.

And then Jeff and his father and mother were all sitting at the table alone on this silent, lame Christmas day. This was supposed to be the best Christmas ever and his dad ruined it because of a candy bar joke. Seriously? Jeff knew not to question his father, but on that day he felt like he needed some answers.

"Why did you kick him out, Dad?"

"He was drunk. He was saying things I don't want you or your mother around."

"So you just kicked him out? On Christmas?"

"It's what I had to do."

"I didn't even get to see my present. It's not fair."

"This isn't about *fair.*"

"Well, it's not right, then, I mean."

"This is bigger than right and wrong. This is about protecting my family."

And this was how his father always governed their household. From the moment he was born until he got Amy pregnant and had to leave, Jeff watched as his father led the family. He didn't empathize. He didn't ask everyone else how they felt. He did what he thought was right.

Now, all of these years later, Jeff could see how many right decisions his father had made. He could see why the Uncle Dales of this world had to be kicked out of the house. Because there are times when you stop worrying about making the popular decisions and instead you make the right ones. And it was time for Jeff to start making those types of decisions. It was time for this to be over. It was time to put Will, the cornfield, and the prophecies behind them. As he drifted off to sleep he looked forward to tomorrow, to getting on with their lives, to right decisions he'd get to make.

The next morning Jeff awoke with resolve. It was time to go back to normal. Sure, normal meant Jeff would have to go back to work, and he was growing more and more tired of his job. The work completely exhausted him; even the thought of work made Jeff squirm. If he saw a car commercial on the television it sent him into a cold sweat, and while most people love the new car smell, it sent shivers through his spine. He imagined it was the same way a Vietnam veteran must feel when they smell napalm.

But he needed to get back. Today was about providing for his family. So he grabbed his work clothes and decided to complete his outfit by wearing his maroon-colored tie with navy blue diagonal stripes. It was the tie Amy bought for him last Christmas. When he'd opened it she'd told him, "That looks like the tie of a man in charge. A man who makes sales. That looks like the tie of a *senior sales rep.*"

As Jeff was tying his tie he looked in the mirror and started to take stock of this whole Will situation. He needed to tell Will no more prophecies. They were hurting the family. Hopefully yesterday would scare him off from giving any more. There were three total, Will had told them, and Jeff didn't want to know (or anyone else to know) what they were. Hopefully that would make things go away. After all, Will had never delivered a prophecy or a vision. The way Will was acting over the last four days was nothing like him. So what happened?

You saw the cornfield. There was stuff—weird stuff—going on out there. Something wasn't right. He had a vision. It came from somewhere. Eleven-year-old boys don't talk like he was talking. Try all you want, but you can't explain it.

Yes, I can, Jeff thought.

Okay, then, explain why Will was saying those things when Mike and everyone else found him?

And so Jeff did the best he could to explain his side of things to the face in the mirror.

Downstairs Amy was making Jeff's lunch the way she always did: Bread slightly toasted, two pieces of turkey, one single of Kraft cheese, and enough mustard on one piece of bread to make the letter *S*. In a brown paper sack with the sandwich she'd include a baggie of Lays potato chips, a strawberry-banana yogurt, and a bottle of water. This was his favorite lunch when he'd first gotten the job at Hansley. He couldn't afford to go get a burger or a steak with the other guys, so she wanted to make sure he'd have a lunch that he liked.

But since he'd started at Hansley, she hadn't checked to see if he still liked this lunch. Maybe he didn't. Maybe he was sick of turkey and didn't say anything because he had this incredible ability to deal with the lot that life dealt him—maybe now he was dealing with a wife that made him nothing but turkey sandwiches.

This rapture, and everything that had happened with Will lately, made Amy realize how easy it was to sleepwalk through life. She realized they'd all been living under the same roof, but maybe they hadn't been talking about the things that needed to be talked about. And as Amy walked upstairs she decided she'd talk with Jeff about the turkey sandwiches and whatever else they needed to talk about.

But when she walked into the room, Jeff was staring into the mirror, his tie half-tied. She wanted to ask him what was wrong, but that's when he blurted out, "Okay, I don't understand why the flashlights burned out, or why my son is acting so freaky, or what happened in that cornfield. I don't understand any of this! Is that what you want to hear? Are you happy now?!"

At first Amy thought he was shouting at her. But quickly she realized Jeff didn't even know she was there. He was shouting this to himself. Out loud. He was shouting in an unstable, mental patient sort of way. Then Jeff's eyes caught Amy's reflection in the mirror. He turned around. Husband and wife stared at each other as if they were complete strangers.

At that moment, Amy didn't know what to say. It didn't seem

like an ideal time to bring up turkey sandwiches. So she just said, "I, um, brought you your lunch." She held his sack lunch up for him to grab. But she kept the rest of her body away from him. "You better go. You're gonna be late," she said.

"Okay." Jeff grabbed his lunch and walked out of the room.

Amy looked down the stairs and saw Jeff standing at the doorway. The door was wide open, but Jeff wasn't moving. It was as if he was debating if he had the strength to leave for the day. Amy called down and asked, "Honey, are you okay?"

"I don't know," Jeff answered, right before he slammed the door shut and left.

Will lay flat on his bed covered in a blanket of graphic novels. For the first time in his life, he really wanted to go back to school. But he couldn't.

"When can I go back?" he asked his mom.

"When this whole situation is over," she answered.

Whole situation.

Whatever that means.

So while he was trapped at home suffering under house arrest, he read his graphic novels. He had everything, from *Batman*, to *Sin City*, to *The Greatest Adventures of the Old Testament*.

His mom had bought him the last one in hopes that he wouldn't read so many of his other "scary books."

For the last two days he'd been flipping through them and staring at images of Batman fighting off Two Face, and Sampson smashing through the Philistines. He read the novels so he wouldn't have to think about everything else. He didn't want to think about how everyone in town assumed he was horrible — a villain. He knew some people were saying that he was threatening the school. And then on the news this morning they said about half the students had gone to school today. They said, "It looks like the threat (might as well have said Will Henderson's threat) didn't come true." But he wasn't threatening the school. He was trying to *save* it. He was trying to warn them. Why couldn't people understand that?

Because that's how prophets get treated.

The thought just kind of popped into his head. And he was right. It made total sense. He'd been reading about prophets in his Old Testament graphic novel. And they were kind of like super-heroes. They were all misunderstood. Like Noah. God told him to build an ark. It didn't make sense, but Noah did it anyway. And then, when Noah started to tell people about the flood, they thought he was completely out of his mind. A flood? They'd never even seen rain. They had no reason to believe him.

It was like that with all the prophets.

Moses predicted plagues and Pharaoh thought he was bluffing. They thought Joseph was just having crazy dreams about fat cows eating skinny cows and stars bowing to moons. After nearly every single prophecy in the Bible, there was doubt. No one believed the prophet until *after* things came true. Maybe that was just the way God designed it. Maybe that was part of what the prophet had to go through. Maybe Will should feel honored that everyone thought he was crazy. After all, no one had any reason to believe him.

But that didn't mean he wasn't telling the truth.

Then Will stopped thinking about himself. His thoughts went in circles and he was tired of them. He didn't want to think any-more. So instead he once again went back to reading his graphic novel about Superman outsmarting Lex Luther and tried not to worry about all of his friends who were trapped inside Jefferson Elementary.

* * *

Emily was relieved things had gone back to normal. It was nice just to sit in trig class today and not have to worry about raptures and news media and her misguided baby brother. Even the weather seemed to reflect her feelings—it had been overcast for the last few days, but today it was sunny and bright and warm and there wasn't a cloud in the sky.

The day seemed so bright because yesterday was such a success. It was a test. She knew there would be hurdles on her way to becoming homecoming queen. And it seemed like Will's incident was her final test. And she leapt over that hurdle—and she'd leapt over it heroically and with relative ease, to be honest. She'd passed her final test with flying colors.

She was a shoo-in for homecoming queen now.

She only had to worry about the little things like what color and type of dress she would wear. It had to be something daring but not *too* daring. No way was she going to wear that orange creamsicle gown her mom had insisted on.

She had been TiVoing every *Red Carpet Special* and every *After the Red Carpet* show where pretty girls and fashion guys in tight shirts debate which celebrities looked daring and chic and which ones looked like train wrecks. She kept these shows on file so she could study them, so she wouldn't have to listen to the uneducated opinions of her mother and her friends when it came to the issue of evening gown fashion.

And now the time was right to start watching these specials and seriously considering what she would wear on the greatest night of her life. She could picture it. She could taste it—it was that close.

Things couldn't be better.

Amy took the laundry from the washer and threw it into the dryer. She remembered once upon a time, when she had first been married, she had to go to the Laundromat to do all the whites and darks. It was actually kind of fun. She and Jeff would go together on Sunday afternoons. They'd bring novels, crossword puzzles, board games, and six loads of laundry, and they'd spend the whole afternoon talking and laughing and hanging out. She liked her life now, but sometimes she missed those days. They were so much simpler. There was so much less to worry about.

Today she couldn't leave the house even if she wanted to. She hadn't left in days—since Will had been placed on house arrest. How could she? She was afraid that if she left to pick up groceries or dry cleaning, she'd be interrupted by a phone call telling her Will had caused another incident that rocked the town to its core.

But that was only one reason she couldn't leave.

She was more afraid *for* Will.

There were still those nasty phone calls.

Some people weren't threatening. Some people called to give their support. They'd even sent gift baskets with fruit and cheese and chocolate. They said they appreciated Will's bravery. Maybe one of those people would know how to council Will through this. Because he needed counsel, didn't he? And not counsel telling him he was wrong or crazy; there were plenty of people saying that. He needed counsel on what to do with these prophecies. He needed a mentor. Jeff couldn't be that for him. Jeff didn't even believe him. Jeff didn't think anything was going to happen. As if this was just some sort of phase. As if the stages of development included potty training, the rebellious teenage years, and the false prophet phase.

For the rest of the morning and into the afternoon this is how things went. The Hendersons kept themselves busy hoping that if they worked hard enough—if they thought about other things—the day would end without incident. Jeff was completely focused. He was on the verge of a sale, but he couldn't let the sweat show. He couldn't let this couple know how much he needed this. He tried to think of calming things like baseball and Emily's first steps and their vacation on Lake Powell eight years ago. He thought of those things so he could keep the smile. The smile that made him look confident. The smile that said, "Hey, I've got a whole line of people waiting to buy this car. If you don't want it, quit wasting my time."

Jeff was flashing that smile to a couple named Andrew and Michelle. They were newlyweds and the first real customers Jeff had all day. They were the first people who actually wanted to talk about pre-owned cars rather than Will and the rapture and that school. Jeff looked at Andrew and Michelle, and he could see the questions forming on their faces: *Can we really afford this car? Is this the right one for us? Is there something better out there?* If Jeff was going to survive the next couple of months, he would have to become a closer — a shark. To be a shark, his job would be to answer every one of those questions with "yes" or "no" or "maybe" or whatever answer the customers needed to buy the car. To a shark it didn't matter what the honest answer was. Because who's to say what somebody actually "needs" or what is actually "reliable" or what is a "good deal"? Any car will get you around, all cars eventually break down, and all cars have a value.

The rest is just semantics.

"How's this thing on gas mileage?" Andrew asked.

Not very good, was the first thought that popped into Jeff's head. Because it wasn't. It was a Ford Tundra. It was a huge truck. Trucks like that don't get good gas milage. Actually, they get horrible gas mileage. And in today's economy, who can afford a car like that? Jeff could just see himself telling this couple everything he was thinking. And they would answer, "Great, thanks for your time." Another salmon would successfully swim upstream out of his grasp. Meanwhile, he and his family were going to starve to death and get their house foreclosed on. He was going to lose his job because Mr. Hansley was going to tell him, "I'm sorry Jeff, I just can't keep a salesman who doesn't make sales. Do you have to be so honest?"

This is bigger than right and wrong. This is about protecting your family, Jeff could hear his father's words popping back into his thoughts. It was almost primal, like his father chiding him and daring him to be successful. The voice was reminding him of what all the business books said—if you want to be successful you have to picture yourself as successful. Think about positive things. Take control of your life. It was time to stop just trying to survive. It was time to succeed—to thrive. To make your life what you want it to be. It was time to stop worrying and caring so much about what you think everyone else needs, and instead direct your life to where you want it to go.

"I mean, how many miles per gallon does it get in city versus highway driving?" Andrew clarified.

"For a truck its size, it gets great numbers," Jeff said. This was true. But nobody gets a truck for its gas mileage. So there was no need to focus on that. "You need to realize what a versatile truck you've got here. Let's say you two want to get to some secluded spot in the Colorado mountains for a getaway. No problem. This truck can get you to where there won't be another soul for miles. Or let's say you want to rent a speedboat and take it to Lake Morgan in Oklahoma. This truck will haul it down there without a hiccup. If a friend needs help moving, you're right there for them if you want to be. Before long, everyone in town will owe you a favor. This is more than just a truck. This is a chance for a better life," Jeff said.

Then he was silent. He let his work sink in.

It looked like Andrew was about to say, "We'll take it," the three magic words every shark longs to hear, when Lisa, one of the receptionists at Hansley, ran over screaming. "Mr. Henderson! You have to come see this!"

"Really, really bad time," Jeff said.

"No, you don't understand. The school—" Lisa said.

And then everything melted away. The sale, the newlywed couple, the truck—it was like they never existed.

"What about the school?" Jeff asked.

"Something's happening," was all Lisa could muster.

Jeff didn't say goodbye to the newlywed couple as he followed Lisa into the breakroom. The room was packed, the attention of every soul in the room focused on the Panasonic TV in the corner. They were watching live coverage of Jefferson. The forecast called for sunny and clear (and Jeff would later talk about how it was sunny outside, right before he started watching the newscast), but the clouds above Jefferson Elementary were black. It was as if thick clumps of charcoal dust hovered above the school.

Nancy Palmer was saying, "Only half the students have shown up today. But—"

And then Jeff couldn't hear the newscast anymore because someone in the breakroom screamed, "It's a funnel cloud!"

"Where?" A junior in Emily's class asked.

"Right there!" someone screamed.

And they were right. Emily could see it on the TV. It was a tornado, right next to Jefferson. It was kicking up everything around it—newspapers, dust, plastic bottles, and other garbage. And then the tornado began to sink its teeth into Jefferson Elementary.

Emily had never seen anything like it. Windows shattered, the plastic paneling on the sides peeled off, and then it was hard to tell exactly what was going on. There were bricks and plastic and glass and God knows what else being spit out by the tornado. It seemed like the tornado was swallowing the school.

Nancy Palmer was trying to comment on what she was watching, but it was impossible to hear her. There was too much screaming. Even through the rushing wind, the screaming children could be heard.

"All those kids!" Some girl in the class was crying. "My—"

"—friends are in there! I tried to tell them!"

Will thought about everyone. Jane, who was so pretty and nice and who looked like such a babe with those blonde pigtails; Nate probably had all of his cool new graphic novels with him; and Mrs. White who always put smiley faces on his papers when he did a good job and wrote "You can do better" when he didn't try very hard.

Was the face killing them all?

Were they all dying right now?

The thought made Will sick. He wanted to turn away—

—but he couldn't. He had to see what was happening.

No one in the breakroom was saying a word. Some of the guys at Hansley had kids who'd gone to school today. Hours before, they'd told Jeff, "Sorry, I just can't believe what your kid's saying. I'm not keeping my kids from school two days in a row. That's ridiculous." And now Jeff looked at those same guys (a lot of them soulless sharks who told crass jokes, ripped off customers every chance they got, and compared their own wives to livestock) and watched as tears rolled down their cheeks. Jeff thought some of those guys probably hadn't cried in fifteen years.

And then sunlight started to rip through the black clouds.

The whooshing and crashing began to dissipate and the tornado quickly followed. Quickly as it had appeared, the whirlwind was gone. But it had done its damage. Entire pieces of the school were missing. The playground had been ripped apart to where only metal poles of the swing sets and half the monkey bars were still intact.

It looked like a bomb had gone off.

Moments later every person in the room was on their phone. They were trying to get through to anybody: their wives, their kids, the school. They were trying to get word of what had happened. Some were trying to find out if there were tornados anywhere else in Goodland.

Jeff didn't take out his phone. He ran into the bathroom, leaned over the toilet, and let everything go. And in between heaves, he thought to himself, How is this possibly happening? How could he know? What are they going to do to him?

What will happen to my son?

Amy put her arm around Will. She brushed the hair off his face and kissed him on the forehead. She said, "It's going to be okay."

And it was going to be okay, Amy thought. They said he was wrong. They said he was crazy and he was makings threats. But God, they all looked foolish now. Because he was right.

Her baby boy had been right about everything.

THE MIDDLE

Two men will be in the field; one will be taken and
the other left. Two women will be grinding with a hand mill;
one will be taken and the other left. Therefore keep watch,
because you do not know on what day your Lord will come.

JESUS SPEAKING TO THE DISCIPLES,
MATTHEW 24:40 – 42 NIV

There is something undeniably attractive about becoming
a born-again Christian ... Every moment of your life is
a search and rescue mission: Everyone you meet needs to be
converted and anyone you don't convert is going to hell,
and you will be partially at fault for their scorched corpse.

CHUCK KLOSTERMAN,
SEX, DRUGS, AND COCOA PUFFS

THE PREPARED

For as long as Goodland has existed, there have been those who knew the Goodland rapture was coming. But they didn't start calling themselves the Prepared until after the tornado hit Jefferson Elementary. And even before they called themselves the Prepared, they understood that God didn't *need* the test market for the rapture. After all, He is God. He already knows everything. He was, is, and forever will be omnipotent. And you don't just lose omnipotence.

The Prepared made it very clear to new members that just because they thought Goodland might be the test market for the rapture, they were not saying that God had lost a step. Nor were they saying that the creator of heaven and earth now needed market analysis rather than just flooding the earth or raining down fire and brimstone with the snap of His fingers like He did during His prime in the Old Testament days.

But there were other factors to consider.

For instance, maybe the testing was more for all of us. Especially in this day and age where human beings test everything. We measure and remeasure and read consumer reports before we make any decisions. And God understands this, so perhaps He's being culturally relevant by testing out the rapture in Goodland. After all, in the twenty-first century, people won't just believe something because everyone else does. This is the age of skepticism. This is the age where the answers to any of life's great questions are just a Google search away. So perhaps humankind will need a sneak preview of what the rapture looks like so they can know how to respond.

And there's also free will to consider. The Prepared don't like to talk too much about this because who really knows just where free will starts and stops? Who knows when a decision is made how much free will has to do with the decision and how much God has intervened? That's for theologians and heads of denominations to debate.

But that's beside the point.

The fact is, once the rapture starts, there are decisions that people will make in how it plays out. With human beings playing a part in the equation, it is possible things can get messed up. There is a chance that God's best-laid plans and intentions can go awry. So wouldn't God want to test out the rapture with the one variable—people—before he took it global? It's not like you get a second chance at the apocalypse after all.

With all of this in mind, one of the main reasons for the Prepared to exist was to make preparations for the rapture in Goodland. There was so much to do. Tree branches that hung over tombstones in graveyards had to be trimmed. What could be worse than the great ancestors of Goodland rising from their tombs and thwacking into tree branches on the way to their immortal destiny? Of course it was entirely possible that the souls would just pass through the tree branch like Patrick Swayze walking through a door in *Ghost*, but the Prepared weren't willing to take that chance.

Then there were their personal lives and possessions to think of. This is why most of the Prepared drew up a document called "The Rapture Will and Testament." This document would bequeath all earthly possessions in case of the rapture. The person who was drawing up this document would usually leave all of his or her goods to the friend or family member who was least likely to be raptured. Along with possessions, the inheritor(s) would also receive a note that explained why the rapture had happened and how it was not too late to save their immortal soul.

Most of all, there was getting the message out. Sure, the Prepared had their souls in good standing with eternity, but many in Goodland did not. So the number one reason they existed was to let people know the end was coming when it was time. And once the tornado hit the elementary school, every member of the Prepared knew how close they really were to the end. Moments after it happened they sprung into action, trimming branches, affixing bumper stickers, finalizing their Rapture Will and Testaments, and sending the message out that the apocalypse was coming soon. They sent out emails and made easy-to-read pamphlets with bright, colorful illustrations explaining what would happen in the upcoming days. One of the wealthy members of the Prepared owned some of the billboards in Goodland. So he had the biggest billboard in town painted black with blocky white letters that read **The End Is Now**. It was a message for all of them. It was a reminder for the skeptics in the town of Goodland to drop their cynicism and get their souls ready for the end.

Because it was time to get ready. One of the Henderson boy's prophecies had come to fruition. There were only two left. And once they came to pass, the test would begin. The Prepared were going to do everything within their power to make sure all of Goodland passed with flying colors.

From the beginning, the idea of the rapture didn't make very much sense to Jeff. He'd never even heard of it before the first time he'd gone to church with Amy. And he'd never been a regular attendee at church before he'd gotten married.

Before Amy, Jeff didn't have strong feelings about religion one way or another. He felt about church the same way he felt about NASCAR racing—it wasn't really his thing but he was cool with other people being passionate about it. Still, like NASCAR racing, there were so many nuances about church that Jeff didn't understand. So many cultural differences. Jeff didn't know what they all were; truthfully he knew very few of them, but even the little bit he did know weirded him out.

For instance, Amy didn't listen to the rock groups he was into like The Cure and Aerosmith and Def Leppard. She listened to Petra and Stryper and Whitecross, which were sort of the same except for all of the songs were about Jesus and the music wasn't quite as good. She said she listened to Stryper because *secular* songs were bad. Jeff didn't even know what a secular song was. The best he could tell, the only difference between secular and Christian songs was that secular songs weren't about Jesus and their music was a little better. But this was just the tip of the iceberg of what Jeff didn't understand about Christianity.

Still, it didn't matter. He'd married into Christianity. And on the first Sunday after they'd gotten married, Jeff promised Amy he'd go to church. He wished he hadn't. He felt completely uncomfortable there. The stained glass windows had all of these freaky images of saints and disciples looking at Jesus. The stories on the stained glass were distorted, colorful, animated versions of the Bible stories he remembered hearing growing up. Jeff felt like a foreigner. Everyone inside the church was (and always had been) passionate, and even fanatical, about church and religion and God and Jesus. And not only was he not one of them, he was the evil wicked teenager who'd impregnated Amy Jones, one of their own — the innocent flower of a girl who spent her summers in their youth camps and on their mission trips. But now, in sort of his own sinful, messed-up, heathen way, he'd married into the church family.

That's how things are in marriage, Jeff realized. You assimilate your spouse's traditions and pastimes into your own life. For instance, at Jeff's house at Christmas it was, "On your marks, get set, go!" and everyone tore into their presents as fast as they could. But at Amy's house they tore into them slowly, one at a time, going around in the circle and admiring and ooing and ahhing about all the wonderful sweaters and toys and Chinese message contraptions. Jeff and Amy agreed that every other Christmas they would rotate how they opened presents, honoring both family traditions.

Jeff's only Sunday tradition was making waffles and fresh-squeezed orange juice. So they decided to merge their traditions. Jeff would go to church. And afterwards Amy would make waffles and fresh-squeezed OJ.

It was only fair.

On his first morning at church as a married man, he walked through the giant oak doors trying to pretend everyone wasn't staring at him. He actually couldn't tell if they were staring at him or his wife, who was with child, or if they were staring at this whole scene. Jeff couldn't tell if people thought that maybe he and Amy were there to make a scene, to flip over the communion tables and snatch handfuls of cash from the offering plates. So he tried to ignore them. He took Amy to find a seat and sat there with a confident smile as if he were completely used to going to church. As if this was what he did every Sunday.

Then, when the service started, Jeff stopped thinking about the other people and started to consider what the preacher was saying. Jeff couldn't tell what Pastor Colby (the former youth pastor who was now the Senior Pastor) was talking about. Jeff didn't know what the preacher meant when he said you have to make *an eternal impact*. That's how he kept saying it. "Live your life to make an eternal impact." Jeff assumed Pastor Colby was talking about taking care of the environment.

But he wasn't.

He was talking about heaven and hell and the fact that people will spend an eternity in one place or another. He was talking about how your actions will get you close to heaven or hell.

Pastor Colby went on, "You see, someday Jesus will come back for all of us. We will be raptured, and we will be held accountable for every decision we've made on earth. Don't you want to be able to stand there, in front of the Father, and feel proud? Don't you want to hear Him say, 'Well done, my good and faithful servant'?"

Jeff thought it would probably be nice to hear Jesus say that. But he had the feeling that for everyone around him, Jesus' saying this wasn't a nice thought—it was a goal. They lived every single day facing the reality of heaven and hell. And Jeff suddenly wondered how everyone lived like this. He looked around the sanctuary and wondered how they all woke up, scanned their offices, schools, the bus stops and supermarkets, knowing that everyone around them was going to one place or the other. Sure, Jeff knew it was possible everyone would end up in heaven or hell, but he also knew it was possible that the ozone layer could melt away; it was possible the local nuclear power plant could melt down; it was possible that on his next checkup he could get diagnosed with cancer and only have six months to live. There was a chance all those things could happen. But you can't live your life in fear of a chance that something *could* happen. It would paralyze you. But for the people in the church, there wasn't the *chance* heaven and hell could happen; they knew better, they knew it was only a matter of time.

"You see, guys, it's real simple. The Bible says nobody knows the day or the time. So one day we're just going to be going along, business as usual, and then BAM," the minister snapped his fingers. "And like that we'll be gone. So we need to live our lives holy and righteous. We need to live as if Jesus actually were coming back any second."

After the service Jeff and Amy mingled with some church members. Jeff was surprised at how friendly everyone was. He was invited to the next week's potluck; he was hugged, smiled at, introduced to everyone, and overall it seemed like he was being welcomed into the church family.

On the car ride home things were better. He drove through the neighborhoods with Amy snuggled up to him, resting her head on his shoulder. It was a spring day and he slowly drove past the kids playing jump rope and hopscotch, past the fathers grilling bratwursts in their "kiss the cook" aprons, past the blossoming trees, singing birds, and elderly couples drinking freckled strawberry lemonade on the porch. Jeff rolled down his window and the breeze tussled his hair, almost reassuring him that everything was going to be okay from here on out. And for a moment he blinked, took a deep breath, and let everything soak in.

But when he opened his eyes, they were all gone.

The kids had vanished and the jump rope slowly fell to the ground. The elderly couple had disappeared and their freckled strawberry lemonade fell to the porch, shattered, and red juice crept across it. Around him he could smell the bratwursts as their skin started to blacken and burn. And when Jeff looked over at Amy she wasn't there. She had vanished along with everyone else. When he felt the place where she was just sitting, it was still warm. He couldn't bring himself to lift his hand up because he didn't want to stop feeling the warmth. He knew it was the last of piece of Amy he would ever have.

Then Jeff shook his head and they were all back: the children, the fathers with grilling utensils, the elderly couple, and Amy. She didn't even notice anything was wrong. She was staring out the window, humming along with the radio.

This was the first paranoid flash Jeff ever had. He thought everything he was seeing was real because he wasn't used to these flashes/paranoid-visions-of-the-future. So at that moment he couldn't make sense of what he was seeing.

Still, he'd had fears before and he knew a little bit about dealing with them. He knew the best way to battle paranoia was to use logic and reason. And when he had the rapture vision he used the same sort of reason. He told himself the rapture wasn't going to happen because, in all honesty, it was nonsense. Was he really supposed to believe that one day every Christian in Goodland would really just vanish? There were so many logistical problems in this line of believing alone. How would God know exactly who to rapture? And if he was doing it all at the same moment, couldn't there be a little confusion and chaos? What if some of the wrong people were raptured? What if God scooped up a few sinners and pagans and heathens by mistake just because the whole thing was happening so fast? What if God grabbed some Mormons and Muslims and Jehovah's Witnesses because they were all in *some* sort of church? Would they have to be sent back to earth? Would there have to be a second rapture to grab all the people who'd been inaccurately left behind?

As Jeff pulled into his apartment complex he decided that if he was going to go to church, he would no longer put any stock or thought or faith in the talk of the rapture. From that point forward the rapture was just an odd footnote in the Christian belief system that he would ignore.

And through the years, Jeff's Sunday morning ritual began to change—once the baby was born, the fresh-squeezed orange juice came from cartons and the homemade waffles became Eggos. "There just isn't time to make everything from scratch," Amy would say. And then a couple of years later the Eggos became Frosted Shredded Mini Wheats because they were high in fiber, and the OJ became grapefruit juice because there wasn't all that needless sugar—but that was okay. He had more important things to worry about than breakfast now. He had become a responsible adult and a reliable parent. He went to church and provided for his family. These were monumental accomplishments he never thought he'd be able to do when Amy first announced her pregnancy. And as part of his new life he even learned that church could give him some of the right things to worry about. He began to concern himself with the importance of being kind to his neighbor. He learned to make sure he never committed any of the horrendous sins like stealing or killing or committing adultery.

He could worry about those things. Those seemed like good, sensible, adult things to be worrying about. Just as long as he didn't have to worry about thousands and millions of souls vanishing in the blink of an eye; graveyards coming to life with all the dead Christians; seven years of hellish tribulation; a one-world government; and last, but certainly not least, just as long as he didn't have to worry about the Antichrist.

As long as he didn't have to worry about any of that, everything would be fine.

Eighteen years later, Jeff suddenly had no choice. The first of the signs of the impending rapture had happened. But before he (and everyone else) could start worrying about the philosophical/apocalyptic ramifications of the tornado that shredded Jefferson Elementary, he had to worry about the practical ones first. That started with getting home and making sure his family was okay.

This would not be an easy task.

Once he pulled out of Hansley Automotive's parking lot and onto the normally quiet streets of Goodland, Jeff realized he was trying to do the same thing everyone else was. *Everyone* was trying to get home. Or at least they were all, in some way, trying to get to their families. Husbands had to find their wives, mothers had to rescue their children, even couples who'd only been casually dating for a month or two were trying to find each other. At that moment everyone needed to hug and hold and talk with and see the people that mattered most to them. And because the tornado hit in the middle of the workday on a Thursday afternoon, it meant everyone was apart—children were at school, homemakers were at home, and fathers and mothers were at their jobs. Everyone had to drive across town to get to their families.

It was chaos.

Jeff couldn't believe all the people on the roads. He'd never seen anything like it. The streets of Goodland just weren't designed to hold the amount of traffic that was on them. It seemed like everyone who had a car was driving it. And even though the drivers of Goodland were normally very cautious and courteous—

State Farm had ranked it the fourth safest city in America, and the citizens of Goodland enjoyed some of the lowest insurance premiums in the country — today all that was thrown out the window. Everyone behind the wheel of a car was driving in a panicked frenzy. The streets of Goodland looked like a third-world country. Not that Jeff really knew what driving in a third-world country looked like. He'd seen movies where there were bikes, carriages, horses, mopeds, small cars and trucks that were honking and crisscrossing and zigzagging through the streets of Bangkok. And this is how Goodland felt.

It took Jeff a minute or two to get used to driving under the new traffic rules. If there were two lanes on a street, the drivers acted as if there were four. Stoplights were only recommendations. Sidewalks were used as the carpool lane. Horns were used wildly and freely. They were held down to give one long beep — horns of the smaller cars cracking as if the beep was coming from insecure, pimply middle school students, horns of the large SUVs were deep and guttural as if the beep were coming from a mustached truck driver in flannel. Other horns were rapidly fired in long and short bursts as the drivers pounded their fists against them to let everyone know they were on the road and in a hurry.

As Jeff made his way home he passed accident after accident. No one in Goodland really knew how to drive in a third-world, Bangkok style. And even though most of the accidents weren't serious, they still made getting home feel all the more dangerous and jarring.

Jeff drove past the accidents, trying to stay focused on the mission at hand, but he couldn't help but notice as some of the other motorists caught his eye. They glared at him. And for a moment Jeff felt responsible for all of this. What if it was all Will's fault? Of course it wasn't, but what if he were blamed for everything? Jeff knew people could sue for anything these days — we live in a society that teaches us to shirk the blame whenever we can. If some woman spills coffee on herself, she doesn't take the blame, she turns around and sues whoever made the coffee for making it too hot. A man whose waistline expands after eating too many Oreos will sue Nabisco for making them too high in fat content. Jeff knew he lived in a day and age where people could sue for whatever reason, no matter how frivolous and nonsensical the lawsuit seemed.

And sure, Will couldn't be blamed for *causing* the tornado—that would be impressive for any lawyer to prove in court. But he probably could be blamed for causing the paranoia. Tornados happened all the time in Kansas—but tornados that marked the beginning of the end, those were special. And it wouldn't be too far a stretch to imagine a group lawsuit. Jeff could imagine some lawyer planting the idea that all of these wrecks were happening because of Will's prediction. He could picture his son in a courtroom with his hands folded as some lawyer in a high-priced suit said, "You see ladies and gentlemen of the jury, it was the paranoia started *by the Henderson family* that caused all of these accidents. No one would have been hurrying home if they didn't think the end was near. And, therefore, it was Will Henderson's irresponsible prediction that caused all of this damage and heartbreak. Not some simple afternoon storm." All of the jury would nod in agreement and find Jeff guilty because their friends' cars were also damaged in these accidents. And even if they didn't find Jeff guilty, he'd still have to pay all of the legal fees to defend himself, and it would break him. His car and house would be repossessed and they'd have to move in with Amy's parents.

Jeff shook his head.

He wasn't going to face massive group civil suits. Even if he was, he couldn't let himself think about that right now. Will. Amy. Emily. That's what was important.

To make matters worse, Jeff began to notice that along with the horrendous driving, everyone was on their phones. They were talking and dialing and redialing and holding their phones in the air to see if they were getting any service. A lot of the phone lines were overloaded, so people couldn't get through, which only made them fidget with their phones more. And Jeff was just as guilty. He was trying to get through to Amy. He dialed and listened and waited, only to hear an automated voice coldly say, "All circuits are busy right now. Please try again." He was going crazy in the car. He was still miles from home, he had to get all the way out to the country, and at this rate, he'd never get there.

He flicked on the radio to get his mind off things. It didn't help. KBOY Country wasn't playing any of the songs he loved; they were giving live reports of the school. Most of the news was good. No one had been killed by the tornado; most had been evacuated before the funnel cloud hit. So far there were about fourteen injuries—only three of those seemed serious and only one of them was critical. "On Tuesday a fifth grade student by the name of Will Henderson told the other students that the school would be destroyed. There was confusion about when exactly the destruction would happen—"

Jeff's phone started to ring. He turned the radio down. He'd heard all the rest before. "Amy!"

"Jeff!"

Jeff smiled from ear to ear. Tears rolled off his face. It felt good to hear her voice, and even better to know that she was okay. But just to be sure, he asked. She said she was fine, good even if you considered the circumstances. "What about Will?" he asked.

"He's holding up, Jeff. He's a lot stronger than I am."

"But the school, the destruction, I mean that's got to be hard for him."

"He knew better than anybody that this was going to happen."

"Yeah, but it's one thing to know and another thing to watch it."

"Honey, he's going to be all right. He *is* all right. He's sad it happened, but he knew it had to happen."

"Well, just tell him to hang in there. I'll be home soon."

As he pulled into the driveway Amy and Will ran outside. Jeff jumped out of his car and grabbed his wife. It felt almost unreal to be holding her, to smell her apricot shampoo, to look into her smiling blue eyes and know that she seemed all right. That she still seemed like the same person he'd been falling in love with over the last eighteen years.

And then he knelt down and hugged his son. "Are you all right?" he asked. When Jeff pulled back, he was startled at how rock-solid his son seemed. Jeff thought maybe Will should be holding him and asking if he was all right.

Will didn't answer. So Jeff asked again, "Come on, Will, I asked you a question? How are you buddy?" Will looked as if he were really considering this question. He seemed to be deeply concerned with what it meant to be okay. But when Will finally opened his mouth, all he said was, "Yeah Dad, I'm fine."

A little later, Jeff, Amy, and Will were in the sitting room. They did not normally use this room. The dining room was where they ate dinner, the living room was where the TV was, and there was nothing in the sitting room except for stuffy, rigid furniture.

"Why do we even need this room?" Jeff once asked Amy.

"It's what dignified people have," Amy said.

So just the fact that they were sitting in this room made the hours after the tornado unusual for the Hendersons. Jeff sat his family in there to debrief what had happened, but before they could get too far into the situation, Emily walked through the door.

Amy ran up to her and they hugged and talked about what they'd seen. They said things like, "Can you believe the tornado hit just like that? In the middle of the day? That was crazy. I've never *ever* seen anything like that." Jeff knew what they had seen was fascinating. But there wasn't time to focus too much on that. Not right now. They needed to know what they were going to say. The town was in chaos and soon friends and neighbors and the media were going to want answers from the Hendersons. They were going to want them to speak about what had happened. And Jeff knew they had to be careful about how they went about that.

But before Jeff could even bring that up, there was a knock at the door. Their whole conversation screeched to a stop. The four members of the family just sat on the rigid furniture and stared at their front door.

"Who do you think it is?" Amy asked.

"I don't know, but let me handle this. I'll do all the talking," Jeff instructed his family. Jeff flung the door open and there were cameras, lights, and a lady with a microphone. They were all aimed at Jeff to record anything he said. Whatever he did was about to be broadcast into every home in Goodland.

"Mr. Henderson, Nancy Palmer, News Channel 4. Can we get your reaction to the Jefferson Elementary Disaster?" the reporter asked.

"Jefferson Elementary Disaster?" Jeff asked.

"It's what the tornado at the school is being called."

"Oh," Jeff said. But before he could say much more, another camera crew and reporter ran through his lawn and up to his front door.

"Mr. Henderson, I'm Laurie Winters and we want to offer Will and his family a chance to be a Channel 9 exclusive," the second reporter said.

"I was here first, Laurie," Nancy Palmer said.

"Did she offer you an exclusive?" Laurie Winters asked Jeff.

"What's an exclusive?" Will asked. He'd popped his head through the door and come outside. This was the last thing Jeff wanted. All the cameras and lights aimed at Will. "Isn't an exclusive when a guy and a girl date each other and no one else?" Will asked.

"Yes, that's one definition," Laurie Winters said, crouching to eye level with Will. "But another definition is your chance to tell your story however you and your dad want you to. You are a very special boy and very special to this town, and they really want to hear from you."

"Okay, that's it. Will, get inside," Jeff said.

"Mr. Henderson, Channel 4 doesn't just want Will. We'd love to interview any members of your family," Nancy Palmer said.

"I'd be happy for you to interview me," Emily said. She'd come outside while Jeff was trying to corral Will back inside. "It would be great for me to get some good PR right before homecoming. That way Goodland could see the caring, family side of Emily Henderson."

At that, all the cameras and lights flicked on Emily. Microphones were thrust above her head. And Nancy Palmer asked, "Emily, have you ever seen Will predicting anything before all of this?"

Jeff thrust his hand in front of the camera. "Enough. Emily, Will, inside now. Everyone else, get off my property. The Henderson family has no comment about the disaster at the school right now."

Jeff had to physically grab his son and daughter and pull them inside. It had been years since he'd had to pull them away from danger. You don't pull a seventeen-year-old away from something the way that you pull a three-year-old away from sticking her hand on a hot burner. But what was outside was a hot burner. It was an Uncle Dale. It was something that seemed so nice and friendly. It took someone of Jeff's years to see how dangerous it was. Emily and Will could have no way of knowing how much those pretty ladies were a threat to their family.

But they were a threat.

They would plaster their faces all over the TV.

Everyone in town was upset, but if they let the news pass on, soon enough there would be another story to talk about. But if they fed the news beast, then all of the rapture fanatics or anti-rapture fanatics would be at their door wanting answers. The Henderson family would be laser-locked in their sights. They wouldn't be safe at home, at the store, at school — anywhere.

Jeff realized all of this in a flash, but maybe this flash was good and helpful. Maybe it was primal. His survival instincts had kicked in and he suddenly knew what he had to do to keep his family safe. It didn't matter if they understood or felt good about it. Someday they would. And in the meantime they would not be harmed. That's what was important.

"Dad, what are you doing? I just want to say a few things. This is my chance to be on TV," Emily said.

"Okay, listen to me, Emily and everyone else. No one says a word to the media. Not to the reporter or newspapers or anyone else. We don't want them talking about us and showing our faces on TV."

"They're going to talk about us anyway. We're like the biggest story in town."

"Let them talk. We'll keep our mouths shut."

"But why, Dad?"

"Because I am the head of this household! I provide for this family, I lead this family, and this is my decision," Jeff snarled. He didn't mean to come off so cold and mean. But he could leave nothing to chance. His family could not put themselves in the line of fire. He didn't want to go into all of the reasons why because that would just freak them out. That wouldn't help anything right now. And when his family could see how serious he was by the look on his face and the sound of his voice, they didn't say another word about the topic.

Dinner was cold and awkward. There wasn't a lot of conversation. There was the clanking of forks against ceramic plates as they ate their pasta with red Ragu sauce, and that was about it. Jeff knew everyone was thinking about the news trucks that were all parked in front of their house. It was hard not to notice the bright white glare from the camera lights that pierced their way through the blinds. Jeff asked Mike if there was any way the news crews could be removed, but Mike said they were legally off the property so there was nothing he could do.

The family wanted to watch the news, but he knew that would just be a reminder of how difficult the media silence was, so he refused to let them turn it on.

As dinner came to an end, they heard three knocks at the front door. Jeff was sure one of the news people had snuck back onto the property and he was ready to tear their head off as he threw his napkin onto his plate and walked towards the front door.

But it wasn't a newsperson at all. It was Mike standing there.

"Can we come in?" he asked.

"*We?*"

"We need to talk," Mike said and stepped back. Standing behind Mike were people Jeff had never met. But Jeff knew who they were: the mayor and his entourage, the chief of police, and Reverend Whitlock, minister at The Church of Hope. Why had

Mike brought these people into his house? He was trying to calm his family down; this was the last thing he needed.

"Is Will here? We need to talk."

"About what?"

"We need to ask him some questions about what he thinks is going to happen to our town next," one of the mayor's men said. He was wearing a charcoal suit and seemed to be the spokesman for the mayor.

"So, you actually believe that he was giving prophecies?" Amy asked.

Jeff turned around to see that all of his family was in the living room. He would have rather they talked to the news than the mayor and his men. This all felt really uncomfortable, so Jeff said, "We don't feel like talking right now."

"I don't think you have a choice," Mike answered.

Jeff glared at Mike. You're supposed to help protect us, he thought. And you bring these men into my home to interrogate us?

"We're just here for a friendly chat," the mayor said. He was a plump, good-natured man who was beloved in Goodland. He was always smiling at the fair and the Christmas parade. But Jeff had never met him in an official capacity and didn't really know what to expect.

"It doesn't feel friendly," Jeff said. And without being invited, Mike, the mayor, and his men walked into Jeff's house. Men like these probably don't think they need to be invited in.

"Well, to be frank, I don't think many people in the town feel friendly right now. And that's why we have to work together on this," the mayor said as he sat on the couch in the living room. The mayor was such a large man, it seemed like he didn't like to stand for long stretches. Whenever Jeff saw him in public events — parades, rallies, the rodeo — he was usually sitting. It was probably just a little much to ask his knees to support that large frame.

"I didn't mean to cause trouble," Will said.

"It's okay, Will," the mayor said. "We know that you didn't mean to. It's just, you've done something very powerful by sharing your prophecy with other members of the town."

"It's actually the face's prophecy," Will said.

"Sure, the face's prophecy," the mayor echoed. "Now, you said the face has more signs, isn't that true?"

"Yes, two more. Then the rapture," Will said.

"When were you going to share the next sign?" the mayor asked.

"I don't know."

"Because you see, we've got to be careful when we share prophecies."

"We do?" Will asked.

"Yes, very careful," the mayor said. Then he got on one knee and put a hand on Will's shoulder. "And that's why we've come to talk to you. We were wondering if you could tell us what your next prophecy is going to be. So we can help the town know how to react and keep things much more orderly."

"We're trying to avoid panic and chaos," Mike added.

"So, if you just tell me what the prophecies are, then I can tell the town. It's not that we don't want the prophecies to be told, we just want to control how the information comes out," the mayor said.

"What's the next prophecy, Will?" the man in the charcoal suit asked.

Will paused. "I don't know, it's kind of blurry."

"Blurry?"

"Yeah, the first one was easy to remember because I told everyone the next day after the cornfields. But now it's been a couple of days, and —"

"You don't have to tell them anything, Will," Amy said. Jeff noticed she'd been watching silently in the background during this whole interview, but these last questions had become too much and Jeff could see her "mother bear going to snap the neck of anyone coming near her baby cub" instinct was now taking over.

"Actually, he really should," the man in the charcoal suit said.

"He's trying to take all of the credit," Amy answered, looking at the mayor.

"I'm what?" the mayor wheezed.

"Come on, Will tells you what's going to happen next, you get the town ready for Will's prophecy, and you look like the big hero."

"Tell me you're not serious. Tell me you're not that paranoid. This is not about looking like a hero," the mayor said.

"It isn't?" Amy asked.

"No, I've got a town in chaos out there. Parents are scared, children are scared, and your son caused a lot of that fear," the mayor said.

"He caused a lot of that fear? If it weren't for my son, you wouldn't have scared children and frightened parents. You'd have dead children and grieving parents," Amy shouted.

"That's not fair," Mike said.

"No, what's not fair is two days ago you put my son on house arrest for spreading panic. And now you want him to tell his prophecies so you guys don't look so completely pathetic—"

"Okay Amy, stop," Jeff said.

"But Jeff—"

"No, this is ridiculous. Will—"

"Yeah, Dad?"

"No more prophecies."

"What do you mean?" Will asked.

"I want you to forget whatever the face told you. I know you said it's blurry, but now I want you to push it out of your head completely. Don't tell it to me or your mom or the mayor or anybody. Don't write it down. Don't whisper it to your comic books when you're alone in your room. You know how you have a really good imagination?"

"Yeah, Dad."

"Well, imagine you were never in those cornfields. Imagine you don't know what the face looks like."

"That's weird, Dad."

"Son, you can do it," Jeff said. Then he looked at the mayor and his entourage. "I know why you're here," Jeff said, looking at Mike more than anyone. "The goal is to keep things under control. No more panic and chaos in this town, right? That's what you want. It's what I want too. So what if I can keep my son quiet? Will you leave us alone?"

"We need to know if something else is going to happen," Mike said.

"Nothing is going to happen. You know that and I know that. The only thing that telling those prophecies will do is stir up panic. Leave us alone. I promise I can keep things quiet on our end."

"You really think you can deliver on that promise, Mr. Henderson?" the mayor asked.

"I know I can."

"Fair enough," the mayor said. "You haven't spoken with the media so far. You haven't fanned the flame and we appreciate that. So we'll trust you. No more prophecies. Not to each other. Not to anyone. And this will all go back to normal."

"Yeah, back to normal," Jeff agreed.

AMY HENDERSON

The moon wasn't making things any better. It was butter yellow and smiling. Jeff was lightly snoring, but Amy's eyes were wide open. Sleep wasn't even an option. She'd never been so awake in her life. It reminded her of her senior year, before she was pregnant, when she took like five NoDoz pills with her friends while they were pulling an all-nighter studying for SATs. She couldn't blink that night. She crammed her mind full of facts and figures and formulas and statistics, and the next day her mind was all jumbled. She couldn't think straight. She bombed the test. She never took it again because, by the time she was scheduled to retake it, she'd found out that she was pregnant, and by then what was the point?

Tonight felt sleepless just like that night. Amy had been drinking cups of black coffee between worrying about the news, the mayor, Will, Jeff, and everything else. She just kept downing the stuff because it was the only thing that would comfort her. But now she just lay in bed, clutching her covers and looking all around the room. The moonlight pierced through the windows and the maple trees created crisscrossing shadows all over the bedroom. The shadows crept all the way onto Jeff's face.

I hope he knows what he's doing, Amy thought. She'd been worried about it all day. She could understand why Jeff didn't want them to talk to the mayor. After all, the only thing the mayor was looking to do was to protect himself. But why didn't Jeff want them to talk to the media? The media could help get the truth out. The tornado happened just like Will said it would. If anything, we should be vindicated. So why does it feel like we're on trial?

Because you are.

Amy wasn't sure where the thought came from. Maybe it was God, or the coffee, or from somewhere deep in her subconscious. It didn't matter. Wherever this thought came from, it was right. She *was* on trial. They all were. Who said predicting the end of the world was supposed to be easy? It was suddenly all so clear. If she just laid there and did nothing, they could miss out.

The first time it was her own lust and flesh and insecurity that made her lose everything. It kept her from her dream of holding little African babies and singing worship songs as the sun set. But now there was something so much more meaningful happening. Her son was the voice and guide and prophet for what was happening at the beginning of the end of Goodland and then the world. People were terrified — so what if God had ordained Will to be the ultimate voice for guidance and comfort? Will would guide everyone toward eternity.

Maybe this was God's ultimate plan A.

Maybe this is what he intended all along. Maybe every single moment of their lives had been adding up to helping Will warn the town about the rapture. Hundreds — maybe even thousands — of souls in Goodland were realizing how close they were to the end. With each prophecy that came true they would understand more and more. Perhaps the whole town would be saved by the time the great trumpet blasted. And then, once they were all gone, the world would understand how serious the rapture was. Will would not only save Goodland, he would save the world.

Jeff probably already understood this. His faith always amazed Amy. Because when they first got married she was so scared. He didn't come from a background with any faith or religion in it. In fact, she knew she shouldn't have even dated him in the first place. They weren't equally yoked. She spent her summers at youth camps and on mission trips and he spent his summers at kegger parties. Her youth group friends (who all ditched her the second they found out she was pregnant) were horrified when she first started *talking* to Jeff. And they were right. She had no business with him. He was popular, cute, charming, funny, and brave, but he wasn't Christian. There were plenty of guys who were cute *and* Christian. Things would have been so much easier if one of them would have gotten her pregnant.

But when she saw how that first service ministered to him, she knew something amazing had happened. He accepted God even though he never had spirituality in his background. And he'd been leading their family with faith ever since.

And today he'd been leading them so fearlessly. He was so wise in understanding that they couldn't give such an important message on the front doorstep with cameras shoved in their face. And they couldn't just give it to that selfish mayor. So he told the fat man what he needed to hear so there could be a right place and a right time for Will's prophecy. But still the time to give the message was now. Who knew when the next prophecy was supposed to come true? It could happen days, or even hours, from now.

What if Jeff wanted to continue to be cautious about this? He'd been so brave, he'd guided them every step of the way since the cornfields, and sure he'd made some mistakes, but he was trying. Still, it seemed that he was scared to make another mistake. And now wasn't the time for fear. Now was the time for action.

You can't expect Jeff to do everything.

This came from nowhere again. And again this thought was right. It was time that she started to carry some of the weight of this. Even though Jeff had been leading them in faith, he still didn't have it *in* him like she did. He needed her. It was time that she made a decision and acted like a helpmate to her husband instead of just sitting back and drinking coffee and expecting Jeff to take care of everything.

Amy lightly crept out of bed and into their office. She booted up their old IBM computer, which was louder than one of those old pontoon planes when it started. It made whirling and clicking sounds until finally the Windows image came up on the screen.

Amy wanted to get online to see if she could find any websites about prophecies similar to what Will had been having. Surely there would be some answers, guidance, and maybe an online community of prophets to help her know what the next steps were. When the computer finally booted up it seemed a little overwhelming to scour the entire World Wide Web for advice on how to coach your son in foretelling the apocalypse. So, to warm up, Amy checked her email.

Her inbox was flooded with concerned, congratulatory, and confused emails about what had happened with Will and the tornado. There was no time to read it all. But she couldn't help but be curious about what they were saying. So she started with an email forward to her with a subject line that simply read **THE END IS NOW.** Amy never really liked forwards, but she couldn't help but read this one.

She clicked open a Quicktime movie and it revealed a nice slide show with warm, friendly pictures. Harp music played behind a picture of the Goodland fair last summer. There were bright balloons, Ferris wheels, and people in shorts and flip-flops laughing and enjoying the summer day. This faded to another happy image of a family of six in a van eating strawberry ice cream. The next image was of a bride and groom facing each other and smiling in a fairytale-looking wedding chapel.

Amy thought the slide show was nice, but kind of uneventful.

She'd give it a second or two longer before clicking on her next email.

Then bright blue cursive text appeared on the screen that read, "We take every day for granted ..." At that the image on the screen went black. The harp music cut out. And dark heavy-metal music began to blare through the speakers. Amy had to crank down the volume, hoping the thrashing guitars didn't wake anyone up. But she was too terrified to take her eyes off the screen as dark red letters popped up saying, "BUT WHAT IF TOMORROW NEVER COMES?"

Then pictures of the same locations appeared.

But everything had changed.

The picture of the Goodland fair had abandoned flip-flops and shorts scattered all about, balloons floating up like souls towards heaven, and everyone left behind was on their knees screaming. The picture of the family in the van now had all the kids missing. The parents looked in the backseats, horrified to see that their children were now only piles of clothes, and the only proof of life that remained was the strawberry ice cream that ran down the seats and windows. The picture of the wedding was now missing the groom, and the bride clutched onto the empty tux as black mascara ran down her face.

And that's when it clicked. Seeing all of those pictures — all of those hopeless people being blindsided by the reality of eternity — made Amy realize this was more than about saving the world. This was about families being separated for an eternity. Loved ones having to deal with the chasm of heaven and hell. It was going to happen. Soon and very soon everyone in Goodland would have to face the afterlife, and like it or not, they would have to answer to the creator of the heavens and the earth. Sure, she always sort of knew the rapture was coming. But it always felt distant and cloudy, something far off to be worried about someday.

In the meantime she'd spent all of her time worrying about non-eternal things, like how much cholesterol was in her diet, and who got to be head coordinator of the Royal Rangers bake sale, and what kind of college Emily and Will would attend. (She wanted the college to be prestigious but not too secular. She'd heard horror stories of her friends' kids going off to college and coming home brainwashed.) But now she felt foolish for wasting so much time thinking about all of this. Over and over again Scriptures refer to the short amount of time we have on earth. It was time she started living like that. From now on there was only the present. And every moment of the present needed to be spent doing whatever it took to get ready for the rapture.

As if to confirm her thoughts, the screen cut to black again and read, "The End Is No Longer NEAR ... The End Is NOW!" Then the music turned to an unbearably quick, grinding beat as one red-lettered warning after the next flew onto the screen.

"The Prophecy Has Come True!" Amy almost screamed when she saw Will's picture come on the screen. Who put this together? Who all has this been sent to? She looked at the top of the email and saw that it had been sent to hundreds and hundreds of recipients.

"The School Has Been Destroyed!" A picture of Jefferson Elementary flashed on. It was hard to look at. Gray rubble and dust was scattered everywhere. It looked nothing like the school she'd dropped her son off at over the last five years. Jefferson was a crystal-clear physical reminder of how real this whole situation was. God had destroyed the school to prove a point. A point that Jeff or Mike or the mayor couldn't argue. Then, over the school's picture, more words popped up: "There Is No Time Left!"

The screen went black. The music cut out. And then the final apocalyptic warning flashed onto the screen, "Repent ... Or You Won't Be Sent!"

After that the video faded out. It gave Amy two options: *Play Again* or *Forward to a Friend.*

Amy's hand quivered as it grabbed the mouse and clicked onto Play Again.

AMY HENDERSON

Amy knew the sun was going to rise in about an hour. It was time to act. She couldn't wait for Jeff. Besides, he would be so thankful when he understood what she had done. She was going to take Will to the news station to explain his side of the story. She wouldn't let him give the next prophecy; she wanted Jeff to be in on that decision. The important thing would be to let everyone know a prophecy was coming soon, that the rapture was real, and that *now* was the time to get things right.

So Amy softly stepped through the hallway and into her son's room. She gently shook him awake and told him they had to get ready quickly. She went to the back of his closet and picked out an outfit for him — tan Dockers, canary yellow shirt, and a navy blue blazer. "Put this on and fix your hair nice. Not that messy look." He grabbed the clothes and marched to the bathroom, staring at nothing but the carpet as he walked. She was happy as he obeyed in silence. He seemed too groggy to ask any questions.

As they left she was a little afraid the clanking of the garage door might wake Jeff up. Amy hadn't taken into account the possibility that Jeff could wake up and think the end had already happened. What if he woke up and thought they'd been raptured? Maybe that would be even better. He'd roll over to her side of the bed and be a little startled when it was empty. He'd fling their bathroom door open and get worried when she wasn't in there.

He'd flick the lights on in Will's room only to see that his first-born son was gone. Then he'd run outside in his pajamas and stare at the sky. He'd wonder if that shooting star was really one of the horsemen of the apocalypse. And at that moment the reality of the rapture would rip through him like shotgun pellets. That moment of clarity might even give him the strength he needed to finish guiding their family through this time.

"Where are we going, Mom?" Will asked, snapping Amy out of her thoughts.

"We're going to the news station," Amy answered.

"Oh," Will said.

"Will, let me ask you a question. What made you go to school and tell everybody about what the face said?"

"Because the face told me for a reason. And if I didn't tell anyone, I was afraid the school would be destroyed with all of the kids still in it."

"That makes a lot of sense," Amy said.

"I thought so," Will agreed. "Why? Are you still mad at me for telling?"

"No, not at all."

"Do you think something's wrong with me?"

"No baby, I think everything's right with you. You listen to me; you have been given a very important gift. The signs the face gave to you are very important. They're from God, and they'll tell us how to prepare for the rapture," Amy said.

"How do you know they're from God?"

"Because they came true."

"So if they didn't come true they'd be from Satan?"

"Um, probably. I don't know, honey."

"I thought Dad wanted me to forget everything the face said."

"Your dad was just trying to get the mayor to leave. He's a little worried."

"Oh," Will said. "Does Dad think the face is Satan?"

"I haven't thought about that."

"He probably thinks the face is Satan. I thought the face might be Satan at first."

"You did?" Amy asked.

"Yeah, but then I realized the face didn't have horns. The face had a beard. And Satan never has a beard. Normally only people who are interested in God have beards. And that's probably because God has a beard. If the face had been clean-shaven I wouldn't have listened to him. It would have been a dead giveaway that he was up to no good."

"So, does the face visit you often?"

"Nope, only that one time in the cornfield. I've asked him to come back but he hasn't. I figure he has lots of other things to do," Will said.

"You're probably right," Amy agreed.

The news station was much smaller than Amy thought it would be. On TV it looked like this large room with commanding oak desks and the sprawling Goodland skyline in the background. But here it was just this tiny set where everything looked plastic and flimsy — the desk looked like it could snap in half if you leaned on it wrong and the background appeared as if it was cut out of a large magazine and pasted on the back wall with a glue stick.

It was a little disappointing. Not that Amy really had a reason to feel disappointed. It was just that her son was about to have his first televised statement, and that should be in a place that was as grand and important as what he was about to say. Apparently, Goodland Channel 4 wasn't that place.

Will and Amy waited for twenty minutes as the producer ran around making one frantic phone call after another. Finally she came up to them and said, "We're really happy you want to give our station the exclusive."

"We just want to get his story out," Amy said. "We want people to know what really happened."

"That makes perfect sense," Monica said. Amy hated how agreeable she was. She knew the producer was just buttering them up to get what she wanted. Then again, Amy was using Channel 4 to get what she wanted, so it probably all worked out in the end.

"All right, so we're just going to ask Will a couple of questions. And Will, you just answer them honestly," Monica said.

"Yeah, okay," Will agreed.

"You can ask him about anything but the next sign," Amy butted in.

"The next sign?" Monica asked.

"Ask him all you want about the tornado, the school, the cornfields, but I don't want him talking about the next sign."

"I guess I didn't realize there was more than one," Monica said.

"Me neither," Nancy Palmer added, scribbling down notes on a notepad. She appeared out of nowhere and Amy noticed how great she looked all of a sudden. When Nancy had first arrived at the station she looked horrible. Monica had called her and told her she had to come in for this interview. Nancy had walked into the studio with bags under her eyes, frizzy hair, and wearing a large dumpy trench coat. Twenty minutes later she had her makeup, hair, and wardrobe done and she looked ready to change the world.

Amy wondered if she could change the world if she had a whole team helping her look great. I look better than Nancy when I wake up, she thought. What if I had a whole hair, wardrobe, and makeup crew? For some reason Amy thought that Nancy made herself up for the nightly newscast. But now she knew the truth: Nancy had a whole team. All she really had to do was read words off a TV screen. Amy wondered what else she had misconceptions about. She'd always been so intimidated by the outside world, but lately she was starting to realize it was all smoke and mirrors. Amy was starting to understand she could have been just as important as these women newscasters and producers—maybe even more—if she hadn't blatantly disobeyed God's perfect will and gotten pregnant when she was eighteen.

"So then, how many signs are there?" Monica asked.

"Three," Will said.

"And the tornado was the first one?" Nancy asked.

"Yeah, that's right," Will answered.

"Okay, I can't ask him specifically about the next sign, but can I ask him how many signs there are?" Nancy asked Amy.

"Yeah, sure, I'd appreciate if you did ask that," Amy said.

"Just out of curiosity, why don't you want Will talking about the next sign?" Monica asked.

"I want his father here for that," Amy said.

"But Mrs. Henderson, Will saved so many lives by telling his prophecy the last time," Monica said.

"I know what my son did," Amy said.

"Then you realize he can save as many lives again."

"What I realize is I can take him to Channel 9 instead and they'll be happy to respect my requests about the interview."

"Okay," Monica said and flashed a smile. Then she turned to Nancy, "No questions about the next prophecy."

Amy sat in the makeup room watching a stylist feather her son's hair. It really was impressive to watch. She sculpted each strand with such confidence, and Amy was amazed as Will's hair went exactly where the stylist wanted.

How come his hair won't do that for me?

Monica popped her head in the door and said, "Okay, we're firing everything up now and we'll be ready for Will in five." Then she left. She didn't even look at Amy. It was probably because she was still upset that they couldn't ask about the next sign. But Amy had her reasons. Right now was about getting him on the air and having him become a friendly, trustworthy face. And then, when the time was right, maybe later today or even tomorrow, they would stand as a family and Will would give them the next sign. And ultimately it would be her family—not the stupid mayor or Mike or anyone else—that would lead Goodland to the end.

It was so exciting.

Amy could almost picture what the day would look like. It would start with all of her family and the rest of Goodland on a hill looking up towards the sky. Maybe they'd all be wearing white. They would hear the trumpets blaring this perfect heavenly blast. The sky would split open, glowing with ultraviolet, crimson, and tangerine hues. It would probably also be lit up with other colors that hadn't even been invented yet. And everyone on the grassy hill would be so enraptured with the colors that they wouldn't notice themselves becoming light as balloons and floating off the ground.

The floating would be the best part.

It'd be better than any amusement park ride ever created. They'd float into the air (maybe it'd even feel like the hand of God was pulling them up) and as they'd float higher, they'd watch their houses, then Goodland, then Kansas, then the entire country become ant-sized and eventually disappear. And soon they'd stop looking at the earth all together. They would look up towards the sky as they passed through the atmosphere and then there would only be heaven and eternity to think about. Of course Amy knew this was a fantasy. She knew the end of the world wouldn't be as romantic as she was picturing it.

When they finally got Will on the set Amy thought Will looked so grown up. And he looked grown up more than just in a my-boy's-growing-up-so-fast way. He actually looked like an adult. She'd always wondered what he'd look like as a thirty-year-old with kids of his own. Of course now with the rapture she would probably never know. After all, we don't become grown-ups in heaven, do we? How old are we in heaven? And as Amy thought this she realized maybe there was something to be sad about with the end of the world. She would never get to see Will and Emily as adults. She would never get to hold her grandkids. She would be in her thirties and Will and Emily would be preteens and teenagers for all of eternity.

So, as she looked at her handsome son in his blazer with his hair done so professionally, she thought this may be the closest she'd ever get to seeing him as an adult. And Amy was glad he looked so grown up, because once the cameras started to roll and the reporter started to talk, she knew he was completely on his own.

"Good morning, Goodland," Nancy said as she smiled and flashed her flawless teeth to the camera. "We're here with Will Henderson, the fifth-grade student who caused quite the ruckus four days ago when he predicted the Jefferson Elementary Disaster. And yesterday his prediction came true when a tornado came out of nowhere and did quite a bit of damage to the elementary school. Now this morning, Will has agreed to give Channel 4 his first public statement on all of the events of the last couple of days." Nancy then turned to Will. "Good morning, Will."

"Good morning," Will responded.

"So, why don't we start with the tornado?"

"Okay."

"How'd you feel watching it?"

"Sad," Will said.

"Why were you sad?"

"'Cause, um," Will squirmed.

What's up with the one-word answers? Amy thought. Was he getting shy? Don't get shy, Will. You've got to be strong and confident if you want people to follow you as a prophet.

"Is it because your friends were in there?" Nancy asked.

"Yeah. I mean a lot of people think just because I said the school was going to be destroyed that I *wanted* it to be destroyed. But that's not the truth. Whoever thinks that is just lying to themselves. And why would people want to lie to themselves?"

"I'm not sure," Nancy answered.

"All I know is I loved that school. I grew up there."

"If you loved the school, why'd you say it would be destroyed?"

"I was just telling everyone what the face told me."

"The face?" Nancy asked, leaning in.

"Yeah, it's a face that I saw one night when I was lost in Mr. Johnson's cornfield."

"Do you see the face often?"

"Nope, I've only seen him that one time."

"Have you ever seen anything else like this face?"

"You mean like angels and demons and supernatural stuff?"

"Yeah, things like that," Nancy said.

"Nope. I've wanted to. I mean, doesn't everybody want to see stuff like that? It's like if God's real and there are all these angels and demons around, then how come we don't see them? Haven't you thought that?"

"I suppose I have," Nancy said. Then she asked, "So, who do you think the face is?"

"God," Will answered. "I'm sort of like the story of Moses and the burning bush. Of course, I've also thought maybe the face is an angel of God. Sometimes they came to deliver messages in the

Bible. Like when the angel told Mary she was pregnant. But I don't think the face is Jesus. There aren't stories in the Bible about Jesus coming back and giving messages. And my mom has told me stories where some people say they've gotten a message from Jesus like his face appearing in a piece of bread or on the side of a wall, but I think those people are just imagining stuff because they're bored."

"So you think some people actually have visions and other people just imagine their visions?" Nancy asked.

"Yeah, I think so."

"Okay, so let me ask you this—how are you so sure you didn't just *imagine* the face?"

"Um, two reasons I guess. The first reason is I know when I'm imagining something and when something is real. And the bigger reason is what the face said came true. I mean, that school has been there my whole life, and nothing bad has ever happened to it. And then all of a sudden it's destroyed around the time the face said it was going to be. That's pretty crazy, don't you think?"

"Yeah, I do," Nancy said. "Let me follow up on that real quick though—why was there so much confusion about the timing of the tornado?"

"That was my fault. I misunderstood what the face was saying. He said three days and I didn't know when the three days were starting."

"Was there anything else the face told you?"

"Yeah, he said there would be three total signs that the rapture was coming. The tornado was the first."

"Do you know what the rapture is, Will?"

"It's the end of everything. God will take all the Christians like that," Will said as he snapped his fingers, "and then everyone else is going to suffer. I think there's going to be fires and wars and Antichrists and stuff like that after the rapture."

"Wow, that sounds pretty bad."

"Not for Christians."

"True," Nancy said, seeming a little awkward about where the conversation was going. "All right, let's go back to what the face told you. There are going to be three signs?"

"That's right."

"The tornado was the first."

"Yes."

"And you can't tell what the next two are going to be?" Nancy asked.

"No," Will said. "My mom said the time's not right. But don't worry, I'll tell you before it's too late."

"Okay, well then let me ask you this. There are still people who are doubting all of this. I might even be one of them. Why should we believe you?"

"Because everything the face said has come true."

"Right, but you've only given us the one thing the face has said."

"And that one thing came true."

"Yeah, sure, that one thing *did* come true. But that's not what I'm getting at."

"What are you getting at?" Will asked. Amy wasn't sure if Will was asking an honest question or antagonizing Nancy, but he was clearly gaining control of the interview.

"There may be some people who are still processing what to make of the Jefferson Elementary Disaster. But does that really mean we should honestly believe that the apocalypse is coming? A tornado equals the end of life in Goodland? It doesn't even make sense. This is Kansas. Tornados come all the time. And most kids have some subconscious fantasy that their school is going to be ruined. It's just those two things happened to line up for once. You had a lucky guess, Will, right? I don't think that means we should all suddenly get ready for the afterlife."

"I'm not sure what your question is."

"I don't have one. I'm just saying I'm not sure I can believe you. I don't see any reason anyone else should either," Nancy said, looking and sounding far more upset than Amy or anyone else had ever seen her. Normally she was always so composed, but Will seemed to be making her unravel.

And the weaker she got, the stronger Will seemed. His eyes became steely and focused as he looked right into the lens of the camera (it almost seemed that he had the power to look *past* the camera and into the living room of every home in Goodland). "You can believe whatever you want. I'll tell all of you what I know when the time is right and then it's up to you how to react. You can believe the rapture is coming. Or you can believe that some crazy little kid is making all of this up. But when the end comes and all the Christians are gone and there is nothing left but fires and wars and beast marks, you might want to blame someone. You might feel like shouting, 'Why didn't somebody tell me this was going to happen?' But you know what, you're not going to be able to shout that. Because someone *did* tell you this was going to happen. Then the only person you'll have left to blame will be yourself. And that will suck for you."

JEFF HENDERSON

The idea that the world could actually be ending came with an un-intended side effect—it turned Goodland into the happiest place in Kansas. Truthfully, you'd be hard-pressed to find a happier place in Oklahoma, Nebraska, Missouri, or Colorado either. And this didn't make sense to Jeff. He thought the idea of Armageddon would send all of his friends and neighbors into a panic. And if there wasn't a panic, he thought families would, at the very least, hunker down, lock themselves into basements and fallout shelters, and wait to see what happened next.

But on the morning after Will's first prophecy came true, Jeff drove to work, dumbfounded to see that the streets were bub-bling with enthusiasm. It felt like Mardi Gras—at least a really wholesome, small-town, Kansas Mardi Gras. People were grilling out, laughing, hugging, and sitting on lawn chairs and chatting away as if the rest of their lives were going to be one lazy Sunday afternoon.

To everyone in Goodland, the rapture seemed like either one big joke or the best news ever.

Jeff noticed a lot of the shops in town were closed for busi-ness. And he wondered if perhaps Hansley Automotive would also be closed. But it wasn't. The pre-owned automotive lot was swarming with people. Jeff was running a few minutes late; he'd overslept because the last few days had taken such a toll on him, so he rushed out of the house before he even talked to Amy or Will. And when he got to work he realized he was late on the one morning everyone wanted to buy a car. They were selling cars off the lot as if they were hip Christmas gifts. It was as if the Lexuses, Audis, and Hummers were Tickle Me Elmos and Cabbage Patch dolls — like every parent knew their families would be disappointed if they didn't walk off the lot with the new car.

Jeff couldn't miss out on this chance to make monster commissions.

His first customer was named Marsha Peterson and she lived just a half mile away from the Hendersons. Jeff had known her for years. And he knew that she was not the type of person he'd even picture in a brand new Hummer. Yet somehow that's exactly what she had her eye on: a bright, shiny, brand-new, sunflower yellow H3.

She was ready to close on it, but before Jeff would close the deal he felt that he had to ask, "Do you really think you can afford an H3, Marsha?"

"No, absolutely not. But think how great I'd look in it," Marsha said. She didn't even look up at Jeff. She was just staring at her reflection in the yellow paint, probably imagining herself driving away in the car.

"Sure, okay, that's true. But there are a lot of other cars, affordable cars, that you would look great in."

"Yeah, but does *affordable* really matter anymore?"

"It kind of does. But Marsha, it's no skin off my back, I mean, I want to sell you this car. I'm going to get a lot more commission that way."

"Great then. It works well for both of us."

"Yeah, but I'm going to feel really guilty in a couple of months when the bank comes and takes the car away."

"It won't really matter by then, will it? We'll all be raptured before that," Marsha said, smiling and sincere.

A little while later Jeff had a big commission and Marsha had a giant Hummer which, granted, she did look good in. But she had to spend her life savings and take out a second mortgage on her house just to make a down payment. She didn't seem to mind. "If the rapture is coming, then, for just once in my life, I want to drive a really great, expensive, flashy car," she told Jeff as she signed the contract.

"But what if the rapture doesn't come?"

"You're not serious, are you? You of all people should know it's coming. Your son's been talking all about it."

Jeff didn't say anything.

"Oh, I see—you're a doubter."

"I'm just saying it's *possible*, Marsha. He could be wrong."

"You'll understand the truth soon. But by then it will be too late for you to buy a Hummer."

And as soon as Marsha drove off with her new Hummer, Jeff turned around and saw a line of people waiting to talk with him. This had never happened before. Jeff never imagined he'd see the day when there were *too many* people who wanted to buy cars. But that day was here. And it presented problems. This was a car lot, not the DMV. There was no line to get in or number to be drawn so the customer could make sure they got their new car in a timely and orderly fashion. So, in most cases, the most aggressive customer got to be next. And the most aggressive customer in Jeff's case was a man named Phil Donald. Phil was one of the leading real estate agents in town and not the type of person Jeff would have assumed would get caught up in the rapture hype. He was a rational, calculating, smooth businessman. If Phil was drinking the Kool-Aid, then everyone else surely was as well. And as Phil was looking at a brand new Audi S8, Jeff walked up to him and said, "Let me guess. You're buying a car while you still can."

"I guess you could say that," Phil replied.

"Are you worried about this rapture stuff too?" Jeff asked.

"No, of course not."

"Then why buy a new car while everyone else is?"

"Because I've been making all sorts of real estate deals since yesterday. There are a lot of people who want to get their dream homes before things *come to an end*," Phil said. And Phil said *come to end* so Jeff could hear the italics or sarcasm or quote marks in his tone. And even though Jeff was relieved that Phil didn't believe the rapture was happening, he was still somewhat uncomfortable that Phil was taking it so lightly. Then Phil leaned in, as if replying to Jeff's thoughts, and said, "Honestly Jeff, I don't know if anyone believes any of this doom and gloom stuff or if everyone's just using this whole thing as an excuse to buy all the things they've always wanted."

"Yeah, I know."

"Either way, doesn't really matter to me. All I know is at the office they're saying the real estate market is up about 2000 percent."

"Wow."

"I should send your son a thank-you note or a bottle of wine," Phil said. "He's making business really take off for me."

"Yeah," Jeff said, wanting to get the subject away from Will as quickly as possible.

"So here's what I'm thinking, while I'm making all of this extra money I want to get something nice to drive around in. Maybe a nice new ride will even help me get a little extra business."

"Maybe so," Jeff said.

"So what've you got for me?" Phil asked.

A half hour later Jeff sold him the most expensive Audi on the lot. And the whole day was a whirlwind like this for Jeff. By that afternoon he had sold a total of ten cars, and on any other day this would have been an all-time record at Hansley. But on that day it was just enough to put him in the middle of the pack. Jeff couldn't compete with Kevin Grabowski who became the day's top salesman. Jeff overheard Kevin as he was trying to make sales of his own, and Jeff noticed that Kevin always greeted the customer by saying, "What do you think about all this rapture business?"

Kevin's question was usually met with one of two responses. Some people would say it was such an honor, they would say what an incredible thing it was that Goodland had been chosen for the end of the world before anywhere else. If the customer said this, Kevin would mimic the customer's mood and everything he said, and from that point forward the conversation would have an air of reverence and awe to it. He would say things like, "We are blessed," and, "I just can't wait to be a part of the glory myself," and, "How beautiful it will all be," before going in for the sale.

Jeff had never heard Kevin say anything like that in his life. Jeff knew Kevin was playing the part, and he couldn't help but be impressed that Kevin was playing it so well.

Other customers would say, "I don't know. It's all a little silly to me."

And Kevin would reply, "Tell me about it! Who knew we were the test market for the rapture?" This would always get a response. Sometimes the customer would belly laugh, other times it would get a polite chuckle, but either way Kevin stood confidently and grinned.

Kevin told this joke so many times (and maybe it wasn't his joke, maybe he'd just heard it from someone else) that the phrase started to stick. That night, in the evening edition of the *Goodland Times*, there was a tongue-in-cheek piece titled *The Top 10 Great Things about Being the Test Market for the Rapture*. And Morry (of Morry's T-Shirts) screen-printed a whole clothing line based on this phrase. Normally he only printed shirts aimed at tourists, shirts that said things like "Kansas: *There's No Place Like Home.*"

But on that day he decided to start printing rapture T-shirts. They were a huge hit — everyone loved them. Some of the shirts contained somber warnings like "The End Is Now" and "Repent or You Won't Be Sent." Others had witty phrases like "In case of rapture I'll be naked." It seemed that the entire town was starting to lean towards one camp or the other. They were either in the repent camp or the naked camp. They either believed that the rapture was extraordinarily serious and coming soon, or they believed it was some myth to have fun with.

And Jeff's final customer of the day must have belonged to the more serious camp because she came in wearing one of Morry's black T-shirts with white lettering that read "We'll Be Gone in the Blink of an Eye."

"Good morning," Jeff said as he reached out to shake her hand. "Jeff Henderson?"

"Mary."

"All right Mary, what kind of car are you looking for? Something flashy?"

"Flashy? No," Mary said. All of Jeff's other customers that morning seemed enthusiastic and bubbly. Mary was sour and serious — she seemed like the type of person who would only get joy from things like sending orphan children to bed without dessert.

"Sure, something more practical," Jeff said.

"Good. Everyone's assuming we're pre-trib. But what if we're post-trib or middle-trib? No one's talking about that, are they?"

"I guess not," Jeff said. But he barely understood what Mary was talking about. From his understanding, post-trib meant the rapture wouldn't happen until after the wars and meteors and Antichrist-led tribulation. Mid-trib meant it would happen in the middle of all that. It seemed most in Goodland had the pre-trib philosophy, assuming God would want to scoop them up before all the pain and suffering really kicked in.

"That's why I want a car with the best possible gas mileage," Mary said. "I want a car that will still be running when all these flashy SUVs are stranded without gas. And even then I will only use it for extreme emergencies. I'm going to be wise with how I use my resources. That's how I'm going to survive this," Mary said.

"So, you believe the rapture is actually coming?" Jeff asked.

"What I believe, sir, are two simple rules: Plan for the worst and hope for the best, and better safe than sorry. Those two rules have kept me alive for a long time, and they'll keep me alive when everyone else is running around like chickens with their heads cut off. Your son said we should prepare for the rapture and this is how I'm going to prepare."

"Wait, my son said what?" Jeff asked.

"He said we should prepare."

"When did he say that?"

"This morning on the Channel 4 Early Edition news."

"Okay, hold on. He was on the news?"

"Everyone has been talking about it all day."

"About what?"

"The interview. Nancy Palmer asked him, 'What should we do?' And he said we should prepare, and if we don't, we won't have anyone to blame but ourselves."

"He said that?"

"Yes."

"This morning on the news?"

"Yes."

"Really?"

"Aren't you his father? Or have I confused you with someone else?"

"Yes, I'm his father. Did he predict what the next sign would be?"

"No. I thought he would, but he didn't."

Jeff couldn't think straight. He yelled, "Kevin!"

"What?" Kevin Grabowski called.

"This is Mary. Can you find her a car with low gas mileage?"

"Hello, Mary," Kevin said, putting his arm around her. Kevin was going to get Jeff's sale, but it didn't matter. There was only one question that mattered at the moment—what was Amy doing? All day long people had been talking to him about Will. But Jeff just assumed it was because of his prediction days ago. No one had come out and said Will was on the news this morning.

But it made sense now.

That's why he was fresh on their minds. That's why they were talking about him all day. He was their link, the spokesman for the rapture. But what exactly had he been saying? How had Jeff not found out about it all day? Was he really running that late this morning that he just rushed out of the house and didn't even notice his wife and son were gone? Was he really that self-centered? Was he that bad of a father?

Jeff saw another flash: Will standing behind a large pulpit. There was an enormous sound system behind him so he could speak to all who'd gathered to hear him. He was screaming warnings to the masses. And the masses ate up every word he said. Jeff could see himself trying to tell Will to stop, but neither Will nor anyone else would listen to him. And finally, when he would try to come up to his son, two large bodyguards would carry Jeff away. Will was now a prophet, and he was too big and much too important to listen to what his small-minded father had to say.

Jeff closed his eyes and shook his head. Stop it, he thought. Will just made a few comments on the news. You don't even know what happened yet. It could be nothing. Yes, that's it, nothing. She was probably just going to get groceries at seven in the morning, and maybe she felt that Will needed to get out of the house. Maybe she thought she could take him to the grocery store in the early hours before anyone would notice him so he wouldn't be hassled by lots of curious customers. And then, maybe along the way, she got inspired and decided to drive a few miles out of the way to the news station. She'd pop her head in to say hi, and then, somehow in a whirlwind of confusion, the news anchors tricked Will into going on the news and making all sorts of statements on the rapture. The news anchors had convinced him to throw a bucketful of gasoline on the raging fire that was the Armageddon paranoia in Goodland.

That's probably what happened.

Because if that isn't what happened, then the alternative was a little difficult to stomach. The alternative would mean Amy deliberately snuck Will out of the house long before he even woke up. She snuck him out because she had no intention of listening or debating or arguing about what should be done about her son. She was going to take control now. She was going to let Will prophecy the signs of the rapture so that he could be a hero, and she didn't care if he or the mayor or anyone else disagreed with what she was doing. She was like the mom of a child star actor who could not see all the extreme psychological damage that was being done. The mom of the child star actor never focused on how the experience would take a toll on the child for the rest of his life—all the child star actor's mother could see were the dollar signs and fame and adoration in front of her. And that hungry parent would do anything to get her hands on the instantaneous riches and glory their child offered.

No matter what the cost.

Maybe she didn't quite understand what the cost was; maybe if she knew she'd put on the brakes and look at the bigger picture. So if Amy were able to step back and see just how damaging her actions were, she'd stop all of this. She'd come to her senses.

Jeff intended to explain all of this to Amy as he flew up the driveway and slammed on the brakes. He jumped out of the car, but before he could even get in the house, Amy was outside to greet him. She gave him a hug and kissed as if they were still teenagers and as if their kids weren't watching.

What is she doing?

"How was work today?" she asked.

"Good. Amy—"

"Because I heard the cars were selling off the lot."

"Yeah, they were. I sold ten."

"You sold ten! That's amazing!" Amy said and flung her arms around him again.

"Yeah, I guess it is."

"Wow, we aren't going to have to worry anymore. Everything's going to be okay now."

"I don't know if that's true. Was Will on the news this morning?"

"You didn't see it?"

"No, I rushed out of the house, and it was such a whirlwind today—"

"You *have* to see it," Amy said. "Will looks so grown up. He was so confident up there. Come watch it. Susan Jackson taped it for me," Amy said as she grabbed Jeff's hand and pulled him toward the house.

"I don't want to watch it. What I want to know is why Will was on the news in the first place. Didn't you think you should ask me about this?"

"Honey, you seemed so overwhelmed with everything else."

"So, what, you didn't think I could handle it?"

"Why are you so upset?"

"You took our son on the news without even asking me. I

168

thought I made it clear yesterday that I didn't want him to give any more prophecies."

"He didn't give any more prophecies. Weren't you just waiting for the time to be right?"

"The time will never be right. Ever. Our son is now the center of all of this. If anything goes wrong we will be blamed. Those fanatics are going to be at our house. And one of those groups is not going to be happy. And do you know who they'll go after first?"

"You were never going to have him give the prophecy?"

"No, I wasn't."

"Even after the tornado?"

"Especially after the tornado. Whatever's going to happen is going to happen. Why should Will have to talk about it?"

"Will saved all of those lives. What if something like that is going to happen again? What if Will can save all of those people again?"

"That's not our problem. End of discussion."

That's when Jeff saw Amy's eyes go cold. It seemed that all the love she ever had for him drained out of them. She spun around, went inside, slammed the door, and dead-bolted it shut behind her.

Jeff twisted the knob and it wouldn't open. He pounded on the door. "Come on, Amy, let me in." Jeff had the deadbolt installed after one of his paranoid flashes about a burglary. He never thought the bolt would be used to lock him out.

Then above him it started raining down clothes. T-shirts and slacks and his toiletry bag hit the ground with a thud. Amy was throwing his clothes out the window.

"Do you need anything else?" Amy asked.

"Anything else for what?"

"You need to stay at a hotel tonight, Jeff."

"I do?"

"Yeah, and probably for a while."

"Come on, Amy."

"You cannot be at this house until you're ready to support what is going on with Will. I can't believe you just want to let people die because you're scared, Jeff."

"This is ridiculous. Let's talk about this. I'm not staying in a hotel."

Amy slammed the window shut.

"Amy!" Jeff shouted, but she didn't answer.

And after about a half hour of knocking on the door, calling inside, and trying to get someone to let him in, Jeff decided that Amy was serious. So he gathered his stuff and hopped back in the car with nothing left to do but see what vacancies Goodland hotels had to offer.

GOODLAND, KANSAS

It was the black ice that made things really spiral out of control. Even without it, Goodland was in a frenzied state. Sure, a lot of people were throwing parties, buying cars and houses, and acting ready to meet the end with a rather cavalier attitude. Nonetheless, it was tough to say at first how many people were really feeling all that carefree, because the day after a tornado seemed like a giant snow day in Goodland. Life felt crazy and carefree simply because there were enough people acting that way, so everyone else just followed.

But by that night, as the adrenaline of the daytime frenzy wore off, a lot of the townspeople of Goodland were sitting around in their living rooms—or in bars, diners, or coffee shops—discussing what the tornado really meant.

There was a lot of debate.

Some said they thought the Henderson boy must have had some sort of operation that made him sensitive to weather patterns. They said they'd heard stories about men who'd come home from Vietnam and had metal plates put in their heads. These men could tell when a thunderstorm was coming *days* before there were any clouds. Maybe it was the same with Will Henderson. Maybe some unnatural thing like a metal plate in his head or knee or arm was there helping him sense when tornados were coming. If he'd lived in Florida he could have predicted a hurricane. If he'd lived in Thailand he could have predicted a tsunami.

A few said that it was a government conspiracy and aliens caused the tornado. Of course these people always thought there was a government conspiracy involving aliens. They didn't know why New Mexico got all of the press because they said all the real UFO activity was in Kansas. What kind of crop-circles can you find in New Mexico? Name one, they'd say. No one was really listening to this crowd. They were just whispering amongst themselves like they always did.

Then there were those who agreed with Nancy, the newscaster, who'd said that this event was just something their intellect couldn't grasp. They said it was just an unbelievable coincidence that all of the events had happened, but that's all. There was no need to go reading more into it. Sometimes there are things that are unexplainable and defy logic. But if we try to decide that we know the cause for those sorts of problems, then we come up with answers like, "The world is flat," and, "The bubonic plague was caused by witches."

And finally there was the growing group who were starting to believe. They were influenced by Will's interview on the morning news and by the frightening email Amy got. They couldn't just pass off all the events unfolding like they did as a mere coincidence. This group of people couldn't help but consider the possibility that the rapture was actually coming. Many in this growing group of believers didn't even know anything about the rapture, so they started to read up on it. They learned that the basic idea was that God would take all of the believers from planet Earth, and as soon as they were gone, everything would spiral into seven years of tribulation. It was hard for them to discover what all the tribulation involved, but everything they read painted a pretty unsettling picture—famines, floods, wars, hopelessness, darkness, until finally the Antichrist came up and united everyone. Then many would receive the mark of the beast and there would be one final battle before all the pagans were damned to hell.

Everyone else would enjoy a thousand years of peace.

And if all of this talk wasn't bad enough, the rain started to come that night. It seemed that the tornado was just the beginning of the storm that was attacking Goodland. The rain started around nine and it didn't let up until about three the next morning. For the first hour the rain simply drizzled, which seemed nice enough. It gave the streets a shiny coat, and the flowers and grass seemed to drink it in. But it was October in Goodland and it didn't take long for things to freeze over. It started getting unbearably cold at about eleven. The few who went outside could feel their bodies shivering and watched as their breath escaped from their lips in tiny little clouds. Then, quickly, the shiny wet coat on the roads turned to an icy sheet, making a mockery of the brakes on every car and truck in Goodland.

The real mess started right before the morning rush hour with a truck driver named Paul Jackson. His son, Nate, was one of Will's best friends. But Paul didn't get to spend much time with Nate. Instead his days were spent driving a semi-truck up and down I–70. And to try to keep himself awake, Paul would spend his days talking on his CB. He liked CBs so much better than cell phones because they never lost service and only one person could talk at a time. "They are the purest form of communication," Paul would always say. And on this frigid night Paul was driving a truckload of unpainted furniture and talking on the CB to some person he'd never met about his number one passion.

"I'm telling you, this is going to make me a lot of money," Paul said.

"What? Trucking isn't paying enough?"

"Trucking is just something I'm doing until my real career can take off."

"Your real career?"

"I'm an inventor," Paul said.

"What have you invented?"

"Nothing yet—but I have ideas."

"Like what?"

"I can't just tell you. I don't know you," Paul said.

"Come on man. It's like five in the morning and I've been driving all night."

"Okay, but you cannot tell a soul. I'm about to get this patented and everything," Paul said. He held the CB in his hand for a moment and then slowly clicked down the button and explained, "It's called the Pregnant Cooler. It's going to make me millions."

"The Pregnant Cooler?"

"You know how you can never get beer or soda into baseball games or amusement parks?"

"Yeah."

"Cause of security, right?"

"Yeah."

"Well, you can now with my invention. It's a cooler that a woman can fasten under her shirt. Makes her look like she's pregnant. And there's no way security is going to check a pregnant woman to see if she's really pregnant. So getting beer into a ball game will never be an issue again. Once the Pregnant Cooler takes off, I'm going to launch a follow-up product for men called the Beer Belly."

As Paul was talking he was envisioning it all. He could see the blue, red, and yellow Pregnant Coolers with foam padding on the outside so it would even feel like the woman was pregnant. He could picture thousands of people flooding into Wal-Marts every spring and fall before football and baseball season to get their

Pregnant Coolers. He could even picture marriages being healed because women would feel they were such an important part of the ball game experience, where before their husbands would just go missing for the whole day on Sundays.

And Paul was so busy picturing all of this that he didn't notice the brake lights up ahead. By the time he realized what was going on, he had to slam on his brakes and that was just too much for his semi to handle on the black ice. His semi jackknifed, flipped, and sprayed splinted unpainted furniture all over I–70. Several cars behind the semi crashed and collided trying to dodge all of the dining room tables and bookshelves that were flying out of the semi truck.

At 5:23 that morning, I–70 was a complete mess on the eastern edge of Goodland. The eastern portion of the city was sealed off.

On the northern entrance of Highway 27, a man named Steve Parker got in his car to make his daily two-hour commute to Colby, Kansas. He'd been fighting with his wife all night long about her going over the maximum minutes and texts in their cell phone plan. He was asking himself, Who needs to send that many texts? and Why would she spend her time jabbering away on her cell phone when there's a land line right next to her? as his Honda Accord swerved out of control and slammed into a power line. The power line was knocked over and its lines danced, spitting sparks all over the icy highway. And with a power line down on one highway and a semi across the other, the people of Goodland woke up the next morning to hear the news that the only two highways out of town were completely closed down.

They were all trapped.

WILL HENDERSON

Will was still a little groggy that morning when he walked down-stairs and saw that the news was on. His sister was watching it so he thought it must be about him or the rapture or something. But it wasn't. Instead it was showing pictures of car accidents all over the place. The caption underneath said "Goodland Sealed Off." There were accidents all over I−70. Nancy Palmer was reporting live from the scene. Then the news cut to her talking to Officer Mike as she asked, "How long do you think until we can get this cleaned up?"

"I don't know. It could be days. It's a real mess out here, and from what we've heard, it's like this up and down I−70 for at least fifty miles in each direction. So it could be hard to get clean-up crews out here. We need them to get something like this cleaned up. But we're working on it."

Will sat on the couch next to his sister and saw his mom walk in. She was talking on the phone.

"Yeah, okay, we will. Yes, right away. Okay," his mom said and hung up the phone. She looked at her children and said, "We need to go to the store."

"Why?" Emily asked.

"They're running low on food."

"Stores don't run low on food," Emily said.

"They do now. I just talked to Mary Beth. She said she just got back from the supermarket and she'd never seen it like that. She said if we want groceries for the next week we better go now."

"What? How does that even happen?" Emily asked.

"Honey, we're about to see a whole bunch of stuff happen that doesn't *normally* happen. Now go get dressed. We're leaving in ten minutes."

Will was the first one dressed. He was excited and kind of scared to see what all the stores would look like when they were running low on food. He sat in the entryway and waited for his mom and sister. This was nothing new. He was always waiting for them. And while he was waiting he heard someone twisting the doorknob on the front door.

Out of habit he opened the door.

His dad was standing there. He was unshaven and his eyes were bloodshot. And when he looked at Will he smiled from ear to ear. Will even thought his dad's eyes might be getting watery. But he couldn't tell if his dad was sad or happy or just really tired.

"Hi son," his dad said.

"Dad."

"You all right?"

Will thought about this question. He didn't feel all right. It was weird having his dad standing there looking like he was a stranger in his own home. It was weird for Will to feel uncomfortable around his own dad. He didn't know what to make of that. He'd never felt uncomfortable around his dad unless he'd done something wrong. But ever since the cornfields, whenever he was around his dad, he felt as if he was always doing something wrong. Still, he didn't want to say that. It didn't seem polite. So he just said, "Yeah, I'm fine."

"Where's your mom?"

"She's getting ready. We're going to stores before they all run out of food."

"Before they what?"

"I don't know, it's just what Mom said. The stores are running out of food."

"So she's going to drive you to the store?"

"Yeah."

"You know the roads are pretty icy out there?"

"Yeah, I saw the furniture on them."

And that's when the conversation stopped because Will's mom walked into the room.

"Jeff," his mom said.

"You're going to the store?" his dad countered. Will didn't like his dad's tone of voice. He knew they were about to get angry at each other.

"Yes, as a matter of fact, we are," his mom answered. "And who let you in?"

"Will."

"Will, why'd you let him in?"

"It was just out of habit. I heard the doorknob twist so I opened it," Will said.

"It doesn't matter. We're leaving," his mom said.

"Honey, have you been watching the news this morning?" his dad asked. "The roads are ridiculous out there and everyone is really panicked."

"I know. I was just talking with Mary Beth. She says everyone's buying up all the groceries in town. To get ready for the rapture."

"That's ridiculous."

"Why? Don't you think it's possible the rapture is coming after all that's happened?"

"When you think about it, Amy, what's really happened? There are some icy roads and a tornado hit in the middle of Kansas."

"Yeah, a tornado that your son predicted," his mom said.

"I actually didn't predict it. The face did," Will said.

"If you take him out there, everyone's going to ask what else the face predicted," his dad continued. "That's why I think maybe we should all just wait here for a while. Why are you in such a hurry?"

"Because we're going to need groceries."

"But after everything that *just* happened—"

"Okay, wait. This all didn't *just* happen. We've been trapped here for three days. Don't you think it's time he got out?" Will's mom said, pointing at him.

"Last time you took him out you sent the whole town into chaos!"

Will was a little startled. His mom and dad didn't shout at each other very often. And Will knew he was lucky in that respect. On the playground, he'd heard stories of nasty fights between his friends' parents. Jane Thompson always told stories about how her parents got into violent shouting matches. They would throw dishes at each other and break furniture. Will always got sad when he heard these stories because that probably meant Jane didn't want to get married. Why would she if she saw marriage as such a horrible thing? Someday, Will thought, he could show Jane how a boy was really supposed to treat a girl. He'd bring her flowers and poems and sing her nice songs. Then maybe she'd warm up to the idea of marriage. But when he told his mom about this, she said Jane probably would rather have a boy that treated her mean. Will asked why. His mom said because that's what she's used to. But that just didn't make sense. Why would a pretty girl pick a mean guy instead of a nice one? His mom probably didn't know what she was talking about. This was just another example of her old-fashioned thinking.

"So, what are we supposed to do—keep him locked up forever?

How long does he have to pay a price for being right?" his mom asked.

"Can we talk in the other room?"

Will watched as his dad brought his mom into the room to talk. They had to know that he would lean against the door and listen anyway. Maybe it just made them feel better if they couldn't see him.

"Do you know what it's like out there? People are really unsettled about all of this. They may try to blame him."

"Blame him? He tried to save them. Every parent who kept their children home from school that day should be kissing the ground he walks on. They should be awestruck to have a prophet in their midst."

"Amy, don't call him a prophet."

"Why?"

"Because it sounds weird."

"Jeff, what does a prophet do?"

"I know what a prophet does. That's not what I'm talking about here—"

"He prophesies. And wouldn't you say that's what our son is doing?"

"Sort of."

"What does 'sort of' mean?"

"Amy, we don't know what's happening. This could all be a coincidence."

"Come on, honey, are you really that naïve?"

"I'm not being naïve here. I'm just not reading whatever I want to into this event. I'm trying to be rational. It appears *someone* in this family has to be."

"This isn't one event, Jeff. It's a whole string of events. And I expect everyone else to be skeptical about it. But the reality is, most people think our son is special. Then there's you. You think something's wrong with him. Something is happening with our son and you should be excited about it—"

"You think this is exciting?"

"God is working through our son."

Will heard the clicking of feet coming towards him. "Where are you going?"

"I told you, I'm going to the store!"

"Fine, but you're going without Will. I'm staying here with him."

"No, I'm taking Will."

"No, you're not," his dad said. He almost snarled it. And then there was silence. Will wondered what was happening on the other side of the door. Were his parents kissing? Gross. He hoped not. That wouldn't make any sense. But sometimes grown-ups didn't make sense. Sometimes they would just be fighting and screaming at each other, and then all of a sudden, they would start kissing in the rain. At least that's the way it happened in movies.

Will listened closely, but he couldn't hear any kissing sounds. He didn't hear anything until his father finally said, "I forbid you from taking Will."

Will was a little startled. He'd never heard his father say something like "forbid." It seemed like a King Arthur sort of thing to say.

His mom must have been equally surprised. Because she replied, "You *forbid* me?"

"Yes."

"Who even says 'forbid' anymore?"

"I'm saying 'forbid' right now because you are not taking *my* son anywhere."

"*Your* son? Okay then, I *forbid* you from sleeping in *my* bed with me. I banish you to the hotel. Again. I thought maybe you'd get the message yesterday, Jeff. But now I'm not letting you in this house anymore until you can act like a caring father and husband."

"Amy, would you just—"

"I'm not finished. I also forbid you from forbidding me to do anything ever again!" And then she pushed open the door. Will jumped back. "Come on. We're going," she said.

"Do I have to come?" Emily asked.

"Yes," Will's mother snapped. "Go get in the car!"

"I'm coming with you," his father said as he followed his mom through the door. "You can't drive on the ice."

"Fine. You can be our chauffeur. Then back to the hotel," she said, snatching her purse and keys.

"Great!" Will's dad shouted back.

Then both parents stared at Will. And he suddenly didn't want to go to the store with either of them. He was afraid both of his parents might be crazy.

As the Hendersons drove to the supermarket, Will sat in the back next to Emily and stared out the window. He thought the icy roads made Goodland feel a little bit like Mars. It seemed uninhabitable, as if it were never intended for human life. It was just an icy wasteland. Tree branches that normally reached towards the heavens were now frozen and pointing towards the ground under the weight of the ice. Jagged icicles hung off the roofs of every house. Drainage pipes had large frozen blocks of ice in front of them. Will wondered how anyone could have ever stayed alive in such a climate before there were things like central heating and cars and houses.

He tried to imagine what it must have been like for the Native Americans living in teepees or for the cavemen when the weather got like this. At least the Indians would have giant Buffalo-skin rugs. What would the cavemen do? There weren't even any caves in Goodland. That must have been horrible. And at that moment, Will felt very glad he was born when he was. Sure, the rapture was kind of scary, but he never had to worry about things like surviving. He never had to be a Native American huddled in a Buffalo-skin rug amongst all of the frozen trees, nor did he have to live as a caveman without a cave.

That was something to be grateful for.

And then, when Jeff pulled into the parking lot of the Super Mart, Will stopped thinking about the Goodland of yesteryear and started focusing on the Goodland of today.

The first thing he noticed was that the parking lot had *never* looked like this. Will was always a little fascinated that there were always so many extra parking spaces in the lot of the Super Mart. Sometimes buses and campers and RVs would park there for weeks because the owners must have known that they would never use all of the parking spaces.

But today every single space was taken.

There were even cars parked in places where there weren't spaces. There were cars on the side of the road, against the building, in front of loading docks, and in the crisscross spaces next to where the shopping carts went.

Inside the Super Mart things were much worse.

When the Hendersons originally started to head towards the supermarket, Jeff thought they might also want to stock up on other non-grocery items: batteries, flashlights, Band-Aids, antifreeze, board games, and so on. Jeff said they'd want to stock up on things just to be safe in case they got stranded or cut off from the city somehow. "There's no way any of that is going to happen," he said, "but better safe than sorry." So he suggested they go to Super Mart instead.

It seemed like everyone else had the same idea.

The people of Goodland were vultures, picking every shelf clean, as if this was the last chance they'd ever have to stock themselves up with Hot Pockets and Children's Tylenol. It reminded Will of when his mom had brought him to black Friday last year after Thanksgiving.

"Think of all the money we'll save. We can get twice the Christmas gifts for half the cost," she had said. They got to the Best Buy an hour before it opened and there was already a line wrapped around the building. And as the doors opened, people flooded in, flanking every aisle, scratching and clawing for DVDs and TVs, and begging to be the chosen ones who were given one of the ten free printers. It was one of the most uncomfortable scenes Will had ever witnessed. He saw his friend's moms (the same kind ladies who had given him rides to soccer practice, the same ladies who insured that every boy on the team was given a Capri Sun and Fruit Roll Up after a game) turn into soulless creatures as they yelled at each other and cussed and snarled "mine" over all of the wonderful deals on electronic merchandise. Will had never seen people act that way, and he learned on that day that every adult was one step away from anarchy.

It was even worse on the day of the ice storm. It seemed that anarchy had arrived. Checkout lines were stretching down every aisle. The shelves were barren. Even clearance items — trinkety things that hadn't been touched in years like Chia Pets and The Clapper — were being snatched up because people didn't want to leave the store empty-handed. And there was no kindness or decency in sight anywhere in the store. Just people, young and old, big and little, doing whatever it took to get what they wanted.

The Hendersons stood frozen amidst all the chaos in the Super Mart. The scene was all too overwhelming. They didn't really know what to do or how to act. Finally, Emily said, "All right, if we're going to shop, we're going to need a cart." She then grabbed a shopping cart, but some short man with a goatee and wire-framed glasses ran up to her and said, "Hey man, what do you think you're doing!"

"Getting a shopping cart," Emily said. Will thought Emily always had this sassy, teenage-girl, know-it-all quality to her. But she seemed taken back by the man who'd run up to her.

"Yeah, sure, whatever," the man with the glasses snorted. "I, like, see this cart across the store, run to it, and you think you're going to grab it from me?"

"She wasn't trying to take it from you," Jeff said.

"Nobody's talking to you, square," the man said. "And besides, it doesn't, like, matter what she was *trying* to do, because what she *did* was steal my cart."

"Oh, okay," Emily said, letting go of the cart.

That was the only invitation the goateed man needed; he snatched the cart and ran into the chaos of the Super Mart.

Will thought the goateed man must have awakened his dad because he cleared his throat and said, "All right, here's what we'll do. We need to stick together and get the essentials first. Bottled water, batteries, flashlights, stuff like that," Jeff said.

What about food, Will thought. Isn't food an essential? He thought about being trapped in the corn maze with his insides eating themselves out because he was so hungry, and he imagined himself like that for days, waiting for the trumpet to sound and Jesus to come. He couldn't bear the thought. They needed food, Will realized. He was starting to feel that he was the only clear-thinking person in his family. Maybe he would need to start taking more action, maybe he needed to grow up a little to help his family survive this crisis.

Jeff went on, "If you see a cart, grab one. Until then, we load up our arms. Now let's go."

"Maybe we should split up," Will said.

"We're not splitting up. It's too dangerous in here," Jeff answered.

"It's just a grocery store."

"Son, have you ever seen a grocery store like this?" Will didn't answer. His dad kind of had a point. "Now come on," Jeff said as he started leading them *away* from the food toward the flashlights. What were they supposed to do, turn the lights on and watch themselves starve to death? This plan was getting worse and worse by the second.

When they got to the flashlight aisle there were only two left and Jeff lunged at one of the last ones. He seemed to have grabbed it at the same time as some lady in a wool coat.

"Excuse me, sir, I had this first," she said.

"No way," Jeff shouted. "I just gave some guy my shopping cart."

"Not my problem. Let go."

"No, it's mine," Jeff said.

Will never found out who won the argument because that was about the time he snuck away from his family and towards the grocery side of the Super Mart. There was no time to argue. His dad would be mad at first, but he'd be happy when Will came back with a cart full of food.

He decided that his best bet would be frozen foods. They would keep for a long time and they would have full hearty meals like Salisbury steak, mashed potatoes, macaroni and cheese, and apple cobbler. He knew that the freezer aisle was aisle 11 and on his way there he tried not to look at everything else that was going on in the Super Mart. He tried to tell himself what to do: Just keep walking. Do not stop and don't be a sissy. All you have to do is get some food for your family. And if you don't want to starve, you better get some before it's gone.

Despite the pep talk he gave himself, he couldn't make it past the produce aisle without stopping. He watched as women with shopping carts grabbed the last of the apples and pears and bananas and put them into their carts. They were all complaining, saying things like, "This fruit is way too bruised to buy. I can't even believe they stock fruit like this. Honestly, if they expect us to pay for this, at *most* these apples/pears/bananas should only be half price." Of course it wasn't really their conversation that shocked Will.

It was the empty produce stands.

There were neon letters on poster boards that said Bananas for 69 cents or Apples $2/lb. But underneath those signs were only empty brown shelves. Will had never seen shelves in a grocery store completely barren. He never even knew that was an option. He never thought about the process of stock boys coming in late at night to restock all the fruits and vegetables so his mom could buy more—because he never had to. It just happened. And the fact that things were not happening normally was starting to unsettle him. The system was breaking down.

What are you doing? Keep walking. You are at aisle one— ten more to go, buddy.

Will locked his eyes and walked straight ahead. He didn't focus on all the grabbing and tussling over cereal and oatmeal in aisle four, or the shouting match that was happening between two large men in aisle nine. It wasn't his problem. All he had to do was make it to the freezer aisle.

Unfortunately the freezer aisle was the most crowded in the Super Mart. Every freezer door was open with two or three people at once trying to grab whatever was inside. Will stood at the end of the aisle and watched as all of the frost-coated doors had hands and faces and legs mashed against them. It reminded Will of when his dad would let him watch detective shows after he was already supposed to be in bed. In those shows they had shelves that slid into freezers where they would put all of the dead bodies. In aisle 11 it looked like all of the shelves had been stood up and now all of the dead bodies were trying to claw their way out.

How am I supposed to get in that aisle? There's no way, Will thought. It's weird and there's too many people and I'm too small.

Are you serious? Is that what you're going to tell your dad when he asks why you snuck away? Are you actually going to tell him, "Sorry Dad, I was going to get food but I'm too small"? Are you really going to let your family starve because the grocery aisle is too crowded?

Of course he couldn't let his family go hungry. It would be fine, no one was going to hurt him, he just had to get in there. He had to be brave. So he marched down the aisle past the worthless things like frozen vegetables and stopped in front of the sign that said "TV dinners." There would be turkey à la king with mashed potatoes and spaghetti dinners with breadsticks. But the frozen TV dinners seemed to be quite the commodity. Everyone was reaching and clawing towards the back to get the last of Super Mart's frozen meals. Will tried to reach in with everyone else, but with little luck. He was too short and just couldn't wedge his way in there. He'd have to let people know he needed in there too.

"Pardon me," he said a little timidly. No one noticed. "Please, I need to get in. I have to get some turkey à la king for my family." A few people looked back but did not give him room. He would have to shout. Everyone here was acting so primal and he would just have to get in and act primal with them. That was the only language they would listen to now. So he shouted, "I have to get food for my family! PLEASE let me in! What kind of people are you? You didn't listen when I warned about the school being destroyed, and now you're acting like this?"

Will realized he probably shouldn't have said that last part. Because at that moment every soul in the aisle stopped the pushing, shoving, and clawing and stared at the little boy. People got out from deep inside the freezers. The frosted doors clicked shut. And then there was only silence as people stood watching Will. The only sound came from a big-boned woman who dropped an entire armful of ice cream. Will didn't know what these people were about to do to him.

Then one man said, "That's him. That's the little boy who predicted the tornado."

"That's not the Henderson boy," another man argued.

"No, it *is* him. I recognize him from the news," the lady with the ice cream said.

"What's happening? Can you tell us what's happening?" someone else asked Will.

More questions started to fly. People in the surrounding aisles could tell something was happening and they started to flock towards the freezer aisle. Quickly people from the store jammed their way into the freezer aisle and both the aisle entrances were overflowing with more customers trying to see what was going on. And even though most people couldn't see Will, they could hear the murmur of the mob saying, "It's him ... the prophet ... the tornado kid ... he's about to say something."

Will heard their questions and he knew exactly what they were asking. They wanted to know what the next prophecy was. He had to give them the second sign. He would just open his mouth and tell them. He had waited long enough. His mom or his dad or the mayor or anyone else couldn't stop him from doing what the face wanted him to do.

He took a deep breath to speak, and that was all it took to make the crowd go completely silent. But nothing came out. His mind was blank. He still couldn't remember what exactly the next sign was. He thought it would all just come back to him when the time was right. But for some reason, it wasn't that simple. For some reason the face's words seemed far away and cloudy.

So he clinched his eyes shut and tried to remember back to the night of the cornfield. He tried to remember the face telling him about the three signs that would predict the rapture. And the face used three words. Will could remember that now. The first word was about destruction. Will could hear the face's strong, thick voice saying, "The school will be destroyed." But what did it say next? What was the next word?

Power.

Yes, *power,* that was it. But what about power? It was coming. No, it was going. Will couldn't remember. It seemed like the night in the cornfield was a lifetime ago. Even now, as he closed his eyes and pictured it, it seemed so blurry and jumbled. It seemed like a dream. Will knew he had to say something, so he finally took a breath and belted out the word, "Power!"

The mob began to murmur questions all around Will: "What about power? What does *power* mean? Whose power? God's power? Power plants? Power Rangers? Power team?"

Then Will answered all of these questions with his eyes still clinched shut. He hoped the face's words would come to him as he spoke. "The power is —"

"The power is what?" someone squeaked.

"The power is leaving. The power is going to leave," Will said and let out a deep breath. He knew there was nothing specific to this prophecy. No timeline, no event, so of course this time no one would believe him. But when he looked around at everyone's faces, that didn't seem to be the case at all — in fact it looked like everyone believed him. They nodded as if they understood — or at least as if they were trying to understand — what exactly *the power is leaving* meant.

And Will decided he would let them figure it out; he couldn't talk anymore. He just wanted to get to his mom and dad. It seemed as if the mob in the freezer aisle understood. They parted like the red sea and let him through. No one touched him. No one even reached for him; they acted as if they were afraid God would strike them down if they did.

EMILY HENDERSON

Emily didn't know why people were cramming themselves into the freezer aisle until Will emerged. As he left the freezer aisle, he was all hunched over and his fingers were crunched tightly together so that, from a distance, it looked like he only had three fingers on each hand. And as he walked away from the aisle, people just kept staring at him like he was Gandhi or Joseph Smith or some other kind of freakish prophet. His eyes were a liquid ice blue, almost glowing, and as they looked up at her, Emily realized something — there is no possible way I'm related to him. We are nothing alike. So who is the stranger in the family? Is it Will or am I the one that doesn't belong?

Will slowly kept sliding his feet across the grimy grocery store floor. As he walked, Emily couldn't handle the way those people in the freezer aisle just kept staring at him. When he got close enough, Emily grabbed her brother's arm and pulled him into the cereal aisle where all the Lucky Charms and Frosted Flakes were now gone. There was nothing but oatmeal left. Emily crouched down next to her brother and looked at him. On closer inspection she noticed her brother's eyes weren't glowing at all; rather it looked like they were coated with that frosting they put on glazed doughnuts.

"What's going on? What happened?"

"I had to tell them."

"You had to tell them what?"

"The next sign."

"The next sign?"

"The next sign that the face gave me for the rapture."

Then a large man in a flannel shirt and puffy vest burst into the aisle. He stared at the two children for a moment. Then he shouted, "Are there any more Rice Krispies down there?"

"I don't think so," Emily said.

"Great. That is just fan-freaking-tastic. My wife is gonna kill me," the flannelled man said as he left the aisle.

"This place is crazy," Emily said.

"I know," Will said. "Those people were crazy. They pressured me to tell them the next sign. That's why I told them."

"So what did you tell them?"

"The power is leaving."

"That's it?"

"That's it."

"What does that even mean?"

"I don't know. The face just gave me the signs. He didn't explain them."

"Yeah, but 'the school is going to be destroyed,' that's at least sort of specific."

"I know. I think that's why the face gave me that sign first."

"Let's just find Mom and Dad. They sent me to find you and I'm sure they're freaking out by now," Emily said.

Once Emily and Will found their parents, they all left the Super Mart. Problem was, they didn't leave with very much. They had a flashlight (with no batteries), a few apples (which had been badly bruised), some yellow and blue yarn (her mom insisted she could knit them all sweaters), and a couple of Salisbury steak microwaveable dinners. They had much more that they had needed to get, but Will's meltdown/prophecy had taken place before they could get anything else.

And on the car ride home they seemed unable to focus on their lack of supplies because everyone was still too angry. Emily couldn't decide exactly why both her parents seemed so upset with Will. After all, they were split down the middle about the prophecy issue. Someone should have been happy with him. And it was pretty clear to Emily that her mom thought whatever had happened in the cornfield was a gift from God while her dad just wished all the prophecy talk would go away. But now, for whatever reason, they finally agreed on something. They agreed Will should not have told everyone his prophecy. At least not in the store. Not like that. And Emily could tell this because they were shouting things like, "Seriously, what were you thinking, Will?"

"We were worried," her mom said.

"Very worried," her dad echoed.

"I thought we needed food."

"But not at the cost of something happening to you. What if something would have happened to you, son?" her dad asked.

"Nobody hurt me."

"But if they did, then how would you feel?"

"I guess I would feel hurt," Will answered.

"Exactly. You would feel hurt."

Emily watched the conversation circle around like this for most of the way home. Her dad insisted that what Will did was dangerous, her mom said that giving his prophecy in the store was poor timing, and Emily decided she'd heard enough. "I think you guys should lay off him," she said.

"We're not laying on him," her mom said.

"Don't you think he's been through enough?"

"Yes, I think he's been through more than enough. He must feel awful," her dad said.

"Could you guys not talk about me like I'm not here?" Will said.

"My point is, I think we've all been through more than enough. That's why I don't want us running around and making prophecies or going on the news or anything else. Why would we put ourselves in harm's way?"

"That makes no sense, Jeff," her mom said.

"It doesn't?"

"No, we're already in harm's way. Have you ever even read Revelation?"

"Amy, don't get started on this."

"On what? The fact that there is going to be fire and plagues and wars and you want to keep us out of *harm's way*? This is too big, too important, Jeff! Will is too important to just tuck him away because people are going to say something bad about him. He has been given a gift and he has a responsibility! *How DO YOU NOT UNDERSTAND THAT?!*"

Emily watched her mom scream this. And it looked like she was a lunatic. Insane. Emily remembered that when she was a kid, her dad loved *Terminator 2*. And he'd let her stay up late at night and watch it with him, but she had to promise not to tell her mom about it because it was rated R. But in order to be a good father, he told her to close her eyes at the really scary parts like when the T–1000's arm becomes a giant sword and stabs the guy through the mouth while he's drinking milk. Anyway, in *Terminator 2* John Conner's mom was crazy, like mental hospital crazy, because she'd been so consumed with the fact that he was going to be this great, important leader. And that's what Emily thought her mom seemed like. She was so consumed with Will's role as prophet, so consumed with the rapture and the end of the world, that she was willing to do anything to prepare herself, her family, her friends, her neighbors, and her community.

And, in a way, Emily could understand why. After all, when put against the end of the world, most other things seem trivial. How do you worry about what people are saying when lives are at stake? Why would you even really worry about a shortage of food and supplies when everyone is just going to be whisked away? Why even worry that much about safety? After all, it isn't *this* life that matters. *This* life only has weeks or days or hours left in it. The only thing that matters is where everyone will spend their eternity. Because an eternity lasts forever — right? So, in a way, Emily could understand why her mother would discard everything in the present for the greater eternal good.

There was just one problem.

The world wasn't coming to end. Not in Emily's lifetime, and probably not her kids' lifetime either. The world and Goodland would go on just like they always had. And this presented a problem. Because it meant that her mother was lying. (Actually, maybe lying was the wrong word. Her mother had been lying about things like the Easter bunny and tooth fairy and Santa Claus. But the rapture did not fit into the tooth fairy category. Her mother actually *believed* in the Goodland rapture. Which made it much worse than lying. It made her mother delusional, or at the very least, extremely naïve to believe in something so quirky and odd and paranoid.)

For the first time, Emily began to wonder what else her mother had been delusional and/or naïve about. Politics, sex, religion, the origin of life, the meaning of life — was it possible that her mother had been wrong about all of these topics as well? Of course it was possible. Anything was possible. But her mother had always seemed so sure. She always seemed so dead set in her beliefs. There had never been any room for doubt.

That might have been part of what made Emily realize her mother was wrong because no one could be right about everything.

Emily wondered what she should do now that she was beginning to fear that so many (if not all) of the beliefs that had guided her life up to this point were hollow. She was like Charlton Heston pounding his fist against the wet sand and staring at the Statue of Liberty, realizing that the planet of the apes was earth all along. She was Alice taking her first steps into Wonderland. Everything was backwards. Right was wrong and wrong was right. Things that were always rock solid suddenly felt like shifting sand.

"Don't you think so, Emily?" her mom said. Her parents had been talking about something, debating and fighting about Will or the rapture or the prophecy or the face, and Emily hadn't heard a word of it.

"I don't know. I just … I don't want to talk about this anymore," Emily said. And even though her mom was looking back at her, she just stared at the floor mat. She couldn't look at her mother. And she couldn't face all of this. Not right now.

"Okay, honey," her mom said. "Jeff, you need to understand, all I'm saying—"

But Emily stopped listening. For the rest of the car ride home she tuned out the argument about Will and the prophecy, and she simply stared out the window feeling completely alone and overwhelmed.

Emily had to get away from her family. She decided to call Curtis because she felt such a connection to him that day when everyone was gathered around Jefferson. And right now she needed to talk with someone she felt connected to. So she called him and told him she wanted to meet at the field out by the fairgrounds.

"You know, it's kind of cold outside," he said.

"Yes, I know."

"Wouldn't you rather go to the mall?"

"Too many people at the mall."

"I thought homecoming queens loved malls."

"They do. But not right now. Can we just meet at the field?"

Emily got to the field before Curtis was there. She parked her car in the empty lot and stared at the abandoned fair grounds. In the summer they were always bubbling with life and Emily loved going there. She could walk around for hours, and laugh, eat cotton candy, funnel cakes, and giant turkey legs. She loved the fairgrounds because it was like Neverland there—life seemed to stop and there were no problems like homecoming dresses and dates and family problems and crises of faith. At the fair the only thing that mattered was how long the line to the Tilt-A-Whirl was.

And even today, looking at the fairgrounds helped melt her problems away. It was beautiful. Icicles hung off the Ferris wheel, making it look like an enormous spider web; frost covered the windows of the funhouse; and the road into the fairgrounds was coated in ice, creating an endlessly welcoming white path. She'd never been out here after an ice storm and she wondered why not—the fairgrounds looked so magical this time of the year, like something out of a Tim Burton movie. So she resolved that in the future she would visit the fairgrounds whenever it got icy just so she could get a mental break and contemplate things like family and faith and the meaning of the universe.

Curtis pulled his car up and Emily hopped outside to meet him. The two stared in the cold for a moment until Curtis said, "Hey yourself." Emily looked at him a little puzzled. Then Curtis stammered, "Normally I say, 'Hey,' and you say, 'Hey yourself,' so I thought I'd just preempt all of that by saying, 'Hey yourself.'"

"That's cute," Emily said in a tone that implied it *wasn't* cute even though she actually though it *was* cute. These are the types of mind games teenage boys and girls play when they're attracted to each other.

"*I* thought so," Curtis said. "So how are you doing?" His nose was already Rudolph red from the cold. It was adorable.

"My family's crazy," she answered.

"All families are crazy."

"My family believes this town is about to come to its end."

"A lot of people believe this town is about to come to its end."

"My family caused everyone to believe that."

"Touché."

"Why haven't you asked me to homecoming?" Emily asked. Then she was a little embarrassed for having asked. It was kind of an abrupt subject change. But she could not go on any longer until she knew the answer. And besides, she shouldn't be nearly as embarrassed as Curtis. He *should* have asked her by now. How could he not see how lucky he was? She was willing to go with him. She was putting herself out there. And she never put herself out there.

"Two reasons I haven't asked. One, I thought you didn't want to go with me," Curtis said.

"Even if I did, I couldn't act like I did," Emily said.

"Okay, well then, I'll be honest and say the second reason is that I don't want to go with you anymore."

"You don't what?" Emily said. It was all she could manage. She suddenly felt like that girl in junior high again — the girl she vowed she'd never become — the girl who was crying and alone in the bathroom. That girl was the whole reason she wanted to become homecoming queen, so she could put all of that behind her. Only now she was morphing into that pathetic, crying girl right in front of Curtis' eyes. How was this happening? He was supposed to be her backup and he was rejecting her.

But it was worse than that.

She needed a boy to like her and care for her and hold her right now. Her family was falling apart. Her parents didn't understand who she was anymore. Her entire belief system up to this point was a sham. She'd been dodging calls from Derrick and Philip because she thought it would be so much more adventurous to go with Curtis, only now Derrick and Philip had other cute, smiley blonde girls who'd wear bubble-gum pink dresses to homecoming. Curtis was her last chance. And he was ditching her, which meant she had absolutely no chance of becoming homecoming queen — and that meant since sunrise that day, every ounce of meaning she'd attached her life to in the last seventeen years had now crumbled into nothing.

"I should probably leave," Emily said.

She fished her keys out of her pocket. She was already picturing her ride home where she would blare love songs and cry and scream when Curtis said, "I don't want to ask you to homecoming, but I do want to ask you something else."

"What? What could you possibly want to ask me right now?"

Curtis got on one knee. His designer jeans were getting ice and dirt all over them, but he didn't seem to notice as he grabbed Emily's hand and asked, "Will you marry me?"

Emily ripped her hand away. "You are a jerk. You reject me and now you're making fun of me?"

"How's asking for someone's hand in marriage making fun of them?"

"Let me get this straight, you won't ask me to homecoming but you want me to marry you?"

"Why waste time with homecoming? What if everything really ends? I know it won't, but what if it does? Wouldn't it be nice to be married? To have our own little place that we could decorate however we wanted, a place where we could invite friends over for Rummy tournaments and wine parties and where we could play whatever music we wanted to play anytime, day or night."

"I can't tell if you're being serious," Emily said.

"All I'm saying is there's some weird stuff going on in this town. It's got me thinking that I don't want to watch it end all alone. I mean, two days ago I was scared about asking you to homecoming. I was actually scared that you would say no. Now today, there are much bigger fears like the town being sealed off, storms ripping buildings apart, and the apocalypse taking us or killing us or doing something to us all. That should scare the freaking daylights out of me. But it doesn't. Because do you know what actually scares me? This could all end and I could have wasted all my time being so worried about being rejected that I didn't ask you out. It scares me that things could come to an end, which would mean I'd never get a chance to get to know this amazing girl that I'm staring at right now."

This is going to end badly, Emily thought. She just wanted a nice boy to take her to homecoming. She didn't want to actually fall in love with him. She didn't want to start caring about him and thinking about him for every waking moment. That was the last thing she needed. And getting married? Did she really want that? No, but then again, Curtis was right. Everyone was doing whatever they wanted, whenever they wanted to. It might as well have become the mantra of Goodland: If it feels good, do it because we're all just going to be raptured anyway.

If my family's going to act crazy, I might as well join them, she thought.

Emily looked at Curtis and smiled. He smiled back, waiting for her to say something. She didn't say a word — she just lunged at Curtis, wrapped her arms around him, and kissed him. She could feel his ice-cold Rudolph nose mashed against her face, but she didn't care. She was feeling warmer already.

GLENN DAVIS

Glenn Davis hated being cold. Even in the dead of summer he liked to have his heater blaring. He liked to walk around his house in shorts, flip-flops, and a Hawaiian shirt in the middle of January because it felt like he was beating nature. He felt almost godlike when he set his house at whatever temperature he wanted despite what was going on outside.

He wasn't sure what he thought about all this rapture stuff; he didn't know if he should side with the Realists, the Prepared, or if there was some other third party he could side with.

But he'd been standing in the freezer aisle with everyone else just trying to get some TV dinners when that Henderson boy walked in and proclaimed that the power was leaving. As soon as that boy left, everyone was yammering away about what "the power is leaving" meant. Everyone in the grocery aisle quickly decided the boy was talking about electricity, running water, and natural gas.

All of that would soon be gone.

And Glenn thought that even if it didn't go out, one of the fanatics would make sure it went out just to prove a point. The thought of no power petrified Glenn. It was freezing outside. He wasn't ready for winter and now ice was everywhere. Having to face that without a heater was nearly enough to drive him insane.

So while everyone else was debating the nuances of what the

boy's prophecy meant, saying things like, "Why did he say, 'The power is leaving' instead of, 'The power will leave'? Does that mean it's leaving right now?" Glenn darted out the door of the Super Mart.

He jumped in his car and sped down the road thinking of everything that was suddenly at stake. Soon microwaves, hair dryers, televisions, iPods, toaster ovens, laptop and desktop computers, coffee makers, lamps, electric razors, Crock-Pots, and cell phones would be rendered useless things of the past.

He realized how used to technology the people of Goodland had become. He'd been around Goodland for forty-seven years, and it was always a town that prided itself on resisting the change that technology imposes on all of us. They wanted to be old-fashioned. They wanted to churn their own butter and farm their own vegetables and slaughter their own organic chickens.

When he was a boy, everyone hung their laundry outside with clothespins even though everyone else in the country had a device cleverly called "a dryer" that would dry their laundry for them. And when technology finally crow-barred its way into their lives, Glenn watched as everyone tried to cling to the old technology even when new and better technology was in its place. They clung to Beta tapes long after it was clear that VHS had won the war, and right after they switched to VHS, DVDs appeared on the scene. They tried to avoid the digital age like the plague.

But they lost every battle.

Glenn didn't care about all of that. He wasn't much for gadgets. But living without heat was unthinkable. So he knew he needed to get a generator as soon as possible. And besides, he realized that once the power went out, all those who had generators would become kings. They'd be like cavemen who'd discovered the secret of fire.

Glenn smiled as he realized how important he was about to

become. For once in his life he wouldn't be inferior. He had no idea what it would feel like to be important. He wasn't smart enough, so he didn't get into the right college. He wasn't good-looking or charming enough, so he could never find the right girl to like him, and by the time he was ready for any girl to like him, it was too late. He was too old and never got married. He didn't have any of the things that society thought were valuable. The only thing that he could control was how hot it was in his house during the winter or how cool it was during the summer.

But things were about to be different.

He would have power when everyone else did not. He could hire bodyguards to watch his generator and supermodels to hang around his house and the best chefs to cook him meals. And they'd all be willing to because he'd be the only one with a working TV. Not to mention that the only alternative would be hanging around a bonfire in the middle of some street trying to stay warm and cook a meager amount of food.

Throughout history there were always equalizers in society. The printing press, the first handgun, Model T cars, the television, and internet stock trading all changed who was powerful in society. With all electricity leaving, the totem pole was about to once again get reshuffled and I'm going to end up on top, Glenn thought as he walked into the supply store.

"I need a generator," Glenn said.

"Wow," the store manager said. "These sure are a hot item today. I only have one left."

"How many did you have?"

"Three. But they've just been sitting on the back shelf all year. Nobody has wanted one until today."

"Well today is a different day," Glenn said. He wondered what his face looked like at that moment. It probably had some sort of diabolical smile on it.

"I guess it is. I'll be right back," the manager said as he walked to the back room to get his last generator. The last generator in town. And Glenn was about to own it. Now he could hardly wait for the power to go out.

SERGEANT MIKE FRANK

Mike finally got to Main Street just as a gang of men—grown, well-groomed men who'd look perfectly natural in suits—picked up a large metal trash can and flung it through the window of Bob's Electronic Superstore. Bob's was a staple on Main Street, but these men didn't seem to notice or care as they watched the glass shatter, jumped through the window, and emerged with armfuls of loot. Mike screamed at them to stop and even fired a shot in the air, but the men just ran as fast as they could, dropping any merchandise that became too cumbersome to run away with.

When the men were gone, Mike surveyed downtown Goodland. It was only a little before noon and already many of the stores on Main Street had been wrecked, looted, vandalized, and picked clean. Tiny fires burned in metal garbage cans; glass, brick, chunks of sheet rock, and trash littered the street that was normally bustling with friendly Kansas folk. Mike had never seen anything like it.

Not in Goodland anyway.

Mike got in his car and clicked the handheld police radio. "Hey Earl," Mike said.

"Yeah, Sarge," Earl said.

"Have you seen downtown?"

"No, I've been out here on I–70 for at least eight hours now," Earl said.

"How's it going out there?"

"Not good. We're trying to keep this roadblock, but people keep trying to get around the thing. Then a couple of miles down the road they end up in a ditch and I've got to send a squad car and a tow truck to get them out."

"Well, downtown's a mess too. We need some men down here."

"I can't spare anyone."

"Well, I'm gonna need you to," Mike said.

"Okay Sergeant, let me get this straight. You want me to keep the roadblock on both ends of town and tell people to stay home because the highway patrol has shut down 70?" Earl asked.

"Yes, I want that, and I need some men to stop the looting and violence down here."

"Well, there ain't enough men for that," Earl said. He was shouting now. For all the years on the force, Earl was the level-headed one. Nothing rattled him. And from the sound of his voice, he was coming off the hinges.

"Well, figure something out," Mike shouted back and slammed down the radio.

He sat in his car and continued to stare at the damage downtown. How did this happen so quickly? What was going on in the hearts and minds of people in this town? This was a friendly place. A safe place. This was nothing like the big cities of Kansas: Salina, Manhattan, and Kansas City, which, of course, was only partly in Kansas—half the city was is in Missouri—and that was probably why it had so much lawlessness and evil. Goodland, on the other hand, was the type of place where you borrowed a cup of sugar from your neighbor, where the bagger kid at the checkout line of the grocery store knew you by your first name, where you never had to lock your front door. And now, after a couple of rough storms, it seemed that everyone was willing to throw all of that away.

Mike wasn't going to let that happen. Not yet. If he couldn't get things done by conventional means, then ...

Mike picked up his phone and dialed. When someone answered he said, "This is Sergeant Mike Frank. I need to speak with the mayor." In all of Mike's years on the force, he'd only personally called the mayor three times. And those were all emergencies.

Well, Goodland had never faced an emergency like this one.

"What is it, Mike?" the mayor asked. Mike could hear his labored breathing over the phone. And he began to explain the problem. Goodland was starting to unravel. They needed more men.

"How many do you need?" the mayor asked.

"As many as we can get. More," Mike said.

"Go out and find the men you need. Deputize them. I'm having an emergency town meeting tonight; the news is making the announcement in a few minutes. Until then, let's have a curfew. Once you have your men, no one is on the streets until it's time for the meeting tonight," the mayor said.

"Yes sir," Mike answered.

When he got off the phone he called friends from the bowling league and guys he'd played poker with. He called guys who were always jealous that he was a cop; men who were born for law enforcement but somehow missed their calling. "Now here's your chance," he told them. He deputized them on the spot and called the men the Emergency Police Force. Morry printed them black T-shirts that read EPF in bright yellow letters—it was all the uniform they needed. Mike made sure they were given nightsticks, mag-lights, and a gun (which was never to be used; it was only for intimidation). Their job was simple: Keep everyone inside.

Mike felt uneasy about deputizing men on the spot. But these were desperate times. And when times get desperate, well, two can play at that game, Mike thought.

By two o'clock that day, a mandatory Goodland curfew was initiated. It was only going to be for a few hours and then everyone was allowed to come to the all-Goodland town meeting that was going to be held at the rodeo stadium at the Goodland fairgrounds. Until then, anyone who was roaming the streets for any reason would be warned, and if they failed to comply, they'd be arrested. No one was allowed to leave their house until six o'clock that night, and even then they were only allowed to go straight to the town meeting where they would get further instructions on what to do until this crisis passed. Most complied. A few were arrested. But either way, by three p.m. that day, no one outside of authorized personnel was roaming the streets of Goodland.

JEFF HENDERSON

Jeff was trapped inside a tiny motel room. It was stale, not a hint of personality. Even things that were supposed to give the room warmth and personality — like the painting of a cabin in the prairies with fresh snow all around it — looked completely generic. It looked like something that belonged on a bottle of maple syrup. This painting was probably in every other room at the motel, as well as in hundreds of other motel rooms across the country. The paintings were just like the lamps and end tables — they were supposed to give the room warmth and personality, but instead they gave the whole room a bland, slapped-together-assembly-line feel.

Jeff should have been at home.

His place had personality. There was that old scuffed-up leather recliner that he loved to read the sports page in; it was the recliner his dad had given him right after he got his own place. There was his kitchen table, his living room, his bed with his pillow that fit perfectly around his head, and best of all, his family was there. And he couldn't be with them because of philosophical differences.

That was insane.

Maybe he should just admit to Amy that she was right. Did it really matter if he believed her or not? Wasn't a white lie to get his family back together the lesser of two evils? Isn't knowing when to back down and say "I'm sorry" a vital part of a healthy marriage? Besides, most of the damage had already been done. Will had already gone on the news and made a scene in the grocery store. The town was now in chaos and it had much bigger things to worry about. And everyone knew there was only one prophecy left, so if Will could just tell that prophecy right away, everyone else would move on and start worrying about themselves.

But what if all three of the prophecies came true, or at least sort of came true? Would the town really just leave him alone? When people feel this paranoid, they look for some sort of leader. And what if they tried to make Will that leader? Even after all the prophecies were over they'd want more, and if Will couldn't give them more, they'd tear him to shreds.

Jeff didn't know what to do. He needed help. He needed answers. He needed God. He sat on the edge of his bed and stared at his reflection in the TV screen. His eyes were glazing over. And then, after a few minutes of staring at his own reflection, something completely unexpected happened.

His reflection leaned forward.

Jeff was unsure if his eyes were playing tricks on him. So he sat perfectly still and watched as his reflection in the motel television folded its hands and tilted its head up. The reflection looked Jeff in the eyes, only the reflection's eyes were steely and determined. Jeff had never seen his own eyes look like that. That's not me, Jeff thought.

Of course I'm not you, the reflection answered.

Jeff looked all around the room. He wasn't even sure what he was looking for. Maybe he was just checking to see if he had fallen into another dimension. He was just looking for something normal and stable. And as he looked around the room, everything was its bland, normal self—the lamps, the end tables, the comforter, the painting—everything was normal except for the image of himself on the television. "Who are you?" Jeff asked the image. And he was pretty sure he said this out loud.

I'm someone who's come to give you advice.

"Advice?"

You were just wondering what you should do about your family.

"How do you know that?"

I'm the reflection in the television that's talking to you, and you want to know how I can see that you're having family trouble? I mean, isn't that a little obvious? Everyone else in town is with their families while you're stranded and alone in some cheap motel room.

"Okay, then how are you talking to me?"

We don't have time for this, Jeff. I can't answer every question you have. I'm not your magic 8 ball.

"What do you have time for?"

To tell you this: you have to let Will give the signs that I've given him. You have to help him get Goodland ready for the end.

"But why should I believe you? Honestly, how am I supposed to believe Goodland is coming to the end?"

I gave Will three signs. These aren't simple little magic tricks. Everyone's going to pay attention to what's about to happen. They'll have to.

"Okay, but here's my thing: Why give signs? Why don't you just appear in the middle of Main Street as a giant ball of fire and tell everyone what's going to happen?"

Come on, Jeff. You know the answer to that.

Jeff didn't know the answer to that. And he wondered why his reflection would think he had the answer.

I know this has got to be a lot for you to comprehend, and I can completely understand why you are overwhelmed by this whole situation. But that doesn't mean I'm still not expecting you to do the right thing. And the right thing is to stand by your son's side and help him deliver the three signs I gave him. That might not seem like much. And you probably feel like a third wheel. I can understand that. Joseph felt

the same way two thousand years ago. But he wasn't a bystander. Well,
he sort of was. But he knew his role was to be a bystander. Maybe it's
time to understand your role.

Then Jeff's head bobbed down and his reflection went back to normal.

Jeff felt groggy. He waved at the reflection in the TV screen and made faces, but the reflection just mimicked every one of his actions. Whatever was there was now gone.

Did I dream that? Jeff wondered. No, dreams are not like that. Jeff had dreamed before and that was no dream. So, what was the alternative? He had a vision? Was he supposed to believe God himself or some power from on high had come down to give him advice on his family life? There had to be some other alternative.

So Jeff sat on the edge of the bed for quite a while trying to think of some other explanation about what had just happened to him. After exhausting every other option, he decided there was only one way to make sense of what had just happened.

God had spoken to him. And now it was time to act.

MARY CRANE

While most were trapped inside their houses during the curfew, others were making efforts with their time. Efforts that would impact eternity. Mary Crane was making those types of efforts because the thought of not being able to see the other girls in her pinochle club for all of eternity was unbearable.

They were like sisters to her.

They laughed and drank Chai tea and talked about the newest quilting patterns. The girls at Tuesday morning pinochle shared stories about what the kids were doing now that they'd left the house. They talked about their marriages, about what life was like when they were young, and they gossiped about everyone. Even though Mary only saw the girls once a week, they were still her family, kindred souls who understood every part of her life.

Every part except one. They did not believe in the rapture and they snickered at folks who did. Mary never admitted that she was one of the believers. And now she may have to pay the ultimate price. She would be separated from her friends and her sisters for an eternity. She would be in heaven while they all rotted in the underbelly of hell, and she would have to look down at them as they screamed, begging to know: Why didn't you ever tell us?

Mary wasn't willing to live with that on her conscience. So, while everyone else was nestled safely at home, warming them-selves from the ice storm and waiting for the meeting that night,

Mary was making a stand. There were members at her church who were actively planning on spreading the word of what was about to happen that night. They would be at every gate passing out pamphlets, and they would have counselors all around the area willing to say a simple prayer with those who were willing to change their eternal destination.

Mary hoped to pass a pamphlet out to every member of pinochle club. She would track them down if she had to. The pamphlet explained the realities of the rapture so much better than she ever could. Mary hoped that each member of the pinochle club would read it, and as they looked up from reading she could imagine their faces as the reality of eternity dawned on them. And then Mary would grab their hands and she would pray with them.

Mary knew she was about to leave her life on earth, but she wasn't willing to leave the girls in her pinochle club. They were her sisters. Her best friends. And they were worth fighting for.

JEFF HENDERSON

Jeff was shaving in his motel room using the complimentary razor and shaving cream he'd asked for at the front desk. The razor was cheap and it burned as Jeff dragged it across his face. It was another reminder of how badly he wanted to go home. But at the moment he had to get ready to go to the town meeting. Everyone, supposedly, was going. And in all of Jeff's years in Goodland, he could never remember a meeting that everyone went to.

When Jeff finished shaving he put on some Old Spice after-shave. It was also complimentary. He was pretty amazed at all of the complimentary stuff that they had at the front desk of the motel. Of course Jeff was hoping that they had Brut, because Amy loved the way he smelled with Brut on, and so to keep the Brut smell special, he only used it for things like their anniversary and Valentine's Day. If he ran into her at the meeting tonight and she smelled the Brut on him, she would clearly understand how much he missed her. He could only hope Old Spice would send the same message.

Once Jeff finished getting ready, he got in his car and drove to the Goodland fairgrounds. As soon as he arrived, he hopped out of his car and started walking across the field with all of the other people in Goodland. His breath billowed out of his mouth like cigar smoke. His face felt burnt and chapped. And far away from the stadium, no one was really talking. Everyone had their faces tucked into their jackets trying to avoid the cold.

As Jeff neared the stadium, it started to crackle with life like a football game. There were two teams, only they weren't football teams—they were two groups: the Prepared and the Realists. Both sides had banners and T-shirts and all other sorts of paraphernalia that made it crystal clear where their allegiances were drawn. And each side was doing all they could to draw converts to their point of view. Many of the Prepared walked around the stadium's entry points wearing sandwich boards with messages handpainted across them like: "Repent!" and "Is Your Soul Ready?" and "There's Room in Heaven for You." Some from the group had pamphlets printed on glossy paper that explained what the rapture was and what could be done about it. There were also counselors and prayer lines outside of the meeting for anyone who was open to getting his or her soul right with God. And the prayer lines were packed. There was quite the mini-revival going on outside the town meeting.

The Realists were just as vocal. They talked about the intolerance of the Prepared. They had pamphlets that explained the bigotry of the rapture and demanded a more equal opportunity rapture where Muslims and Buddhists and Scientologists could also be scooped up and taken to eternity. But the Realists' main message was simple: Stop the madness. They said that if God's going to come, let Him come, but why tear apart the town with fear and paranoia in the meantime? They begged the Prepared to stop being so vocal, to stop trying to influence every policy and decision that was made. They said the Prepared were leading people towards lawlessness and it was time to start being realistic about the future.

As Jeff entered the stadium, representatives from both sides tried to recruit him. They offered him pamphlets and gave him petitions to sign. He ignored them easily. He didn't really have time to care about whose side he was on at the moment. There were more immediate things to worry about as he entered the stadium. Like where his family was.

As he wandered through the stadium's corridor, there were so many faces—women, children, and teenagers who all looked and sounded the same, bundled up in bright scarves and mittens and skull caps. There was no way he could find the needle that was his family in this haystack of people. He supposed he could try to shout out for them, but it was so loud in the stadium. There were so many voices talking and shouting that Jeff could barely hear himself think. And when Jeff thought it couldn't get any louder, rain and drizzle started tapping against the steel roof of the old stadium.

Jeff didn't know what else to do to find his wife and son and daughter. He asked everyone he knew and no one had seen them. He tried calling Amy's cell phone, but for whatever reason she wasn't answering.

Still, he needed to talk to her. He found a chair in the top row in a corner of the arena and tried to call his wife again. She still didn't answer. So he kept calling. He called twenty-six times, and every time his calls went to voicemail after a couple of rings. It was driving him crazy. He had so much to tell her. And since he couldn't tell her anything in person, he left her messages.

Lots of them.

He said, "Something happened and I want to tell you about it. Call me."

"Hey, there's some pretty serious people here. I mean, everyone is pretty freaked out. I want to protect Will. It'd probably be best if you gave me a call."

"Okay, I know why you're not calling me back. But listen, I understand now. Honestly, I get it. I'm sorry for being so awful. Give me a call."

"A miracle happened in my motel room, Amy. Well, maybe

not a miracle. I don't know what classifies as a miracle. I think someone has to be healed or bread has to be multiplied. But it was a supernatural event. Okay, that sounds really *X-Files*. Just give me a call."

"Amy, why aren't you answering? Please call."

"Lot of people here. It's like a freezing-cold rodeo — without livestock. Can you imagine if they tried to ride those bulls in this weather? They'd be sliding all over the place. Kind of funny, huh? Um, anyway, I have my cell on me so just call whenever you get this."

"Did your battery die? I told you to buy a car charger. It's going to be tough for you to call without a battery."

"Okay, I'll tell you a little of what happened to me. The face that visited Will ... it also visited me. In the motel TV. That's all I'm going to say. Just a little teaser if you will. You'll have to call if you want to find out more."

"Wow, look at this stadium. I didn't even know there were this many people in Goodland. I bet someone here has a phone you can borrow if you ask them. Everyone's pretty nice and they understand this is an emergency, so I'm sure they'd be willing to let you use a phone so you could call your husband."

"Okay, well, um, I'll just keep an eye out for you. But I have my phone on me if you want to call."

Those were the messages he left. And he thought he might try to give her a call one more time and leave her one more message just in case, but that's when the mayor stepped up to the podium and began to speak. At the sight of the mayor's jolly, overweight frame, the stadium's loud, chaotic murmur turned into a whispering hush and the only sound left was the drizzle on the roof.

"Goodland is not a city. It's not a metropolis. It's not a bustling center of commerce. It's a town," the mayor said, like an upset father scolding his children. "What separates us from everyone else? Our community. Our trust and respect for one another. That's why people move here. That's what people love about this town. And I can't believe we are willing to give that up so easily. I cannot believe my town has split in two so quickly. We need to find some compromise. Some middle ground.

"Most of all, we have to stop acting like it's every man for himself. We have to stop raiding the stores and hoarding all of the food and supplies and generators for ourselves. So we are taking some steps to make sure no one goes hungry. And the Goodland Utility Company has assured me the running water and electricity will not be going out anytime soon. But if by some unforeseen and/or unpreventable reason the power does 'leave,' we are finding ways of backing things up. We are going to make it through this time, together. I know there are differing views as to what's happening, but we must stop being divisive and learn to live with and respect one another."

That's a nice thing to say, Jeff thought. But it doesn't play out in reality. The two sides are in direct opposition to each other. The Prepared think the world must be saved and the Realists think there is nothing to be saved from. The Realists don't want to be told how to live. They want to keep to themselves. So how are they supposed to coexist? By their very nature, the Prepared have to tell people they aren't going to be raptured and the Realists want them to just shut up. There's no respectful coexistence in that.

"I know some of you don't believe in the prophecies. Others are terribly worried. So that's why, just to be safe, we've worked on the power. And to get the final prophecy out there, we've brought Will Henderson here tonight."

You've brought *who* here tonight?! Jeff thought. He almost screamed it. But neither his body nor his vocal cords could move as he watched his son led out of the pen normally reserved for the bulls and their riders during the summer rodeo. Will was guarded by two secret service–looking men wearing black suits, sunglasses, and with earpieces squiggling out of their left ears. Emily was also there, and Amy followed closely behind her children with a proud smirk.

Jeff was sure it was a smirk.

And he was sure she caught eyes with him the second she left the pen. She knew exactly where he was, she had seen him there squirming and worried the whole time. She wouldn't answer his calls because she didn't want him stopping her from her plan. And what kind of plan was this? Yesterday she was dead-set against helping the mayor out in any way and now they'd all teamed up against him. What was going on? The second he goes away, she starts working directly with the government? Was she that dead-set against him? It wasn't his plans, it wasn't his ideas that she was against — it was *him*.

And that, more than anything, made him furious. He wanted to shout at her from the top row of the arena. He wanted to ask her how she could have let — invited, even — so much come between them. But at the moment, he couldn't scream or shout or say anything. He could only watch. He was no longer the head of his family — he was, instead, alone and completely helpless.

"I know there are differing views about what went on at Jefferson Elementary on Thursday," the mayor said, "but no matter what your views are, we must all acknowledge that Will Henderson is a hero. His brave actions saved the lives of hundreds and hundreds of our children. And I think, for that, he must be applauded." At that, most of the stadium burst into applause. Many stood and cheered.

"So tonight I've asked Will Henderson to unveil the final warning sign. And then I assure you, your government will do whatever it takes to ensure that we are protected from whatever's out there. I know some of you think there is nothing to be protected from. And that's fine. I know others of you think there is no way to protect ourselves. To both sides I say, we are just looking to guide this great community through this time, so that everyone is provided for. And you will see over the next couple of days, this is exactly what will happen. Then maybe we can go back to being the town that I have grown to love so much.

"So, without further ado, ladies and gentlemen, I present Will Henderson."

There was more polite/raucous applause. Jeff looked at his son who seemed petrified by the crowd, unable to move with all of those eyes staring at him. Finally, Will crept up and took the microphone. He held it in front of his face but did not speak. He mustered a "Hi," and then stood for a few more moments. "My name is Will Henderson. I'm eleven years old and I'm the one the face gave the three signs to." The mayor stood confidently behind Will, his hand on Will's shoulder.

That should be my hand, Jeff thought.

Will went on, "Okay, so one night in a cornfield a week ago I got three signs. The first sign was *destroy.* The school was going to be destroyed. The second sign was *power.* The power is—"

At that moment, Jeff knew exactly what was going to happen. Will would say, "The power is leaving" one more time and then the stadium lights would just shut down. Flash, they would just burn out. Then the power would be gone. In the parking lot every streetlight would burn out, one by one. Lights in homes would just die. The sound system would go silent. And like that, Goodland would be set back five hundred years, into the Dark Ages. Who knows what sort of riot would take place in the stadium? People would claw and scratch and trample one another in the darkness.

Jeff could see this all happening in a flash. He knew he had to get down there and protect his family. This was what the reflection in the mirror was telling him to do. He was just waiting for the right moment to spring himself out of his chair and run down to stand beside Amy and Will. But the right moment wasn't coming. Because as Will continued talking, something odd happened—the lights in the stadium kept on burning bright and the sound system kept pumping out sound. They were using as much power as ever. Even though this seemed like the optimal moment for a sign from on high, the sign wasn't coming.

"—leaving. And I'm pretty sure the final sign is," and Will stopped. He seemed nervous to say another word.

The mayor crouched next to Will and told him, "It's okay, son. Just take your time." Then the mayor gave Will another squeeze on the shoulder.

Who is this guy? Jeff thought. He comes in and takes over my family and now he's crouching next to Will and squeezing his son's shoulder like he's Mr. Cleaver and Will's the Beav? How did Amy do this to me? How did she replace me with the mayor? If the power does go out, and I'm alone with the mayor, I may make it so he doesn't walk out of here.

Jeff snapped out of his thoughts. He watched his son take a deep breath and say, "Okay, the final sign is, the rooster crows before the harvest." Jeff almost thought he could see a thought bubble over every head in the stadium asking what "The rooster crows before the harvest" was possibly supposed to mean. Will tried to answer them by saying, "I don't know what that means exactly. I wish the face would have been more specific or he would help me to remember better. But honestly, I'm still trying to understand what *the power is leaving* means."

And that's when the mayor collapsed. His legs simply buckled and his body slipped to the ground with a quiet thud. He grabbed at his chest and rolled on the ground for a few seconds, and then went still as a corpse. The entire stadium gasped. Will dropped the microphone and turned to stare at the mayor. Quickly, assistants and agents and God knows who else swirled around the mayor. Even from the top row Jeff thought he could read the lips of one of the other assistants as she whispered, "I think he's dead."

AMY HENDERSON

As the mayor grabbed another leg of fried chicken, dipped it in country gravy, and took a generous bite, Amy thought that no one should be eating that much fried chicken. Certainly not the mayor who was already far heavier than a man of his height should be. He probably didn't care. His jolly, overweight frame was one of his trademarks. It was like the city of Goodland was being led by John Candy or Chris Farley. Everyone loved that he was overweight. He played Santa Claus at the Christmas parade every year, and it seemed like the whole town had cheered like fraternity boys and sorority girls when they danced among the disco lights at his inauguration ball.

But Amy didn't find the mayor to be jolly or happy or a whole lot of fun. To Amy, the mayor looked like the Godfather or that big guy from *The Sopranos.* Amy felt like a mafia boss was sitting in her kitchen. It was as if she was about to make a deal with the devil. But she was running out of options. And when he called and asked if he could come over so they could talk things out, she felt like she didn't have much of a choice. First of all, they didn't have any food. Their trip to the grocery store couldn't have been more of a disaster. They left without a single item of food or any helpful supplies. Even worse, Will had given his second prophecy in the grocery store.

The grocery store.

God had given him such an important message, a message the whole town needed to hear, and Will gave it in aisle 11? Certainly God's plan A for Will and His message did not entail giving his prophecy in the middle of some freezer aisle where he could barely be seen or heard. If it was up to her, Will would have delivered his prophecy — well, she didn't know where exactly. And maybe that was the problem. She didn't have a plan. Now two of the three of his prophecies were gone. There was only one left.

To make matters worse, the town was going crazy. Her friends and neighbors had turned into frightened children. No one was using this time to get themselves ready for the afterlife; they were acting childish, indulging their every desire. So what would happen once they started running out of food? Right now there was looting and violence and Lord knows what else going on outside of her house. But when food became scarce and the power went out, what would happen then? What would everyone turn into when things went dark? She needed to make sure she was protected. And Amy had to make sure the final prophecy could be delivered at the right place and at the right time. Jeff couldn't help protect her and he didn't want to help Will do what God had asked him to do. That's why Jeff was gone. He had forfeited his right to lead his family. But she needed someone's help.

She couldn't do this alone.

And as much as she hated to admit it, the mayor could help her. The mayor could make sure Will delivered his prophecy on the right stage — a stage where everyone could clearly hear what he had to say. And who really cared if the mayor didn't believe Will? Didn't God work in mysterious ways? Hadn't He used Jezebel and Pilate and Herod and all sorts of other people in His master plan? Maybe God was just going to use this faithless mayor in the same way. So when he called and said he could not only help, but he also had food, Amy knew she had no choice but to invite him over.

"I just love fried chicken," the mayor said.

"I can see that," Amy answered.

The mayor wiped the gravy off his fingers and then threw his napkin on the plate in the midst of the chicken bones. "Your boy caused quite a stink at the grocery store today."

"With all due respect, Mr. Mayor, the grocery store was already in a stink."

"I'm not saying it was your son's fault," the mayor said, looking at Will's plate probably because Will hadn't even touched his chicken, "I'm just saying the town's clearly panicked. We've had to create a whole new police force just to keep things under control. This isn't a game anymore. I need your boy to tell me the final sign."

"That's just not going to happen," Amy said.

"Then what are we doing here, Mrs. Hender—"

"But what I can do is have Will give the final sign at the meeting tonight."

"You *want* him to give it?" the mayor asked and then leaned back in his chair. It creaked and groaned under his weight. "Okay, I'd be fine with that. It might even *be better* if he gave it."

"He can give it on two conditions," Amy said.

"I'm listening."

"First, you must give him full credit for saving the lives in the elementary school. There are a lot of mixed feelings about that event. And I think the town would look at him like a hero if you paint him as one."

"He is a hero," the mayor said.

"Good. Then the second condition is that I want police protection until the rapture comes."

"I don't think the city can afford to pay an officer to guard your house for that long."

"It's a lot closer than you think."

"So you say. Where's your husband anyway? Shouldn't he be protecting you?"

"He's not in the right mind to protect us or be here right now."

"Dad doesn't believe me," Will chimed in. "He thinks Satan gave me the signs."

"Will, the mayor and I are talking."

"I was just going to explain about the face and the fact that it had a beard and that's how I knew it was God and not the devil and how Dad doesn't understand that."

Amy blushed. "That's not the reason Jeff's not here. He's not here because ... it doesn't matter why he's not here. The issue is, we have a panicked town and some people could blame Will for what's happened. But that would just be shooting the messenger. He didn't cause the storms or anything else to happen. If anything, he's trying to save lives. So tonight I want you to paint Will as a hero. After that, then you will give us police protection until the rapture happens or until you can get this town under control. Whichever happens first."

The mayor said he couldn't give them police protection until the rapture, but he could give them police protection for the next two weeks. Amy thought it was the same difference, but she didn't say that to the mayor. She just told him they had a deal. As soon as that happened, there were a bunch of aides on cell phones trying to get everything ready for the meeting tonight. And within the hour Amy and Will were in a private limo driving to the rodeo stadium in Goodland.

Amy had never been in a limo before. And not only was she in a limo, but she was in a stretch limo with the mayor and other important people, while everyone else had to walk through the bitter cold up to the stadium. Amy tried to feel bad for all of those other people, but how can you feel bad when you're being treated like

Cinderella? Inside the limo it was perfect. The heater was blowing a constant stream of warm air against her hands and face.

This is what it's like walking in God's best, Amy thought. When you're walking in God's steps he treats you like a princess. She wondered what other things she'd missed out on by not walking in God's will.

When they got to the stadium, two large metal doors were opened so they could pull inside. Once the limo was parked, a gentleman wearing a black suit, sunglasses, and with a squiggly wire coming out of his ear opened the door for her. He took her hand and escorted her into one of the holding pens where all the bulls and horses were kept during the rodeo. But inside it didn't feel like a holding pen. There were space heaters, bottled water, Perrier, fresh fruits and cheeses, and plush couches and chairs. They hung out in there for the next half hour or so. Amy relaxed on one of the leather couches while Will was snacking on strawberries and Swiss cheese.

After a while, Amy thought she should get up and peek through the fence to see how many people had gathered in the stadium. More than she'd imagined. It seemed like everyone she'd ever known was there, as well as hundreds, maybe thousands, of people she'd never seen. Goodland's a small town, she thought. How can there be this many people I've never met?

As Amy continued to look around the stadium, she saw Jeff. He was alone and shivering. And he was scanning the stadium with a cell phone pressed to his ear. Everyone else had families and friends they were talking to, but Jeff was completely alone, looking so helpless and frazzled. Amy watched as he kept dialing his phone and scanning the stadium. He's looking for me, Amy thought. And her heart almost broke. She should run up there and save him; she should bring him down here and he could stand by

Will's side as he delivered the prophecy. He was probably ready for that now.

Amy might have gone to him if she hadn't heard a familiar voice say, "Mom."

"Emily," Amy answered. "What are you doing here?"

"I'm with Curtis."

"Curtis?"

"I went to his house after the grocery store. He's taking me to homecoming. I guess his dad is someone important," Emily said as she gestured to some official governmental-looking folks. Amy recognized one of them. He was the man who was wearing a charcoal suit and asking all those uncomfortable questions the first time the mayor visited. And now Emily was dating a government man's son? Amy suddenly remembered Pastor Colby saying that sometimes it was difficult to walk in God's best plan because of the decisions that your parents made. That was called a generational curse. Sometimes our parents can make a decision before we are even born that can affect us. That always made Amy mad at her parents. How could they be so insensitive as to go around sinning before she was even born? But now she had done this to her own daughter. Amy had dated a heathen like Jeff. Jeff found God eventually, but when she first started dating him, he was a heathen. Of course Emily would want to date someone godless as well.

It was in her genes.

Amy looked over again at the man who was always with the mayor. She said, "Curtis' dad, he's with the—"

"—mayor. Yeah, he's been at our house before," Emily said. "His name's Mr. Clayton. I guess he's one of the mayor's right-hand men."

"And you're dating his son?"

"He's really cute."

"Emily, do you really think you should be — "

"Mrs. Henderson," the man with the black sunglasses said, "I'm sorry to interrupt, but it's time."

"Oh," Amy said and followed the man with sunglasses out on to the stadium floor. Even more people had arrived while she was talking with Emily. As Amy walked out behind the mayor and all of the other dignitaries, she looked up at Jeff and smiled at him. She wanted her smile to say *Everything's okay. I still love you.*

Then the mayor started to speak. He said the government was doing everything they could to protect them. He acknowledged Will as a hero. Amy could only stare at the floor. When the mayor called Will up to give his final prophecy, Amy couldn't help but peek up and look at her husband as confusion and rage and hope-lessness crawled across his face. She couldn't blame him for those feelings. Surely Jeff still had mixed feelings as to why his son was up there delivering his prophecy. But once he again saw how many lives Will saved and what good he was doing, even Jeff wouldn't be able to deny what was going on any longer.

Amy was so lost in her thoughts about her husband that she missed much of what Will said at the town meeting. She refocused and listened as her son said, "And I don't know what that means exactly. I wish the face would have been more specific — " Amy smiled. He was doing such a great job. He wasn't just telling people what was going to happen, he was saying things with such charm and charisma that there would be no way everyone could ignore the message. This was the first prophecy that wasn't coming to them secondhand. It was coming straight from the messenger. And maybe now that everyone could hear it, they would stop second-guessing his motives, but rather listen to the message and get themselves ready.

Amy continued to smile in the way only a proud mother can as her son finished his message. "Honestly, I'm still trying to understand what *the power is leaving* means." And as Will finished speaking, Amy stopped smiling. Because right in front of her, the mayor had fallen down. He was twitching and grabbing at his chest. He sounded like a man who was drowning, trying to draw in deep gasps of air to stay alive. At that moment Will's second prophecy flashed through her thoughts like neon lights on a billboard: *THE POWER IS LEAVING*.

Amy realized that, right before their eyes, Will's prophecy was coming to fruition. It was nothing like they thought it would be. This was the power of God. Even when you think you know exactly what's coming, you really have no idea. Everyone in town was foolish for thinking they could understand exactly what the prophecy meant before it happened.

But everyone understood now. Amy watched with everyone else as all the mayor's aides and attendants rushed around and tried to save him. It occurred to Amy at that moment that this is what *had* to happen. In the span of ten minutes the whole town had heard one prophecy in person and now they had witnessed another come to pass. She was amazed how people could keep hearing about miracles and prophecies and keep denying what they saw.

Even the mayor was arrogantly ignoring the reality of this situation as he said he was going to protect everyone. But perhaps he'd just done something much greater than protect them. He'd shown them the truth. This was bigger than a power outage. This was about eternity. This was life and death. And through the mayor's death, he'd drawn a line and shown what exactly was at stake. Now not a soul in Goodland would be able to deny the reality of what was about to happen to all of them.

EMILY HENDERSON

Emily lay curled against Curtis on a giant teal green beanbag in the basement in his house. As she rested her head on her new boyfriend/fiancé's shoulder, she tuned out the MTV show about bratty, skankily dressed teenagers and instead imagined what it would be like if she married Curtis and became Emily Clayton. She thought they'd have cute kids, and he came from a well-to-do family, so they'd always have a nice house, and they'd probably be able to take really expensive vacations to the Hamptons or wherever it is that rich people vacation.

It would be great. Life would be so different because she'd have a completely new family. A new worldview. For her whole life it seemed that every conversation always became about something religious sooner or later. Maybe not about the rapture, exactly (even though the fear of life ending like the snap of an index finger against a thumb was always there), but conversations about God, morality, church, and all other things religious seemed ever-present in the Henderson household. Emily thought it would be so nice to sit down at a Thanksgiving dinner and talk about normal things. Not that she knew exactly what normal family things were, but she couldn't wait to find out.

But then Emily realized something. Sure, *she* could hang in a normal conversation with a sophisticated family like the Claytons. But if they got married, their families would get together for holidays. And before long her mom would start talking all about the rapture or something crazy like that. She'd talk about it as if it were perfectly normal. As if everyone believed in it. And eventually when the Claytons would say, "We don't believe in the rapture" (or whatever other crazy faith thing her mom was talking about), it would get really tense in the room. Insults would fly. It would get personal. Her mom would say something like, "Jeff, we're leaving," and they'd storm out.

In the aftermath, Emily would help her new family do the dishes. And with her hands covered in soap she would have to say, "I'm not like that. I'm nothing like my mother. I don't believe any of that." Then her new mother and father would wrap their arms around her. Once she disowned her parents, she'd finally be in a family where she felt she belonged.

Emily buried her face against Curtis. She tried not to think of the distant future anymore. She'd just have to worry about that day when it came. In the meantime there were plenty of other worries.

For instance, the whole town was on lockdown. She could understand why. She'd seen the way people were biting and clawing and scratching over cans of soup and AAA batteries at the grocery store. And now she was trapped at Curtis' house. Even if she wanted to get home, she couldn't. Things had gotten much worse since the grocery store this morning. Anyone out on the streets for any reason would be arrested. At least that's how Mr. Clayton had put it. He'd said, "If you are out on the streets for any reason, you will be arrested."

"Arrested?" Curtis asked.

"Yes," Mr. Clayton answered.

"Just for being on the streets?"

"Afraid so."

"Is that fair?"

"This has nothing to do with fair. Fair flew out the window once Goodland citizens started destroying their town. This is about order," Mr. Clayton said. He went on to explain that there was looting, fighting, fires, car wrecks, and all other sorts of lawlessness that needed to be squelched in the streets of Goodland. That's why they had to deputize so many citizens. He said, "Every soul in the city of Goodland has to know the strong hand of the law is nearby. They have the right to *believe* whatever they want. But once their *actions* start damaging lives and property, that's another thing. That has to stop. That has to be met with consequences."

Then he went back to the phone. Mr. Clayton had answered one call after another as soon as Emily had arrived. She overheard some of his conversations. He kept insisting that he was the mayor's right-hand man and it was his duty to make sure order was restored. His last conversation ended with him saying, "I'll be right over."

As Mr. Clayton was putting on his jacket, he looked at Emily. "I'm going over to your house."

"My house?"

"The mayor wants to talk with your brother over a fried chicken dinner. He wants Will to give him the next sign."

"Oh," Emily said.

"Do you want to come with me?"

Emily thought about it for a moment. It was a ride back to her family's house. She could be with them. When they needed her. But they were about to have the mayor over. She would just be shoved into a corner. Will was the important one right now. He'd become the most influential and powerful member of the Henderson family. And maybe that was okay. Deep down somewhere, she still loved her parents, and if they had Will to focus on they wouldn't miss her so much. So she told Mr. Clayton, "No, I think I'll hang out with Curtis for a while."

"Okay," Mr. Clayton said. Then he looked at Curtis, "Stay in the house. There's a town meeting tonight at six. You should be ready to go by five."

"Yes sir," Curtis said. And Mr. Clayton left the house.

Before long she and Curtis had to get ready for the meeting and they had to really bundle up because it was so cold outside. He let her wear one of his coats and she thought it was a nice gesture, but the coat smelled like boy and it was *so* not cute on her. She thought she looked frumpy in it but Curtis insisted she bring it just in case. She really didn't want to, but Curtis said, "It's gonna get really cold out there." Emily and Curtis went back and forth like this for a while, and then once they stopped talking Emily realized that they'd had their first fight. Maybe marriage wasn't all it was cracked up to be.

But she couldn't stay mad at him for very long, because they got to ride to the town meeting in a really nice car, and once they were inside they were taken to a very fancy room where a bunch of politician-type people were. They were talking about policies and a bunch of other things that were boring to Emily. She just wanted to eat all of the tasty food. She poured herself a glass of wine but she noticed one of the gray-haired men staring at her as if to say, "I know how old you are," and so she handed it to one of the politicians.

Then, before Emily knew it, she ran into her mother. She felt guilty seeing her there. Her dad wasn't even around and she knew her family was falling apart. Emily could tell that her mom wanted to get into some sort of intense conversation. Luckily, it didn't go on for very long. Quickly, all of the mayor's people said it was time and then she and her old family and her new family were standing in front of all of Goodland. The mayor started to talk. And then he introduced Will to give his prophecy to the whole town. He was talking about a rooster crowing and a harvest coming and Emily couldn't help but think this is all so crazy; his last prophecy hasn't come true, and they're all still clinging to every word he says like he's Abraham Lincoln or Jesus or someone like that.

And that's when the mayor fell down. There was a soft thud as he hit the ground. And then he started gasping for air like he was drowning. And this was all happening in front of Emily. She couldn't have been more than ten feet away from him.

"He's dead," one of the assistants said.

"What do you mean he's dead?" another assistant asked.

"I mean he's not breathing, he's not moving and he doesn't have a heartbeat or any other signs of life that *alive* people normally have."

"So he's dead."

Emily looked up from the mayor. She looked at all of the people in the arena. Nearly every person she'd ever known was there. She could see them all bundled up with scarves, hats, and mittens. She could see her teachers, neighbors, parents' friends, the paperboy, the milkman, and every student who had hopefully elected her homecoming queen huddled together.

And now they were all staring at the dead mayor.

Emily had to back away quickly as paramedics, EMTs, and other professional-looking-type personnel were rushing around the mayor. They were shouting orders and pulling out all kinds of medical equipment. But if the mayor's assistants were right, then all of this work was in vain—there was nothing for the trained professionals to do other than put the mayor in a body bag and zip it shut. Maybe the paramedics were putting on a little show because they didn't want the town to worry.

This was all so unbelievable.

Just moments ago everything seemed so calm. Emily had

watched the mayor explain what was happening and what had to be done. His words were so great that she wondered if Mr. Clayton had written them himself—they were the words of a seasoned politician and she'd never seen the mayor talk that way, but Mr. Clayton talked that way all the time. He probably wrote everything the mayor said that night. He probably wrote *all* of the mayor's speeches. She felt powerful that her father-in-law-to-be could write such great speeches, and because his words were working. They made her feel like everything was going to be all right.

But then the unthinkable happened. It almost seemed like God struck the mayor dead. Does God still do that? Does he still strike people dead? Isn't that a little Old Testament? It seemed a little unkind and erratic of God if he did strike the mayor dead. What did the mayor ever do to God?

Emily got frustrated with herself for thinking this way. Thinking everything has to do with God is how her mother would think.

As Emily watched the medical staff wheel the mayor on a gurney through the dirt on the rodeo floor, suddenly some man darted out of the stands and started running towards the stage. He was bundled up and he looked crazy. He was screaming. He was waving his hands. Emily feared that maybe he was coming to assassinate her new father-in-law. As the crazy man got closer, Emily could hear what he was screaming. He was screaming, "We'll! We'll! *We'll!*"

We'll?

We'll what?

It seemed like this crazy man thought of himself like some sort of prophet. Doesn't everybody these days? He was trying to tell the town of something "we'll" soon be doing. But Emily had no idea what they'd be doing. We'll be dead by morning? We'll know the truth soon? We'll be raptured at any moment?

As Emily thought this, the crazy man was suddenly very close. And that was when she realized two things: One, the man wasn't screaming "We'll!" he was screaming "Will!" and two, that crazy man was her father. She didn't know whether to be completely mortified or if she should go out to help him. While she was trying to decide, two of the mayor's secret service agents in black suits ran out and tackled him. Emily's dad actually landed a couple of punches on the secret service agents, which kind of impressed Emily because she'd never seen her dad stand up to anyone, let alone punch them. But he didn't last long. Quickly, they had her dad on the ground and the whole scene looked like the calf tying at the rodeo in the summer, with the secret service agents playing the part of the cowboys and her father playing the part of the helpless calf. The agents handcuffed her father, and as they were carrying him out of the stadium, he looked at Will and said, "I understand now, Will. I saw the face in the TV. It told me everything." Then Jeff looked at Emily. "Hey honey, I love you. We'll talk soon."

At that moment Emily thought maybe she'd picked the perfect time to join a new family.

After her father's outburst, the stadium was starting to stir like spooked cattle. It started with whispers, but quickly the whispers turned to murmurs, which turned into a few people standing up and shouting. Emily could hear them crying out, "There's nothing we can do. We can't stop this with nice plans and government systems!" "They're going to take us all!" "I'm sorry. Whoever you are. I'm sorry for everything! Take me too!"

Emily took a deep breath and clutched Curtis' hand. She'd seen those soccer games in Europe where the whole stadium went wild, where flares flew onto the field and police with riot gear and shields threw tear gas into the crowd. Usually in those scenes someone got trampled near a fence and a whole bunch of people got hurt. Emily didn't want to get trampled near a fence. She wished the whole town would just calm down. And that's when Mr. Clayton stepped up to the microphone, and in a commanding voice, said, "The mayor is receiving medical attention right now. We are doing everything we can to take care of him. But in the meantime, these outbursts have to stop! If we're going to survive—"

"We're not going to survive!" a woman in the crowd screamed.

"—*If* we're going to survive," Mr. Clayton continued like a parent scolding his children, "you have to have faith in me and we must start working together. We must coexist. And since we seem to be unable to do that without guidance, we are putting some systems into place to ensure our safety. These are the same systems the mayor himself was planning to put in place before he became incapacitated. Because he is not here, I will be leading these new initiatives.

"First, the heads of households will be assigned an odd or even number. Those numbers will be put onto everyone's hands with what is called a henna tattoo. It cannot be washed off right away as to ensure that no one will switch numbers, but it will wash off in about two to three weeks so you can rest assured that it is not permanent.

"Even-numbered citizens will be allowed to get rations of food and supplies on Mondays and Thursdays. Odd-numbered citizens will be allowed to get rations on Tuesdays and Fridays. The heads of households will be the only people given numbers, so they can get food and supplies for their families on the appropriate days. Hopefully, within a week at the most, we will have stores restocked and we will no longer need the numbers.

"Secondly, we are starting a curfew from sunset on until this city can get back to normal. Business owners may go and work on repairing damage and get your shops ready for business again, but please, everyone, let's be respectful of everyone's property. We will not be allowing any rallies and large public gatherings for the next week. I respect the first amendment as much as anyone, but I do not want any more riots or mass paranoia. We need to put an end to this mob mentality. Leaders of all groups, I ask that you respect this policy, and if you do not, then you will be prosecuted to the fullest extent of the law.

"I know these new rules are a bit harsh and even a little extreme, but hopefully they will only be put into place for a couple of days. Then we can get back to normal. But if that's going to happen, we need a little dose of reality, everyone. Now you're dismissed. If you're the head of a household, you may get your number and then take your family home. And be careful out there, the roads are still very slick," Mr. Clayton said and then walked off the stage.

Emily smiled and squeezed Curtis' hand. Mr. Clayton did such a good job. She thought everyone received what he had to say rather warmly.

GARY & GAYLE

Drivetime with Gary & Gayle was far and away the most popular morning radio talk show in Goodland. And it turned out that Gary's views lined up politically, religiously, and philosophically with the Prepared's, while Gayle's views were straight down the line in sync with the Realists. Gayle laughed lots and lots on air while Gary was always somewhat gruff and serious. It's ratings magic. The people of Goodland couldn't get enough of their banter. And the night after the town meeting they had to have a special edition of *Drivetime*.

There was lots to talk about.

Nothing was more pressing than the mayor's death and Adam Clayton. Gary was somewhat confident that the new mayor was the Antichrist. Mr. Clayton had the right characteristics: He claimed that he could do miracles and signs and wonders. (He didn't exactly claim he could do miracles but he did claim he could restore order back to Goodland, which was kind of like a miracle, and he told the town that they should depend on him and his systems instead of trusting in God, which was definitely a delusion of grandeur.)

"A delusion of grandeur?" Gayle asked.

"Absolutely," Gary answered. "Did you see him up there? He was so smug. He was acting like it was such a gift that we had him."

"He was acting like a man who's trying to lead a town that's been rattled by death and natural disaster."

"Let's see what the callers think. We've got Desmond from east Goodland. What do you think, Des?"

"Until tonight I've never heard of Adam Clayton. Which is why he's clearly the Antichrist. Second Thessalonians says, 'He,' meaning the Antichrist, 'will oppose and will exalt himself over everything ... and now you know what is holding him back, so that he may be revealed at the proper time.' *The proper time.* I mean, come on Gayle, what time could be more proper than when the town is scared out of its mind?" Desmond said.

"Thanks for your call, Desmond," Gary said. "Let's take another call. Mary Crane from south Goodland."

"Hi Gayle and Gary. Love your show."

"Thanks Mary."

"I just didn't like the way he said, 'If we're going to survive, you have to put your faith in me.' That seems like the type of thing the Antichrist would say."

"But Mary, don't you think he was extremely nervous under those circumstances. Do you really think we can read into every word he said?" Gayle asked.

"He didn't seem nervous to me. He seemed very confident. Almost creepy confident given that our mayor had just died. He was *Antichrist* confident," Mary said.

"Antichrist confident. So, if you show a little bit of leadership, you're the Antichrist? Would it have been better if he stuttered a little? If his hands shook? That would have let us know that he wasn't some supernatural being?" Gayle asked. "Let's take another call."

"I agree with you, Gayle," the caller said. "How much more can these people stretch everything? It's absolutely crazy. They aren't thinking straight at all, they are just taking two things that have nothing to do with each other and saying it has something to do with the apocalypse."

Gary had to butt in. "Okay, first of all we're not talking about the apocalypse, we're talking about the rapture. The apocalypse is just what you people want to call it because saying *rapture* makes you feel uncomfortable. And frankly you might as well call it that. Because for us it will be the rapture, while everyone left behind will have to deal with the apocalypse. So, good luck with that," Gary said. Gary then hung up the line and took another call.

"Yeah, okay, I think the most obvious reason Adam Clayton is the Antichrist hasn't even been talked about yet. The mayor has asked us to get marks on our hands. And not just marks—he wants us to get *numbers.*"

Gary then interrupted the caller. He took a moment to explain to the audience Adam Clayton's complicated number system. It went like this: For half of the town, the number one was tattooed on the hands of the male heads of households and the number three was tattooed on the hands of female heads of households. The odd numbers were allowed to get supplies on Mondays and Thursdays. For the other half of the city, the number two was tattooed on the hands of the male heads of households and the number four was tattooed on the hands of female heads of households. The even numbers were allowed to get their food on Tuesdays and Fridays.

"So, yeah, okay, you can see where I'm going. You do a little bit of simple math and you can see the frightening ramifications of these numbers. On even days the number two males and the number four females would be standing next to each other. Two plus four equals six."

Gary could see where the caller was going so he jumped in. "Okay, but then we all know men don't listen to instructions very carefully. So it's perfectly rational to think that on the first Monday of the system a few of the number two males, who were supposed to get their food on Tuesdays, would not understand and so they're gonna mix in with the number one males and number three females. So then the food shelter is filled with people with the numbers one, three, *and* two. And even a second grader could tell you that one plus three plus two equals six."

"Right," the caller said. "And what about when everyone goes back to work? Two single mothers who work at the Goodland coffee house could both get their food on Mondays and Thursdays. Three plus three equals six. The three garbage men in Goodland all got their food and supplies on Tuesdays and Fridays. That means every home in Goodland would be passed by with a truck carrying three men with the number two tattooed on their hands. Three multiplied by two equals six."

Gayle had to chime in, she couldn't take it anymore. "Okay. That's cute. I get where you're going. The mark of the beast."

"Think about how our new leader has tattooed our town with the most evil, dark, and wicked of all numbers: 666. He has placed the Mark of the Beast on our skin," Gary said. "How are we supposed to not respond to that? One or two of these things, sure, its just a coincidence. You add them all up and this new mayor is looking a lot like the Antichrist."

"I could kill that new mayor for what he's done to our town," the caller said.

"Yeah, but you don't actually mean *kill him*. Do you?" Gayle asked.

"Yes, that's exactly what I mean," the caller said. His voice sounded like ice water. "Think about it. Osama, Hitler, Saddam, all these guys. Think about how much better off we all would have been if someone had just had the courage to kill them early on. Millions of lives would have been saved. And a lot more lives than that wouldn't have been destroyed. But if someone had stepped up like a man and assassinated those rulers, it would have saved the world from so much evil."

"Okay, I think we've heard about enough from you," Gayle said and hung up the phone. It was one thing for a caller to stir up a little controversy, quite another for him to be advocating murdering the mayor of their town over the airwaves.

"Let's take our next caller," Gary said.

"I don't know why we would kill the mayor," the caller said.

"Thank you," Gayle responded.

"I mean, if the Prepared are so itchy to kill someone, why don't they kill that little boy? Did you see him up there tonight? He keeps getting this town much more freaked out. And then the mayor died right when he said, 'The power is leaving.' If you ask me what's wrong with this town, it's that Henderson kid."

"Okay. Goodbye," Gayle said and hung up the phone again. She and Gary looked at each other. They'd never gotten calls like this.

"All right, I'm going to ask all our listeners out there for a favor. Can we not talk about committing acts of violence over the airwaves for the rest of the night? Can you all do me that little favor?" Gary asked.

But as the night went on, the callers didn't oblige. They talked about murder, lashing out, and fighting back. The calls got worse and much more unthinkable. Gary and Gayle were shocked. Sure, they knew the town would be scared — there had been some apocalyptic storms and the mayor had died — but they were, after all, talking about religion and politics. These were bloody things. That was nothing new.

What was new was how Goodland was responding to them. Gary and Gayle were just trying to do the same thing they always did, stir up a little healthy debate. But this town was beyond debate now. It was time for action. And as Gayle and Gary packed up for the night, they'd never felt filthier. The things they'd heard over the airwaves tonight, the thoughts that were flying through people's heads, were otherworldly. This was Gayle who'd noticed that, and she was the agnostic. But even she had to admit that something wasn't right with their fair town. And she needed to get home and be with her family. They both did. After that night, after listening to the way the entire town was talking, Gayle and Gary thought the only safe thing to do was gather up their families and lock themselves in the basement until this all passed over.

That was assuming, of course, that this was just going to pass over and not be the beginning of something that would stay with the town forever.

JEFF HENDERSON

Jeff woke up on Saturday morning with a horrible crick in his neck. He'd spent the night in a jail cell sleeping on a concrete slab of a bed. Other than the bed, there was nothing in the cell except a toilet that was so grimy Jeff could no longer tell what color it was supposed to be, and a tiny window that was over seven feet off the ground. Jeff had to stand on the tips of his toes and careen his neck just to see out the window. The only reward he got for his efforts was to see the feet of officers and the emergency police force as they walked towards their squad cars.

He couldn't believe he'd spent the night in a jail cell. He couldn't believe he'd charged the field like that last night. Then again, he couldn't stop himself. After the mayor died, he could see the town was furious and scared out of their minds about the mayor's death, and he could see them blaming Will for predicting it. They'd be so furious that they'd storm the field and want answers; when Will couldn't give them what they wanted, they'd rip him limb from limb. And that was more than Jeff could bear to see.

He'd sprung up from his seat and shouted for his son.

No one else moved. They all just stared at him like he was a moron. He felt naked, he might as well have been streaking across the stadium floor. But what was he supposed to do? Go back to his seat? Was he supposed to say, "I'm sorry, I misjudged you and thought you were about to tear my son apart like a pack of blood-thirsty vampires?"

No, he couldn't go back. He needed to be with Will. The reflection said he needed to help his son. Maybe the way to do that was to stand with him. Maybe all the reflection was trying to say was he needed to stop trying to protect his son and instead just encourage him. Maybe the reflection's only message to Jeff was this: Be a father.

Jeff had sprinted towards Will, wanting more than ever just to scoop him up and tell him he loved him. He wanted to tell him, "I'm sorry I've always been a little closer to Emily." It wasn't like he purposely tried to be closer to Emily, it was just he could understand her ambition — she wanted to be homecoming queen, she wanted to go to college and change the world. All Will ever wanted was to read comic books and play video games. There wasn't much to him. Or so he thought. But the courage and the heart that Will had shown in the last couple of days was greater than anything Jeff had ever done. To be able to stand in front of an entire stadium —

Wham!

That's when he'd been tackled by men in suits. He didn't know who they were or why they were tackling him. The whole experience was really jarring. And he felt embarrassed that he punched one of the secret service guy and he felt mortified as he was being hog-tied in front of the entire stadium. But he didn't want to seem embarrassed. He wanted Will and Emily to know he was okay. So he said hi to Emily and told Will about the reflection.

The night ended with him being shoved into a jail cell and told, "You're being charged with disturbing the peace, assaulting an officer, and possibly an assassination attempt on Mr. Clayton."

"Assassination? With what, my bare hands? Mean words?" Jeff said.

"I can't discuss the specifics of your case."

"I was trying to help my son."

"Save it for the judge," the officer replied.

"When's my case going to be tried?"

"After the rapture," the officer laughed as he walked off into the distance. That was the last Jeff had heard from anyone official.

Now Jeff was trapped in this cell. He had no way of knowing what had happened last night. How were Emily, Will, and Amy? What was going on in Goodland? Was it still in one piece? Was everyone okay? How had things at the town meeting ended up? He needed to know.

"I want my phone call!" Jeff shouted, his face pressed against the bars of his jail cell. He was staring down a long hallway with what must have been five different cells connected to his on one side and a concrete wall on the other. At the end of the hallway stood a rusty green metal door with a window the size of a mail slot.

"I want to talk to my lawyer!" Jeff shouted. But no one opened the rusty door. No one peeked through the mail slot. "I deserve some answers."

"It doesn't matter what you deserve," a voice answered. "There is no justice or due process anymore."

"Oh," Jeff answered. "Okay." He was a little startled that someone else was in one of the cells. He hadn't heard or seen anyone else since he'd been dropped off last night. But since there was no one else to talk with Jeff asked, "Why isn't there any more justice?"

"Because this town is being run by the Antichrist."

"Oh," Jeff said again. He hadn't gotten the memo. "You sound familiar. Do I know you?"

"This is a small town. We all know each other."

"Then tell me, who's the Antichrist?"

"Adam Clayton."

"How do you know?"

"Well, his initials are A.C. for one."

"AC?"

"Anti Christ. Adam Clayton."

"Seriously, that's why you think he's the Antichrist?"

"It's *one* of the reasons. It's not the *only* reason."

"Okay, besides Sesame Street letter-of-the-day reasons, what else do you have?" Jeff was surprised to hear himself coming off so sarcastic. But he was tired and he'd been freaked out for his family's safety for what seemed like weeks. He'd seen too much and been jerked around for too long to be moved by anymore Goodland paranoia.

"What about the Mark of the Beast?"

This was just getting better and better. "The Mark of the Beast?"

"Yes, he placed the Mark of the Beast on the hands of those who were willing."

"What is the Mark of the Beast exactly?"

"Henna tattoos."

"Henna tattoos?"

"They're like tattoos."

"Okay, but what's the difference between a Henna tattoo and an actual tattoo?"

"Henna tattoos wash off."

"Oh, so it's like those tattoos they give away in packs of gum."

"They're a little more intense than that. They last for weeks."

"Weeks. Wow."

"Weeks are a big deal when that's all we have left."

"I know, that's why I said wow," Jeff said. "Okay, so let me guess, he had you tattoo the number 666 on your hands?"

"No."

"No," Jeff said, "then what number?"

"He used the numbers one, two, three, and four, which can all easily add up to six."

"They can also add up to seven, eight, and nine," Jeff said. And that's when Jeff stopped himself. What sort of conversation was he in? Was everyone actually saying Mr. Clayton, who had the guts to step up and be the leader at a difficult time, was the Antichrist because of his initials and bubble gum tattoos? This was insane. The whole town had gone crazy.

"I can see you're skeptical, Jeff," the voice said.

"Yeah, actually, I am," Jeff agreed because that was the first thing this person said that made a lick of sense. He was skeptical. Not because he didn't try, though. No matter what Amy, or this guy in the cell, or anyone else thought, he did *try* to believe. He tried to have a supernatural experience in his motel when the reflection in his TV talked to him. And he thought he had had an experience. At the time it was making a lot of sense. It told him to help his son deliver the last prophecy. He was moved by the reflection's words. He was touched that something so grand and great as the rapture was happening and his son was right in the center of it all. The Hendersons would change the destiny of this town.

So what happened?

Amy, the mayor, and Will all made a plan without him. Will gave the prophecy and the mayor died. Jeff was told he needed to help his son deliver the final prophecy but he never had the chance to act. It all went on as if he didn't even exist. The reflection had been wrong. Actually, that wasn't entirely true. The reflection hadn't been wrong. The reflection hadn't been there at all. Jeff was so alone and desperate that he would believe anything. And Goodland was the same way. They were so freaked out and desperate for answers that they'd believe a tornado in Kansas and the death of an overweight mayor could mean the end of everything. Goodland was the problem. Jeff had to get out of this cell. And as soon as he did he'd find any excuse he could to load his family into the car and drive out of this place. He'd drive all the way to the east coast.

He'd drive across the Atlantic Ocean if he had to.

"Be a skeptic if you want. You'll know the truth soon," the voice said.

"I will."

"Yes."

"And what is it? What is the truth?" Jeff said. He was surprised to hear himself still talking. But what else was he supposed to do? Sit and think? He'd done all the thinking he needed to do. It was now time for action. And he would do something as soon as someone in authority walked in here. Until then he needed to pass the time.

"The truth is, we've been chosen for something special," the man's voice said.

"You honestly believe God has chosen us as the test market?"

"That's a crass, twenty-first-century way of putting it. That's the way the Realists are putting it."

"How would you put it?"

"That we've been given a great honor."

"Which is?"

"To warn the world," the voice said as if it were obvious.

"About the rapture?"

"About the end."

"Right. Excuse me if I'm not as excited as you are."

"Why not?"

"Because I just wanted to have a good, regular life. I've never been able to have that. Everyone else gets to have this great life, they get to take their families on vacation to Disneyland and buy their kids the hottest new toy every Christmas. They get to have nice houses and stable jobs. They get to laugh with their friends and drink bottles of imported beer on lazy Sunday afternoons. I never got any of that. I always had to work lame jobs and buy my kids Christmas gifts at the dollar store. I didn't have any friends because I worked the jobs that only teenagers were hired for because I wasn't educated enough to work the jobs guys my age were doing. And now that everything's finally getting better you're telling me that the end of the world is coming. Well, that's just great. And you're telling me I'm supposed to be excited about it? Honestly? Pardon me if I'm not delusional enough to see all of the signs you all seem to. I just want be left alone with my family."

"You can't be left alone anymore. The world is growing smaller and more fragmented, my friend. There are men leading countries with armies and tanks and weapons. These men are less stable than that guy in high school who wore a black trench coat and sniffed Sharpie markers in the corner of your chemistry class. These leaders are stocked to the teeth with nuclear weapons and God knows what else that could level entire countries with the push of a button. The polar ice caps are melting and the ozone is ripping to pieces like a cheap white sheet. Hurricanes, floods, and tsunamis are getting worse and worse every year, destroying entire cities. Here in the U.S. of A., husbands and wives are cheating on each other and not even lying about it anymore and our kids are loading up with 357s and gunning each other down in the streets.

"And you want to go to Disneyland?" the man asked. "But you know what, Jeff, I used to be like you. I wanted to get the sale and take care of my family. But the worse part is, I wasn't even taking care of my family. I realized that when I stood in the breakroom and saw that tornado ripping apart the school. I thought my little girl was going to die in there, and the worst part is, I've been so busy trying to earn money to take care of her that I don't even know her. And when I finally got to hold her, when I got to see and touch all the bruises and cuts on her, it snapped for me, man. I tried to ignore it at first. The next day I tried to go on like I was the same guy. But then the ice storm, the mayor, I couldn't deny it, you know? I had to admit something's going on here. And so I made a decision: I wasn't going to be that old guy anymore. I wasn't going to turn a blind eye anymore."

Jeff actually felt for this guy. He talked with so much conviction. And his voice was so familiar. Who was he? A neighbor? A manager at the grocery store? Whoever he was, Jeff thought maybe he could talk some sense into him. "No, friend," Jeff said, "*I* used to be like *you*. I wanted to believe something big was going on here. But it doesn't make sense. At all. Why would God choose Goodland? Don't you think that if he was going to warn the world, he would do so in New York City or London or Tokyo? It would make sense to have the rapture tested in a big city. But Goodland's so off the map, how would anyone even notice? Don't you see how crazy it is? And why does the world even need to be warned? Why not just end it all?"

"If the rapture happened in New York City it wouldn't be a test market—it would actually bring about the end of the world. New York is *too* big. If that city shut down, it'd have global effects. Same with Tokyo, London, or any other major city. But when the rapture happens in Goodland it won't have any global effects. Everyone can keep on going like they are if they want. However, people will know what happened here. Don't you understand, Jeff, with the internet and twenty-four-hour news coverage, everyone will see what happened to our town and they will have a decision to make. And God wants everyone to see because he gives us every chance he can. The end is so close, not just for Goodland, but for all of us. No one can see it because we're too worried about the Crate and Barrel decorations in our houses and waxing our new shiny red cars. No one can see how close everything is from unraveling because we're too comfortable. We need a wake-up call. And God has chosen us to deliver that wake-up call. It's how God works. He didn't just flood the earth, He had Noah warn everyone, He had Jonah warn Nineveh that fire and brimstone was going to rain down on them. Don't you understand? Planet Earth is Nineveh and Goodland is Jonah."

Jeff didn't respond to this at first. He was letting these words sink in. But he was also trying to figure out who he was talking with. And that's when Jeff said, "Kevin?"

"Yeah, Jeff."

"Kevin Grabowski from Hansley?"

"The one and only."

Kevin was the most cold-blooded shark Jeff had ever known. Kevin would sell expensive cars to customers who couldn't afford them. He'd lie, smile, tell Yankees fans he hated the Sox and Sox fans he hated the Yankees. Kevin once looked a client in the eyes and told her that he, too, had lost a child to cancer, just so he could get a sale. Kevin was the guy who originally started joking that Goodland was the test market for the rapture. This same Kevin was now preaching to him? Jeff hadn't been able to tell it was Kevin's voice throughout the conversation because it sounded nothing like him. Kevin's voice was always gruff and direct and to the point. It was a trademark. The voice that had been talking to him was a soft, compassionate whisper. Only during that speech did the old Kevin come out.

It freaked Jeff out that Kevin was defending the rapture so adamantly. Now he knew what people in zombie movies felt like when they were already in a stressful situation, only to do a double take and realize that an old friend had also turned into a zombie. It was still their face but it wasn't them anymore — their eyes were yellow and their skin was rotting and all they could think about was eating brains.

That was Kevin now. He'd become a zombie.

Jeff pulled on the bars of the cell with every muscle, so desperate to get out, that for a moment, he envisioned himself pulling the bars apart and freeing himself. But the bars didn't budge. They were metal. They were designed to keep prisoners in. Jeff should have known better. But he couldn't think. He needed to get out. He'd go crazy if he were in here any longer. And in the first stroke of good luck that Jeff had in days, that's exactly when Sergeant Mike walked through the green, rusted metal door.

"Officer, let me out, I have work to do," Kevin said.

Mike didn't even look at him. Instead he walked straight up to Jeff's cell and said, "How are you?"

"I want out of here."

"You shouldn't have charged the field like that."

"I know."

"You freaked a lot of the top brass out."

"I'm sorry."

"They want to press some serious charges."

"Okay, fine, but can I get out of here on bail? I don't know what's going on out there, Mike. My family needs me."

"You can get out of here on bail, but it's going to take a while, Jeff. It's taking everything we have just to keep this town under control. But that's why I'm here. I can help you out right now if you can help me with something."

"Anything."

"We need some extra men for the Emergency Police Force. If you'll serve on it with us until things get back under control, I can let you out right now."

"Don't do it," Kevin shouted from his cell. "They want you to join their side, Jeff, and that's not where you belong!"

Jeff didn't say anything back to Kevin. He just looked Mike in the eyes with the desperate sort of look that only a father could have, the look that said "I'd join the Nazis and follow Hitler himself if I could just be with my family." Jeff nodded that he'd join. He'd do anything Mike asked of him.

And that's when Mike fished the keys out of his pocket and said, "All right, come on, let's get you out of here."

THE HENDERSONS

Amy sat at the kitchen table staring at the coffee pot. It was brewing a new pot, but it was taking an eternity. We need a new pot, she thought. I asked Jeff for one last Christmas and he didn't get me one because he thought we should all pitch in for a new TV. And now I have to deal with this coffee pot that takes a lifetime to brew a pot of coffee.

Amy needed the coffee. It was the only thing giving her strength. The only thing that would allow her to think straight. There was so much to do.

First of all, Emily was nowhere to be found, and she needed Emily to stay with Will so she could go find Jeff, but it seemed like Emily was barely even a member of the family anymore. Fine, so be it, Emily, Amy thought as she stared at the drip, drip, drip of the coffee. But I need to find my husband. He was carted off last night in front of God and everyone else like he was Lee Harvey Oswald. What did they think he was trying to do? He's a local businessman, he pays his taxes, attends church; he's been a valued member of this community for his whole life and they lasso him like he's a stuck pig.

The nerve.

Amy picked up the phone and called the police station again. She'd lost track of how many times she'd called. And again it was the same teenage-sounding kid whose voice cracked with every other word, and who said, "I'm sorry ma'am. I've already told you I can't answer any specifics about your husband's case. You'll have to wait until someone in authority gets back."

Amy asked, "When is someone in authority going to get back?" All the teenager said was, "I'm not sure ma'am."

Amy slammed the phone down. Jeff, Emily, how have you done this again? How have you left me to clean up your mess? She wasn't sure if she was thinking all of this or saying it out loud. She wasn't even sure what cup of coffee she was on. Her twelfth? Thirteenth? Her hand shook as the pot finally finished brewing so she could pour herself another cup. She drank it and it didn't even taste warm anymore. Or maybe it was warm and her mouth had gone numb so she couldn't tell the difference between hot and cold. She needed to stand up. She needed to do something. Everything around her looked grainy and blurry like a VHS tape that's been watched one too many times.

She went to the bathroom, washed her face, and when she looked at herself in the mirror, she saw that her eyes were so bloodshot that she couldn't tell if there had ever been any white in them. She needed to sleep. She'd tried to sleep. But sleeping just made things worse. She saw the same image over and over when she closed her eyes: she and Will were standing on a cloud wearing white while Jeff and Emily were miles below them screaming out and engulfed by flames.

It was the direction her family was heading.

They'd been torn apart and needed to be reunited. But to do that she had to get out of the house. And she couldn't get out of the house without Emily. She needed her daughter to watch Will. There was no way Amy was going to take her son to the police station to see all the crime and filth and the underbelly of Goodland. He'd seen more than his share of disturbing things already. It was starting to weigh on him. Last night on the way home he actually asked, "Mom, did I kill the mayor?" Amy tried to tell him of course he didn't. That's crazy. It was something that had to happen, and Will nodded at her as if he understood. But she was not so sure that she understood herself.

The more Amy thought about things, the more she experienced this deep-down, primal need to reunite her family. She was the mother and that was her job. She took a swig of coffee, picked up the phone, and dialed Emily's number again. And to Amy's surprise she answered. "Hi, Mom?"

"Emily, there you are. Where have you been?"

"I stayed at Curtis' house last night?"

"You what?"

"Don't get all freaked out, we stayed in different rooms and we didn't even do anything."

"Have you done something before?" Amy knew she was going off track but she had to ask this question. This was the roller coaster of being a parent. One moment you're so happy just to be talking with your daughter. And then the next your daughter says something like, "We didn't do anything." It was as if Emily was saying we did things other nights, but last night we abstained. And that made Amy feel like a first-time skydiver who'd just jumped from a plane and forgotten her parachute. "Emily, have you? Have you done something before? Anytime before?"

"Gross! No, Mom."

"Okay, why didn't you come home?"

"Because, I don't know, everything's been crazy at home. I wanted to get away."

"Oh, it's been crazy at home. I'm so sorry. Has it ever occurred to you it's been crazy for all of us?"

"I understand, Mom. I know it has been."

"Do you realize your father's in jail right now?"

"Still? Are you sure?"

"What do you mean, am I sure? Of course I'm sure. If he wasn't in jail he'd be home by now."

"It's just, I talked to Mr. Clayton and he said he was going to get Dad out of jail."

"You talked to who?"

"Mr. Clayton."

"As in Mayor Clayton?"

"Yes."

"As in the Antichrist mayor?"

"Mom, you don't know that he's the Antichrist."

"You don't know that he's *not* the Antichrist. And why were you talking to him?"

"Because I was at his house and I told him about Dad—"

"Wait, you're dating the Antichrist's son?"

"We're not dating exactly, we're just going to homecoming together."

Amy didn't say anything for a moment. She took another drink of cold/hot coffee (she still wasn't sure which it was—but at this point it was fuel) and then said, "Emily, I need you to come home right now. Thing are getting very tense and you need to be with your family."

"Mr. Clayton says things are going back to normal."

"Well, he's the Antichrist, honey. He would want things to go back to normal."

"The Antichrist wants things to go back to normal?"

"No, the Antichrist wants you to *think* things are going back to normal. You know what, I don't have time to argue. Come home so you can watch your brother and I can find your dad."

"I'm sorry. I can't. I'll check with the mayor and make sure he gets Dad out. I love you, Mom." Click. She hung up. Just like that. On her own mother. Amy was ready to dial her again but that's when the phone rang.

"Mrs. Henderson?"

It was that kid from the police station. "Yes."

"I have good news. Your husband's been let out."

"When was he let out?"

"I think about three hours ago."

"Three hours? You couldn't have called me sooner?"

"I'm sorry, it's been very busy around here." And that's when Amy slammed the phone down. Jeff's been out for three hours and he hasn't come home? Hasn't even called? Enough of this. Enough sitting around and waiting while her town was falling apart and her family was out there doing God knows what.

"Will, honey, come on. It's time to go."

Will's mom wouldn't tell him where they were going. Wherever it was, she seemed like she was in a hurry to get there. As soon as he was awake, she told him to get ready. As soon as he was ready, they got in the car and drove. On their way to wherever it was they were going, they saw something funny. They drove by Nate Jackson's house and his whole family was in the driveway. Mrs. Jackson was cramming their car topper and trunk with suitcases, portable appliances, groceries, cats, dogs, hamsters, goldfish, and any other possessions that would fit inside. It looked like they were packing anything they owned that would spoil or die, like they were planning on leaving for a long time.

His mom pulled the car to a stop, rolled down the window, and asked Mrs. Jackson, "Where are you going?"

Mrs. Jackson walked up to the car and peeked inside. "Oh, hi, Amy," she said. "Are you okay? You look—" Mrs. Jackson, stopped, as if she was searching for the right word, "—tired."

"I'm all right. It's been a tough couple of days," his mom answered.

"That's why we're leaving," Mrs. Jackson said. "We just can't handle all of this anymore."

"You can't leave now. We need people like you."

"I know, but all of this," Mrs. Jackson said, looking towards the Goodland skyline, "is more than we bargained for. After Paul's accident and everything else, it's more than we can handle, Amy. We're not strong like you are." Mrs. Jackson looked over towards her husband. He was wearing a neck brace. And their car was packed now. Will could see Nate inside reading a comic. He wondered if he'd ever see his friend again. "Listen, I'll see you later Amy."

"If the Lord tarries," Will's mom said.

"Yes, if the Lord tarries," Mrs. Jackson said and then got in the minivan with her family.

"Let's go, Will." Amy rolled up the window and sped away from the Jacksons' house.

"Why is Nate leaving?" Will asked his mom.

"I'm not sure, honey. Probably because they're scared of the unknown. That's what happens even to people of faith," she explained. "They get tested. Sometimes it's too much and they give in to their fears. That's why we must be brave in these final hours."

"Okay, Mom," Will said. It was in the same tone of voice that he used when he said that he'd brush his teeth or that he'd do his homework. He thought he should use a different tone of voice when it came to being brave about the rapture, but he didn't have a brave rapture tone yet. He'd have to work on that in the next twenty-four hours.

After Nate's, they continued to drive. Even though his mom seemed in a hurry, she also didn't seem to know where she was going. She turned up Main Street and began to drive through downtown Goodland. That's when they saw a gathering of people—maybe 250 or 300. It was some sort of rally. A large banner hung over the old movie theater and asked, "Are You Prepared?" There were people ringing enormous bells and wearing sandwich boards that read, "The End Is Now." Some were handing out pamphlets and fliers. Others in the group preached at people as they walked by. And a few in the group were smiling and handing out flowers and last Christmas's leftover candy canes as folks walked up to the information booth. Even though everyone was doing something different, to Will it looked like they all had one goal—to attract as much attention to themselves as possible.

Amy parked the car and started walking towards the rally. Will asked if they should be looking for Dad and Amy answered, "We can't just sit around and wait for your father anymore. Time is too precious." She seemed very tired and even more frazzled as she said this. Her eyes were glassy and focused on nothing but the rally. If Will was honest with himself, she didn't even seem like his mom. He thought he knew why she was acting like this. It was because they weren't all together, they were only half a family, and what's the point of being raptured as half a family? In the last few days his mom had talked about how great it would be to lead Goodland though these final turbulent times as a family, but now they couldn't even lead themselves. And in the process him mom stopped seeming like herself. She was more like some depressed, stressed-out stranger. Will didn't understand people who could get so depressed. He had a friend at school who often got very sad for long stretches and for no reason at all. He had to take medicine called Prozac.

"What does Prozac do?" Will asked his friend once.

"It makes you feel better," his friend said.

"So it makes you happy?"

"Not exactly."

"Oh. Okay."

"Let me explain it like this: Have you ever burned your hand with a lighter just because you were so sad? Just because you wanted to feel something?"

What kind of person wants to burn their hand on purpose? It can get infected and cause gangrene, and Will learned in Boy Scouts that if something gets infected with gangrene, then it sometimes has to be amputated. Seems pretty stupid to do that to yourself just because you can't feel anything. If you weren't sure if you could feel, you should go to the doctor. But Will had the feeling that when his friend asked the question — *just because you wanted to feel something* — he meant it in the deeper teenager way. It was something one of Emily's friends would have said. Will didn't quite understand the deeper teenager questions yet. And because he didn't want his friend to feel even worse or to get more depressed, he answered, "Yeah, I've felt like that before."

"Well, that's what Prozac does. It keeps you from feeling like that."

"That makes sense," Will said, even though it didn't make a bit of sense. But what also didn't make sense was his mom being so sad. She'd gotten what she wanted. He gave the prophecy in front of the entire town last night and she was so excited about that, and yet ever since then she'd seemed hopeless. It was probably because his dad got arrested. But if that was the case, they should be looking for him. They should get him out of jail. But she didn't seem interested in doing that. The only thing she seemed interested in was being sad. Sad enough to burn her hand with a lighter.

Maybe she needed Prozac.

When Will and his mom came up to the rally they were greeted by a man in a white cowboy hat with a raspy voice. "Well, if it isn't the little prophet," the man said. He grasped Will's hand and gave it a violent shake. Quickly everyone noticed Will. They dropped their flowers, pamphlets, and candy canes and gathered around him. They all wanted to shake his hand and hug him.

They said things like, "Thank you for being so brave last night. Thank you for being so wise. So fearless. Thanks for sharing everything you've seen. Did you know that was going to happen to the mayor? That he was going to die just like that? How did you know? What's going to happen next?"

"I didn't know he was going to die, and I don't know what's going to happen next," Will answered. "I gave the final sign last night."

The crowd seemed deflated by this admission.

"Do you think today is our last day in Goodland?" someone asked.

"Last day?" Will replied.

"The rooster crows before the harvest. The corn harvest begins tomorrow, right?"

"I think so," Will answered. He wished people would keep their questions to only the prophecies. Even though he didn't know much about the prophecies, he knew a lot less about the corn harvest or anything else farming related.

"Well, the harvest is tomorrow," another voice explained.

"Okay," Will said.

"And the rooster always crows at sunrise," the person stated.

"Right," Will answered, though he'd have to take this person's word for it. They didn't have a rooster so Will didn't know exactly how they worked.

"Well, if the rooster crows at sunrise, and the end is before the harvest, then we can pinpoint exactly when the rapture is."

"Really?" Will said, finally finding himself curious for the first time in this whole conversation.

The person went on to explain, "The almanac has sunrise at 6:11 on Sunday, the day the harvest begins. If that's the case, then we can know exactly when the rapture will hit. We can give people that moment to prepare themselves."

"That's why we're here today," the man with the raspy voice and white hat said. "We want Goodland to know they can now set their clocks, and if they do not get things right before 6:11 on Sunday morning, then they will be separated from God and perhaps from their own families for all of eternity."

Will was ready to respond, but he noticed the eyes of all who were just looking at him were now looking past him. Will turned around and he saw that police cars and members of the EPF were everywhere. Sirens blared. Their cars were coming up in force and circling around the movie theater. They were barricading the rally. Officers with giant shields, clubs, gas grenades, helmets, and face masks started to get out of their cars. One officer shouted into a megaphone, "Disperse immediately. This meeting is in violation of the mayor's assembly code."

"We're not listening to any code that comes from the Antichrist!" one person shouted. And then he threw something.

That was all it took.

The officers charged, and everyone in the rally grabbed something to fight back with. It looked like one of those scenes from *Braveheart* or *The Patriot* where two armies collided with each other at full speed. Those movies were rated R, but Will was only allowed to watch them because they had Mel Gibson in them and his mom said anything with Mel Gibson in it didn't actually count as being rated R. But Will was glad he'd seen those movies because it helped him make sense of what this scene looked like.

He knew from those movies that he could get attacked from anywhere and he should duck for cover. But before Will could think of where to go he was grabbed by an EPF officer and thrown into a police car. The officer slammed the door. Will was forced to watch the scene through the window of the car. He watched as a bottle smashed off the head of an officer. One man got hit with a club. The man in the white hat grabbed a folding chair and cracked it over the back of an officer. Then one family who was just standing by got plowed down by officers with police shields.

Things were out of control. And that might have been why the officers uncorked their gas bombs and threw them into the crowd.

Everyone was coughing, gagging, and covering their mouths and eyes. The masses were screaming and running into each other as they scattered for cover. The clouds got so thick that Will could no longer see what was going on. And then through the clouds another officer appeared, dragging Will's mom. He opened the door and threw her inside.

She was coughing and crying and she threw up on the floor of the car. Will had never seen his mom throw up before. But every time he was sick, she sat there with him, rubbed his back, and held his hair off of his forehead. It always made him feel better. So he parted his mom's hair to one side, held it out of her face, and patted her on the back.

"It's going to be okay, Mom," he said. She threw up again. It smelled like coffee. Will wanted to do something more for her and he remembered that whenever he was sick, his mom always got him some Sprite. Will pressed his face against the cage separating the back from the front of the police car and shouted, "We need to get some Sprite!"

The officer didn't acknowledge Will. He just flicked on his sirens, put the car in drive, and sped away from the scene. "Did you hear me? My mom's sick. We need some medicine. Or at least some Sprite."

The officer still didn't answer. He was completely focused on the road, on speeding away from the scene. Amy was still coughing and hunched over. It seemed like she'd gotten really hurt out there. The officer didn't seem to notice or care.

Once they'd driven for a few more minutes, Will asked, "Where are you taking us?"

The officer slammed on the brakes. He took off his helmet, slowly, like Darth Vader would. But when the man turned around, it wasn't an officer at all.

It was Will's father.

"I'm taking you and your mother away from Goodland. We're getting out of here forever. They can have this rapture without us."

Jeff Henderson put his helmet back on, stomped on the gas, and the police car sped down the highway like a bat out of hell.

THE END

The Lord himself will come down from heaven,
with a loud command, with the voice of the archangel
and with the trumpet call of God, and the dead
in Christ will rise first. After that, we who are still alive
and are left will be caught up together with them
in the clouds to meet the Lord in the air.
And so we will be with the Lord forever.

1 Thessalonians 4:16 – 17

It ain't the parts of the Bible that I can't understand
that bother me, it's the parts that I do understand.

Mark Twain

THE REALISTS

The Realists had a bumper sticker of their own. It read, "In case of rapture, can I have your car?"

They wanted the rapture to just go away. But it wouldn't. One Realist had counted eighteen rapture predictions in the two-hundred-year history of Goodland. Nearly one every ten years. But even the oldest members of Goodland couldn't remember the town being this worked up before. Sure, there'd been predictions that they'd seen in their lifetime. But nothing like this. They'd never seen the whole town get so wrapped up, shut down, and halfway destroyed.

Which made every member of the Realists think the same thing — this has to stop. Now. The religious paranoia that has cast a shadow over Goodland must come to an end. This was the twenty-first century. Hadn't we moved past thinking the world is flat, burning witches, and worrying about the sky falling?

The Prepared would say no, and insist that the floods, storms, fires, and violence were just getting more and more intense as the years went on and would eventually lead to The End.

But this was nonsense. There were no facts to back this. If you looked back a short time ago you could see much more catastrophic earthquakes, floods, fires, bubonic plagues, and wars where an uncountable amount of lives were lost.

The Prepared would also insist that, more than anything, morality was worse than ever.

But some Realists could remember a day not too long ago where segregation, racism, and sexism were common, if not encouraged, practices. In those days so many people were treated like animals. Immorality was just manifesting in different ways nowadays.

The only thing that has changed has been the Prepared's reaction to all these things. They have been getting more and more adamant that the end is near. This time, they have been vocalizing every fear, and this lack of reality has affected public policy and created an unstable economy. The Prepared were acting like a rock band, trashing the hotel room of Goodland because they'd be checking out tomorrow.

The Realists were tired of it. It was time to push back. It was time to take a stand. It was time to send a message so that tomorrow, when the rapture didn't come, the Prepared would see how destructive and foolish this all was. So that they wouldn't try to pull this stunt again. Or maybe that was too much to ask, but at the very least, the Realists wanted to send a message so the Prepared wouldn't try something like this again in their lifetime.

That seemed fair.

THE HENDERSONS

Amy and Will had been sleeping for an hour or so after giving in to sleep about twenty miles on the other side of Hayes. At first they didn't want to sleep. They used all the energy they had left protesting. "Turn around!" "What are you doing?" "Let us go!" "Take us back!" "Stop this!" and things like that. Jeff didn't say anything. He just stared straight ahead.

Because what was there to say?

He had to get them out of Goodland. The time for discussion was over. Maybe if they said, "Dad, thank you so much for taking us from Goodland!" or "Honey, you are so wise for rescuing us from that horrible, horrible place!" then Jeff would have said something like, "You're welcome." But no one seemed to be in the complimenting mood. They couldn't understand the bigger picture.

After a while no one said a thing. The only sound was the hum of the car sailing down the road. But once Amy was asleep, Will asked a question Jeff knew he should answer.

"What's going to happen to Emily?"

This was a fair question. Jeff had thought about stopping to get Emily, but she was at the mayor's house. Lord knows what stopping there would have meant. In his short time on the Emergency Police Force, Jeff had heard about Mayor Clayton's place. It was surrounded by rottweilers, armed guards, and infrared cameras.

He couldn't risk taking Amy and Will there in a stolen police car. They were too high-profile. The guards would recognize them and they'd all be back in jail.

So Emily had to be left behind.

Jeff would call and check on her as soon as he could. She had chosen to leave the family. So be it. No one would harm a hair on her head as long as she was in the mayor's fort. That's all he could hope for. He'd get his family out of Goodland for a while, and in a couple of weeks he'd go back for Emily. But he couldn't explain all of that to Will. The poor kid already had been through so much. There was no need to worry him more. It was time to rest, time to look forward. They'd escaped from Goodland and if they looked back they'd turn into pillars of salt. So he just told his son, "I know you're worried about your sister, but trust me, she's going to be all right."

Will didn't say another word. He just hunched against the police door, defeated, and by the time Jeff looked back again he was out cold. Jeff rolled down the window and let the breeze rush through his hair. Every mile made him feel more relaxed. Liberated. Carefree. He was in high school again, cruising down the highway without a care in the world.

The tank didn't run low on gas until Salina. Jeff wanted to make sure he refueled as far away from Goodland as possible, and luckily he was deep in the eastern part of the state before he needed to stop for anything. It briefly occurred to him that he should drive all the way into Missouri before he stopping, just so he could be sure other places in the United States actually still existed. But the car wasn't going to make it without gas. And running out of gas in a police car from Goodland would raise a few eyebrows to say the least.

So he pulled into a Stuckey's on the outskirts of Salina, Kansas. Whenever Jeff took road trips, Stuckey's was the only place he'd stop. Stuckey's is an institution in Kansas — a combination of all the things a Kansas tourist could ever want. At this particular Stuckey's there was a gas station, convenience store, arcade with Miss Pac Man and QBert, DVD rental center (where 60 percent of the DVD collection consisted of Steven Seagal martial arts films — Jeff assumed the truck driving community must worship Seagal), a Dairy Queen, and a souvenir store where tourists could buy small personalized Kansas license plates with their names on them and *Wizard of Oz* T-shirts.

As he pulled up to the gas pump, Amy and Will awoke in a haze. They blinked, rubbed their eyes, and slowly looked around in a way that people do after they've been passed out in the car for hours.

Jeff craned his neck towards the backseat and told the remainder of his family, "I'm going to the restroom. I'd recommend you go too. After this we're not going to stop until we leave the state. If you need anything to eat you can grab something in there as well. You have five minutes." Then Jeff opened the rear doors of the police car and walked into the Stuckey's without saying another word.

As Will watched his dad walk into the Stuckey's, his stomach had the same feeling it did as he was plummeting down a roller coaster at Worlds of Fun. My dad has lost his mind, Will thought. Where does he think he's taking us? What does he think he's doing? How can we leave Goodland *now* — right before everything is about happen?

"Where are we going, Mom?" Will asked.

"Honey, I don't know. I really don't."

"What is Dad doing?"

"I don't know," his mom said. Her face was green and her eyes were hollow. She seemed to have no energy left. She was always the one fighting so hard for the truth of the rapture in Goodland, and all of a sudden it seemed like she didn't care. Or maybe she couldn't care. Maybe there's only so much a person could take and his mom had experienced all she could handle.

But still, what about Emily? If the rapture did happen tomorrow like everyone thought, then Emily would be grabbed and taken into heaven just like everyone else. Like that, his sister would be gone. He wouldn't be able to see her for the rest of his life. This made Will want to cry. She wouldn't be there to give him advice and joke around with and see him graduate. She wouldn't be able to interrogate his fiancée when he finally got engaged and he wouldn't be able to know if he'd really found his wife without Emily's stamp of approval.

Was Will really supposed to just go into the gas station, go to the bathroom, get a Dilly Bar, and then hop back into the car while his dad drove him away? Was he really supposed to just let his sister die? Well, not *die*, she'd be taken to heaven, but it was practically the same thing. Of course his dad wasn't going to do anything about it because he didn't think the rapture was going to happen. His dad also hadn't thought the school would be destroyed, so what would have happened if he would have listened to his dad about that too?

Then Will realized something: Superheroes do the right thing no matter what. Superman helps the people of Metropolis even when they're ungrateful and Batman helps Gotham even when they think he's a villain. What people say never, ever, dictates a superhero's actions. A superhero makes a choice only by what is right. And the right thing — the *heroic* thing — to do was to save his sister. Even if his dad didn't want Will to save his sister, Will couldn't listen to him. At this point his dad was just like the ungrateful people of Gotham who had no idea what they were really talking about; his dad would probably vote the Joker into power.

"I'll be right back, Mom," Will said.

He expected his mom to ask where he was going, but all she said was, "Could you shut the door behind you?"

"Sure," Will said and slammed the door shut.

Finally, Amy could just lay her head on the window again. She was so tired. She just wanted to sleep. Somewhere deep inside of her, something was screaming that they had to get back to Goodland, that they were needed for the end, but she just didn't have it in her to listen to that voice right now. She didn't have the energy to fight the town anymore. She had thought the town would be grateful for the salvation that her son was bringing. But they hadn't been. They were always second-guessing him, Amy always had to defend Will, and she just didn't have the strength for any of it anymore.

She wanted to sleep, but when she closed her eyes, sleep wouldn't come. Even sleeping seemed like too much effort. The only thing that seemed right to Amy was pressing her face against the cool window of the police car. As she looked around the front of the Stuckey's, she noticed how carefree all of these people were. Most were on road trips of some sort. Families on trips to theme parks, fathers taking their daughters to college, and so on. Life seemed so uncomplicated for these people. It was like they'd never even heard the word *rapture*.

And as Amy continued to scan the exterior of the Stuckey's, she saw something frightening. She had to blink and close her eyes to make sure she wasn't hallucinating. Will was talking to some bearded, potbellied trucker wearing a black shirt. Will was frantic as he talked. He waved his hands all over the place. The trucker nodded as if he understood and then opened the passenger door and let Will in. The trucker glanced to his right and to his left, looking as guilty as a shoplifter, as he closed the door behind Will.

Why is my son getting into that truck? What is he doing?

"Will!" Amy yelled. And she pulled on the handle to get out. The door didn't budge. She pulled again. But of course, she couldn't get out. She was in a police car. It was designed not to let the strongest of detainees out, and the grate between the front and the back seats kept Amy from jumping into the front seat and letting herself out.

"Will!" Amy shouted again. "Will!" She was screaming now. "Somebody help! That man is taking my son!" The red semi truck was pulling away. It was pulling away with her baby inside it. "Please someone! ANYONE!" Amy looked all around but the families on road trips just kept filling their cars up with gas. "Oh my God, he's taking my baby, he's taking my baby!" Amy said as she watched the truck pull away from the Stuckey's and back onto I–70.

Within seconds it was out of sight.

Then there was a tapping on the window of the opposite side of the car. It was a police officer. A real police officer. Not a fake one, like Jeff.

The officer opened the door and stared at Amy. "Ma'am, I need you to calm down and tell me where the officer is who arrested you? Normally detainees aren't supposed to be left alone."

Amy opened her mouth to explain everything, but words wouldn't come out. She just broke down sobbing. It was more hysterics than sobbing. Deep down in her mind she knew she had to gain control to explain herself. Will needed her. She wanted to stop crying but she felt like she couldn't. It took her well over a minute—an eternity when your son's just been kidnapped—to calm down enough so she could tell their story to this officer.

SERGEANT MIKE FRANK

Mike Frank swears he's never had a dream in his life. When he goes to bed at night he lays there until the darkness overtakes him, and when he wakes up in the morning there is nothing but grogginess. As he brushes his teeth he never remembers any dreams, he never remembers flying or standing on the school bus in his underwear or any of the other dreams people claim they've had a thousand times. When he tells people that he's never dreamed, they all say that's impossible, you have to dream, everybody dreams. But Mike just feels skeptical, like they're trying to convince him of something that simply doesn't exist.

It seemed like everyone was trying to do the same with the rapture. They believed in it so strongly and talked about it so passionately, but just because someone desperately wants something to be true doesn't mean it is. Cubs fans always believe that this is the year they really will win the World Series, mothers believe that their child really was the best and should have been cast as the lead in the school play, and half of the people Mike pulls over believe they weren't speeding. And people don't just believe these things — they're fanatical about them. And the more fanatical, pushy, and insistent people are about something, the more Mike believes it just isn't true. Everyone was fanatical about the rapture which, deep down, made Mike think the whole thing must be some elaborate hoax.

At the moment, Mike was laying in bed trying to sleep. He must have been lying there for hours with his eyes closed yet unable to drift into the darkness. He knew he needed to get some rest after the ice storm, the riot outside this morning, and all of the chaos at the town meeting the night before. He felt stretched so thin. And he could expect the same from his men — they were tired, worn out, and exhausted. They didn't know how much longer they could hold up law and order in Goodland.

If Mike was going to lead them, he needed to sleep, but his thoughts were racing so quickly. How can everyone just be destroying our town? How can they be looting and wrecking and burning every corner in Goodland? I know all of these people. They're good and decent. How are they really resorting to this?

And then his alarm clock blared. He opened his eyes and looked at it. It was seven p.m. It was time to wake up and start making the calls to the men on duty for the night. Normally it wouldn't be an issue — if they were scheduled, Mike had no question that his men would be there. But the rapture was taking a toll on all of them. So he decided it would be best if he double-checked.

He picked up his phone and started calling through his roster. He started with Charlie, a longtime friend, a man who'd been on the force for the last ten years. "Hey Charlie, just checking in to make sure you know you're on duty with me at eight."

"Yeah, I know," Charlie said.

"Okay, great."

"But I don't think I'll be there."

"You what?" Charlie had never turned down a request from Mike. Ten years on the force and Charlie had always helped out Mike whenever he asked.

"I've helped enough. My family needs me now," Charlie said.

"Yeah, and the best way you can make sure your family's okay is by protecting this town."

"No, the best way to make sure they're okay is by making sure they're prepared for tomorrow morning. Goodbye, Mike," Charlie said right before he hung up.

Mike wanted to call him back and yell about loyalty and duty and the oath to serve and protect that they'd made. But Mike feared his sermon wouldn't get through to Charlie. From the sound of his voice it seemed that another set of beliefs had already taken over Charlie's thoughts and his life.

So Mike kept calling the men who were scheduled to help him protect the town. He called Earl and said, "Earl, you know you're on duty at eight, right?"

"Yeah, I need to talk to you about that, Mike."

"About what?"

"I've been talking with some other guys on the force," Earl said. Mike didn't really know what he meant by *guys on the force*. Before all of the prophecies there were five full-time officers in the department. But now, with all of the emergency police officers, who knew where they were taking the conversations.

"And what have the guys been saying?" Mike asked.

"That this fear is spreading like a cancer. That this is a good and decent town with good and decent people. But when the rapture talk comes up, everyone goes crazy."

"It'll be over in the morning. We need to stay stable. We need to serve and protect until then."

"It won't be over in the morning. Once this prophecy doesn't come true, there'll just be another. I think it's time we did something proactive."

"Proactive?"

"Yeah, send a message."

"What kind of message?"

"Don't worry about that. Just promise to stay out of our way."

"I don't know if I can do that."

"Then I guess you're going to have to stop us," Earl said, and then the phone went dead.

Mike couldn't believe that everyone was turning their back on him. But all the guys reacted either like Charlie or Earl did and said they were staying with their families until the end or that they were doing something "proactive." There was no loyalty left. Not a soul had a sense of duty. Mike was the only person who still cared about such things.

Mike knew it was up to him to stop whatever it was that all the men on the force were planning. But he didn't know if he could. Because what frightened him the most was realizing that maybe Earl was right. Maybe the fear of Armageddon was a cancer in Goodland, and the town would never be stable and whole and healthy again until that cancer was cut out.

THE HENDERSON CHILDREN

The sun was once again setting over Goodland. It didn't paint the Goodland skyline in crimson reds and oranges like it usually would this time of year, but instead glowed an ashy gray.

As Emily looked at the Goodland skyline, she could see the damage the last few riots had caused to local businesses. Smashed-in windows were covered in duct tape and trash blew across the deserted streets. It didn't feel like Emily should be driving to homecoming. She didn't know what it did feel like, but certainly not like homecoming. Certainly not like the most magical evening of her life.

But that's exactly where she was going. She was in the car with Curtis—her hair was fixed perfectly, her silver dress was beautiful, and she had a red rose corsage strapped on her wrist. This was supposed to be the most important night ever, the crowning moment of her life, but all of this rapture stuff had upstaged it. There was a dead mayor and riots and people talking about the Antichrist, and half of the town convinced that the rapture was coming tomorrow morning—6:11 tomorrow morning, it had been said—probably about the time she and her friends would be at the Waffle House ordering omelets after partying all night.

According to the Prepared, this was the last night of her life. It was the last night of everyone's lives.

So shouldn't they be at homecoming living it up? Emily knew she certainly would be. She'd been waiting six years for this.

But as she walked into the high school gym she was horrified. Maybe all of those kids at the popular table would get the last laugh because after all of the build up, the hoping and dreaming, homecoming was so *lame*. Not that it was decorated lame; the homecoming committee had actually done a pretty decent job. There were silver, blue, and pink lights all over the place, shimmering streamers, great music, and a disco ball to add a little classy ambiance.

But the gym of Emily's high school felt so flimsy and lame because at most, half of the junior and senior classes were there. And most of them were Realists. The Realist parents insisted that their children go to homecoming because skipping homecoming was exactly what the Prepared would want them to do. "My mom says the Prepared want to disrupt our lives in any way they can," one girl explained to Emily.

Emily was deflated. The dance floor was sparse. The mood was somber. This is what a zombie homecoming must feel like, she thought. It would feel all helpless and lame and gross just like this.

Perfect. Just perfect.

The homecoming game had already been cancelled last night because of the town meeting. And now this. She was about to be named homecoming queen in front of a hundred people. Big deal. What was the point? Did it really matter if she was crowned queen if no one was there to fawn over her? If nobody was there to see it?

Emily Henderson would not let that happen.

"Don't worry, more people will show up," Curtis said.

"Take out your phone," Emily said.

"What?"

"Get out your phone. We're making some calls."

Emily took her phone out of her purse and hit a number on her speed dial. "Veronica, where are you?" Emily listened. "No, there's a lot of people down here." Emily listened again. "I don't care what you're wearing, get down here now. This is the last night of our lives, and even if it isn't, we're going to act like it is."

Will had never ridden in a semi truck. Or a helicopter. The most exotic thing he'd ever ridden in was a minivan with third-row seating, and that was hardly anything to brag about. Under different circumstances Will might have been impressed with the walkie-talkie and the fact that there was a bed right behind the seats for the trucker to sleep. If things weren't so dire Will might have been fascinated with the life of a truck driver.

But things were dire.

His sister was in trouble. And now that it was pitch black outside, Will realized he might not have thought through his plan carefully enough. What if he got back to Goodland and he and Emily couldn't get out in time and they were raptured while his mom and dad were away? That would be horrible.

Heaven suddenly never seemed scarier.

And if that thought wasn't bad enough, he was in this truck with a creepy bearded guy whose breath stunk like Funyuns. The trucker said he'd take Will back to Goodland, but maybe he'd have said anything to get Will in the cab. This man was a stranger after all. And when Will was younger he'd been taught about the danger of strangers. When he was six he thought the world was full of killers and kidnappers and child molesters. That's the way his Boy Scout safety class made it seem. "Never talk to any adult you don't know. No matter if they offer you candy or video games or a ride home. Stranger danger!" the Scoutmaster always said.

So for a long time Will would walk around the mall scared out of his mind of all the dangerous adults lurking around. He'd look at one lady and think *she's probably a kidnapper* and he'd look at some man and think *he probably kills children and puppies.*

Will didn't think like that anymore, though. There comes an age when you're too old for kidnapping. A little after third grade you either become too strong or not cute enough to where parents would pay lots of money to get you back. But tonight he wasn't positive he was too old to be kidnapped.

Will looked over at the trucker. The trucker turned his head and smiled at him. His eyes seemed really white. They were piercing through the darkness. It made Will feel uncomfortable. It was the same feeling Will had the night he was lost in the cornfields when he thought he could hear someone behind him breathing. He remembered that his mom had said that when a demon walks into a room you can actually feel the whole room turn evil. That's what was happening in the truck. It was turning evil.

Still, he had to be brave for his family. They were so close to Goodland now, and if he could just get this freaky trucker to take him to his sister, he could make sure they were okay. She could drive. They could get out of town before the rapture happened at sunrise.

Will told himself to be calm and brave as the trucker looked at him again. The trucker said, "So, why isn't your sister with your family?"

"She's at homecoming."

"And something bad's going to happen to her at homecoming?"

"Kind of. It's hard to explain."

"Try me." Will didn't like where this conversation was going. He wanted to tell this Funyuny-smelling trucker that his sister was in trouble, and that's all of the information that he needed to know. But the trucker had been nice enough to give him a ride.

And they were getting really close to the city limits. So maybe if Will told the trucker everything that was about to happen he would just drop Will off and get away from Goodland as quickly as possible.

"Well, the whole town's in trouble."

"The whole town?"

"Yeah, you see a couple of days ago there was a tornado. And it wrecked my elementary school."

"Okay."

"But here's the thing. I knew the tornado would happen. Well, I thought it would be a laser. Or at least kids at my school thought it would be a laser. But no matter what it was, I knew something bad was going to happen at my school."

"Really," the trucker said, looking at Will. "And how did you know that?"

"Because a face —"

And that's when something appeared in the middle of the road. At least *appeared* is the best word Will could use for what happened. They were driving along, and suddenly this figure in a full white robe with a long beard was just standing there. It could have been an angel or maybe God himself, but most likely it was a good guy because it had a beard. And as the truck was barreling toward the white-cloaked figure, it locked eyes with Will. It was the face. Sure, this time it had actual eyes instead of cornhusk eyes, but it was still the same face.

Will was sure of it.

Will looked at the face, trying to read what its eyes were saying: Was it mad because he was telling an outsider about the rapture? Did he get the last prophecy wrong? Was there something else he needed to know, something he missed? And the face looked like it was about to speak, to answer all of those questions and maybe more, but that's when the trucker yanked on the steering wheel. The truck started to rock back and forth and Will clung on to the door handle, scared the whole thing was about to tip over. And then Will clenched his eyes shut and wasn't sure exactly what happened next. There was rocking, the smell of burning brakes, the trucker yelling the most unholy combination of swear words Will's young ears had ever heard. There was a loud screeching noise, and finally a crash.

Then silence.

Within the hour, homecoming was packed. Emily's phone calls had worked. People just started to arrive. Most of the new arrivals weren't wearing formal attire. They were in jeans and T-shirts, or they were in their pajamas because it was already eleven at night and they were planning on getting a good night's sleep before the rapture.

But Emily convinced them sleep could wait. And all of the people wearing all of the different clothes were actually helping to make homecoming memorable. It was bringing the magic back. Because there was something so carefree in the air. It was like everyone had nothing to lose. It was as if all of the songs the DJ played had some deep underlying truth. They could lose themselves completely in one song after another. The high school students were almost all collectively thinking—

It really *is* fun to stay at the YMCA.

It *is* getting hot in here. We *should* take off all our clothes.

And the people just kept coming. Nearby college students and guys who Emily knew had graduated one or two years ago were sneaking into the auditorium. Soon it was standing room only. The DJ was feeding off the energy in the room and the whole gym was bouncing with students jumping in their jeans or pajamas or suits and dresses. Everyone was pumping their fists in the air, sweating, and singing and yelling the words out to each one of the songs. The room was in a fever. Emily had heard about the crazy clubs in New York and LA, and she thought this must be what they're like. This type of energy was usually only found in the biggest cities of the world. But it was here tonight, maybe because deep down everyone really did fear it was the last night of their lives on earth.

And Emily was about to be crowned queen of everyone here. She was basking in the thought as her phone vibrated. When she pulled it out of her purse she saw "Mom" on the caller ID.

Not now, Emily thought.

"Hello," she said.

Her mom was saying something on the other end of the line and she sounded frantic, but Emily couldn't hear her with all of the singing and screaming and shouting in the background.

"Hold on," Emily said as she walked out of the gym. When she was outside she said, "What's going on?"

"Will's been kidnapped," her mom said through the sobs.

"What do you mean he's been kidnapped?"

"We were at Stuckey's in Salina—"

"What were you doing in Salina?"

"Your dad took us away this morning. He wanted to get us away from everything. We didn't want to go but we were trapped in a police car."

"Dad took you in a police car?"

"I don't have time to explain all of this, honey."

"Okay, so how did Will get kidnapped."

"He was so worried about you! He was so worried that you'd be raptured without us. Your dad said he kept talking about that."

"Okay," Emily said.

"So he either got in some creepy trucker's semi or he was forced in. I'm not sure. But I think he's looking for you."

"Mom, this can't be happening right now. They're about to announce the homecoming queen."

"Well, this *is* happening right now, honey. We need you to find your brother."

"I've got to go," Emily said as she snapped the phone shut.

When she stepped back inside the gym, the dance was crazier than ever. And Emily wanted to be a part of it all. She wanted to dance and crowd surf and make out with Curtis. More than anything she wanted to hear the cheers and see everyone's adoring, jealous faces when they put the crown on her head and declared her queen.

Will was going to be fine. This was just another case of her mom being overly sensitive. Her paranoia wasn't going to ruin this night, because if Emily let that happen, then her mother's paranoia may just take over the rest of her life. So Will had gotten into a truck. Big deal. He was hitching a ride back to Goodland and he'd probably end up at Nate Jackson's house, and when she got there they would be reading comics. She would stand in the room in her silver dress, with mascara running in rivers down her face because she was crying so badly about missing her one opportunity to make her high school years count for something.

The reality was, nothing was going to happen to Will. At least, probably nothing would happen.

WILL HENDERSON

When Will slowly opened his eyes, he saw a cloud of dust, and as it cleared, he realized they were well off the road. He opened the door to the truck, hopped out, and saw that a bunch of the truck's tires had blown out. The trucker must have yanked the truck off the road and rolled into the middle of this field. They'd even barreled through some barbed wire on their way down. It looked like some of the wire had wrapped its tentacles around the tires and the underbelly of the truck. The trucker stood next to Will, his nose bleeding some. He didn't seem to notice. He was just looking at all the damage done to his semi.

"What was that?" the trucker asked.

"You saw it too?" Will said.

"Yeah, but I'm not sure what it was. Was it a deer?"

"Most deer's don't wear white cloaks and have beards."

"It was blurry. It happened fast."

"Yeah, but it looked a lot more like a person than a deer," Will said.

"If it was a person, then where's he at?" the trucker asked, pointing up towards the road. And it was true, there was not a person or a car or anything on the road. It was empty and lifeless.

"I don't know. But it wasn't a deer," Will said.

"Whatever. I'm going to get us some help," the trucker said, walking back to the cab. Disbelief is already sinking into him,

Will thought. All the time, adults wonder why they never see angels and demons or anything like that. But maybe they do, and when they see them, their minds instantly try to tell them they saw something else. Maybe that's why adults live in such a faithless, serious world. Maybe that's why even people in my own town are having such a hard time believing in the rapture even after every one of the face's prophecies have come true.

Will walked up to the cab and saw the trucker clutching the CB, trying to get an answer. "I said, this is Clyde. Is anyone out there? Over," the trucker said. But no one on the other end answered. There was only static. Clyde kept trying the CB, but every time he was met with static silence. If there was someone out there listening to his pleas for help, they weren't answering. And the trucker finally got the hint. He threw his CB down and started walking up to the road.

"Where are you going?" Will asked.

"We've got to walk into town. Apparently every trucker on the planet turned their CB off and there's no phone service out here. What is it with this town?" the trucker shouted.

"I don't know," Will answered. He'd been wondering the same thing himself.

Will followed him up the slope. When the trucker got to the top of the road, his eyes became as big as baseballs. A week ago Will might have thought the trucker was looking at the four horsemen of the apocalypse or something else rapture related, but luckily Will knew better now. He knew the rapture was still hours away.

Finally Will saw it too. He didn't realize they were that close to town, but there, across the road, were Mr. Johnson's cornfields, and about a half-mile down the road, next to the cornfields, was a large group of people. There were bonfires and people shouting and who knew what else.

"What are they doing?" the trucker asked.

"I have no idea," Will said. And Will didn't want to know. Whatever was going on out there, Will thought he should be at least in the eighth grade before he saw it firsthand.

"Come on, maybe there's someone there who can help us," the trucker said.

Will knew he shouldn't go anywhere near those people. It was the same feeling of things turning evil. There was a little voice inside him that was shouting to stay away. But what was he supposed to do? Sit on the side of the road and wait for the rapture to come first thing in the morning? Not an option. He'd been brave and it had gotten him this far. He just had to hope his bravery would take him a little farther. So he told the trucker, "Okay, let's go."

They started walking toward the last place on earth Will wanted to be. Will hadn't been back to the cornfields since the night the face had appeared to him. He hadn't even been near them. When he had to go into the city he insisted his mom go the opposite direction. It wasn't the thought of the face exactly that made his stomach sink, it was the fear, the feeling of being trapped, the thought of death closing in on him, the thought of starving and thirsting to death. He knew that just seeing the cornfields would remind him of all of that.

As they got closer, the shouting got louder and the fires burned brighter. Two men with torches saw Will. One of them shouted, "That's him! That's the Henderson boy!" Will didn't even have a chance to run. Two men grabbed Will from behind and started dragging him into the mob. Will didn't know what was going to happen next. He didn't even want to know. All he could do was shut his eyes and pretend this was all a nightmare that he would wake up from at any moment.

* * *

The DJ at homecoming could tell the room needed a break. He told the senior class president that now would be a good time. The class president stepped up to the microphone with two officers of the student council. One officer was holding a dozen roses and a sparkling white sash that read, "Homecoming Queen." The other officer was holding a crown.

The class president said, "It is now time to announce this year's Homecoming Queen and King. First, the Queen. Drumroll please." Many in the room slapped their knees, mimicking a Letterman-like drumroll. "I'm proud to announce that Emily Henderson, you are Washington High's Homecoming Queen!"

At that the room erupted into wild applause. Everyone knew what a victory this was for Emily. They started chanting her name.

"Get on up here, Emily," the class president said.

Everyone in the gym kept chanting. But Emily did not appear. The room quieted down into a hush. "Where are you, Emily?"

Emily did not answer. Everyone was looking around now. There was a murmur in the room. One person was asking another if they'd seen Emily. "Has anyone seen Emily?" the class president asked.

No one answered. Even Curtis, her date, looked baffled. Emily was nowhere in sight. She was not outside the gym or in the bathrooms.

She had simply disappeared.

JEFF HENDERSON

Jeff was in handcuffs, sitting at the police station in downtown Salina. All around him phones rang and actual criminals — vagrants, pimps, drunks, drug dealers, and prostitutes — were being booked, fingerprinted, and photographed. This is what the rapture had reduced Jeff to. A common criminal. He was about to be put in jail for the second time in twenty-four hours.

When Jeff asked what he was being charged with, they said impersonating a police officer and stealing a squad car for starters. And if they thought about it, they were sure they could come up with more. For instance, they didn't know if locking your wife up in a police car while impersonating an officer of the law counted as spousal abuse, but if it did they were willing to charge him with that as well.

"Where is my wife?"

"Don't worry about her. She's being taken care of. My partner's asking her a couple of questions."

"We don't have time for questions."

"Trust me buddy, you got all the time in the world."

"You don't understand —"

"Yes, I do. You've said it like fifty times, your son's in trouble."

"Well, he is. I have to rescue him."

"From what?" the officer said.

This was a tricky question. Jeff still didn't know exactly how to explain it. When the officers first found him outside of Stuckey's, Jeff had been reluctant to explain everything. He kept thinking he could just rationally talk his way out of this. He thought if he told them what was going on in Goodland it would make him sound crazy.

But it was getting late.

Will had been gone for at least an hour now and if Jeff didn't get out of this station soon he might never see his son again. Who knows where that trucker would take him? Jeff couldn't think about it. He needed say whatever it took to get him out of custody.

It seemed like the truth was Jeff's last option.

So Jeff told the officer everything — the rapture, the Antichrist, the mark of the beast and the food rations, the mayor's death, the ice storm, the tornado, the cornfields, the Prepared, the Realists, and the prophecies. As Jeff told his story the officer looked at him with furrowed brows. Jeff thought this was probably the same look this officer would give to a schizophrenic homeless man talking about the FBI tapping phones, and government conspiracies, and the town being overthrown by vampires. Jeff was trying to talk in a tone of a voice that said, "I'm not one of those guys." A voice that said, "I'm not homeless and I'm pretty sure I'm not schizophrenic."

Jeff finished up by saying, "My son thinks he's a prophet. But the crazy part is, half the town is sure he's a prophet as well."

"That's the crazy part?" the officer said.

"Well, one of the crazy parts," Jeff said.

Then the officer's partner walked into the conversation. He was a lot younger than the officer Jeff was talking with. Jeff thought the younger officer was probably the one who wanted to get into all sorts of crazy car chases and shootouts while the older cop was just trying to stay alive long enough to get his retirement pension. But at the moment Jeff didn't care about any of that. He just wanted one of them to let him go so he could save his son.

"You'll never believe the story this guy's telling me."

"Tornado, cornfields, and Armageddon?" the younger officer replied.

The older officer looked surprised.

"His wife had the exact same story."

"What do you think? You believe them?"

"Sarge, I don't know what to believe. But I'll tell you this, I ran away from home once when I was a teenager. When I got back, my ma had that same look in her eyes. Whatever's going on, that woman really believes her son's in trouble. Only a mother can have that look."

"Take us back to Goodland," Jeff begged. "If everything's not exactly how we say it is, then lock me up for as long as you want." The officers just looked at Jeff. But he could tell they were considering it. "I'm just trying to save my family."

EMILY HENDERSON

Emily couldn't stay at homecoming any longer. It wasn't right. It didn't matter how crazy her parents were. They wouldn't lie about Will, and that meant Will was out here somewhere. That meant she had to be his big sister and protect him. She should have been protecting him this whole time. She knew that now. He didn't have anyone else and he needed her. But she had been so obsessed with Curtis and homecoming — well, it was more than obsession. It was her image. If she couldn't control that, if she couldn't make something of herself while she was in high school, how did she ever hope to make something of herself once she graduated? There were just a couple of pretty girls she had to compete with in high school, but in the real world she'd have to compete with everybody. If she couldn't be homecoming queen in a small town, what did that say about her chances of ever doing something anywhere?

Emily cleared her thoughts.

She had to stop it.

Homecoming was over now. There was only the future. And what would the future be like without her brother? Saving Will, that was the important thing. Because if something happened to him, if he got scarred or damaged for life or worse, she'd never forgive herself. She wouldn't deserve forgiveness.

She wasn't going to let that happen. She was going to find

him. Problem was, she didn't know where to look for him. Luckily, Goodland wasn't that big of a town, so she just combed one street after another until she ended up near the cornfields, where she found hundreds of people gathered. There were bonfires, flashlights, a few torches, and a giant herd of people. And most of them were looking up at the billboard that read, "THE END IS NOW."

And sitting underneath the "O" of "NOW" was a boy gagged with duct tape and tied to a chair. Emily hopped out of her car and glided with remarkable grace and quickness (considering she was wearing three-inch high heels) up to the crowd. She looked closer at the boy.

Who else could it have been but Will?

Emily could see he was struggling. He was using all of his strength to pull against the ropes, but they weren't going to budge. It must have been ripping his arms up to be pulling like that against the ropes, she thought. And as Emily stared at her baby brother she could see that he was crying, and not just a single tear running down his face, but tears and snot and everything else. He was in hysterics. How long had he been up there?

The whole crowd was silently staring at him. Emily had noticed that whenever crowds had gathered over the last week, they were either bubbling with enthusiasm or brewing with anger. But this crowd was lifeless as a stadium during the national anthem. It was almost as if putting Will up on the billboard was an unpleasant but necessary chore for the crowd.

"What is he doing up there? Let him down!" Emily screamed. It just kind of burst out of her. And the crowd quickly turned to look at her. She suddenly felt extremely uncomfortable in her high heels and silver gown, glitter on her eyelashes and her hair loaded up with so much spray that every piece was cemented into place. This was not the way she imagined people staring at her in her homecoming gown. She always thought they'd look at her with jealousy, she always thought they'd be awestruck by her beauty. And they were awestruck. But her beauty didn't seem to be the primary reason.

Still, since Emily already had everyone's attention, she said, "What kind of sicko freaks are you? He's just a kid."

"We're not trying to do him any harm," a voice said. And then a man stepped out from the crowd. Emily didn't expect to see someone in his position here — a part of all of this. But he seemed to be more than a part. He seemed to be leading the crowd. "But we can't let him down. He's the messenger for all of this, Emily. He spreads fear and ignorance. He gives them permission to act this way. Permission to destroy the town, to act out, to bring everything to a halt in the name of doom and gloom."

"What he is is a kid in the fifth grade. You can't do this to him," Emily shouted.

"I'm afraid we can." the leader said.

AMY HENDERSON

Amy was in the back of the police car biting her fingernails. There was so much nervous energy coursing through her veins. She'd tried to call Emily at least fifty times and she had only answered once. And that one time she answered all she said was, "They're about to announce homecoming queen." Amy could picture Emily standing there with a big smile and a sash holding a dozen roses while God knows what was happening to Will.

"Jeff, she's still not answering," Amy said.

"She probably turned her phone off," Jeff said.

"Well, she needs to turn it back on."

"I know that, honey, but there's nothing we can do about that now."

"Wow, that is a really helpful attitude. Thank you, honey. Thank you so very much," Amy said. Or maybe she screamed it. She was getting so tired it was tough to control the tone of her voice. It was tough enough to control *what* she said, and after this many hours/days with so much fear yet not much sleep, it was impossible to control *how* she said it.

"What do you want me to say?" Jeff shouted back.

"I want you to think of something helpful, not just criticize me."

"I wasn't trying to criticize."

"Not what it sounded like to me."

"Could you two *please* stop yelling?" the older officer asked. At that Jeff and Amy slouched back to their sides of the police car. The older officer looked at Jeff, "Is there anyone you could call in Goodland to check on your kids?"

"Yeah, but he's really not going to want to talk to me."

"Why?"

"Because he's a sergeant on the Goodland police force. And I stole the police car," Jeff said.

"Let him know that the car's being towed back to Goodland at your expense." It had to be expensive to tow a car all the way to Goodland. Amy almost hoped that they would be raptured just so they wouldn't have to pay that bill. But she didn't bring that up to the police officers when they negotiated that as part of the agreement to get back to Goodland. She thought the not-paying-the-bill-because-of-the-rapture thing was best left unsaid.

Besides, at the moment she wasn't sure if she still believed the rapture was going to happen. The further away she'd gotten from Goodland, the more the rapture seemed dreamlike. She didn't know how it was possible. How one thing could seem so real and true at one moment, yet at the next seem so empty and hollow.

Naïve even.

She suddenly couldn't remember why she was so sure the rapture was ever going to happen. Maybe because it seemed like it was time for things to end. The streets were crawling with immorality, and the news every day talked about the threat of nuclear war, terrorist bombings, school shootings, and natural disasters. It was almost like God was allowing all of this to happen because he was ready. It was as if it would be better for everyone if the world just stopped. But she'd started to question all of that in the last hours as she'd grown so nervous for her kids. Because if she actually believed that tomorrow morning they'd be raptured and in heaven with Jesus where he could wash all of the bad memories away, then none of this should matter.

But that was the problem. It did matter.

It mattered so much that the Goodland rapture seemed like the second most important thing in her life. A distant second. Making sure her kids were okay was first. And she really hoped Jeff could get ahold of Mike so that he could help them.

"He's still not answering," Jeff said.

"Is there anyone else we can call?" Amy said, reaching across the chasm between them and grabbing his hand. He squeezed her hand back. Relief rushed through her body. It reminded her suddenly of being back in high school and being so nervous about having a baby. Her life seemed over. But Jeff grabbed both of her hands and looked her right in the eyes and said, "I love you, Amy. Everything's going to be okay. I promise." It was the first time he'd even ever said "I love you." When he said that, it was weeks after she found out she was pregnant and it was the first time in the whole process that she felt like things were okay. Like there was an ounce of hope.

And, now, the way he squeezed her hand and looked at her this moment, it was like he was ready to be her hero one more time.

"Yeah, there's got to be someone at Hansley that can help." Jeff said as he dialed a number. And then he added, "Everything's going to be okay." Amy was waiting for an *I promise* to follow and it didn't. She understood why. He couldn't promise anything.

JEFF HENDERSON

Jeff was still trapped in the back of the squad car and his skin was sticking to his clothes. I must stink, he thought. He hadn't been home for days, his eyes were bloodshot, and there was this constant buzzing in his head. It was like his brain had overloaded from processing and worrying too much. It reminded him of high school when he went to see Poison, the greatest hair band of all time, in Kansas City. The show was so amazing, but so loud. When he lay in bed that night after the show, there was this ringing in his ears that wouldn't stop. It never got louder or quieter, it was just a constant, high-pitched hum. He later learned that the ringing meant part of his hearing was dying. Now, in the back of the police car, Jeff felt like his thoughts seemed to have the same high-pitched ringing. He wondered if part of his brain was dying.

It probably was.

The last road sign said they were forty-seven miles from Goodland. Still too long to just sit and wait. But what choice did he have? So Jeff looked out of the window and stared at the moon. It was unusually bright and cast a white pasty glow onto every corner of Kansas. It was as if God was using it as a flashlight so he could clearly see every corner of the stars to ensure that everyone was behaving. He wondered if God was happy or angry with what he saw.

Not that it mattered; even if you were a firm believer in the

Goodland rapture, God wasn't going to do anything until morning. God was going to take the people who were ready and leave the people who weren't. Happy and angry had very little to do with it. So, in the meantime, Jeff continued to stare out the window with his mind flashing between thoughts of God, his children, and his wife. None of his thoughts were very clear. It was as if the ringing in his brain was keeping him from feeling much.

Then finally he saw the most important sign, the one that read "Goodland City Limits." The officer pulled off I–70 and Jeff directed him to the cornfields. Jeff had called Kevin Grabowski who'd just gotten out of jail, and Kevin told Jeff that's where he should go. There was some sort of big rally outside of the cornfields and Kevin had heard that Will was there. Maybe Will was there with Emily celebrating or praying with a group from the Prepared on the night before the rapture.

When they got to the cornfields, they saw a crowd, a frighteningly large crowd, standing amidst bonfires and looking up at a billboard. They looked so interested in what was on the billboard. They were pointing and shouting at it. The billboard had been there for days with its simple, foreboding message, "The End Is Now."

But then Jeff could see what they were yelling at. There was a girl with black hair wearing a shiny silver dress. Two men were carrying her up a ladder like King Kong climbing the empire state building. Everyone in the crowd was yelling and pointing at this girl.

"What are they doing?" the older officer asked.

"Are they about to sacrifice a virgin?" the young officer asked.

"Is that what you do in this town? Virgin sacrifices?" the older officer said.

"No, we don't sacrifice virgins," Jeff said. Though, by the way things had been going the last couple of days, he knew it could be entirely possible that a virgin was about to be sacrificed.

"Well then, what are they doing?"

"I don't know," Jeff said.

They were so far away that Jeff couldn't make out who the girl was. But then Amy shouted, "That's Emily!"

"That's not Emily. How can you tell that's Emily?" Jeff asked. Amy was probably just being paranoid.

"That's her homecoming dress."

"Someone else probably just has a dress like hers."

"No. No one does. Emily made sure of that. She ordered it from New York," Amy said.

"So, your son's been kidnapped and now they're about to sacrifice your daughter," the young officer said.

"They're not going to sacrifice my daughter."

"Then what are they doing?"

"I don't know," Jeff said, pulling on the handle of the back of the police car. "Let us out and I'll see."

"We need to call for backup," the young officer said.

"We're in Goodland. We're hours away from backup," the older officer said. "Get the shotguns." He opened the back door of the police car. "Come on."

Jeff helped his wife out of the car and they ran with the officers down the trail. Jeff could see the young officer's hands were wrapped tightly around his gun, and he was breathing heavily.

As they approached the mob, Jeff could hear members of the crowd yelling at the billboard, "You see what happens? No more of your fear and ignorance. That's what happens to fear and ignorance." On the billboard, Jeff saw Will sitting on a chair. He was tied to it and had duct tape over his mouth. Emily was next to Will in her silver dress and tied in the exact same way. Amy shouted, "Will! Emily!"

Every set of eyes spun around and stared at them. Amy might have run into the crowd and climbed up the side of that billboard if Jeff hadn't grabbed her. He held onto his wife tightly to make sure she didn't make things any worse for them. But things were about to get worse anyway. The crowd was starting to circle around them like hungry zombies. They didn't say anything, but they were thirsty for something.

The older officer could see the crowd closing in. He held up his shotgun like an action hero and shouted, "Everyone needs to go home. Now. There will be no virgin sacrifices tonight!"

"We aren't going to sacrifice a virgin. But we're not going home either," Mike said, stepping through the crowd. He was in his uniform, but he was not himself. Jeff couldn't believe he was here. He was always holding up law and order at all costs, but at the moment he didn't seem like a man who was only concerned with the law. He had this cold determination in his eyes that Jeff had never seen before.

The older officer seemed to have a more difficult time aiming the 12-gauge at someone with a badge.

"What's going on here, Mike?" Jeff asked.

"Hello, Jeff. Glad you could make it."

"What have I made it to? Why are my children up there?"

Mike looked at his watch. "Because in about two hours now, the rapture is going to occur. Only, something funny's going to happen. There's not going to be any rapture. Time will go on like it always has. God will not scoop up even one person from our town unless he does so through death, the good, old-fashioned way."

"So why not just let it come and go? Why tie up my kids and create bonfires and a demonstration?" Jeff asked.

"Because Jeff, once the rapture doesn't happen, all we'll have to show for our misery here is a wrecked town. Businesses and homes and college funds will have been destroyed. And we're going to have to clean it up once again. Sure, that will calm everyone down for a while. But then some of the Prepared will begin to forget and soon enough, in no time at all, there will be another prophecy. I can't take it anymore, Jeff. I can't keep cleaning up this mess. Goodland would be a great town if it wasn't for this fascination with the rapture. And sure, tomorrow will come and go, but this is all going to start again because no one has the courage to say *enough*. I didn't want it to come to this.

"But these are desperate times and my men have convinced me they're going to take desperate measures. And when nothing happens, we have your son up there so we can say to everyone, 'Remember this. Next time you want to spread your fear and paranoia, remember his face.' And hopefully they will, Jeff. Hopefully this will make them think twice and Goodland can be the great town it was meant to be."

Mike's speech seemed to have pacified the older officer. Maybe he's won him over, Jeff thought, because by the time Mike's speech was over the officer's shotgun was almost aimed at the ground.

And that was all the invitation someone in the crowd needed. One in the faceless mob reached out and punched the older cop and knocked the shotgun out of his hands. Another man lunged at the young officer, but the officer ducked and dodged the tackle. Instead of drawing his gun and fighting back, the young officer burst through the crowd and sprinted down the road, toward the squad cars, and out of sight.

This all happened in seconds, but it seemed like slow motion. And by the time the dust settled, the older officer was being held hostage, and the crowd started to close in on Jeff. But somehow the officer's shotgun lay lifelessly on the ground near Jeff's feet. Jeff lunged at it, picked it up, and fired a blast in the air. Everyone froze. Jeff then took the barrel of the gun and pressed it against Mike's forehead.

Mike's face turned Casper white.

Jeff thought he'd be completely frightened being in this position, aiming a gun at another man, but he was surprised by how natural it felt. Before tonight, he'd only held a gun a couple of times, and that's when he went duck hunting with Mike every now and then. He usually missed every duck he shot at, while Mike knocked them down like it was a video game. So maybe Jeff felt so confident at that moment because he was pretty sure he wasn't going to miss Mike at this close of a range. And what scared Jeff the most was that he might just pull the trigger if he had to. He would end his best friend if that's what it took to free his children.

With the entire crowd staring at him, Jeff knew he had to say something. These moments happen in movies all of the time, where it's the hero versus the world, and somehow the hero manages to speak with such noble, grandiose words at those moments. But Jeff couldn't think of any of those words right now. All he could think was, *I just want my kids back.* And so that's exactly what he said.

The crowd stared, waiting for him to add more. So he said, "You can do whatever you want, make whatever statements you want, argue whatever you want. But it's not your kids up there. And you have no idea what it's like to be down here with your kids crying and trapped up there. They're so frightened and they need their dad. And that's me. I'm their dad. So I'm going to get my kids, and then my family and I are getting out of here. You can do whatever you need to after that. But in the meantime, if you get in my way, I will do whatever it takes to get through you," Jeff said, and pumped the shotgun still aimed at Mike's head.

Jeff didn't know he had such a speech in him. And pumping the shotgun was an especially nice touch, he thought. It let the crowd know he meant business.

However he wasn't sure what the next practical step was. He couldn't put his gun down and climb up on top of the billboard. That would leave him pretty vulnerable. To keep control of the crowd he'd have to leave the gun pointed at Mike. Everyone else would have to do the dirty work.

"Earl," Jeff said, looking at one of the other officers on the force. Earl wouldn't want anything to happen to Mike. "Can you climb up there and untie my kids?"

Earl looked at Mike. "Do it," Mike said. Earl then climbed the ladder on the side of the billboard up to the level Will and Emily were sitting on.

"You know, Jeff, you of all people should be empathetic to our side of things," Mike said.

"I really, really don't want to talk about this with you."

"I know you don't want to talk about this at all. Am I right?"

"Pretty much," Jeff said.

"I was thinking of *you* when I decided that the men were right, that I had to help organize this. I'm trying to help you, Jeff," Mike said, looking at the crowd who was gathered around.

"Wow, thank you. Next time why don't you just torture my dog and burn my house down," Jeff said. *Trying to help me, how could he possibly be trying to help me?* He was supposed to be the levelheaded law and order person in Goodland. Now he was tying children up on billboards and telling their father that he was doing him a favor. If he'd lost his mind this badly there was no hope for anyone else in Goodland.

"Jeff, no one's going to have a more difficult time putting this behind them than your family."

"I already told you I don't want to talk about this."

"Well, you should get used to it. Because you're going to be talking about it for the rest of your life. Your son will always be this prophet, and people will always, *always* be asking him what his next prophecy is. When he has kids they'll ask his kids what the next prophecy will be. You can't run from this. As long as you're in Goodland this will hang around your neck. Can you leave? Sure, but do you really want to leave the one place where your life is? Where your friends and family and your home are? If you want to be able to keep a life in Goodland you can take a stand with us tonight. I know this is hard, but if everyone can see that Will's own father has the courage to say, 'My son is just a kid. He's not a prophet and the end of the world is not coming!' then that will make an impact.

"And you have the courage to say that, Jeff. But the only way to make sure your message is heard is to keep your son up there. Keep the gag on his mouth as a symbol of silencing the fear that everyone is needlessly spreading. Now, I know what you're thinking: I can't do that. But ask yourself this: What's a rough couple of hours so that he can put this behind him for the rest of his life?"

That was a good question.

Maybe everyone got it wrong, maybe *Mike* really is the Antichrist, Jeff thought. He was talking so eloquently even with a shotgun pressed against his forehead. And what was worse was he was making sense. A lot of sense. This wasn't just going to go away after tonight. Jeff had tried to escape Goodland and he couldn't. The more he'd tried to keep Will out of the spotlight, the brighter the light burned on his family. Maybe this wasn't something he could do by himself. Wasn't it possible that he needed someone like Mike to help him out of this mess? And truthfully what was a small sacrifice of a couple of hours when compared to the rest of their lives?

The thought of keeping Will up on the billboard came in a flash to Jeff. He could see himself going up there and explaining things to Will. He'd whisper to his son that this was for the greater good. He'd tell his son that he loved him. And then he'd stand by Mike and everyone else as the sun rose and the possibility of the rapture disappeared.

This would be the safe thing to do.

The sensible thing to do.

And then the flash disappeared. Jeff put it behind him. He wasn't interested. He knew that he may never be able to protect his family from the outside world, but that didn't mean he was going to stop trying. Maybe every time he tried to protect his family, forces would push back at him. He'd just have to learn to push back harder.

Jeff took the shotgun off Mike's head and fired a blast in the air. "I'm done talking. Mike, the next time I fire this gun it will knock your head clean off," Jeff shouted, loud enough for the crowd to hear. Then he looked up at Earl, "Get my kids down! Now!"

Earl quickly started to untie Emily. When Earl took the duct tape off Emily's mouth, she shouted, "Daddy!" And Jeff wanted to cry. Even tied up like that she still looked like his little princess. "I'm right here, honey. We'll have you out of here in no time," Jeff shouted.

Then he turned his attention back to the crowd. They were too close to him. Someone could try to be a hero and grab the gun. He could shoot Mike on accident. So he shouted, "Back up! Everyone! Just keep backing up until I say stop."

The crowd complied; they started to walk backwards, away from this crazy screaming man holding a shotgun at a police officer. Some backed up all the way until they had disappeared into the cornfield. Quickly, there was breathing room around Jeff and he felt better.

No one would be able to sneak up on him now.

But suddenly Jeff saw a man who wasn't sneaking at all. He

was charging like a possessed rottweiler. And Jeff could hear this man shouting/snarling, "The message must go on. The message must go on." He just said it like that over and over, charging at Jeff.

Jeff did not want to take the gun off of Mike's head. He said, "Stop! Don't make me pull the trigger!"

But the snarling man didn't even slow down. His eyes were glowing and he was staring at Jeff, repeating to himself that the message would go on. Jeff took the gun off Mike and aimed it right at the guy charging. "Take another step and I *will* shoot. I swear to God I'll shoot you right here!"

But it was pointless. The charging man wasn't going to stop. He wasn't going to slow down. He was going to tackle Jeff or die in the process. So Jeff aimed the gun right at him and put his finger over the trigger. He didn't want to kill this guy. But he gave him ample warning. Pulling the trigger was the only option. So, Jeff stood there with the gun aimed at this man, waiting for the courage to pull the trigger and save his family.

The courage never came.

Before Jeff knew what had happened, this man had barreled into him and sent the shotgun flying. Jeff was knocked clean off his feet and his head thwacked against the gravel road.

And that was the last thing Jeff remembered for a while.

When Jeff came to, everything was blurry. He tried to move his lips but they were taped shut. He tried to move his arms but he could feel ropes pinning them to his body. Eventually, Jeff's eyesight came into enough focus that he could see everything around him. He could see Emily on one side of him tied to a chair and Amy on the other side also tied down. Next to Amy was Will, somehow looking brave and strong as ever.

Jeff looked off the edge of the billboard and could see everyone scurrying around like ants. Jeff had never been on top of a billboard before, but he was amazed at how high it was. Their chairs were on a lip that jutted out from the billboard, but the lip wasn't very wide. It was made for guys to stand on while they plastered a new image on the billboard. It was not made for a chair. At that moment Jeff could see himself falling off the billboard and breaking every bone in his body. How embarrassing would that be? So Jeff tried to think about keeping his body perfectly balanced.

And he tried to think about how he could get his family off the billboard. But the ropes were on really tight. What sort of boy scout tied these? He wasn't getting out of them anytime soon. There was no choice but to sit with his family and watch this from on high. At least they were together. Still, he wished he knew what time it was. He wished he knew how much time was left. By the looks of things, not much, because there were a lot more people gathered beneath the billboard now. And as Jeff stared at the group below he realized there were two groups now.

Jeff strained to try and hear what the groups were saying to each other. He knew one group was the Realists. They wanted his son and now his whole family up here to prove their point. And it didn't take too much imagination to guess who the second group was. The Prepared had heard what was going on underneath the billboard and they were gathering to see what was going on. Jeff wasn't sure, they may have been gathering here anyway. In his couple of hours as a member of the Emergency Police Force he'd heard rumblings about where the Prepared would gather to wait for the end.

Some of the guys said the Prepared would gather in a graveyard because conventional wisdom was that the dead would be raptured first. That's how it would all start. And what a sight that would be. But how would it work? Would the dead rip out of the ground and pull themselves out of their coffins like vampires? Or would it be much simpler? Would they pass through the ground and up towards heaven like friendly ghosts? Some of the Prepared wanted to see for themselves. Others weren't that interested; they would go to bed for the night and they never planned to wake up in the natural sense. They would just sleep, and while they dreamt, God would grab onto them and take them home.

And some were determined to gather in the cornfields. Many thought that "The harvest will begin when the rooster crows" meant that God's harvest of souls would begin in the cornfield, where, of course, the actual harvest was supposed to begin as well.

Still, it seemed like a lot of the Prepared were there at that moment. Jeff thought this was probably because the ruckus the Realists were making with all of the bonfires, shouting, and the family tied to chairs probably drew out some of the Prepared who were just going to sleep or hang out in the graveyard while they waited to see how things would play out.

And as Jeff continued looking at the crowd underneath the billboard, he realized it stretched down the road as far as the eye could see. It was as if the outside of the cornfield was a large amphitheater and his family was the opening act.

The newcomers were saying things like, "This is an abomination. How can you leave that family up there? God will strike you down."

"No, he won't!" someone from the other side of the crowd was shouting. "That's the whole point. He's not going to do anything." Arguments like that were breaking out everywhere. Jeff could pick out bits and pieces of them. And they were all the same: You're wrong and we're right. You're foolish and we're brilliant. You don't understand and we do.

After a while Jeff grew very uninterested in the conversations.

The skyline was starting to glow. It would be 6:11 soon, the sun would rise, and one way or another, this would all be over. If God was up there, he was stretching his fingers and getting ready to make his opening move. And as Jeff sat up straight, looking down on all of his friends and neighbors, he wondered for the first time in his life what it would be like to be God. What would it be like to have a bird's eye view of these arguments every single day from the beginning of human history until today? Watching people shouting and accusing and pushing back at one another but never listening or trying to understand one another. It must be maddening. Jeff would want to bring on the apocalypse too if he were God. He would want to end this all.

Jeff took his focus away from the crowd down below. He caught eyes with his son and tried to give him a look that said everything. A look that said, I'm so proud of you and you've shown me so much in the last week, saving your school when no one else would, protecting your mom, and coming back for your sister because your father couldn't think straight enough to save her.

Jeff looked at Emily. He looked her straight in the eye and thought, You, you look like a princess. You probably would have been crowned homecoming queen. But you left it all to save your little baby brother, and they pulled you up here and tied you up and I'm so sorry, honey. But I'm proud of you, Emily. And I love you.

Then Jeff looked at his wife. He locked eyes with her and he'd swear he could see Amy's eyes smile back at him as a tear rolled down her face and over the duct tape on her mouth. Jeff wanted to reassure her. He wanted the look on his face to say, "I know things haven't been easy from the moment we met. I know it's been such a difficult and frightening journey. But I've loved every step of it. I've loved taking every step with you. I'm so grateful that you were brought into my life."

Jeff knew that sometimes a look and what's left unsaid can be much more powerful than words. Still, he wished he could pry his arms loose and rip the duct tape from his mouth and tell his family everything. He hoped he'd get a chance to someday.

But all of a sudden he knew that chance would never come. Not in this life anyway. Because that's when a light appeared from heaven. It was as bright as the sun itself. Maybe brighter. It was shining right on all of them. And Jeff could see everyone below cease their bickering and stare at the light. The wind started to rush over the crowd and everyone's hair seemed to toussle from side to side.

And as they all stared at the light, Jeff knew this was it. This was his last moment on earth. He was going to be sucked up into eternity and he was so incredibly frightened. He wasn't ready to face God. And then for a moment he thought, What if God doesn't want me? God could read his thoughts, couldn't He? He is God, after all. God would know that Jeff had been such a cynic since the beginning. God would know that Jeff never had any real faith in the first place. God could see through his soul with X-ray vision. And when God knew the truth, He would leave Jeff behind. He would take Jeff's whole family and leave Jeff to sit alone on the stairs and read his Bible like in that really bad rapture movie Amy had made him watch one time.

And then the light spoke. It told the crowd, "Everyone needs to go home. If you do not, you will be placed under arrest."

Jeff didn't know God placed people under arrest.

Quickly, the light twisted, and Jeff could see that it wasn't from heaven at all. It was from a helicopter, a police helicopter from Salina. It was hovering above with its spotlight pointing down on all of them. Then Jeff could hear the sirens. Lots of them lapping over one another. Screaming, letting everyone below know that law and order was coming. A line of cop cars appeared, casting red and blue light all across the cornfields and everyone who was gathered. Cops with riot gear jumped out of the cars and shouted at everyone to cease and desist. Jeff saw the young officer from earlier jump out of his cruiser and start pointing with authority.

Jeff and his family watched the aftermath of the police arrival safely from atop the billboard. Some in the crowd fought back and were arrested. Some just ran away down the road or into the cornfields. Many jumped in their cars and drove away while others peacefully talked with officers, probably trying to explain their side of things and what had happened and/or what was about to happen.

Then the young officer climbed the side of the billboard and began to cut through the ropes. He took the duct tape off their mouths. There was so much to say once they were free, but all any of the Hendersons could manage to say was, "Thank you."

When they were off the billboard, the officer told Jeff, "Take your family home. I know a lot's happened tonight, but I can cover for that. You just take your family home." Jeff looked at the skyline again. It was getting brighter. The sun was about to rise.

"You were our ride," Jeff said.

"Right," the young officer said. He fished some keys out of his pocket. "Take my car. It's right over there. I'll come get it later."

"Okay," Jeff said. "What time is it?"

"Just a little after six," the young officer said.

Jeff gave the officer an understanding nod, and then the rest of his family followed him down the road and towards the car. As they walked, Jeff only looked back at the cornfields once. He saw a number of crows that had perched themselves on top of the cornstalks to watch all of the chaos—they were the only peaceful living thing in sight.

Once they got to the car, the wind began to rustle through the cornfields. Maybe God was drawing in a deep breath and about to blow the trumpet. After all, the Bible says the end will come when we least expect it, and this moment with all of the police and everyone scattered seemed like when they would least expect it.

But Jeff didn't care. He couldn't think about it anymore.

So he just unlocked the car for his family. When he got inside he looked at his kids in the rearview mirror. Emily was in her tattered homecoming dress and Will was wide awake and staring straight ahead. Jeff glanced at Amy and saw that she couldn't help but look back at the cornfields. She needed to see what was about to happen.

Jeff twisted the key in the ignition. The clock on the radio lit up with neon blue numbers. It was 6:10. Less than a minute until the end.

And he was ready for anything at that moment. He was ready to float up towards the sky through the clouds, space, time, and different dimensions until he was standing in some heavenly realm for an eternity. Or he was ready to find some bacon and waffles, drink freshly squeezed orange juice, and see what the rest of the day had in store.

EPILOGUE

So, in the end, the question left is this: How does one define a successful test market anyway?

By nature they're risky. Most are prone to failure, and even if the test is a success, the person running the test can only hope that everyone else in the country (or the world in this case) reacts the same way the control group did. And that, of course, is never guaranteed.

For instance, when Crystal Pepsi was tested, everyone loved it. They thought that having soda pop that was normally colored a dark brown, but then, somehow, through the miracle of modern science, that same soda pop became see-through, well, that was just *wonderful*. They enjoyed every sip of the clear Pepsi. They gave the good people at Pepsi two thumbs high in the air. And that gave Pepsi, who'd spent millions of dollars and months of time on the test market, the confidence to take Crystal Pepsi everywhere. When it was launched, everyone was pretty sure that colored Pepsi would soon be a thing of the past.

But now it is only Crystal Pepsi that is a distant memory. Most people don't even remember the doomed soft drink.

So was the Goodland rapture another Crystal Pepsi? Surely not. Because first of all, unlike Crystal Pepsi, which was tested in Dallas near all sorts of major markets (and therefore gave Pepsi all sorts of false confidence because of media hype), Goodland is far more isolated and, therefore, the test gave much truer results. Kansas is smack dab in the middle of the country, perfectly close, yet perfectly far, from everywhere else. And even though the rapture could have gone better, even though it would have probably been seen as more of a "success" if people were actually raptured, that is just a cynical and pessimistic way to look at it. Most people thought that the tested rapture still gave God lots of answers and data to look at.

Still to this day there is a lot of debate about what actually happened that night and morning of the Goodland rapture. Some say that God was ready to pull the trigger and begin Armageddon until the Realists and the police from Salina made such a mess of things. If the point of the Goodland rapture was for the town to be a signal flare and a sacrificial lamb for the entire planet, it was just too hard for that to happen in the middle of the police riot. How could God make a big grandiose gesture in the middle of all that? He is a gentleman and He isn't going to upstage everyone else. The rapture is supposed to happen only when there's peace and quiet and it's barely expected, not in the middle of absolute chaos where it would hardly be noticed.

Some say that the police and helicopters and the actual chaos *was* the rapture. It was a metaphor. They were there to show how crazy and hopeless planet Earth would become once the tribulation began. The rapture was never going to *actually* happen. Not just in a small town. That's nonsense. It was more like a fire drill or a test of the emergency broadcast system. And what's important in these tests is how people are going to react. That's what God wanted to see. He wanted to see what was in their hearts. Because once Armageddon began, He would have to assume complete control. The time for human decision would be over. Hence, God's intention from the start was to give Goodland a good old fire drill and warn about what was to come. He just wanted one more chance to let everyone know it's not too late for you, but it will be soon.

And inevitably there are some who say that the signs were misread. The real harvest was the one that happened only once every five years, and that harvest was in sync with the Mayan calendar. So when the boy said, "The rooster will crow at the harvest," that's what he was talking about. Even that interpretation caused debate, but the bottom line from that group was that they were sure the rapture was coming. There was just a sign or two that had been misread, and once they were figured out, everyone would know the *true* date of the rapture.

And then there are the Realists, who felt both vindicated and embarrassed when Sunday came and went without a single soul floating towards heaven. They thought they were just as bad, maybe worse, for reacting like they did, strapping the Hendersons up on that billboard. Most never gloated about the rapture not coming. Most denied that they were ever there that evening watching the family on the billboard under the glow of the bonfires.

Those who did admit to what they did said they got swept up in something and they felt the need to apologize to the Hendersons.

One family even bought an expensive cheese basket loaded with a variety of cheeses and jellies and crackers. They weren't sure if a cheese basket was an ample apology after having just strapped their children to the top of a billboard, ridiculing them, and then driving Jeff almost to the point of murdering a police officer and his best friend. But they thought a cheese basket was better than nothing.

They came with their cheese basket early on that Sunday afternoon. They were the first family with the courage to face the Hendersons. To look them in the eyes and say, "We're sorry." They knocked on the door and waited in a cold sweat. Would the Hendersons scream at them and say, "How dare you show up here?" Or would they embrace them and admit that everyone had made some mistakes over the last week and it was time to move forward?

The family with the cheese basket never got to find out.

They knocked and waited, knocked and waited, but neither Will, Emily, Amy, or Jeff ever showed up at the door. The father walked around and opened the back door. Inside, the Hendersons' house was messy, but lived-in messy; it didn't look like they were robbed or like it had been invaded by spies looking for secret microfilm or anything like that. There were clothes strewn about but it was hard to tell if that was because they were doing some last-second packing or if Amy just hadn't had time to keep up with the housekeeping. She was probably quite busy with all of the prophecies and what-not, but some of the clothes weren't even in the laundry basket, and that's embarrassingly messy. You never know when someone's going to break into your house looking for you, so you should at least try to keep your house clean enough for those instances, the father with the cheese basket thought.

When he walked into the garage he saw that both the Hendersons' cars were nestled safely inside. "Jeff?" the father said as he shut the garage door, but the only sound he was met with was the ticking of an old clock. And that's when the father called the police.

Soon the police were all over the Henderson house, and by that night, they had officially declared Jeff, Amy, Emily, and Will as missing persons. Everyone all over Kansas was on the lookout for them.

But no one ever found them.

The Henderson family was never heard from again. Some said it was because everyone was looking in the wrong place. The Hendersons were the only ones who'd deserved to be raptured and there was no way anyone was going to find them because heaven was nowhere near Kansas. Others liked to think the Hendersons ended up on some beach in Mexico, spending the rest of their days basking in the sun, building sand castles, and watching the surf endlessly roll up onto the shore only to be sucked back into the sea.

The Hendersons became a legend around Goodland — another exhibit in Miss May's rapture museum. They became part of Goodland mystique. An outsider could every now and again hear the people of Goodland talking about the Hendersons. If outsiders waited around coffee shops and diners long enough they would hear bits and pieces of the story about the family who'd created the apocalypse and then afterwards promptly vanished. And the outsider would occasionally ask questions once they heard the story. But they'd get different answers depending on whom they talked to. The people of Goodland could, and did, say whatever they wanted about the Henderson family. They shaped their own stories. Because at the end of the day, there was no way of knowing what was fact and what was fiction, and there was no way to prove what was a prophecy and what was simply a coincidence.

I would like to thank in advance the actors who would be ideal to portray the characters in the summer blockbuster adaptation of *The End Is Now*. I'd like to thank Bill Paxton for playing Jeff Henderson because he's Hollywood's best everyman. Diane Lane will play Amy Henderson because she's the type of actress who's beautiful, sophisticated, and sympathetic when she's trapped.

I would like to thank Ellen Page for playing Emily Henderson. However, by the time this book goes into print, and certainly by the time it is green-lit by the Hollywood studio system, Ellen Page will be far too old for this role. Does she have any younger siblings with that spunky, know-it-all vibe?

And speaking of younger siblings, I have no idea who could play Will Henderson. Macaulay Culkin would be perfect. So would Haley Joel Osment. But they are old and completely uncute now. Are there any Culkin kids left? Weren't there like fifteen of them at one point? Maybe Macaulay will have a kid and he and his son will make *Home Alone 5* where Macaulay's family leaves him home around Christmas because he's too busy at his office and flirting with the secretary. Then the whole movie will be about this thirty-seven-year-old man who has to battle through his alcoholism and childhood demons to find the true meaning of Christmas. There won't be a single joke in it. It will be on the Hallmark Channel. And at the end, right when Macaulay is standing on the edge of a bridge and ready to take his life, Joe Pesci will show up and give Macaulay the perfect advice he needs to hear. I would like to thank the Hallmark Channel for making that movie.

I'd also like to thank Andy Meisenheimer, my editor, for once again being Yoda and Captain Kirk rolled into one. Thanks for your friendship, advice, and pushing this story to what it needed to be. I'd like to thank Becky Philpott for making sure my prose snaps, crackles, and pops. I'd like to thank Marcy Schorsch and Karen Campbell for their brilliance in helping *The End Is Now* get out into the world. And I'd like to thank Chip MacGregor for his wisdom and guidance in the literary business.

I'd like to thank all the author friends I've made along the way: Patton Dodd, Mick Silva, Steve Rabey, John Bolin, Glenn Packiam, Joel Kneedler, Matthew Paul Turner, and Michael Snyder. Processing writing and bouncing ideas off of you guys has helped immensely in shaping this novel and my career.

I'd like to thank Kevin Beck and Tim King and Jason Boyett (to name a few) for their expertise on eschatology.

And finally, I'd like to thank Sarah and Julianna and Claire for being so understanding whenever I snuck away to write and for being so loving when I return home. I hope I'm never raptured without you.

The Almost True Story of Ryan Fisher

A Novel

Rob Stennett

Meet Ryan Fisher — a self-assured real estate agent who's looking for an edge in the market.

While watching a news special late one night, he sees evangelical Christians raising their hands in worship. It's like they're begging for affordable but classy starter homes.

Ryan discovers the Christian business directory and places an ad complete with a Jesus fish. His business doubles in a week.

But after visiting an actual church, Ryan realizes that with his business savvy, he could not only plant a church — he could create an empire.

The Almost True Story of Ryan Fisher is a hilarious, spot-on, and often heartbreaking satire in the tradition of Kurt Vonnegut, Tom Perrotta, and Douglas Adams.

Softcover: 978-0-310-27706-4

Pick up a copy today at your favorite bookstore!

9 : 0 2 P . M .

I'm locking myself in tonight.

And no, I don't mean I'm getting ready to snuggle up with a glass of wine and a good book on the bearskin rug by the fire or lying on the couch to watch a nice romantic comedy while I chow down on a pint of Cherry Garcia—no I mean I'm literally locking myself in.

I live in one of those Los Angeles apartment buildings where all the paint is peeling on the outside, and there's always a bright yellow sign hanging over the balcony that announces the "Move-In Special!" This is the type of place that will soon be condemned, the type of place where you never feel safe, where the door to one apartment is rattling with the thumping of hip-hop gangster rap while another apartment always has girls with fish-net pantyhose and way too much make-up coming and going.

I live in apartment 517 B. If you walked down the hallway toward my apartment you'd notice the carpet is warped, green, and it smells like old people. The walls are constructed of synthetic wood paneling. The numbers on the doors aren't metal or raised gold; they're simply stickers and half are on crooked or partially torn off.

I've seen a lot of strange things happen in this hallway.

Which is probably why no one stops me as I return from Home Depot. I walk down the hallway with brown plastic bags full of everything I need: power drill, screwdrivers, deadbolts, chains, latches, and locks. I spend the next hour drilling and twisting and attaching them to the door of my apartment. One or two people glance at me funny as I work on my door, but most just walk right past me. They look at me like this is just normal apartment maintenance.

It isn't.

I have no idea what I'm doing. I've never installed locks before. But now, here I am with seven of Home Depot's most heavy-duty burglar-proof locks lining my front door—"the Kingston series" is what the bearded guy in the orange apron called them. The door's a complete mess now. But it's fine, it doesn't have to look nice, it just has to work.

It has to keep me inside.

Once all the deadbolts and latches are in place, I stop this guy named Rick who lives just down the hall from me. We never really talk but I see him all the time. He's always wearing a track jacket and running shoes, but I've never seen him looking all sweaty like he's just returned from a jog or anything—come to think of it, I have no idea what Rick does. But that doesn't stop me from asking him a favor.

"Rick," I say. He's trying not to stare at my destroyed front door.

"Jonah." I'm amazed he even knows my name.

"Listen, I need you to do me a favor."

"Uh—" Rick says, all awkward and condescending as he inspects my door—"you screwed those in backwards."

"No, I did that on purpose."

"On purpose?"

"Yeah, I'm going to shut the door. Then I need you to lock it behind me. All seven locks. Just bolt them shut."

"You know you're going to be locked inside if I do that," Rick says.

I'm suddenly very glad I've never tried to become friends with

Rick. "Yeah, I know, it's just, I'm doing this thing, it's nothing weird, it's for my own safety really, so if you locked the door behind me it would really help me out." Here I am trying to explain myself to Rick, the guy with the running shoes who never runs, and it makes me think to myself, wow, how low have you sunk?

"Yeah, sure, I can lock the door," Rick says.

"All the locks."

"Yeah, all the locks."

"Thanks, I really appreciate this," I say right as I close the door.

Then I listen. I hear the latches start to fasten. I count each latch as he finishes up—four, five, six, and then there it is, number seven. I'm locked in now.

That was kind of Rick, I admit. I shouldn't have been so hard on him. Even if I was only hard on him in my thoughts. Of course it might not have been me who was mocking his wardrobe, his lifestyle, and his haircut. Did I mention Rick's hair? It's also pretty hideous and embarrassing. It's oily and long in the places it should be short and short in the places it should be long. But you see, it might not have been me who thought all of this, it might have been—

How do I say this?

I guess there's no beating around the bush. You're going to find out sooner or later so I might as well just come out with it: I'm demon possessed. I have been for much of my life, but then I was free and on the wagon and now I've relapsed. That's the worst part. I'd beaten my inner demon (and just so we're clear by "inner demon" I don't mean some sort of tough feeling or really hard struggle. No, I mean an *actual* demon that can turn my eyes into glowing emeralds and speak through me) and now he seems to be back and worse than ever.

So about an hour ago I called Pastor Martin. He's the only person I've ever met who knows how to deal with my demon. Pastor

Martin told me he was in his car and on his way, but it's a six-hour drive from Tempe to Los Angeles. So he told me, until then, stay tight—and lock myself in. Hence the Kingston series outside my door. On my way to Home Depot I gave him another call and told him I didn't know how much longer I could stay in control. He said something else but his voice was garbled like he was losing service. I didn't know how much longer I'd have him on the line.

"I can't do this," I said.

"Jonah, you can. Center your thoughts."

"How?"

"Maybe you should write your story."

"My story?"

"Yeah. Write it down. It will take you awhile and it'll keep you focused on something other than—" and the line went dead.

Now I have no one else to talk to except you. I'm talking to you because I can't actually write my story down. I type like an eighth grader and my hand will cramp into a deformed E.T. shape if I try to write down everything that happened. Which is why after I left Home Depot I stopped by Wal-Mart to get a hand-held voice recorder. It's like one of those old tape recorders that private detectives and news reporters used in seventies movies. You know, the type where the reporter would always click it and say, "Note to Self," followed by some sort of witty or interesting or insightful comment. This is what I'll use to tell my story, and maybe along the way I can explain myself to anyone who will listen, and especially to everyone I've hurt along the way. Pastor Martin told me that if I was going to tell this story I should begin at the beginning. Sounds kind of overly simplistic to me. But maybe it's good, sound advice. I've never been much of one to listen to good, sound advice, but I suppose there's a first time for everything.

This is Jonah Adams' story of how I used my demon and how he used me. ❖

335

Share Your Thoughts

With the Author: Your comments will be forwarded to
the author when you send them to *zauthor@zondervan.com*.

With Zondervan: Submit your review of this book
by writing to *zreview@zondervan.com*.

Free Online Resources at
www.zondervan.com

Zondervan AuthorTracker: Be notified whenever your
favorite authors publish new books, go on tour, or post
an update about what's happening in their lives.

Daily Bible Verses and Devotions: Enrich your life
with daily Bible verses or devotions that help you start
every morning focused on God.

Free Email Publications: Sign up for newsletters on
fiction, Christian living, church ministry, parenting, and
more.

Zondervan Bible Search: Find and compare
Bible passages in a variety of translations at
www.zondervanbiblesearch.com.

Other Benefits: Register yourself to receive online
benefits like coupons and special offers, or to participate
in research.

ZONDERVAN®
.com